Her Grace

A Pride & Prejudice Vagary

By Shana Granderson, A Lady

CONTENTS

DEDICATION

This book, like all that I write, is dedicated to the love of my life, the holder of my heart. You are my one and only and you complete me. You make it all worthwhile and my world revolves around you. Until we reconnected, I had stopped believing in miracles, but now I most certainly do, you are my miracle.

Acknowledgement

First and foremost, thank you E.C.S. for standing by me while I dedicate many hours to my craft. You are my shining light and my one and only.

I want to thank my Alpha, Will Jamison and my Beta Caroline Piediscalzi Lippert. To both Gayle Surrette and Tish Holmes for taking on the roles of proof-readers and detailed editing, a huge thank you to both of you. All of you who have assisted me please know that your assistance is most appreciated.

My undying love and appreciation to Jane Austen for her incredible literary masterpieces is more than can be expressed adequately here. I also thank all of the JAFF readers who make writing these stories a pleasure.

Thank you to Rob Bockholdt: wyndagger@gmail.com, who was commissioned to create the artwork used for the cover.

INTRODUCTION

This is a story of survival and overcoming the greatest odds.

Elizabeth is forced into an unwanted marriage and this book chronicles her life and grace as she encounters each obstacle and overcomes them.

Rather than protect their daughter like any good parent should, first Fanny and then Thomas Bennet push their 16 year old daughter Elizabeth into a marriage with a much older man who happens to be a duke.

Fanny is seduced by the fact he is a duke, even if he is not interested in Jane, something she cannot believe at first, and his willingness to dower her remaining four daughters. For Bennet when the Duke offers to break the entail on Longbourn, after a certain condition is met, his opposition to the match dissipates.

At first, Elizabeth refuses to marry the man, and is adamant even if dragged to the church she will never recite her vows. However, after a private meeting with the vile duke, she agrees. The question is why would she change her mind so drastically.

Read on to discover how ODG survives her ordeal.

PROLOGUE

Early 1806

His Grace, Archibald Winston Chamberlain, the Duke of Hertfordshire and Marquess of Hertford Heights, whose main estate Falconwood straddled the Hertfordshire-Buckinghamshire border, was in desperate need of a wife.

It was all his idiot son's fault. Not six months previously, his son, Archibald, the younger, Marquess of Hertford Heights, died from the French disease, which had returned his title to the Duke. He was to marry, but when the damned Earl of Tamarin, father of the girl his son was to have as his wife saw evidence of the pox, he dissolved the engagement.

This fact was what led Hertfordshire to be seeking a new bride. He had his mistresses and was busy with some, on the women's side, involuntary affairs—cuckolding other men was the greatest sport—but that would not give him an heir and he refused to accept he would be the last in his line, the final Chamberlain.

Finding a new wife should not have been as hard as it seemed to be.

Yes, he was no longer a young man. He was well into his sixth decade, but not counting the royals, he was second in wealth only to the Duke of Bedford which should have made him highly eligible. One would have thought the families of London's polite society would have been falling over themselves to marry off their insipid daughters to him, however, that was not the case. He was not welcome in any homes of his fellow peers and members of the *Ton* just because two of his wives had died, supposedly from his abuse. How could he abuse property which belonged to him? It was his right to treat his wives as he saw fit.

~~~~~~~/~~~~~~~

The first one, he did not even remember her name, he had married in 1765. She had been a pretty little thing, but far too docile for him. Where was the fun in breaking a docile mare? It was so much better when, like a horse, there was spirit to break.

It was not his fault he had given her a light push and she had not been able to maintain her balance and had toppled down the stairs.

He married his next wife, Lady Felicia Eggerton, in 1774. She was the daughter of the Earl of Gryffinwood. Felicia had been even more beautiful than his first wife and had vivacity, spirit, and was somewhat impertinent. She had represented the exact kind of challenge in which Hertfordshire revelled.

For the first two years, he treated her well, never lifting a hand to her until she delivered him an heir. He had learnt from his experience with his first wife and had left Felicia be until a boy was born. As soon as little Archie had reached the age of one the Duke had been sure he would survive.

That was when he began his campaign to break his spirited wife. It had not taken as long as he had expected it would, only about a month. How was it his fault she fell off her horse while making a jump just because he had spooked the mount? She had fallen and broken her neck. By April 1778, he was the father of a son and was without a wife again.

~~~~~~~/~~~~~~~

As long as his son was healthy, the Duke decided not to trouble himself with a wife for a third time. Five mistresses and two to three dalliances with married women at any one time were more than enough to keep him entertained.

His mistresses he could hit occasionally. They were living by his largesse so it was his right. The women he was having affairs with were a different story. He had to leave them unblemished so regardless of the rumours, there would be no marks leading back to him. So what if he forced himself upon them. He was a duke and it was his right!

Money and rank were wonderful aphrodisiacs, and he exuded both. However, as the years went by and his reputation went from bad to worse, married women resisted him so they had to be *convinced* to do his bidding.

It angered him greatly that Lord Sedgewick Rhys-Davies, the Duke of Bedford, was wealthier than he was. His estate of Falconwood, which was on both sides of the Hertfordshire-Buckinghamshire border, was on par in size to Woburn Abbey. However where he owned seven additional estates—the biggest of which was Castlemere in Derbyshire, Bedford had ten. He owned shipbuilding yards, but so did Bedford. That which propelled the Duke of Bedford's wealth far beyond Hertfordshire's was the latter's shipping line, Dennington Lines.

As wealthy as he was, it never sat well with him that he was the second wealthiest. Archibald Winston Chamberlain hated not being first in everything he did.

In May 1798, the Duke's son had graduated from Oxford —barely. His Grace had to use his money and influence to affect his son's completion of his studies. The son took after the father insofar as he loved wenching. He spent more time in brothels with courtesans than in class.

Unfortunately, the idiot was not very discriminating in the ladies of the night he frequented so by mid-1802, the Duke was made aware of the fact his son had contracted the French disease.

In 1805, the Duke convinced (with a huge bribe) the

3

Earl of Tamarin to engage his only daughter to the Marquess of Hertford Heights. Four months later, clear evidence of the pox was visible on Archibald the younger's person and the engagement had been ended.

At the age of eight and twenty, at the end of 1805, his son died from his malady. As angry as he was at his son, the Duke had mourned as would be expected of him, for six months.

~~~~~~~/~~~~~~~

April 1806

Accepting that no family in polite society who knew him or of him would allow their daughter to become his wife —the one earl he had leverage on had no unmarried daughter, the Duke turned to looking in small towns.

The first place he decided to look was in Hertfordshire, in the market town of Meryton, only a few miles from Falconwood's northern border. As it was the nearest town to his estate in that county, he decided to begin his search for the woman he would honour as his duchess in the small market town where he was sure no one would know of him.

Chesham in Buckinghamshire was the closest market town to his main estate but he was too well known there. Talk of what had happened to his previous wives was still rife in that town.

~~~~~~~/~~~~~~~

The Bennets of Longbourn owned an estate next to Longbourn Village about a mile from the market town of Meryton in Hertfordshire. It had been occupied by the Bennet family since shortly after the Conqueror became King William in 1066. Thankfully, the Bennets traced their roots to Norman descent which had led to them being awarded a very large estate in Hertfordshire.

Thomas Bennet sat in his study, for once not paying

attention to the open book on his desk. As often happened ever since his fifth daughter had been born and the news his wife would never be able to bear another, he was lost in his thoughts.

He could feel the scorn of over eight hundred years of Bennet ancestors heaped on his head as he would be the last Bennet to preside over Longbourn as its master.

The estate was a fraction of the size it initially had been all thanks to a profligate son of his great-great-grandfather, his own great-grandfather's older brother. The man had been an inveterate and terribly bad gamester.

By the time the man's father had instituted the entail to heirs male, which forbade the sale of any remaining Bennet land and after disinheriting his eldest son, almost eighty percent of the original estate had been sold off to satisfy the dissolute man's debts. The result was the creation of four other estates with the lost land.

The largest was Netherfield Park, then Haye Park, followed by Purvis Lodge, and lastly what used to be named Bennet's Folly—as an insult his ancestor had richly deserved— but now renamed Lucas Lodge.

The man who had caused all of the Bennets' losses had been most indignant he should be disinherited and had somehow convinced some unsuspecting lady to marry him. He had then assumed her maiden name of Collins as retribution to his father and the brother who had, in his mind, usurped his rightful place as heir. According to the letters and family history Bennet had read, the man who had caused all their woes—including the infernal entail, as his wife termed it —had broken with his family once he was named Collins and the remaining Bennets had not mourned his loss.

Up to and including his father's generation, there had always been at least one Bennet son, sometimes two. Bennet had been the only son of James and Elizabeth Bennet. His father had passed before his mistaken marriage and his mother was gone these twelve years at least.

As it often did, his train of thought led him to the mean of understanding, shrewish, vindictive wife he had been trapped into marrying. He took a long draw on his glass of port as his mind took him back to that damned assembly.

~~~~~~~/~~~~~~~

Autumn Assembly Meryton 1786

Frances Gardiner, called Fanny, was on a mission. She had tried every art and allurement her mother had taught her and, to date, the reasonably handsome master of Longbourn had not looked at her.

This assembly was the first one the new master of Longbourn would attend after coming out of mourning for his father. She had been happy for William Lucas, the son of the owner of Meryton's general store to pay attention to her—she loved attention from men, but he was lost to Sarah Huntington. The fact she had only been thirteen at the time did not phase Fanny. The loss of the owner of the Lucas Emporium had spurred Fanny to make sure she made a much better match than the woman she counted as a rival.

By the time she was sixteen Fanny set her cap for Thomas Bennet. Sarah Lucas was welcome to her tradesman husband; she would marry a member of the gentry. The fact her father was the town solicitor—also in trade—and her brother who was at Oxford intended to go into trade as well, did not discourage the youngest Gardiner.

For Bennet's part, before his father had passed he had thought about Fanny Gardiner as a mate for a few minutes. Being a very studious man who was a confirmed bibliophile, he could not countenance ever being tied to one as vapid and empty-headed as the solicitor's youngest daughter.

Her failure to induce Mr. Bennet to offer for her had led Fanny to her plan for this evening. She had enlisted her older—by six years—sister Hattie as her accomplice. Hattie was engaged to their father's law clerk, Frank Philips.

Hattie knew what her sister planned was underhanded and wrong and was extremely uncomfortable with it. The problem was she had never been able to resist her younger, more forceful, and far prettier sister. Due to her looks, Fanny was their mother's clear favourite. Hattie had always sought their mother's love and approval and found the easiest way was to follow Fanny which gained her the much desired attention from their mother who valued looks above all else.

It was well known Thomas Bennet eschewed dancing, so Fanny had a plan to catch him unawares on his way to the cardroom. She was not intelligent, but Fanny did not lack in cunning.

As soon as her victim made his walk down the short hallway towards the cardroom, Fanny fell into his arms as Hattie waited in the shadows. On cue, Hattie screeched bringing men out of the cardroom as well as many dancers from the main body of the assembly hall.

Fanny pushed her body against the shocked Thomas Bennet and made it seem like he had been kissing her. "Thomas I enjoyed your kisses, but we do not have an understanding yet," Fanny stated innocently.

"Bennet, I will see you in my office first thing in the morning!" *Elias Gardiner thundered. He had been in the cardroom when he heard Hattie's scream.*

"B-b-but I-I d-did n-not touch her," Bennet protested as he came out of the stupor.

"Hattie, you saw all did you not?" Fanny demanded. Unable to look at anyone, the eldest Gardiner sibling nodded. "Did you see my Thomas kiss me?" She knew she would be consigned to hell, but nevertheless, Hattie nodded again.

~~~~~~~/~~~~~~~

The present

7

There had been no escaping his fate and now here he sat, nineteen years of being in a hellish marriage later, with five daughters, and no son, and there would never be an heir.

Knowing he needed a son, Bennet had performed his distasteful duty but instead of a son, a daughter had been delivered in October 1787, a little over a year after the wedding. She had been named Jane.

Their daughter had her mother's golden blonde hair and deep blue eyes.

By the second half of 1789 Fanny was again in the family way and told everyone who cared to hear—and those who did not—she was carrying the heir who would end the entail.

His wife was very frightened of the entail once she understood if her husband died without male issue she would lose her home—in her words, be thrown into the hedgerows. Bennet had to admit, if only to himself the idea of Fanny cast out without a home was not unattractive to him.

Her prediction was disproved when another daughter was born on the fifth day of March 1790. She was smaller than Jane had been as a babe and had a head full of dark hair, just like her Grandmother Elizabeth's.

Fanny had berated the *disobliging* girl for not being born a son. She had wanted nothing to do with the *wilful* girl. As her colouring was similar to his mother's, Bennet named her Elizabeth Rose, who he and Jane would call Lizzy. His mother had always been disgusted with his wife, and now more so than ever with her son's wife's attitude towards an innocent babe.

Elizabeth Bennet took on the care of her namesake and with funds from her own jointure, made sure a wetnurse was employed.

Bennet had started to value peace and quiet in his home, something his sly wife was well aware of. If he ever tried to assert his authority and deny her something she desired, she would make the home a living nightmare with caterwauling and remonstrations so Bennet learnt to simply give in, like he had with her treatment of Lizzy. By the time little Lizzy turned six months of age, she had the same striking emerald-green eyes as her paternal grandmother.

Next to be born was Mary in April 1792. She too had blonde hair, but not golden like her mother and eldest sister, rather it was a sandy blonde. She started off with blue eyes, but by her fifth month she had hazel eyes with some flecks of green and gold in them.

Fanny pronounced her plain because Mary did not have the colour hair and eyes she herself did.

The next lying in resulted in the fourth Bennet daughter in November 1793. This daughter was named Catherine after her mother's late aunt. Strangely enough, for her own inexplicable reason, Fanny did not hold the daughters after Lizzy to blame for not being sons as she still did her second born.

The year 1794, had been a year of great losses. In the early part of the year, Elias Gardiner succumbed to a heart ailment. He was followed three months later by his wife, Lydia Gardiner who had fallen in front of a carriage.

The greatest loss to both Bennet and Lizzy, who was then four, was when Grandmama Beth—as she had been called by her granddaughters—slipped away in her sleep the first week of December of the same year.

By February 1795, Fanny Bennet felt the quickening for the fifth time. Again she was positive she would finally have a son. It was not to be. In early July, another Bennet daughter arrived. Before Fanny could reject her like she had Elizabeth, she saw how much like a Gardiner the mite looked. She even had the same birthmark below her left shoulder as Fanny's late mother.

The new babe was named Lydia after the late Mrs. Gardiner and became her mother's instant favourite. The fact she was told she would never bear another child due to the damage wrought by Lydia's enormity at birth did not dim Fanny's enthusiasm for her newest daughter.

As she grew, Lydia looked more and more like her namesake only endearing her to her mother that much more.

~~~~~~~/~~~~~~~

Although he believed being out at fifteen was far too early, Bennet had not had the wherewithal to stand up to his wife who proclaimed a match to a wealthy man was the only way to secure her and any unmarried daughters' futures.

Hence, when first Jane and then Lizzy had been pushed into society he had not objected much. In April of the coming year, it would be Mary's turn.

Being aware he should be standing up to his hated wife, and doing it were two different things. He remained silent as she spent all of their available remaining profits. Regardless of how many times Edward Gardiner, his wife's brother, had begged him to save and invest for his daughters' futures, Bennet had done nothing.

Peace was better than telling his wife her spending habits would be restricted.

~~~~~~~/~~~~~~~

The Darcys of Pemberley were an old and very wealthy family. The first Darcy had in fact been a D'Arcy and had joined William, the Duke of Normandy in his invasion of England during the war of 1066.

As a reward, Pierre D'Arcy had been granted a huge swath of land in Derbyshire. When William became king, the monarch had offered his loyal subject Pierre a noble title. Pierre wanted nothing more than to be a farmer as he had been in Normandy; he politely refused, and the King had not insisted, increasing his grant of gold instead. Over the centuries successive Darcys had also refused titles.

Pierre embraced his new country with open arms and as such married a native Englishwoman and anglicised his name to Peter Darcy in 1089. As much as he loved farming, Peter was enamoured with the written word.

Once there was peace, he had sent some men to his old home in Normandy to bring his large collection of books to him and made sure that his library had a place of prominence in his house.

~~~~~~~/~~~~~~~

Over the years the wealth and holdings of the Darcys increased significantly. By 1806, they were second only to two other residents of the county in wealth. One, the wealthiest was the absentee landlord who owned the estate Castlemere which had a common fence along Pemberley's western border, the Duke of Hertfordshire. The Duke resided all of the year either at his primary estate Falconwood or at one of his London homes. Given the Duke's dissipated and cruel behaviour, there was no friendship between him and the Darcys.

The next wealthiest was the Duke of Devonshire whose estate of Chatsworth, while a little smaller than the Darcys', boasted a much larger mansion.

The current master of Pemberley was Robert Darcy. He was an only son and had two younger sisters. Edith Portnoy was four years her brother's junior and had married Mr. Ernest Portnoy in 1778. They lived on a large estate in Nottinghamshire. The youngest sister, Leticia, was married in 1780, to Hubert Barrington, a very successful barrister in London who lived at a Darcy estate—Rivington—in Surrey when they were not in Town.

Over her older sister's objections because he was not titled, Robert married the love of his life, Lady Anne Fitzwilliam, the daughter of the Earl of Matlock, sister to the current Lord Matlock. For some reason Lady Catherine Fitzwilliam, eight years Anne's senior, thought she had the power to command all to her will—all evidence to the contrary.

Robert had married his lady love in 1781, with everyone else in the Fitzwilliam family's blessing and approval—other than Lady Catherine's. Robert Darcy and the current earl, Reggie, had been best of friends for many years prior to the former's interest in the latter's youngest sister.

A year after her younger sister married, and after not *taking* for eight seasons, Lady Catherine had married Lewis de Bourgh, the only man who had offered for her. Unwilling to be married to the untitled de Bourgh, Catherine pressed her father until he finally petitioned for a knighthood for his son-in-law. His estate of Rosings Park in Kent was nothing to Pemberley or Snowhaven—the estate of the earls of Matlock—but he was, in her opinion, acceptably wealthy.

The old Earl had passed away in early 1779, his wife followed him not three months later. Lord Reginald Fitzwilliam, with his beloved wife Lady Elaine at his side, had assumed the Earldom and his son Andrew, two-years-old at the time, had become the new Viscount Hilldale. A second son, Richard, had been born in February 1782.

Lady Catherine had come to Snowhaven in order to dispense her advice (orders) after her father's death, but had been sent away almost immediately by her brother who had no time for her officious pretentions.

In January 1783, Fitzwilliam Alexander Robert Darcy was born. He was a rather serious lad by the time he was eight or nine, taller than most boys his age with dark, wavy hair. William as he was called, also had the piercing blue eyes of all the Fitzwilliam family—except for Lady Catherine—who had brown eyes.

Lady Catherine had delivered a daughter, Anne, in June 1786. With no pressure to produce a male heir as Rosings Park was unentailed, since Anne's birth, she had locked her door to her husband and never allowed him to come to her again.

Having been roundly refused to securing an engagement between Andrew and her daughter, she tried to force one between Fitzwilliam—she refused to call him anything but Fitzwilliam—and Anne. The result was the same. Adamant refusal. A seething Lady Catherine had been sent back to Kent with much resentment that no one would obey her commands.

Between William's birth and early 1795, Lady Anne Darcy had multiple miscarriages. She came to believe they would never be blessed with another child. When she had felt the signs of being with child in September - October 1794, she had said not a word to anyone. Then close to Christmas of that year she had felt the quickening. It was on the morning of Christmas day when Lady Anne told her husband her news. Until she entered her lying in on the third day of March 1795, Robert Darcy had been very watchful over his wife's health.

After a long and arduous birthing process, on the fourth day of March a little girl, named Georgiana by combining her late paternal grandfather's and her mother's names—with hardly a hair on her head had been born. She would be called Anna by all her family and friends.

Anne Darcy had been assisted by three of her sisters—the three she enjoyed being with—through the lying in. It had been Edith who had come to collect her brother to come see his wife.

It had taken a while for his beloved Anne to recover, but recover she had. In the meanwhile little Anna captured all of their hearts, especially that of her older brother.

In May of 1800, Sir Lewis de Bourgh had taken a journey to inspect some holdings of his on the Orkney Islands. Everyone knew it was one of his ways to have some peaceful time far away from his wife. There had been a sudden and unexpected storm and the ship and all hands and passengers had been lost.

Due to Lady Catherine de Bourgh's continued insistence on an engagement with one of her two firstborn nephews, and her continued attempts to order the lives of those in the family, after the funeral, it had been the last time the Derbyshire and Staffordshire family had been in her company. An empty coffin had been placed in the family crypt as the body was never recovered.

Sadly, Anne de Bourgh was a rather sickly girl. She had a serious bout of scarlet fever she had when she was seven. It was unfortunate she did not have contact with her aunts, uncles, and cousins, but as long as her mother behaved as she did, it would not be possible.

It was sad, but it was the cost of not being in Lady Catherine's company. Any requests to have Anne come visit her family in London or the north had been rebuffed by Lady Catherine, of course, unless there was agreement to an engagement.

~~~~~~~/~~~~~~~

In 1786, Robert Darcy had employed a new steward, a man who had been a law clerk in Lambton. He had joined the staff at Pemberley with his wife and son. George Wickham was almost two at the time Lucas Wickham took up his new post.

In the years since Wickham had become his steward, George had been added to the group of friends which included Andrew, Richard, and William. The group expanded when the Portnoy and Barrington male cousins were present.

Unfortunately, as George aged, Robert saw jealousy and resentment being stoked in the boy. His son and nephews had not wanted to tattle on the steward's son, but when confronted by their fathers and asked pointed questions, they had not dissembled.

With the mischief coming to light, Darcy had to have

a hard conversation with his steward telling him he felt it best for there to be no more contact between George and the children of the family. Lucas Wickham was not blind to his son's faults nor was he unaware that his avaricious wife was the one who had influenced George's behaviour.

He promised his master to make sure George caused no more mischief at the estate. To that end, after his mother passed away in August 1803, George was sent to live with his father's sister in Devonshire.

~~~~~~~/~~~~~~~

The whole family—excluding the irascible Lady Catherine de Bourgh—were at Pemberley to celebrate Easter which would fall on the sixth day of April 1806.

As he did each and every day, Robert said a prayer of thanks to the good Lord above for the fact his Anne was as healthy as she had ever been and not been taken after Anna's difficult birth.

Although he was not active in the *Ton,* he had heard the rumours regarding the disgusting Duke of Hertfordshire's search for a new wife. He was certain a parent would have to have little love for a daughter in order to agree to marry her to such an abusive brute.

CHAPTER 1

William was not happy, even though he respected Richard's choice of career, that his cousin was in the army—the Royal Dragoons of the regulars—and was a Captain.

Over the years, there was not one of his male cousins he was closer to than Richard Fitzwilliam—they were separated by less than a year with Richard being four and twenty and William three and twenty. William had been somewhat close to Lawrence and Warren Portnoy, four and twenty and one and twenty respectively, and Anthony Barrington, two and twenty, not to mention Andrew Fitzwilliam who was six and twenty,

Being there was less than a year in age separating Richard and William, they had done everything together as they grew older, brothers in every way except not being born of the same mother. Richard could have entered Eton a year ahead of William, but he had elected to wait for his slightly younger cousin. As such, they had been together from the first day they had begun at Eton until the day they graduated from Cambridge when William had been one and twenty and Richard one year older.

Since the first year they had begun their studies away from home, Richard had insisted he would join the regular army.

His parents, his brother, his Darcy aunt and uncle, and even Anna had tried to convince Richard to select a different path for his profession. None had argued longer and harder than William.

Eventually, William recognised Richard had made his choice. From that point on, as much as he hated the idea of Richard being in harm's way, William supported his brother of the heart completely.

The stubborn horse's arse which was his cousin had refused to accept any commission purchased by his father above second lieutenant. He was adamant he would earn his promotions from that point on. It had not taken Richard long to attain the rank of lieutenant. He was well suited for the army and William had to admit Richard was not built to make sermons or be a fiery orator as a barrister.

On the eighteenth day of May 1803, all of William's and the family's fears for Richard's wellbeing had become much more real when war had been declared on France, led by the little Corsican, who became the self-anointed emperor in May 1804.

So far Richard, who had become Captain Fitzwilliam in 1805, had been in the peninsula with his company once, for six months.

Much to William's and all of the family's relief, Richard had returned to England sans any wounds of which to speak of. All he and the rest of the family could pray for was for the same to continue and for Richard to be protected from any serious harm, or worse.

~~~~~~~/~~~~~~~

Over the years as daughter after daughter had been born, Fanny Bennet had been plagued by what she called her nerves. Not a day went by she did not bemoan the entail and curse the Bennet who had instituted it.

Her opinions on the unfairness of entailing an estate away from its rightful owners was something on which she harped almost as much. In her mind, the heir presumptive was nothing more than a thief. The name Collins was considered an expletive in the house.

Bennet had no face-to-face contact with the Collins family for many years, who by now were very distant cousins. The current patriarch, one Clem Collins, who was illiterate, had a letter written for him some years past in which he had gleefully announced the birth of a son, named Clem William Collins.

Each time news had spread about another daughter for the Bennets, said illiterate man had someone write a letter of *congratulations*. Bennet hated the name Collins almost as much as his wife did.

On this particular day, the Friday after Easter, Bennet was especially thankful for the thick oak door which separated his sanctuary, which was his study, from the rest of the house. His wife was screeching at Jane and Lizzy about the gowns they would wear to the spring assembly that very evening.

Two hours since his wife had invaded his peace, he imagined he could still hear her voice reverberating around his study regardless of how much he would have liked to forget it.

The study door had been flung open without so much as a knock. If Bennet thought it would have made a difference he may have taken the time to voice his objections to his wife bursting into his study in such a rude manner.

From past experience Bennet knew it would only lead to even more screeching, so he said nothing in order to keep the frail peace.

"Mr. Bennet, how well it is for our Jane," Fanny had exclaimed at high volume.

"Mrs. Bennet, of what do you speak?" Bennet had enquired. "I am not aware of what you are referring to. What has whatever you are on about to do with Jane?"

"How you like to vex me. My sister was here not an hour ago and told me that a man of exceptional wealth, and possibly a peer of the realm has taken all of the rooms at the Red Lion Inn for his exclusive use," Fanny blabbered.

"Mayhap I am a simpleton, but I still fail to see what that news has to do with us."

"Hattie heard from Lady Lucas, who heard from Mrs. Goulding, who heard from Mrs. Browning..."

"Who is Mrs. Browning?"

"The landlady of the Red Lion Inn! Why do you not pay attention when I tell you important news from the neighbourhood?"

Bennet knew the only way he would have his study for himself again was to allow his wife to relate her fantastically important piece of gossip. "Go ahead Mrs. Bennet, I am all ears and in great anticipation of this wonderous news."

As always, sarcasm went right over his silly wife's head.

"According to what Hattie was told, the man is single and more importantly his heir is no longer alive so he has to marry to beget an heir."

"Just like you gave me," Bennet riposted in sotto voce.

"What was that?" Fanny demanded.

"Nothing Mrs. Bennet, I was clearing my throat. Please continue this earth-shaking news so I may return to my work."

"He prefers a lady from the country rather than some stuck up woman from so called polite society! Do you not see what this means for Jane?"

Bennet was aware at eighteen Jane was an unrivalled beauty, except for Lizzy that was. He could not voice his opinion about Lizzy rivalling or possibly exceeding Jane's beauty, which when you took her vivacity and intelligence into account made her a far better catch than her older sister. If he voiced his opinions on the matter he would never hear the end of it from his wife who told one and all, whether they wanted to know or not, Lizzy was nothing in looks to Jane. Anyone with eyes in the neighbourhood knew his wife was wrong, but over the years they had learnt to keep from saying anything contradictory to the Bennet matron.

That was not only to keep her from a vitriolic diatribe. But out of view of others, Fanny would find some way to punish Lizzy for the crime of others thinking her beautiful.

"I still do not know what this means for Jane."

"Why do you try to vex me? When he sees Jane's beauty he will have no choice but to offer for her and we will be saved! If he is wealthy enough to take the whole of the inn then he will be able to afford to save me...us from the hedgerows."

Fanny had waved a lace square as the excitement of her Jane being married to a peer of the realm became a sure thing in her mind. "Is that all, Mrs. Bennet?" Bennet queried shortly.

Thankfully his wife had been too far lost in her imaginings to pick up on his tone of voice. "To Meryton! I must purchase more lace!" With that Fanny turned and almost ran out of the study screeching for Mrs. Hill to attend her as she did.

As she had not closed the door, Bennet stood and did so, except this time he turned the key in the lock. He knew his wife had almost as much lace in the house as the local haberdashery, but he had stopped himself from commenting on that fact.

Here they were, his wife screeching for more lace to be added to Jane's gown while giving orders, only to contradict them not a moment later.

He did not pay the Hills, the long suffering butler-valet and housekeeper, nearly enough money to put up with his wife's mercurial moods.

~~~~~~~/~~~~~~~

His Grace, Lord Archibald Winston Chamberlain sat in the largest chamber at the god-forsaken inn in this nowhere town.

If only his idiot son had not been discovered to have the pox before the fool died. Had he married, if his son had not been up to the job, he himself would have been able to impregnate the girl. Damn the Earl of Tamarin and spreading the information about Archy's malady to one and all.

It was thanks to his former fathers-in-law, first the sanctimonious Baron, Lord Maidenhall, and then the Earl of Gryffinwood who had spread the rumours of his so-called mistreatment of his wives which had led to all doors of members of the *Ton* to be closed to him leading him to this backwater.

At almost seven and sixty—in his own opinion—he was a fit and virile man.

The inconvenient truth was he was corpulent, sometimes had a hard time catching his breath, had a ruddy complexion, and partook in many dangerous activities, the most of which was forcing himself on married women.

Like other men of rank and wealth, Lord Hertfordshire believed his money and standing would always protect him from his own actions.

He would lower himself to attend the local assembly this evening. He had to see if there was one, who would come close, to meeting his criteria he wanted in his third wife. He was not confident, but one never knew.

She needed to be pretty, that was for sure, he would not bed a homely woman, but vivacity was, and always would be, the most important thing. Some intelligence would not hurt.

As he thought of what he sought, the Duke salivated thinking of how much pleasure he would take in breaking such a woman—after she had delivered an heir of course. As much as he hated to restrict his pleasure, his first priority was the all-important son. He would do whatever he needed to in order to insure he was not the last of his line. If that meant he would have to tamp down his own inclinations until his son was at least one year in age, so be it.

There was no doubt in his mind he would have his new wife in the family way within a month of his marriage. He had not decided where yet, but he would banish his wife to one of his many estates when she was confirmed with child, that way he would reduce the temptation to begin her education before the boy's first birthday.

There was a knock on the chamber door. "Come," Hertfordshire rasped.

His valet and the young man who would do anything the Duke asked of him entered the chamber. Both gave him respectful bows.

"Well?" the Duke prompted.

"The best looking girls in the area are sisters named Bennet. Only two of them are out, one is a little older than eighteen and the other sixteen," the valet reported.

The fact he was almost fifty years one's senior and more than that for the other meant nothing to Hertfordshire. "Characters?"

"In my enquiries I discovered the older, a bland, blonde, willowy one with blue eyes, is very serene and far too compliant for you, however, the younger one, dark hair, rather petite with emerald-green eyes may have the gumption you seek," the younger man informed his employer.

"Then it seems this may not be a complete waste of my time," Hertfordshire stated as he steepled his fingers in thought. He waved his men away and began to mentally prepare himself to mix with those so far below him at the assembly upcoming.

CHAPTER 2

Preening like a peacock, Fanny Bennet led her unwilling daughters into the assembly hall. She knew she was still a handsome woman and felt Jane's beauty was a direct compliment to herself.

Her eyes swept the hall, but unfortunately, she saw no one she did not recognise. She understood the man who would marry Jane was not in attendance yet. Fanny saw her sister speaking to Mrs. Long and Lady Lucas—it still irked that Sarah Lucas was titled. All her husband had done was make a speech to the King and Queen some years ago when he had been mayor of the town. In Fanny's mind, the fact the King had knighted William Lucas for some ridiculous speech only confirmed the rumours of the Monarch's madness.

As much as she hated having to call the former Sarah Huntington, Lady Lucas, Fanny did so. Other than herself and her sister Hattie, Lady Lucas was one of the foremost purveyors of gossip in the Meryton area and Fanny would never give up a good source of tittle-tattle regardless of how much she disdained the woman.

Wanting to feel superior to Sarah Lucas made attaching Jane to a peer of the realm all the more important. Once Jane was married to such a man, she—and of course, her mother by extension—would be far higher than a lowly knight or his wife.

While their mother made her way to speak to their aunt and some of the other matrons, Jane and Elizabeth sought out Charlotte Lucas.

Charlotte—a best friend to the two eldest Bennet sisters —was two and twenty, and as their mother loved to point out, was considered fast approaching being on the shelf. The Bennet girls would have a *whole* one thousand pounds each, and only when their mother passed away, but as far as was publicly known, Charlotte and Maria Lucas would have a mere six hundred pounds to share between them.

More than once when they discussed their relative economic fortunes Charlotte had opined her father had been precipitous in selling his business after his knighthood. In her opinion, had he kept it and employed a manager, they would have had an income which approached Longbourn's rather than less than half.

Another thing the Bennet matron loved to point out was Charlotte's lack of beauty. She was wont to say even Lizzy was prettier than the eldest Lucas, who she called plain.

After Charlotte, there came Franklin, who was home for the Easter term break from Oxford and aged twenty. There was Johnathan—called Johnny—who at sixteen was a few months older than Lizzy, and the youngest Lucas was Maria who was eleven.

"Jane and Eliza, how do you both do this evening?" Charlotte welcomed her friends.

She knew her friends did not agree with their mother's cutting words regarding herself, not even in the smallest measure, something which warmed Charlotte's heart.

"We are all aflutter to meet this mythical peer of the realm Mama has been atwitter about," Elizabeth responded sarcastically.

"He is not a myth," Charlotte informed her friends.

"How would you know that?" Jane enquired.

"You know my Papa," Charlotte inclined her head to Sir William who was fulfilling the role of master of ceremonies, as he always did. "He took himself to the inn to welcome the visitor on behalf of the town."

"And? What did he learn?" Elizabeth asked impatiently.

"For once the rumour mill has the right of it. He and his party have indeed taken every room at the Red Lion Inn. And he is no mere peer, he is the highest rank below royalty," Charlotte revealed.

"A Duke!" Elizabeth exclaimed. "Did he deign to meet Sir William?"

"Papa said he waited for the best part of an hour, but then he did in fact meet His Grace, the Duke of Hertfordshire, Marquess of Hertford Heights. His name is Lord Archibald Winston Chamberlain and..." Charlotte hesitated. "When he arrived home, Papa looked at his copy of Debrett's Peerage. Based on the information of his birth, the Duke is almost seven and sixty years old and, on top of that, he is rather corpulent," Charlotte reported.

"Much older than either of our fathers," Jane stated.

"Surely then Mama's saying he is looking for a wife is false," Elizabeth hoped. "Why would he need to marry at that age?"

"The only thing we have discovered is the Duke's heir passed away with no issue. It was about a year or so past," Charlotte informed her friends.

"So he needs an heir," Elizabeth realised. "I am sure he is too old to seriously consider anyone of our ages, so it is certain we are safe, if he is looking here and not in London for his next duchess that is."

"I am sure you have the right of it, Lizzy" Jane assured herself and her sister both.

The whole room went quiet and all eyes swung to the doors, where an old man, very corpulent, not tall, and with no hair on the top of his head, stood there surveying the crowd with a critical eye.

Next to him stood two men, one younger and rather handsome and the other older than the younger one, but obviously much younger than the Duke.

~~~~~~~/~~~~~~~

For not the first time that hour, Archibald Chamberlain cursed those who had turned all of the *Ton* against him making it impossible for him to find a wife from the upper reaches of England's societal structure.

At least his man had identified one who may meet all of the attributes he was looking for in his next duchess. It was something. Hertfordshire hoped his man's information was in fact true as he would hate to have to search in too many more of these little backwaters. Up to now, the man was usually accurate in his reports.

How fortuitous had it been just over two years ago to find his current man who was only nineteen at the time. The man he replaced, who like the new man, had been willing to do whatever was required of him—including procuring unwilling married or unmarried women for Hertfordshire to bed—had been disposed of when he had failed to procure him the wife of a man who had slighted him.

At first, he had thought his new man was too young, but when he saw how the man was willing to use his good looks and charms to convince others to do what he wanted, the Duke had known he had found the ideal man for the job.

His man took pleasure in causing pain to members of polite society all because—as he had told it—he had been ill used by some member of the *Ton* who had convinced his own father to banish him from Derbyshire to Devonshire.

George Wickham had no qualms as long as he was well paid, there was no task he would not perform for his master. At least he could use his own name thanks to his father's master repaying what he had *borrowed* from his former employer.

Hence as he stood and admired himself in the mirror,

the Duke had high confidence in Wickham's information. When he was happy with the way his valet had dressed him, he made his way downstairs where Wickham and one of his guards were waiting for him. He nodded to the two and they led their master out of the inn for the short walk, but twenty yards distant to the assembly hall.

His plan this night was simple. He would ask to dance with three or four young ladies, the one Wickham had identified being one of them. He would say nothing of his plans this night. If she was the one he chose, he would summon the father to him in a day or two.

When they entered, all conversation ceased, as was his due, of course. It was only right these peasants should be awed in his presence. The Duke looked over the crowd disdainfully.

First, he saw the very pretty blonde. He looked to Wickham. "Sister to the one you want to know, she is the serene, compliant one," Wickham said softly so only his master could hear. "The shorter one next to her."

The Duke turned his attention to the petite one next to the blonde. She was in looks exactly as Wickham had described her. In an instant, he knew she would be the one. Rather than look away like her sister had, she lifted her chin and held his eyes with a challenging look.

"Welcome to our humble assembly, Your Grace," Sir William simpered in welcome. "May I introduce you to my family and some of the principal families in the area?"

Hertfordshire was about to refuse when he noticed a matron, somewhat pretty still, summon—rather loudly—the two girls he had been looking at to her side. "Yes, I believe that will be in order," the Duke granted.

Sir William, feeling the compliment of the Duke agreeing to meet his family very keenly was almost bouncing on the balls of his feet as he led His Grace to where his wife, sons, daughter, and three Bennets were standing.

"Your Grace, Lord Archibald Chamberlain it is my pleasure to present my wife, Lady Sarah Lucas, Miss Charlotte Lucas, Franklin and Johnathan Lucas to you." Sir William was about to stop there when he saw the Duke's pointed look at the Bennets. "Also Mrs. Frances Bennet, Miss Jane Bennet, and Miss Elizabeth. Family and Bennets, the Duke of Hertfordshire, Marquess of Hertford Heights."

Fanny had to fight to maintain her equilibrium. She did not miss the way the Duke—a duke!—made sure Sir William introduced him to her and her daughters as well. Jane would be a duchess! She always knew Jane could not be so beautiful for no reason. She was destined to be the mother of a duchess. Thoughts of how she would be set up for life while lording that over Sarah Lucas were swimming in her head so she almost missed the Duke's words.

"Mrs. Bennet if your husband does not object, may I have the honour of a set from you, and then from your pretty daughters, one each?" the Duke requested as he inclined his head to the matron.

Catching herself before objecting to Elizabeth being described as pretty, Fanny beamed at the Duke. "Why Your Grace, how you honour us. I accept for myself and my daughters. It is very gallant of you to include Lizzy as a dance partner when you have Jane's beauty before you."

Elizabeth blushed red at her mother's thoughtless words. It was nothing she was not used to, but it was not usually before their friends in the middle of an assembly.

Sir William and Lady Lucas could not but be disappointed to be ignored by the Duke once he met the Bennets. Sarah Lucas was aware there would be no end to Fanny's boasting about herself and her two eldest being asked to dance with a duke.

"Lizzy, I am sure Mama did not mean to slight you so," Jane asserted once the Duke had led their preening mother to join the line currently forming.

"You think that if it gives you comfort," Elizabeth bit back with a hard edge to her voice. She did not miss the way Jane's face fell. "Sorry Janey, I did not mean to take my hurt out on you. One day you will have to start seeing the world as it is and not how you want it to be. Do not forget, I committed the cardinal sin of not being born a son."

"But there were three more girls born after you, Eliza. Why is your mother's displeasure directed at you?" Charlotte asked a question she had wanted to ask for many years.

"Somehow, in my mother's way of thinking, because I *refused* to be born a son, it caused her to be cursed with only girls," Elizabeth explained. "Of course, her inability to bear a child after Lyddie was my fault as well and had nothing to do with the fact she was born so huge."

Jane was about to protest when she saw her sister's arched eyebrow challenging her to dispute a word of what had been stated. Jane could not.

~~~~~~~/~~~~~~~

"Your husband was not introduced to me," the Duke observed as they danced.

"Mr. Bennet does not enjoy this kind of activity and is at home with our three younger girls," Fanny averred.

"Five daughters, and no son?" the Duke pressed.

"Correct Your Grace," Fanny conceded. "And we suffer from an entailment to the male line."

'*Good information,*' Hertfordshire told himself. '*If there is resistance, I may have some leverage.*' "What of dowries?" he asked aloud.

Fanny relayed the pertinent information to the man never considering how indecorous the conversation was with one newly met.

'*Another thing which may be useful,*' the Duke told

himself.

The couple was separated by the dance. Fanny preened as she went down the line seeing the jealous looks on not a few of her neighbours' faces. When she saw the sour look on Sarah Lucas's face, her night became so much better.

"If you would like to dance two sets with my Jane and not with Lizzy, I will understand, Your Grace," Fanny proposed when the dance brought them together.

"Madam, let me be rightly understood, it is me and me alone who will decide who I partner for a dance, and when!" the Duke barked.

Not wanting to upset the man, Fanny said not another word, for which her partner was greatly thankful.

'*What a stupid woman. Once I have the father's agreement to wed the dark haired one—and he will not deny me, I will have Wickham bring this creature to me. She is still pretty,*' the Duke told himself as he smirked at his dance partner. '*I am almost decided. The final test will be the dance.*'

~~~~~~~/~~~~~~~

At the end of the dance, Hertfordshire led Mrs. Bennet back to her daughters who were still standing near the nodcock of a knight and his family. The knight's plain daughter was not even a consideration to dance with, never mind anything else.

Jane had been returned by the Goulding heir when the Duke arrived with her mother. He led her out to the line while Elizabeth followed with Franklin Lucas.

The dance with the pretty, but insipid blonde was exactly how the Duke had expected it to be. Wickham had been wholly accurate in his assessment of this one. A pretty face, but an empty vessel. Not any challenge there. She would be far too compliant.

Ultimately he wanted compliance, but only after he had broken a wild filly and remade her as he desired. If it was not for the anticipation of dancing with the sister, the Duke would have left the blonde in the middle of the dancefloor and taken his leave. He felt relief when the second dance came to an end. Relief and excitement. He was about to dance with his third duchess.

As much as she would have preferred not to dance with the old man—she cared not if he were a duke—Elizabeth did not want to sit out the rest of the night as she already had a full dance card. To make sure he never asked her again, she decided to demonstrate her impertinence at its finest to him.

Hertfordshire led the one named Lizzy to the line.

"Your Grace, are you sure you do not need to sit out after dancing two sets, one after the other?" Elizabeth challenged with a raised eyebrow. "You are not a young man after all."

'*I do not intimidate her in the least!*' the Duke realised and felt himself becoming aroused by that fact. "I trust I will survive this dance," he responded aloud.

"If you need to rest, please do not hesitate to tell me, I will assist you back to one of your men," Elizabeth shot back.

'*Yes, little Lizzy, you will be perfect! You will bear me an heir and then, after he is one, I will take my time and pleasure to completely break you. The chit could not have done more to show herself to be the perfect candidate if she had attempted to.*'

"You know what Miss Elizabeth; I have seen all I needed to see here tonight. If your offer is sincere, may I escort you back to your mother?" Hertfordshire requested.

"Please do, Your Grace," Elizabeth averred.

Without another word, the Duke led his future wife to her mother and then farewelling no one, he and his men departed to make the short walk back to the inn.

"What did you say to the Duke to displease him?" Fanny demanded as she pinched her second daughter's upper arm.

"Not a word, Mama. He was fatigued after dancing with

you and Jane and felt he needed to rest," Elizabeth claimed.

"If you have spoilt your sister's chances of becoming a duchess, you will never hear the end of it," Fanny threatened as she released her daughter seeing that not a few neighbours were looking at her disapprovingly. Fanny sniffed and went to find her sister.

"Are you well, Eliza?" Charlotte questioned concernedly.

"I will be well," Elizabeth replied as she rubbed her upper arm. "It is not the first, and nor will it be the last time something like this has occurred."

As much as she would have loved her father to protect her from her mother's nastiness, Elizabeth knew he did not have the gumption to stand up to his wife.

~~~~~~~/~~~~~~~

"A glass of Brandy, Wickham?" the Duke offered.

"Thank you, Your Grace, much appreciated," Wickham responded.

"You did well," the Duke raised his glass to his man once Wickham held his libation in his hand. "She is perfect. There will be a bonus in it for you."

"As always, you have my gratitude for your munificence," Wickham drawled.

"Wickham, once I have the father's agreement to wed his daughter, bring the mother to me. I would like to take a tumble with her."

"It will be so, Your Grace."

CHAPTER 3

As soon as the front door closed, Fanny rounded on her second daughter. On the way home she had convinced herself the wilful disobliging girl had done something which would cause the Duke not to shower Jane with his attention.

Fanny grabbed Elizabeth by the arms. "Tell me what you said to the Duke!" Fanny screeched her mouth only inches from her daughter's face showering Elizabeth with spittle. "I do not believe you said nothing…"

"**MAMA!**" Jane yelled.

If her mother had not been digging her nails into her arms, the look of shock at Jane's shouting would have been comical. Thankfully, her mother released Elizabeth's arms and turned towards Jane with a dumbfounded look.

"Jane what has your sister done to upset you so…" Fanny began and then closed her mouth in surprise with the strident response from her beautiful Jane.

"Lizzy told you the truth about why the Duke departed, I was dancing close to her in the line and I heard him say he was tired," Jane asserted firmly. "It is you and your treatment of my most beloved sister which has disturbed my equanimity, not Lizzy."

Elizabeth was overjoyed, not only that Jane was standing up for her, but she was standing up at all and not trying to look for some positive reason for their mother's cruel treatment of herself.

"B-but Jane…" Fanny tried again.

"Mother, do you really believe Lizzy could have chosen whether she was a boy or a girl?" Jane demanded. "Is it not time to leave that behind us now? My sister has been blamed for that over which she had no control for sixteen years, it is enough."

She was sure this outburst was somehow caused by her wilful second daughter, but now was not the time to upset Jane. Fanny was certain the Duke would be calling to see Jane on the morrow, after all, it was Jane who he had danced a complete set with.

Her eldest, most beautiful daughter would be a duchess, oh what joy would flow from that. If only Lyddie was older. With her liveliness, the same as both Fanny's late mother and she herself had, she was sure Lydia would have turned the Duke's head. There was nothing for it, at only ten it was not possible so all her hopes would rest on Jane.

Bennet stood inside his study with his door cracked. When he heard Jane yell he was about to join his wife and two eldest daughters to see what the ruckus was all about.

That Fanny was once again blaming Elizabeth for something she did not do was a normal occurrence. He felt guilt regarding the fact it was serene, normally docile Jane who had finally said what he had wanted to say to Fanny for years. The feeling of culpability passed as soon as it had appeared.

Peace in the home was paramount and he was well aware of the living hell his life would become if he ever tried to check his wife's excesses, either in spending or—especially— with regard to her irrational treatment of Lizzy.

He did what he could to protect his second daughter. She was welcome to join him in his study anytime she chose to. After all, she was one of the only ones in many years who had been able to best him at chess. In addition, she was able to debate many subjects with him and cause him to stretch his intellect. Lizzy was not only a beautiful girl, but she had an overabundance of intelligence.

He watched as his daughters were waved away. Seeing his wife was headed to his study, Bennet pulled the door closed and was seated behind his desk before the harpy marched in. He waited patiently while his wife walked circles on the carpet as she tried to marshal her thoughts, such as they were.

"Once Jane is married to the Duke…" Fanny began and stopped when her husband raised his hand.

"No one has come to ask for Jane's hand, duke or otherwise," Bennet interjected. "Of what do you speak?"

Looking at her husband as if he was a simpleton not to know, Fanny related the events of the assembly and the fact the Duke danced with none other than herself, Jane, and part of a dance with Lizzy before she caused the man to leave the ball.

"He has not been yet, but I am sure he will, as soon as the morrow," Fanny asserted.

"Jane is only eighteen years old, how old is the Duke?"

"I was married at barely seventeen, Jane is older than I was, besides, she will be nineteen in October." Fanny did not answer the question.

"Excuse me if I do not like your way of catching a husband," Bennet responded sardonically. "I asked about his age."

"Hang his age! He is fabulously wealthy and when he is married to Jane I…we will never have to be concerned about the future after you go to your eternal reward."

"So he is an old man. I will not force Jane to marry where she is not inclined. Besides, this is all theory. There is nothing which says he will offer for Jane, or any other woman in the area. What if the gossip regarding his seeking a wife is wrong?"

"Gossip is never…" Fanny did not miss her husband's raised eyebrows at the statement she began to make. She had to admit tittle-tattle was more often in error than having the right of it. "I am sure it will be as I say."

With the last said, Fanny turned around, leaving the door open, made for the stairs, and headed for her bedchamber.

~~~~~~~/~~~~~~~

"Jane, I have never been more proud of you nor more thankful either," Elizabeth hugged her sister once their shared chamber door was closed.

"What you said at the assembly may have taken hold," Jane admitted shyly. "I love you far too much to stand back any longer and allow Mama to hurt you."

"As I love you, Janey. You know I would do anything in my power to protect you, do you not?"

"That is well known to me, Lizzy. All I can do is beg your pardon that I allowed my desire to see things as I hoped they were, to cause me not to stand up for you before tonight. I am the older sister and it is my duty to protect my younger sisters." Jane held up her hand and smiled as she saw Lizzy about to interject. "Yes, I know you are a strong girl and can defend yourself, but I cannot stand back and allow Mama to keep treating you as less than the rest of us."

"If only Papa had agreed to allow me to go live with Uncle Edward and Aunt Maddie in London," Elizabeth stated wistfully.

Elizabeth had been four, not long after her beloved Grandmama Beth had been called home to God and the Gardiners—Uncle Edward was newly married to Aunt Maddie —had been visiting.

She had been pretending to read a book—Elizabeth had always felt an affinity to them even before she could read— and her mother, not knowing her brother and sister-in-law were observing her, had pulled the book out of Lizzy's hands. As any child of four would, she began to cry. Her mother had rewarded her with a pinch on her arm for having the temerity to disturb her peace, which only caused the little girl to cry even louder.

The Gardiners had been outraged at what they witnessed. Even more incensing was the fact Bennet had done nothing about it. It was then Gardiner had asked his brother to allow Lizzy to come live with them in London.

Not wanting her disobliging daughter to have the enjoyment of living in London with her brother, Fanny had refused and let Bennet know how strenuous her ongoing complaints would be if he agreed. Bennet had capitulated and refused his permission. They had reached a compromise of sorts. Jane and Lizzy would visit the Gardiners together for a few months a year.

It had taken four years before the first Gardiner child— Lillian called Lilly—was born. Edward, called Eddy, had arrived in February 1801. It was not until the third child May had been born in August 1804, that the Gardiners had begun to shorten the amount of time their two nieces came to visit them.

Both Jane and Elizabeth were well aware their comportment, manners, and most of their accomplishments had been learned from the examples they had seen and been taught when visiting Gracechurch Street in Town.

"As much as I understand your life would have been better living with the Gardiners, I would have missed you every day," Jane admitted. "At least we were the lucky ones who spent much time with them."

"I suppose what you say is true. I cannot imagine my life without you in it every day. At least Mary has been open to the lessons we have passed on. I am afraid Lyddie will grow up to be wild and ungovernable with the way Mama spoils her. Where Lydia leads, Kitty follows."

"As much as I am loathe to criticise our sisters, I have to agree with you," Jane owned. "I have known for a time Mama does Lyddie no favours by indulging her, but as you know, she will hear no one speak against the way she parents Lyddie, not even from Papa."

On the tip of Elizabeth's tongue was the retort their father would do nothing which required effort, but she did not want to push Jane too much. This was the first—and Elizabeth hoped not the last—time Jane would stand up for what was right. Not necessarily just for her advantage, but in general.

The sisters—as they did each night—assisted one another to prepare for bed. They climbed under the covers and Jane extinguished the final candle.

~~~~~~~/~~~~~~~

Robert Darcy was working on his ledgers and the projections for the coming harvest based on the spring planting which had been completed not many weeks past. His steward was sitting with him as the two men poured over the columns of numbers.

"Enough Wickham, it is time for us to end the work day," Darcy decided as he closed the ledgers. "Will you join me in a glass of port?"

"Yes, thank you, Mr. Darcy, that would be welcome," the steward averred.

The study at Pemberley was of a larger proportion than the average one. It was almost as wide as it was long. At the end opposite the door was the master's oversized, highly polished mahogany desk. Darcy's well-padded high-backed chair, the one the man had just vacated, was behind the desk. In front of the desk were two comfortable armchairs. One of which Wickham had just been sitting in.

Behind that was a bank of bookshelves which started on the sidewall next to the side of the desk, ran along the back wall, and ended on the other side just before one of the two floor to ceiling windows.

Very few, not even the steward, knew one of the units of shelves behind where the master sat, opened to reveal the thick steel door to a secure vault. It was not only the bulk of the Darcy jewels stored within—inside rows of velvet lined drawers stacked six high—but a few thousand pounds in cash and important documents.

Certified copies of all documents were also held in London in the offices of the solicitor who served the Darcy family's interests.

There was a second floor to ceiling window—the view from the windows was across Lady Anne's pride and joy, her rose garden, to the park beyond, and the lake which began where the grass ended. Between the windows was a comfortable settee with low tables on either side of it.

Opposite were three wingback chairs arranged in an oval facing the settee. On the wall behind them, close to the end of the bookcase on that side of the room, was a sideboard on which sat various decanters and glasses on the silver tray.

While the steward sat in one of the wingback chairs, Darcy stepped to the sideboard, unstopped the decanter containing the port, and poured a measure for himself and the member of his senior staff.

"Thank you, Sir," Wickham said appreciatively when Darcy handed him one of the glasses with the dark red wine within.

"To another productive year," Darcy toasted. The two men saluted one another with their glasses and then each took a pull of his port. "Any word regarding George?"

The steward's wayward son had been employed as a clerk in Clovelly in Devonshire, a town not far from where his sister and her husband resided. Less than two and one half years past, Wickham was notified his son had absconded with all of his employer's funds which had been meant to pay the next three months' wages for the employees.

Since then, neither hide nor hair of his son's location had been discovered. Wickham hoped more than believed his son—who had a rather resentful nature and easily decided he had been ill-used when no ill-usage existed—had left England's shores with his ill-gotten gains.

Refusing to allow his steward to repay him, Darcy had sent the employer the full amount George had stolen from him. That receipt and some other debt markers were among the documents kept in the vault. Not only had he made the employer whole, but it had caused the search for George to cease as rather than a theft, it was now a matter of a debt owed to Robert Darcy.

"Unfortunately nothing, which may be a good thing. I can only hope my son is not bedevilling anyone else." Wickham needed to change the subject to a more pleasant one. "How does Master William in London? I thought he did not enjoy the season."

"He is at Darcy House with his mother and sister. That Bingley fellow, affable chap, had invited William to reside at his brother-in-law's house, but William refused. He refuses to be under the same roof as his friend's unmarried sister."

The master did not need to say more. Charles Bingley had been invited to Pemberley summer last. He had, apologetically mind you, arrived with his two sisters and the older one's husband in tow, even though he had been the only one invited.

The younger sister, Miss Caroline Bingley, had obviously set her cap for the Darcy heir, regardless of his opinion of the matter. She had been in residence three days before she had stoked the ire of one of the most gentle ladies in the world, Lady Anne Darcy. Evidently, the harpy decided to act as the *de facto* mistress when she thought she was unobserved.

Not only had she been seen by the mistress, but she had been caught being rude to Pemberley's housekeeper, Mrs. Reynolds, who was more family than servant.

The very next day the Bingleys were on their way out of Pemberley with a flea put in Mr. Bingley's ear. He was told in no uncertain terms if he ever arrived at any Darcy property with more than those specifically named as invitees, he would be turned away and no further invitation would be forthcoming.

"Excuse me if I am speaking out of turn, but has that woman with her flaming red hair not received the message Master William would not be interested in her if she were the last woman in England?"

"You would think, but it seems Miss Bingley has the same ability my sister-in-law Catherine has. To see and hear only that which suits her desires."

Wickham knew all about the termagant named Lady Catherine de Bourgh. Out of respect to his employer, he listened when his master spoke of her and her foibles, but never made his opinions of the woman known.

"If it is agreeable to you, I think I will turn in for the night."

"Go Wickham, I will see you in the morning before I depart to join my family in London," Darcy stated.

~~~~~~~/~~~~~~~

Bennet was seated in his study in the early morning the day after the assembly, as was his wont.

That time of the day was the most peaceful as his wife and two youngest daughters only woke a little before the family broke their fasts at half after ten. The only other one awake would be Lizzy who would be out rambling over the estate's paths, more than likely sitting on a rock on the summit of Oakham Mount waiting to welcome the sunrise.

Thus, he was greatly surprised when Hill knocked on his study door and presented him with a note. Bennet dismissed his man and broke the ostentatious seal.

11 April 1806
Red Lion Inn, Meryton
Mr. Bennet:

I am Lord Archibald Winston Chamberlain, the Duke of Hertfordshire and (until I have an heir) the Marquess of Hertford Heights.

One of your daughters has caught my eye. Hence, I require that you present yourself to me at the above inn at midday on the morrow, the 12th day of April. You do not want to suffer my wrath and be ruined if you are late or ignore my summons.

For His Grace, the Duke of Hertfordshire, Marquess of Hertford Heights

Could it be Fanny was correct in her assertion Jane was to be a duchess? It seemed so, regardless of how unlikely Bennet ever thought it would be.

Under normal circumstances, he would have ignored the note, but this was the type of man you neither ignored nor refused. Bennet was rather sure the explicit threats were not idle ones. The only question was whether he could agree to engage his eldest daughter to a man of an age greater than his own.

He would say nothing to Fanny and go to the meeting. If Jane left, at least he would have Lizzy at home with him.

CHAPTER 4

At the time and day demanded by the Duke in his note, Bennet presented himself at the Red Lion Inn. He was met by a man who called himself Wickham who would show him to the parlour where the meeting would take place.

Bennet was led into the largest sitting room on the second floor. The man he saw was balding, corpulent and, he could easily see, was considerably older than himself. His first instinct was to turn tail and run as fast as his legs could carry him. However, he quickly discounted that option as he looked around and saw that besides the man who had shown him up, there were rather large guards in the hallway outside the room and one more behind him in the sitting room.

"Your Grace, I present to you Mr. Thomas Bennet of Longbourn. Mr. Bennet, Lord Archibald Chamberlain, His Grace the Duke of Hertfordshire, Marquess of Hertford Heights," Wickham intoned.

Bennet gave a deep bow while the Duke who had remained seated barely inclined his head towards him.

"You have been summoned hither as I am about to bestow an honour on your family which you could not have expected in your wildest imaginings," Hertfordshire drawled.

"And what, Your Grace, would that be?" Bennet asked.

He did not know how he could give Jane to this man in matrimony. What Fanny wanted was immaterial, he was old enough to be her *grandfather*.

"I have selected one of your daughters to be my

duchess," the Duke related matter-of-factly.

"B-but y-Your Grace, Jane is only eighteen summers old, somewhat younger than yourself," Bennet stammered as diplomatically as he was able.

The Duke looked past Bennet to where Wickham was standing. "Wickham, who is this Jane?" he demanded. "I thought her name is…?"

"It is Elizabeth, Your Grace," Wickham corrected demurely. "Mr. Bennet is under the misapprehension you mean to make his eldest, the blonde one you danced with, your duchess."

Now he had to fight to keep from casting up his accounts. Bennet was frozen, it was not Jane but Lizzy the Duke was demanding. He knew Lizzy's disposition and she would never agree to marry this old man.

"There must be an error, surely you do not want to marry my second daughter who is but sixteen," Bennet managed.

"I most certainly do," was the indignant response.

How could this man who was lower than horse dung on his boot be resisting the honour he was bestowing on his family? If he did not need the man's agreement he would have had his men dispose of him.

It was easy to see the Duke was becoming angry at his opposition to his desire. Bennet was sure Lizzy would refuse and even if she was forced into the church, she would not recite her vows. His second daughter did not allow anyone to intimidate her. Much like he did with his wife, Bennet chose the path of least resistance.

"Please accept my abject apologies, Your Grace. I was not prepared for the high honour you desire to bestow on my family and specifically my second daughter," Bennet bowed to the man to show his deference. "Would you be willing to come to my estate later today?" Seeing the Duke was about to berate him Bennet elucidated. "I am sure a man of your discernment realises he must speak to the lady in person and convey the honour of his proposals. As soon as Lizzy has agreed then we will solidify our agreement."

Hertfordshire cogitated for a moment. Seeing the girl—having only been in her company for their truncated dance—would tell him if she was as impertinent as he believed she was.

"I will grace you with my company in two hours. Before you depart, I have a question." The Duke wanted to know how much the man loved his wife, that way it would increase his pleasure when Wickham brought her to him and he took her.

"Ask what you will, Your Grace," Bennet replied evenly.

"So I can understand the environment she was raised in, is yours a happy home? Is the relationship between yourself and your wife a good one? Was it a love match?" Hertfordshire probed.

He had not been ready for the burst of derisive laughter from the nothing country squire.

"Please excuse my outburst, Your Grace," Bennet bowed again. "My eldest daughters are who they are in spite of my wife who entrapped me into marrying her, so you can imagine my union is the farthest from a love match you could find. If that disqualifies Lizzy—Elizabeth as a potential bride, I will understand."

Any desire he had to bed the man's wife was washed away in an instant when the Duke understood this was a man who could not care less if his wife was taken by another. "No, it has not changed anything." The Duke waived Bennet away.

He signalled Wickham to remain when the other guard showed the father of the girl from the room.

"No Mrs. Bennet?" Wickham verified. He had seen the change in his master as soon as Mr. Bennet related the truth of his feelings for his wife.

45

"You know me well, Wickham," Hertfordshire growled. "If you ever try and use anything against me, you will not live to see the next sunset."

"Your Grace, you must know you have my complete loyalty," Wickham assured his master.

He felt a cold shiver travelled down his spine. He was all too aware the Duke would have him disappear if he even suspected disloyalty. Wickham had to keep proving his worth to the man. As soon as the Duke decided he was not useful any longer, he would meet his end. Thankfully he was good at procuring the man that which he wanted. His secret hope was the Duke would expire before the time he was deemed of no more use.

~~~~~~~/~~~~~~~

"Janey, please do not cry so," Elizabeth pulled her older sister into a hug as she tried to console her.

Their mother had summoned Jane as soon as Papa departed for his meeting and whatever Mama had told Jane had upset her terribly—Elizabeth knew not what that was as Jane was crying too much to tell her anything—and she had returned looking sadder than Elizabeth had ever seen her. As soon as Jane entered and Elizabeth asked her what ailed her, Jane burst into tears and now, more than ten minutes after entering the bedchamber and falling into her younger sister's arms, she was still sobbing.

Jane was usually the one who guarded her emotions closely. Elizabeth had seen her cry a few times before, but never as her dearest sister was now. It was breaking her heart and she knew not what to do to make Jane feel better.

"Janey, did Mama say something to upset you?" Jane nodded. Her crying lessened somewhat. "Will you not tell me what hurt you so much?" More nodding. "Would you like me to ask Sarah to bring a pitcher of water and a glass for you?" Again her older sister nodded her head.

With the deluge of crying reduced to a trickle, Elizabeth went to the chamber's door and looked out into the hall. She did not want to leave Jane. Luckily she saw one of the upstairs maids and called her over and requested she ask Sarah—the maid shared by all five sisters—to bring the water. The maid bobbed a curtsy and went on her way to fulfil her charge.

Elizabeth closed the door and sat next to Jane on the bed and gently rubbed Jane's back. The crying was reduced to sniffles by then. Knowing Jane would talk as soon as she was ready, as hard as it was for her to exercise patience, Elizabeth waited.

There was a knock at the door. On opening it, Elizabeth stood back for Sarah to enter carrying a tray with a pitcher and two glasses. The maid placed the tray on the dresser, bobbed a curtsy to the Miss Bennets and withdrew, pulling the door closed behind her.

Jane had kept her head turned from Sarah so she would not see the evidence of her crying. The last thing Jane wanted was for word she was upset to reach her mother. She knew if it did, Mama would automatically blame Lizzy and even if Jane told her it was what she had been told earlier that morning which devastated her, Mama would have ignored her and yelled at Lizzy anyway.

She gratefully took the glass Elizabeth handed her. Her instinct was to gulp the water down, but Jane forced herself to take small sips.

"You remember the Duke we danced with at the assembly?" Jane enquired as she began her tale.

"How could I forget that old man and the way he was ogling us. I felt like I needed to bathe after my, thankfully, short dance with him." Elizabeth paused suspiciously. "I know he is a duke, but surely Mama would not try and match you with a man much older than Papa!"

"Mama told me…" Jane hiccoughed, "the Duke and Papa

are meeting this morning because…" Jane burst into tears once again. "She said she found a note on Papa's desk."

"Janey please do not tell me Mama thinks the Duke wants you as his wife." Jane gave a watery nod. "Did the note to Papa say that?" Jane shook her head. "Then this is all in Mama's head. She knows not why Papa is meeting with the Duke and is stating what are her desires. They are assumptions. Even if Mama is right for once, surely Papa would never force you to accept a man so much older than himself. We promised we would only marry for the deepest love and respect, and that is how it will be!"

As much as she wanted to believe her own words, Elizabeth was not blind to the fact Papa never stood up to their mother. All she could do was pray that if Mama's supposition was accurate, for once their father would act to protect his daughters.

The tears dried up as Jane endeavoured to believe Lizzy's words. Mama had things wrong more often than not, so there was hope she would not be sacrificed.

~~~~~~~/~~~~~~~

Fanny was waiting for her husband at the front door when he arrived home.

"Well?" she demanded. "Did I not tell you he wanted to marry Jane? How many times have I said she could not be so beautiful for no reason! Why did you not have me join you? I read the note!"

Exasperated, Bennet responded, "Do you think I can have something to drink and then we can meet in my study rather than here where all the servants can hear?"

The woman could not be more vulgar if she tried to be. Bennet did not wait for an answer from his wife. As soon as Hill took his outerwear, he made for his study. As he suspected she would, his wife followed him into his sanctuary.

"Do not make me wait, he wants to marry our daughter,

does he not?" Fanny insisted as soon as her husband closed the door to the study.

"He does," Bennet confirmed.

"My beautiful Jane will be a duchess! Just wait until I tell Lady Lucas, she will turn green with envy. What pin money, what carriages, homes, and jewels. I will go distracted," Fanny babbled.

Bennet was not looking forward to the manic swing in his wife's behaviour as soon as he delivered the news he knew she would be loath to hear. It had to be done before his wife decided to go call on their neighbours to boast to one and all.

"Mrs. Bennet, the man is a Duke, he is rich to be sure, but he is closer to seventy than sixty. I thought you loved Jane, why would you want to see her shackled to such a man?"

"How you enjoy vexing me! To save me...us from the hedgerows when you go to your reward. He has more than enough wealth and mayhap he will set us up at one of his estates," Fanny responded dreamily as she again imagined all the riches Jane would have access to.

"It is not Jane the Duke wants to marry," Bennet related.

Fanny Bennet stood frozen, staring at her husband as if he had the head of a wild animal on his shoulders. After some moments she discovered the power of speech once again. "Lyddie is too young and they have not met, surely he cannot want any other than Jane."

"He wants to marry Lizzy," Bennet said almost softly knowing the explosion which was about to occur.

This time she stared at her husband as if he was an insane person who belonged in Bedlam. "**WHAT DID YOU SAY! DO NOT DARE SPORT WITH ME IN THAT FASHION!**" Fanny screamed at the top of her voice.

She had heard him.

"I was as surprised as you are, it is Lizzy he wants, not

Jane."

"What did that wilful, cursed girl do to distract the Duke from her sister?"

"Mrs. Bennet did you not tell me he danced a set complete with both you and Jane, and only a portion of a single dance with Lizzy?" Fanny reluctantly allowed it was so. "By your own statement, Lizzy was in His Grace's company for no more than five to ten minutes. Please explain what she could have done in that time?"

Each time Fanny began to speak, she stopped. The truth was she could not come up with anything to support her claim. "I will not stand for that underserving hoyden becoming a duchess when Jane will not!" Fanny finally bit out.

"Firstly, I seriously doubt Lizzy will accept his proposal. By the way, he will arrive to make it in little more than an hour. Secondly, do you really think a man who is obviously used to getting whatever he wants, will pay heed when you try to redirect him to Jane, who he has already decided against?"

She had no answer for her husband, but of one thing she was sure, she would do everything in her power to make sure the Duke amended his choice when he called later. That ugly child would not be a duchess!

Bennet knew he needed to distract his wife. "We are to entertain a duke, should you not prepare the house to receive one so high? It is not every day we have a peer of the realm at our house."

Whatever vitriol Fanny was about to spew was forgotten. Without another word, she lifted her skirts a little and ran out of the study screeching rather loudly for Mrs. Hill to attend her.

By the time Fanny had issued orders to prepare to receive a duke into her house and verified everything was up to standard, there was a scant twenty minutes before the rich man was to call. Her frenetic running around had allowed her to convince herself it was Jane the Duke was calling for.

Unfortunately for her, there was not enough time to have Jane change before her suitor would arrive. At first, Fanny arrived in the drawing room with only a fearful Jane with her.

Regardless of his wife's opinion about which daughter should be present, Bennet sent Hill to summon Lizzy. Fanny glowered at her husband. She would make him pay for crossing her later.

Barely a minute after Elizabeth sat next to Jane, and gripped her sister's hand in a show of support, the knocker was heard striking the front door.

CHAPTER 5

Hertfordshire had not been impressed by the small size of the estate of Longbourn. Even less so by the pile which was the manor house he spied when his coachman brought his large travelling coach to a halt near the front door of the house.

As it was below him to do so, he had Wickham rap on the door with the knocker. The door was opened by a manservant. His lack of uniform and wig told the Duke the Bennets did not even have the wherewithal to employ a butler. This fit with what the vulgar woman had told him at the assembly.

"His Grace the Duke of Hertfordshire, Marquess of Hertford Heights to see Mr. Bennet," Wickham told the man who opened the door.

"Please follow me," Hill intoned as he bowed.

Hill led the Duke and his man to the drawing room.

As he walked, Wickham was of the same opinion of his employer that there was no money here. Seeing that told him there would be no resistance to the Duke's overtures.

Hill announced the Duke and stood to the side. Being almost as wide as he was tall, the guest barely fit through the doorway without touching the doorframe on either side of him. Only years of learning to school his features stopped Hill from smiling at the corpulent man almost not fitting through the door.

The three ladies gave deep curtsies while the Bennet father bowed to him. The Duke did not respond with even an inclined head.

The Duke stopped and looked between the girls standing between their parents. The blonde insipid one was next to her mother. Why she was present, he knew not, but he would soon set things to rights. The lady of the house was smiling like the cat who got the cream, and his soon to be wife stood between the blonde one and her father.

Seeing the defiant look in his intended's eye thrilled the Duke. He reminded himself he would need to keep his desires in check until she had birthed him an heir and said child had been alive for a year. Then and only then he would take his enjoyment.

"Why are both sisters here? Did I not make myself clear when you called on me as to who it is I want to speak to?" Hertfordshire drawled as he sat on a settee without invitation.

"You see Mr. Bennet," Fanny hissed. "You have upset the Duke by having that hoyden Lizzy here. If you have spoilt Jane's prospects, I will never forgive you."

Jane was praying hard her father had angered the old, very large in girth man and he would leave without proposing to her.

"Did you not tell your wife?" the Duke demanded.

"In fact, I did, Your Grace," Bennet averred. "Unfortunately my wife did not believe you are here for Elizabeth."

Before anyone could speak, an outraged Elizabeth, who had paled considerably, did. "I am not ready to marry anyone, and certainly not one as old as this!" she insisted pointing at His Grace.

Rather than injure him, the Duke was even more convinced of his choice at her outburst. She showed no fear at all. His anticipated pleasure when he broke her increased exponentially.

"B-but Your Grace," Fanny blurted out, "surely you

cannot be in earnest. Jane is a beauty and will be the perfect duchess. Miss Lizzy is wilful, disobedient, impertinent, a hoyden, has manly pursuits, and is nothing to my Jane in looks."

"All of what you listed are in fact the things I am attracted to," the Duke responded disdainfully. "And if you think the lacklustre one," he cocked his head to Jane, "is prettier than Miss Elizabeth, then I suggest you need spectacles."

"I care *not* what you say, I will never marry you! I know the law! If I do not recite my vows there will be no valid marriage!" Elizabeth said with meaning. She was standing, her arms at her sides and her fists clenched.

Bennet breathed a sigh of relief. He knew his Lizzy would never agree to be married to the man, and neither the Duke nor his wife would be able to blame him if she refused to open her mouth at the wedding ceremony.

"You see, what did I tell you," Fanny crowed triumphantly. "Why would you want that…"

"**SILENCE**!" the Duke thundered. "Are you so simple you do not know when to keep your mouth closed? He turned to Bennet. "Remove this dunderheaded woman and her blonde daughter."

Already scared by the Duke's shouting at her, Fanny allowed Hill to lead her and Jane out of the drawing room without a word of complaint.

When the door was closed, the Duke nodded to Wickham who almost dragged a most unwilling Elizabeth to stand in front of his master. An outraged Elizabeth looked to her father for protection, but he just stood in place, doing what he always did—nothing!

"You will marry me," the Duke said as a way of a proposal.

"Never. You may do what you will, I will never marry

you," Elizabeth shot back. She kept her eyes on the man, never lowering her head or showing any fear.

"I did try to warn you, Your Grace," Bennet stated with much relief. "Once Lizzy makes up her mind, she will not change it."

As attractive as her resistance was, if she refused to recite the vows of her own free will, she would never be his wife. After the display she was putting on she had to be— would be his wife.

"In two days I will return and we will revisit this subject," the Duke commanded.

"There will be no wavering on my part, not in two days, two years, or two millennia! Never will I be your wife," Elizabeth insisted, her arms akimbo, chin up as she looked at the disgusting man in front of her.

Without comment, the Duke had his man assist him to stand, and he then walked out of the drawing room without another word.

~~~~~~~/~~~~~~~

Elizabeth had not waited for her father to speak, with tears of fury running down her cheeks, she had run out of the drawing room, through the house, and out of the kitchen door. She did not stop running until she reached Oakham Mount.

Still crying in frustration, she stomped up the path to the summit. When there, she began to rapidly pace back and forth.

If her father had not been so selfish, he would have allowed her to go live with the Gardiners years ago and then she would never have been the object of the disgusting man's attentions.

She would not, could not, marry such a man. Elizabeth intended to honour the vow she and Jane had taken to only marry for the deepest love. Forgetting the age of the man, she did not even like him—yes, she had only met him in the last two days—in fact, truth be told, she hated the very sight of him! He was a man she could never respect as she had been witness to a union without respect, that between her parents, and it was something she would never accept for herself.

Until today, she had believed Papa loved her. Mama she knew did not, so anything she said or did would not be surprising to Elizabeth.

The scales had fallen from her eyes. Papa was unable— or unwilling—to protect her. Not one word had he said, other than an *I told you so* to the old man. If he knew she would refuse him, why did Papa allow the Duke to come to their home and importune her in that fashion?

She knew the truth, Papa was weak. She had seen the examples of his ineptitude over the years when it came to checking Mama's excesses and he never did. Elizabeth could clearly see how Mama manipulated Papa. All she had to do was caterwaul a little and Papa would give into anything she wanted.

Elizabeth could only pray Mama would remain opposed to her being married to the Duke. If she somehow changed her mind, then the pressure on Papa would be relentless, which would translate to him demanding she marry the ancient man.

Mama would never change her mind. She would not allow herself to see the daughter she disliked with intensity become a duchess and not Jane.

For whatever reason, and Elizabeth could not fathom what it was, thank goodness, he did not want to marry Janey. As long as Jane was safe, Elizabeth would endure the slings and arrows directed at herself. She knew her own strength and would not be bullied into changing her mind regardless of what Papa demanded she do.

Hopefully, the old man would be so repulsed with her behaviour he would quit Meryton and leave both herself and

Janey in peace.

Feeling somewhat more sanguine with things and with her confidence in her own willpower high, Elizabeth began to relax. She seated herself on the bolder near the eastern edge of the summit.

She untied and removed her bonnet and then placed her hands behind her for support as she rested, her body at an angle, allowing her arms to keep her in that position.

With the sun warming her, Elizabeth forced herself to forget about the situation at home—for a short time.

~~~~~~~/~~~~~~~

"You were not making sport with me, that man wants to marry Lizzy," Fanny stated.

As soon as the Duke left their house, Fanny had sought out her husband. She had found him in the study. As much as she did not want Elizabeth to become a duchess over Jane, Fanny had realised the advantage to herself would still be great.

"As you saw," Bennet responded tiredly. "You also heard Lizzy say she will never marry him, and you know Lizzy is not one to weaken her resolve."

"Did I not always say that ungrateful girl was wilful?" Fanny paused as she thought about solutions. "If you command it, she will have to marry him."

"You may believe that if it makes you feel better. Mrs. Bennet, regardless of what I command, I cannot force her to recite her vows as she has promised she will not. There cannot be a marriage if one of the two does not speak their vows."

"We will have to find a way!" Fanny intoned shrilly. "This is too important for my...our future! That disobliging girl will do her duty to her family and she *will* obey. Did I not tell you she was overindulged by you? That is why she thinks she will be able to refuse to do that which she must! I will not allow her to anger His Grace! If his judgement is so lacking to

SHANA GRANDERSON A LADY

want Lizzy as his wife, then have her he will."

Bennet knew a response was not required, so he made none. He also knew nothing would sway Elizabeth from her chosen path. It was what he was relying on.

~~~~~~~/~~~~~~~

"She is magnificent," the Duke mused after he and his party returned to the inn. "Wickham," he looked to his man.

"Aye, Your Grace," Wickham gave a bow to the man as he stood.

"Go use your charms and find out as much as you are able about Miss Elizabeth, her likes, dislikes, and her family. When we return in two days not only will I offer her family financial incentive, but I want something to use as leverage in case the little spitfire still refuses to marry me," Hertfordshire ordered.

Wickham bowed and headed into the town to begin to fulfil his master's instructions.

~~~~~~~/~~~~~~~

"Lizzy, I am so sorry Mama berated you as she did tonight. I would never be able to stand strong like you did," Jane said admiringly.

Jane Bennet was under no illusions, not only was Lizzy much more intelligent than herself, but she possessed an inner strength Jane would never have. If anyone could resist their mother's machinations and the insistence she marry the Duke, it was Elizabeth.

"I am happy he chose me and not you," Elizabeth stated stoically.

"How can you say that, Lizzy? You dislike the old man as much, if not more than I do!"

"That is not a fact I will dispute, Janey. But we both know if Mama was insisting you marry him, eventually you would have."

"I do not have the core of steel you possess my dearest sister," Jane acknowledged. "What that man said about you being as pretty, if not more so than me, is true Lizzy. I care not what Mama will say if she hears me articulate it, but it is a fact."

"Janey, what codswallop. You are ten times more beautiful than the rest of us combined!"

"Lizzy, how can you allow what Mama says to influence your opinions of your beauty?"

"After hearing her diatribes for over sixteen years, I suppose I have given her statements much more weight than I should have." Elizabeth sat and stared off in the direction of the heavens.

"What will you do if he renews his addresses in two days when he returns?"

"Refuse him as vehemently as I did today. They can truss me up with rope, force me into the church, and drag me up the aisle, but still, I will refuse to recite my vows. Nothing can make me change my mind!"

~~~~~~~/~~~~~~~

By the next afternoon, Wickham had spoken to many in the town. He used his charm and good looks to loosen tongues and what he discovered he knew, beyond a shadow of a doubt, was exactly what his master needed as leverage.

Wickham reported his findings to the Duke who was well pleased with the results. "Perfect, Wickham. You have once again proved your worth to me." The Duke nodded to his man of business who was in the room. "Give Wickham here fifty pounds for his stellar work."

"Your generosity knows no bounds, Your Grace," Wickham bowed to the Duke. '*The old stingy bastard could have given me a hundred times that amount and not felt it!*' he told himself.

Hertfordshire waved his man away. Absent mindedly he

said aloud, "it is a pity there was one more day to wait. I cannot show any weakness by asking for the date to be changed. I will return there on the morrow as planned."

The only part of the inn which was open to the public was the taproom which is where Wickham headed. Mayhap there would be some games of chance. He had a good amount of money in his pocket and winning more would be just the ticket.

~~~~~~~/~~~~~~~

That night, knowing the extremely old man would be back on the morrow, Elizabeth did not find any comfort in Morpheus's arms. Her mind was far too active.

She wanted tomorrow to be over already. The sooner the man was on his way and out of their lives the better. She cared not for all of Mama's screeching. She was a sixteen year old girl, and it was not her duty to save the family, that rested with her parents.

Nothing would make her do that which was abhorrent to her, and she could imagine nothing worse than being leg shackled to that revolting man. He could have been a royal and nothing would have been different for Elizabeth. What was it to her if he was a duke? She would not under any circumstances allow her free will to be subjugated to him.

At least since finding out she was not the object of the Duke's interest, Janey had relaxed. She was no longer in fear of being sold off to the man like so much chattel.

Yes, for Janey, Elizabeth would bear this nonsense and continue refusing his every entreaty.

CHAPTER 6

All of her hoping the Duke would not return had been for nought. Elizabeth was led into the drawing room by Mrs. Hill, where the corpulent old man sat in her mother's favourite chair on this unwelcome visit, which thankfully was rather wide, but he still had trouble fitting on it.

Her parents were standing before him, just like they had the day before, the only difference was Jane was thankfully not present on this occasion.

It was the only positive Elizabeth could grasp for this day. Jane would be spared the spectacle of having to see the farce which would play out in the drawing room. How she wished she too was with her older sister, but it was not to be. Elizabeth raised her chin like she had the previous visit and looked at the Duke unflinchingly. She did not curtsy or say anything in greeting.

Fanny did not miss the blatant disrespect aimed at His Grace by her undeserving daughter. She made to move towards her daughter but the Duke raised his hand stopping her in her tracks.

"But Your Grace, how can I allow her rudeness in not greeting you to stand?" Fanny beseeched.

"If I feel something needs to be done, you must trust I have the capacity to make that decision," Hertfordshire drawled.

'*What a pity*,' the Duke told himself silently. '*If the husband had cared about her it would have been fun to take a tumble with her. What a waste of a pretty woman.'*

"Yes, Your Grace," Fanny demurred. Inwardly she was furious. If Miss Lizzy did anything to spoil things... Her musings were interrupted by her daughter's speaking.

"Am I to assume you are still determined for me to marry you?" Elizabeth enquired. She knew she was being rude to the man, but she cared not. She would do anything she could to convince him he would not find a bride at Longbourn.

"As you can see," the Duke averred.

"Why would you, a man of above sixty years..." Elizabeth stopped as the duke interjected.

"A man of soon to be seven and sixty years," the Duke clarified.

"Then why are you pursuing a young lady, one who will not marry you mind you, who is more than fifty years your junior?" Elizabeth demanded.

"Elizabeth Rose Bennet, how dare you speak to a duke in that fashion," Fanny screeched. She could not allow this blatant disrespect to stand.

She pulled her arm back intending to deliver a well-deserved slap to her second daughter's face. Seeing his master nod, Wickham moved with speed and caught the shrew's hand before she was able to strike the future Duchess. Fanny felt her arm in a grip which did not allow her to move.

"Let me be rightly understood, no one in this household will lift a finger against my soon-to-be fiancée," the Duke thundered.

Fanny shrunk back in fear. The Duke should have been angry with her wilful daughter, not herself. She thought about disciplining Miss Lizzy once the Duke and his men had departed, but she remembered his words and did not want to take a chance he would back them up with actions.

"As to your question, Miss Elizabeth, my reasons are my

own. Although I will inform you there are certain attributes I sought in a wife, and you have all the ones I desire," Hertfordshire explained.

"And what are these *attributes* I supposedly possess?" Elizabeth insisted on knowing.

Bennet watched silently, as he had yester-afternoon. As long as Lizzy did not give in, there was nothing the man could do. He may be a duke, but the church would not change its law for him or any other, save the Monarch.

There was no surprise her father was not defending her. It was no less than Elizabeth expected. She would have to defend herself.

"Do you love your family?" the Duke asked a seemingly incongruous question.

"Of course I do," Elizabeth bit back. "What sort of simple question is that?"

"Allow me to tell you what I will do for your family if we marry." Seeing the firebrand was about to protest, he raised his hand. "All I ask is allow me to complete what I desire to say, thereafter, you may say what you will." Elizabeth gave a tight nod of acceptance. "This estate is entailed to the male line, is it not?"

"It is Your Grace," Bennet confirmed.

"Am I correct the beneficiary will be some distant cousin, named Collins?" This time Bennet nodded to the Duke. His Grace turned back to Elizabeth. "If we marry, with one condition, I will have the entail broken..." He held up his hand again to stem the words which were about to be loosed by Miss Elizabeth. "I am not done. In addition, each of your sisters will be dowered to the amount of five and twenty thousand pounds, dependent on the same condition being met."

Before Elizabeth could respond, her gleeful mother interjected. "What is the condition?" Fanny trilled.

No more entail, massive dowries for her deserving

daughters—even Mary and Kitty, little did they need it. Fanny could not believe her ears, such massive dowries! It would have been even better had there been an increase of her portion as well, but she would make sure to commandeer some of the funds meant for Mary's and Kitty's dowries for herself. That way, she too would be wealthy.

"Your daughter birthing me a son. As soon as there is an heir and he attains the age of one, I will do as I have now promised. Until then, I will present a draft for ten thousand pounds to Mr. Bennet, to be split between the four remaining daughters, who will after all be my sisters." The Duke looked at Mrs. Bennet pointedly. "There will be restrictions on the money. No one will be able to divert it for any other purpose."

Her joy diminished somewhat, but her daughters would be rich and there would be no more entail. There was still much for Fanny to be glad about. She could only imagine Sarah Lucas's face when she revealed her daughter's wealth to her.

"As much as I would like to see the entail broken and my sisters well dowered, I am not a cow in the dairy to be bartered and sold," Elizabeth responded icily.

With the possibility of the entail being broken, after a slight pause and a flush which revealed his shame, Bennet said quietly: "That is rather selfish, Lizzy."

"In the extreme," Fanny screeched as she saw her dream of no more entail and her daughters becoming heiresses being blown away to nothing like light wisps of smoke on the wind.

"I desire to speak to Miss Elizabeth in private," the Duke demanded.

"There is nothing you cannot say in front of my traitorous parents," Elizabeth spat out.

As much as she knew her father was indolent and weak, she never expected him to be willing to sell her like a piece of furniture.

"Leave us," the Duke commanded.

Elizabeth began to leave with her parents when the Duke's man stopped her by holding onto her upper arms. Her outrage at her father grew exponentially as he and her mother exited the drawing room and closed the door without looking back at her.

~~~~~~~/~~~~~~~

Not many minutes passed before the man named Wickham summoned the Bennet parents back into their drawing room.

Bennet felt guilt when he saw his daughter's tear streaked cheeks. "Lizzy, did someone hurt you?" Bennet asked with genuine concern.

"Other than you Mr. and Mrs. Bennet, no one has harmed me physically." Elizabeth glowered at the smug-looking duke when she spoke.

"Your daughter has something to tell you," the Duke reported with an evil grin.

"I agree to marry His Grace," Elizabeth informed her parents through gritted teeth.

"My man will hie to London to acquire a special licence and we will marry as soon as it arrives. On the day we marry, I will present you with a bank draft for the amount I agreed to provide before the birth of my heir," the Duke revealed.

His daughter would not look at him, and Bennet remembered she had called him Mr. Bennet, not Papa. "We must meet at my brother-in-law Philips's offices for the settlement. Without one, I will not sign the document giving my permission for my daughter to marry and then there will be no license."

"Agreed. We can make for the solicitor's office directly. It will be far quicker than travelling to mine in London," the Duke allowed.

Her part done, Elizabeth fled the drawing room for her

and Jane's bedchamber.

~~~~~~~/~~~~~~~

An hour later, Jane found her sister sobbing on the bed. Never had she seen Lizzy half as upset as she was now.

"Lizzy, what has occurred?" Jane enquired as she sat on the bed and began to rub her sister's back to try and soothe her hurt.

"I...am...to...marry...that...reprehensible...old man," Elizabeth managed between sobs.

"No Lizzy, please tell me it is not true," Jane begged.

"W-wish...I...could."

"What happened? I thought you were the one of us who would never give in on this."

"Do...not...want...to talk...about...it."

If anything, rather than subside, Elizabeth cried even harder than she had been before. Jane was at a loss to understand what had occurred to make her sister agree to marry the very old man.

If it were her, Jane knew she would not have been able to withstand the pressure from her mother, but Lizzy would never give in to anyone. So why had she now?

~~~~~~~/~~~~~~~

The Drawing room, an hour or so previously

"Talking to me alone will in no way change the fact I will never marry you, no matter what you offer my family as the price for my purchase," Elizabeth insisted.

"Do you remember I asked if you loved your family?" the Duke questioned.

"I do, unlike you, I am still young enough to remember what was said minutes ago," Elizabeth riposted.

Rather than get upset as she hoped he would, the Duke and his man, the one she had already grown to hate, Mr. Wickham, only grinned like fools.

"According to Wickham here," the Duke inclined his head towards his man, "you love your older sister the most and will do anything in your power to protect her, will you not?"

"Who would not do what they could for one they love?" Elizabeth hedged.

"Indeed. If you continue to refuse me, I will tell your mother she is correct, I chose the wrong sister and I will propose to Miss Bennet. We both know she does not have the fortitude you do," the Duke stated nonchalantly as he flicked some imaginary lint from his oversized waistcoat.

The fact he would never marry one as meek as Jane Bennet was not something the object of his desires needed to know. He had always been good at bluffing—and when needed, cheating—when playing cards.

The instant angry tears began to roll down her cheeks, Lord Archibald Chamberlain knew he had won. She would be the challenge he had wanted and he would take pleasure in bedding her to beget an heir.

"If I am to be forced to marry a vile old man, then I have some terms which are to be added to the wedding settlement..." Elizabeth had laid out a few things without which she would not agree to marry him.

"Agreed. I will have those items written into the marriage settlement," he confirmed. "You do not want to know how much I will settle on you?"

"I care not." Elizabeth spat out as she wiped some of her tears of anger from her eyes.

"After we marry, you will be presented at court, and then we will retire to my main estate of Falconwood," the Duke related.

"Please summon Mr. and Mrs. Bennet back in, the sooner I am out of your company the better," Elizabeth stated with a hard edge to her voice.

One thing she resolved, as she waited for those who had given her life but were certainly her parents no longer, was that she could not tell Jane why she had agreed to marry the heinous old man. Jane would never recover from the guilt which would plague her if she knew the truth.

~~~~~~~/~~~~~~~

Elizabeth stuck to her resolution. She told Jane nothing regarding her reasons for accepting the old man. It was her burden to carry.

Eventually, Jane's gentle ministrations to her back relaxed Elizabeth to the point she was overtaken by sleep. When Jane noted the change in her sister's breathing indicating she was slumbering, she continued to rub her favourite sister's back.

She could not even imagine the pressure which had been brought to bear on Lizzy to cause her to capitulate.

~~~~~~~/~~~~~~~

Philips pulled his brother into his private office, leaving the Duke dictating the terms of the settlement to the law clerk.

"Bennet, you cannot condone my niece's marriage to a man who is practically of an age to be our fathers!" Philips exclaimed.

"You see the advantages to us aligning with him. The entail, dowries..." Bennet began to answer.

"With conditions," Philips interjected.

"There are one or two more than I expected, but nothing I am unwilling to agree to." The guilt of Lizzy marrying this man was already lessening.

The Duke had restricted the money for his daughters as he had said he would, but the interest from the four per cents would most probably be paid out to Bennet. Another four hundred pounds per annum, which Fanny would be unaware of would purchase many books and much port after Lizzy was married.

"Does our Brother Gardiner know you are selling Lizzy for your and Fanny's comfort?" Philips interrogated.

"Not yet, soon…" Bennet began.

"You can be sure I will be sending an express to Edward and Maddie this very day," Philips insisted.

Bennet would have preferred to have more time before another disapproving brother remonstrated with him, but the settlement would be signed in the next hour or two so there would be nothing anyone could do to stop things. Not that Gardiner would have been able to even before the documents were signed.

Philips had had some reservations about the wording of some of the outside of the norm items which had been incorporated in the settlement, especially the additional document Bennet would have to sign. However, his disgust with his brother-in-law was so great he decided to hold his peace. If Bennet wanted to accept the terms as they had been laid out, then so be it.

The duke was settling two hundred thousand pounds on Lizzy, but what would that be worth if she was suffering in an unhappy marriage. Philips had never been more disgusted with his Bennet brother and sister.

An hour later, the settlement was signed. Also, an express rider was well on his way to London.

~~~~~~~/~~~~~~~

"I cannot believe they would do this!" Gardiner exclaimed when he read the express from Philips.

"Edward, what is it?" Maddie enquired worriedly.

"We leave for Longbourn at first light," Gardiner told his wife as he handed her the page.

"Yes, indeed we do," Maddie agreed with a moue of distaste aimed at the Bennet parents.

CHAPTER 7

Sleep would not claim Elizabeth that night. Knowing Jane would wake if she were not still, she lay without moving for as long as she was able before she slipped out of the bed she shared with her dearest sister. Once she had wrapped her robe tightly around her, Elizabeth sat in the window seat, allowing the curtains to fall behind her back.

'It was my choice to protect Janey so I can never allow myself to resent her for the fact I will have to marry the brute on the thirtieth day of April,' Elizabeth thought to herself as she looked out of her window onto the park which was bathed in moonlight from an almost full moon and very few clouds blocking the light. She looked wistfully at the ancient oak in the middle of the park. Although the branches hid it, she knew the swing was hanging there, the one she and her sisters had enjoyed so much over the years, and now in less than a fortnight she would not see it again.

Elizabeth had no expectation the old man would ever allow her to *lower* herself to visit Longbourn once she was married to him. How she hated the fact one of the vows she would recite on that terrible day was to obey him.

At least she had gained a small concession in return for consenting to marry him, he agreed to have the wedding at the end of the month. He had wanted it in a few days and she had wanted to delay it as long as possible. Almost a fortnight was better than days, but all it did was delay the inevitable.

'I can only pray I bear him a son as soon as possible because then at least he will not need to come to me any longer.' That

thought made her think of the speech her mother gave her that evening.

Not long after she had joined Jane in their chamber for the night, Mrs. Bennet had called her to attend her in her bedchamber. She had explained what happened between a man and woman on their wedding night and thereafter. From books she had seen in Mr. Bennet's study and living on a working farm having seen animals mate, Elizabeth already understood the mechanics of the act.

There was no doubt in Elizabeth's mind about the glee with which Mrs. Bennet explained the pain which would be felt the first time, and more than likely thereafter as well. She was told to lie still and submit to her husband whenever he chose to claim his rights.

Only once she did her duty and became with child would her husband cease coming to her.

She resolved that each time he came to her, she would keep her eyes shut tight, she had no desire to see more of the disgusting man than she had already seen. It was a strong motivation to want to be in the family way as soon as may be so she would be able to be free of his attentions.

'Sisters I still have, but I am an orphan. Those who did not protect me from my awful fate cannot be bestowed with the honour of being called parents. I have been sold into slavery!'

With this last thought the tears began to fall once again. Elizabeth had thought she had cried all of her tears earlier and there were none left, evidently there was an endless supply. Even though she made no noise, her body was wracked with sobs.

Her life as she had known it to that point, was over.

~~~~~~~/~~~~~~~

The Gardiner carriage had barely stopped in front of Longbourn's manor house when the door burst open and an infuriated Edward Gardiner shot out.

Hill did not miss the thunderous look on Mr. Gardiner's countenance so he stood back wordlessly to give the master's brother-in-law a clear entrance to the house. The Hills and all of the servants were beyond disgusted with the master and mistress for selling Miss Lizzy to an old man, regardless of the fact he was a duke. It seemed Mr. Gardiner shared their opinion of the matter.

Gardiner pushed the study door open with such great force it crashed against the bookcase behind it causing books to rain down from the shelves.

Bennet had been sitting with a book and some port, as was his wont, when the door flew open. It caused him to start, spilling his port over the front of his coat, waistcoat, shirt, and cravat.

He stood up just in time to see the fury in his brother-in-law's face and before he could duck, Gardiner threw his right hand forward, his hand in a fist and planted a facer.

The force of the punch threw Bennet back colliding into a bookcase. He then crumpled to the floor as blood began to flow from his mouth, books raining down on his head. Gardiner was not a violent man, so why had he struck him in that manner? His answer was quick in coming.

"You selfish bastard! You are so far beyond contemptuous. *HOW COULD YOU SELL YOUR DAUGHTER* to a man old enough to be your father?" Gardiner spat out as he stood over Bennet ready to hit him again if needs be. "Maddie and I wanted to adopt Lizzy, but you wanted her here with you regardless of how much she suffered from my sister's mistreatment. You are not a man; you are a weak shell of one. What have you to say for yourself you nodcock!"

Bennet removed his handkerchief from his pocket and while still seated on the floor wiped away the blood still trickling from his mouth. He was sure there were two or three loose teeth from the force of the blow Gardiner had delivered.

His head ached from where some of the falling books had struck him.

"Lizzy was sacrificed for the good of the family..." Bennet got no further because Gardiner reached down, grabbed him by his lapels and lifted him.

It caused Bennet to cower as he suspected Gardiner was about to deliver another punch, or more than one.

"For your good, not the good of the family! Had you pulled your head from your arse after you married Fanny, and yes, I know she entrapped you, you would have given over her portion for me to invest for you and sent me some of your profits each year.

"But no, you have not the backbone to stand up to my sister and you allow her to spend you into oblivion, not to mention your extravagance on books and port! Now because you would not bestir yourself to take the trouble to plan ahead, you sell Lizzy to this horrendous man. Did you even check as to why he is seeking his next duchess here and not in London?"

"N-No," a much frightened Bennet managed.

In disgust, Gardiner released Bennet with a little push causing the man to fall back into his chair behind the desk. "You know not that not one member of the *Ton* will allow their daughters to marry him because both of his first two wives have been killed in suspicious circumstances. There was no one who would bear witness against him being he is a duke, but it is an open secret in Town." Gardiner related what had caused the Duke's late son to die.

By now Bennet's pallor was decidedly grey. "How was I to know?"

"If you had taken the trouble to leave the confines of your study you would have been able to discover all with ease. It would have taken a letter to me, or even having Philips investigate. But no, I am sure you were reading a book you have read ten times before and were *unable* to leave your *vastly important work* to do something to protect your daughter."

As Gardiner had struck at the truth of the matter, Bennet would not look him in the eye. He rather dabbed his mouth, which had all but ceased bleeding than try and defend that which he knew was indefensible.

"It is too late now; the marriage settlements are already signed. Besides that, the other four will eventually receive dowries of five and twenty thousand pounds each," Bennet explained churlishly.

"You disgust me, Bennet. It would not have been too late if you had acted as an even halfway decent parent. When we leave here today, Jane and Lizzy will accompany us and thereafter, besides seeing our other nieces, all connection between us is broken. From my sister, I expected this sort of thing, but not you. I always thought Lizzy was your favourite. Evidently that all changed when you were presented with a way to break the entail with no effort to yourself!" He paused as he thought about leaving any children at Longbourn. "One thing, you will sign a document giving me guardianship over the remaining girls for as long as I see fit. Not even the younger ones should remain under your care."

"I cannot," Bennet began to reply and blanched as Gardiner seemed to get ready to strike him again. "Speak to Philips…" Bennet related the reasons to Gardiner.

"In that case, you will sign and permit me to keep the girls in the meantime. I will *NOT* leave my nieces here at your and my sister's mercy. Who knows which one you will sell next if you need more books and port? Also, you will give me control of their dowries when the initial amount is paid." Gardiner noticed the look on Bennet's face and that he was about to object.

"You planned to use the interest for yourself, did you not? Not only will you not, but you will pay me forty pounds per month for their upkeep. You and my sister will not profit from what you have allowed!"

With a defeated look, Bennet wrote out his permission, agreed to the monthly sum to be paid for the girls' upkeep, and signed the document.

With that in hand, Gardiner turned and marched out of Bennet's study.

~~~~~~~/~~~~~~~

"Sister," Fanny exclaimed when Madeline Gardiner entered the drawing room. "Have you come to congratulate me that my most undeserving daughter is to be a duchess?"

"Congratulate you for selling Lizzy for your comfort. You and your grasping, mercenary ways disgust me," Madeline averred with asperity.

In the hall outside, Jane and Elizabeth heard the words from within. Jane squeezed Lizzy's hand.

When Jane had woken this morning, she had found the spot in the bed where Lizzy would normally be cold. Before Lizzy went for a ramble, she always woke Jane and told her what direction she was headed, and she had not done so this day.

As much as Jane would have sympathised with her, she did not believe Lizzy would have run away without telling her goodbye.

Jane had looked and found Lizzy's clothing for that day still where it had been left before they went to bed and nothing else was missing from either her closet or dresser. Jane was at a loss as to where her beloved sister was when she noticed the curtains had a rather distinct bulge.

On opening them, it had revealed Lizzy curled up as tightly as she was able and asleep on the cushions of the window seat. As gently as she could, Jane had woken her younger sister.

Lizzy had explained she had not been able to fall asleep

and came to sit and look out over the park to commit as much of it to memory as she was able. She did not remember lying down, but based on where Jane had discovered her, she had obviously done so.

Due to the fact Lizzy refused to sit at the same table with —as she now called them—Mr. and Mrs. Bennet, Jane had asked Sarah to have two trays delivered to their chamber. If anyone asked, she was to say Miss Bennet was indisposed and Miss Lizzy was keeping her company.

Until they saw the Gardiner carriage stop in the drive, the eldest Bennet sisters had resolved to remain in their chambers for the rest of the day using the excuse Jane gave to Sarah as the reason.

They had readied themselves as speedily as they had been able which had brought them outside the drawing room in time to hear Aunt Maddie berate their mother.

For the first time since being forced into accepting the brute she was to marry, Elizabeth showed a ghost of a smile in reaction to hearing her aunt stand solidly at her side. She was about to enter the room when Jane placed a restraining arm on her wrist and shook her head. Elizabeth understood Jane wanted to hear what else was said. For her part she too wanted to know, so Elizabeth stopped and stood with Jane.

The three younger girls sat with gaping mouths at the way their normally mild-mannered Aunt Maddie had attacked their mother.

"How dare you speak to me in my house thusly. That ungrateful, disobedient girl will save this family, as it is her duty to do as she refused to be born a boy!" Fanny screeched.

"So you sold Lizzy to the worst kind of man because of that nonsense you hold onto, that Lizzy, or any babe has the ability to choose the sex it will be born," Madeline shook her head at Fanny's abject stupidity and ignorance. "Following your logic, why is it you do not blame any of your other four daughters for not being sons? And what of Lyddie, it was her size which made it impossible for you to birth any more children. Should we blame her for that over which she had no control as well?"

"Mama, the bible teaches children are a blessing from God, so how could Lizzy determine to be born a boy or girl?" Mary, who had turned fourteen a few days previously, pointed out.

"Hold your mouth! What do you know? A girl as plain as you has no room to talk about anything!" Fanny bit out at her middle daughter nastily. She turned back to her sister-in-law. "And you miss hoity-toity, you are just jealous my daughter will be a duchess and I will move in society much greater than the wife of a tradesman..."

Fanny Bennet had always been jealous of her brother's wife. Madeline had been raised a gentlewoman whereas she was the daughter of a solicitor. Everyone liked Madeline and she was too intelligent for a woman; hence Fanny disliked her.

"NO YOU WILL NOT!" Elizabeth, who had slipped into the drawing room unnoticed, insisted at the top of her voice. "If you think you will ever be in my presence again after I leave this home, you, Mrs. Bennet, are delusional."

"Do not dare to speak to me in that fashion, I am your mother!" Fanny screeched as she began to stand intending to slap her rude daughter as hard as she was able.

"Fanny Bennet, if you attempt to harm Lizzy in any way, I will do the same and worse to you," Madeline threatened.

Fanny did not like the determined look in her brother's wife's eyes so with no good cheer, she sat back into her chair.

"You and Mr. Bennet are no longer my parents," Elizabeth retorted once her aunt had said her piece. "Anyone who is willing to sell their daughter into slavery cannot be considered such. We both know if the Duke had not for whatever his unknown reasons are, chosen me, you would have been quite happy to sell Jane to him. You have always professed your love for Janey, yet you would have consigned her to the terror I am to endure as his wife. Is that how you would have demonstrated your love for Janey, marrying her to an old man who has the makings of being a brute?

"So no, Mrs. Bennet, you will not join me in Town, you will never be invited to any of my husband's houses or estates. Once I leave this house I will never know you or Mr. Bennet again."

"Lizzy, what do you and Aunt Maddie mean that Mama and Papa sold you to the Duke?" Lydia asked confusedly.

"You know your sister tells tall tales," Fanny tried to hedge.

"It is nothing but the truth, Lyddie," Jane spoke up. "If he had not wanted to marry Lizzy, Mama would have put me forward, in fact, she tried to have him take me instead."

"Jane, how could you," Fanny averred with put on sadness, her hand over her heart.

"Because it is the truth, and you know it is," Jane shot back.

Now it was Elizabeth's turn to squeeze her sister's hand in support.

Just then Gardiner entered the drawing room and nodded to his wife. "Girls, go and pack as much of your things as will fit into two trunks, the rest will be sent to you on the morrow," Gardiner instructed. His wife placed a restraining hand on his arm.

"Of what do you speak? **MY GIRLS ARE NOT LEAVING ME**! I suppose you can take Mary and Kitty, and of course Miss high and mighty Lizzy. The sooner I never see her again the better," Fanny stated disdainfully.

"Lizzy, after what you have been through, we do not want to take more choices away from you than has already been done." Madeline, ignoring Fanny, looked directly at

Elizabeth. She turned to address the other four girls. "We would like all of you to come live with us, you until you marry Lizzy, the rest of you for the time being. Your father has given his permission, in *writing*."

"The sooner I am away from Mr. and Mrs. Bennet, the happier I will be," Elizabeth accepted.

"I feel the same," Jane added.

"Me too," Mary agreed.

Jane looked at the two youngest Bennets. "We will not leave you two alone here. I promise you this is a very good thing."

The three youngest Bennets stood and headed for their chambers to pack while Fanny stared at them with her eyes wide-open, and a gaping mouth. She was about to tear into her husband's study to demand he rescind his permission if he had in fact given it. Before she could stand her second daughter addressed her with ice in her voice.

"When my fiancé or one of his despicable men come seeking me, send them to Gracechurch Street." Elizabeth turned and cut her mother and she and Jane went up to pack.

~~~~~~~/~~~~~~~

"How dare you send my Lydia away!" Fanny screeched as soon as she pushed the study door open.

The door slammed against the bookcase for the second time that day and Bennet flinched thinking Gardiner was returning to beat him again. He was almost relieved it was his wife instead.

"It is done and done for the best," Bennet stated as he returned to his book.

"You tell them you have changed your mind, **NOW**!" Fanny screamed.

"Yet I will not, as I have not," Bennet averred evenly. "You may caterwaul all you want; it will not change the facts.

We will have an estate with no entail one day, but no children."

Bennet did not explain anything to his wife who stood staring at him as if he was mad.

Fanny screamed at him for so long that by the time she tried to stop her brother from removing her children, she was in time to see the retreating Gardiner carriage.

CHAPTER 8

"You brought this on yourself," Hattie Philips told her younger sister. "How did you think the rest of us would react when it became known you sold one of your daughters to a man so very old, and even worse, from all accounts, an absolute reprobate."

Fanny had been convinced her easily led sister, the same one who had assisted in her compromise of Thomas Bennet all those years ago, would never stand up to her in this way.

"How can you be so disloyal to your sister?" Fanny demanded with asperity. She did not enjoy Hattie having her own opinions.

"My first loyalty is to my husband, who I married without any subterfuge, unlike you who with all of your beauty and charm had to entrap a man into marriage," Hattie shot back.

Her husband had informed her about her brother's removal of her nieces from Longbourn. At first, she had felt sympathy for her sister, but the more her husband revealed regarding Thomas and Fanny's callous and mercenary behaviour, the more she had come to opine it was no more than her sister and brother-in-law deserved.

A look of outrage was returned by Fanny, but unlike in the past where a display of anger would make her sister waiver, there was no effect now.

There was one thing Fanny knew her sister would not be able to resist, tears. "You have cut me to the quick," Fanny moaned as she squeezed out some crocodile tears. "How can you be so heartless when I suffer so?" She dabbed her eyes with her delicate lace handkerchief.

"If you think I will be swayed by your fake crying any longer, you are sorely mistaken, Sister!" Hattie stated firmly. "It has been some time now since I realised I should never have participated in any of your dishonourable schemes, not the least of which was your entrapment of your husband."

Fanny Bennet was reeling. Not only had she lost her children, but now her sister's support—something she had counted upon all these years without question. At least she still had her friends in the neighbourhood. She would enjoy boasting of how she would soon be the mother of a duchess.

"I take no leave of you, Fanny, you deserve no such compliments. My husband and I will not admit you or Bennet to visit us socially any longer. My Frank will continue to act as Thomas's solicitor for the good of your children. That is the only contact we will allow." With that, Hattie turned on her heel and marched out of her younger sister's drawing room without a look back at Fanny.

She stood frozen to the spot. Hattie had just broken all connection with her, and then cut her. Fanny was reeling.

"You are just jealous!" Fanny screeched at the spot where her sister had stood. "Regardless of what Miss Lizzy says, I *will* be in the Duke's company and he will get my children back for me. Him a brute! What stuff and nonsense! Other than not having the good sense to choose my Jane over Miss Lizzy, he is a very proper gentleman."

Pushing the visit out of her head, Fanny ordered the butler to have the carriage readied. It was time to go lord her daughter's soon-to-be rank over those in the neighbourhood, starting with Lady Lucas.

How jealous that lady would be. Her husband was only a lowly knight while she would soon be the mother of the Duchess of Hertfordshire!

~~~~~~~/~~~~~~~~

"I know it is not ideal as we only have two chambers for the five of you," Gardiner told his nieces the next morning.

Jane and Lizzy had shared the bed in the smaller room while Mary, Kitty, and Lydia shared the one in the larger bedchamber. None but Lydia had raised a word of complaint regarding the sleeping arrangements.

From the day Lydia had been moved from the nursery, at eight rather than ten, or in Elizabeth's case twelve, she had been given a large bedchamber which she did not have to share. At Longbourn, Jane and Elizabeth always shared, as did Mary and Kitty. Their mother had never hidden her favouritism of the youngest Bennet.

"I still do not see why I have been taken away from Longbourn and Mama," Lydia whined.

"Lyddie, we will address this later, let us hear what Uncle Edward has to say first," Jane suggested.

She pouted, but Lydia clamped her mouth shut.

"Thank you Jane dear," Gardiner smiled. "Some months ago, I purchased the house next door to us, the one which shares a wall with this house. I had intended to create space for offices there, but your Aunt Maddie and I have spoken. With our three and you four who will remain with us for the foreseeable future once Lizzy is married to *that man*, we will open the walls between the two houses and make one big dwelling. There will be more than enough bedchambers for each of you to have your own and when Lilly, Eddy, and then May move from the nursery, they will have their own rooms as well."

"Is there nothing which can be done with regards to my marriage?" Elizabeth asked.

"If I had known of this before your father," Gardiner noted his niece's scowl when he referred to Bennet in that way. "Excuse me, before *Mr. Bennet* signed the settlements, there may have been a way, but now there is not. If you refuse to marry him, he will assume guardianship of all five of you. He has enough wealth that he would be able to beat back any challenge."

Elizabeth felt like she had to ask. She was well aware of the terms of the settlement and that she had sacrificed herself to protect Jane. If she could have been assured Jane would be safe, she would have run away already. She would never do that to her most beloved sister.

"But why must I stay with you?" Lydia whinged.

"Lyddie, did you not hear what was said in the drawing room at Longbourn yesterday?" Madeline who had been silent up to now enquired.

"Yes, but Mama tried to say it was not true," Lydia claimed.

"Mrs. Bennet was prevaricating," Elizabeth stated stridently. "Do you think a parent who is willing to sell one of her daughters for her own future comfort truly loves any of her children?"

"But Mama never liked you; she would not have done so to the rest of us," Lydia reasoned, with much less confidence than she had before.

"Did you not hear Aunt Maddie remonstrate with Mama because she had wanted me to be the one to marry that ancient man...I am sorry, Lizzy," Jane rebutted.

"Please Jane, you, and any others, may insult that man as much as you choose. It is after all nothing but the truth," Elizabeth allowed.

"W-was t-that t-t-true?" Lydia queried tremulously. "I-I thought M-Mama loved you well, like m-me."

"It was all true Lyddie..." Jane told her sister exactly how their mother had tried to push her forward as the one to be sacrificed. "She only became sanguine with Lizzy being the one to be offered to the man when he offered to end the entail and dower the rest of us."

The tears fell freely from Lydia's eyes. It was not easy to see the pain it caused her to have her illusions shattered regarding Mrs. Bennet being a loving mother—at least to some of her daughters.

~~~~~~~/~~~~~~~

Robert Darcy had been in London for two days when he saw the announcement in the *Times of London* that the dissipated duke was taking another bride. That her name— Miss Elizabeth Bennet of Longbourn in Hertfordshire—was unknown was no surprise.

Rumour had been circulating according to his brother Reggie Fitzwilliam that Hertfordshire had turned to look in the countryside for his next bride when he had come to realise all doors in polite society were closed to him. No one he knew of would allow their daughter to become the Duke's next victim regardless of his rank or wealth.

The announcement said nothing of the young lady's family. Darcy wondered how old she was knowing the Duke was past five and sixty years.

He made his way to the main drawing room where his wife was entertaining their sister, Lady Elaine Fitzwilliam, Lady Sarah, the Countess of Jersey, and Lady Rose, Duchess of Bedford.

Darcy bowed to the ladies. "Anne and ladies, I just saw a distressing announcement in the papers, Hertfordshire is to be married again," Darcy shared.

"Do we know the lady?" Lady Anne enquired.

"No Anne, she is a Miss Elizabeth Bennet from an estate in Hertfordshire." Darcy turned towards the Duchess of Bedford. "Lady Rose, as your main estate is in Bedfordshire, have you heard of this family?"

"No, it is not a name known to me. Mayhap Sedgewick knows of them, but I doubt it," Lady Rose averred.

"It is obviously a family who only saw his rank and either did not know of his reputation or cared more for the societal advantages of such a match," Lady Jersey opined.

"We can only pray this lady has the strength to survive where his previous wives did not," Lady Anne stated sadly. "If her family did not know what he is, then they were wilfully blind."

"Or they cared not enough for their daughter and were seduced by his rank and wealth," Lady Matlock surmised.

There were sad nods from those in the room. It was a fact of life that there were parents who would sacrifice one of their offspring for purely selfish motives.

"Such a pity the King did not act when my husband and others tried to have the disgusting man hobbled," Lady Rose sighed.

A few years back, the Duke of Bedford and the Earl of Jersey, among other peers had applied to the King to have Hertfordshire's rank and wealth stripped from him. The King had been disinterested—part of his malady in the peers' opinions—and nothing had come of it except an angry and vengeful Duke of Hertfordshire once word got back to him.

Given the group who had applied to the King were made up of dukes and a few earls, there was nothing—so far—other than bluster Hertfordshire had been able to do.

"If we are able, we will assist the new Duchess," Lady Matlock stated. "However, I expect he will isolate her from society like he did his other wives."

No one disagreed with her.

~~~~~~~/~~~~~~~

As soon as he had arrived in London, Hertfordshire had the settlement papers sent to his solicitor. Yes, he had agreed to some things which raised his lawyer's eyebrows, but he fully intended to survive his new wife like he had the others so it was of no consequence to him.

The same day he sent Wickham to deliver the notices to the papers. If only he could have been present in the homes of members of the *Ton* when, despite their attempts to hobble him from finding a new duchess, they learned he had successfully secured a fiancée.

The next two days he spent between two of his mistresses. How it pleased him to be able to exercise his power over the doxies. As much as he would have liked to have Wickham procure him a wife of some peer or another, he knew he needed to refrain until after he was married. He did not want to give the Bishop of St. Paul's reason to deny him being married at that church.

Before returning to London after the summer upcoming, he would need to get the spitfire with child. Once she was sent away to one of his estates for the duration of her confinement, he would be able to enjoy himself and take his pleasures.

On his third day in Town, the Duke remembered he should send an engagement ring to his fiancée. He was at the largest of his four homes in London, Hertfordshire House on Berkeley Square. Hertfordshire pulled a bell pull. When the butler entered he told him to summon Wickham for him.

While waiting for Wickham, he swung the painting opposite him on the wall open and opened the safe behind it. Without paying attention he pulled open a drawer of rings and grabbed one from the top.

It was a gold band with a large emerald surrounded by smaller diamonds.

By the time Wickham knocked and was bade enter, the safe was locked and the painting back in place. "Ride to Long... whatever the name of the estate is, and present my fiancée with this ring." Hertfordshire tossed the ring at his man carelessly. Luckily Wickham caught it.

"It will be as you wish, Your Grace," Wickham bowed and then inspected the ring. "If I may point this out, Your Grace, your betrothed's fingers are somewhat thinner than this ring, it will not fit her."

"What care I, tell the father to have it made smaller then. Away with you." The Duke waved Wickham away like he would anyone of no consequence.

Wickham schooled his features, bowed and left the room. In short order, he was on a horse headed to Longbourn.

~~~~~~~/~~~~~~~

"The Duke of Hertfordshire's man to see Mr. Bennet and Miss Elizabeth," Wickham told the butler who opened the portal after he had let the knocker fall against the oak door.

Without a word, Hill made his way to the study. He returned anon and led Wickham into the room. Wickham looked around, other than at Pemberley and the Duke's libraries—and that man disdained reading, his libraries were to impress—he had never seen so many books in one place.

"My daughter is no longer here," Bennet stated gruffly without standing and greeting his guest.

"You have allowed her to run away?" Wickham thundered. "His Grace will be most displeased and you will feel his wrath…"

"I said she was not here, not that I do not know where she is," Bennet interjected.

"Then where is she?" Wickham demanded.

The worst thing for his health would be to return to Berkeley Square and report Miss Elizabeth was gone.

"She is at this address," Bennet proffered a piece of paper.

Wickham read:

Edward Gardiner

23 Gracechurch Street

London

"Why did you not write and tell His Grace she is in London?" Wickham insisted.

"I knew one of his lackeys would call." Bennet blanched when he saw the man bunch up his fists. "You are correct, I should have done so. With everything which has occurred of late, it was an oversight on my part." Not wanting to be hit again, Bennet had used a more conciliatory tone of voice for the latter part of his speech.

Wickham relaxed and opened his balled-up fists. "Good day," he intoned and then was gone.

Bennet breathed a little easier. He had avoided another beating.

CHAPTER 9

"Lizzy, how is it you did not write to us about all of this before? Your uncle and I would have come to attempt to put a stop to this madness before it was too late," Madeline wondered.

It was just aunt and niece sitting in the former's private sitting room. The rest of the Bennet sisters were with their cousins, the governess, and nursemaids at the park opposite the Gardiners' house. It was a nice spring day, perfect for a walk and feeding the ducks in the park. Madeline had requested Lizzy remain at the house in order to speak to her.

"But I did, several times," Elizabeth protested. "You never received one letter from either myself or Jane did you?"

Madeline shook her head. "If you wrote them then someone..." Madeline began to say.

"Removed them from the post before they were taken into Meryton," Elizabeth completed. "I am sure it was Mr. or Mrs. Bennet! I should have thought to take a letter to the Red Lion Inn myself."

"Did you not tell me the Duke had rented the entire inn for his stay?" Madeline verified. Elizabeth confirmed with a nod of her head. "Do you not think the Duke would have had his men be on the lookout for letters from Longbourn?"

"I thought myself so intelligent and I did not think of that either," Elizabeth berated herself. "I should have taken the post coach to Hatfield to send a letter."

"Dearest niece, why would you have suspected your parents to be so duplicitous?" Madeline questioned. "You hold no blame here, the only thing I am not reconciled to is why my niece who never changes her mind and will do nothing she does not want to has agreed to marry this man."

"If I tell you, I need you to swear you will tell no one, especially not Jane," Elizabeth insisted.

"You know I have no secrets from Uncle Edward," Madeline reminded her niece.

"I am sanguine with your telling Uncle, but not another living soul." Madeline agreed.

Elizabeth told her aunt what the Duke had used as a threat if she refused to marry him. She made sure her aunt was completely aware she did not resent Jane in any way as it had been her own choice to do what she did. Jane would never have asked it of her and would have sacrificed herself for the family which Elizabeth could not allow her to do.

"So I did in fact choose to marry for the deepest love, my love for my dearest sister and best friend in the world."

"My dear girl, never have I been party to hearing about such a brave and selfless act of protection." Madeline pulled her now crying niece into as warm a hug as she was capable of giving. "It was you who insisted some additional terms were added to the settlement, was it not? Uncle Frank mentioned something, without going into the details, to Uncle Edward."

"It was," Elizabeth confirmed with a watery smile.

Madeline decided to change the subject without asking Lizzy about the terms. "You have heard Uncle Edward and me speak about how the Duke treated his previous wives, have you not?"

"Yes, I am aware I am about to be shackled to the worst kind of man. If it had been my free choice he would be the very last man in the world I would ever be prevailed upon to marry."

"If I were to guess, he will do nothing to hurt you until you deliver an heir. If he does not do this anyway, you must have him send you to his estate in Derbyshire, Castlemere, while you are increasing. From there, after you deliver your babe, if we have to, we can assist you as I know many people in the area. You have heard me speak of Lambton where I grew up, have you not?"

"Many times," Elizabeth agreed.

"My brother, Adam, is the rector there, he took over after my father passed some four years ago. He and his wife Eve," Maddie smiled when she noted Lizzy's reaction to Adam and Eve, "do not look at me so, it was by chance he fell in love with Evangaline, she has always been called Eve." Elizabeth giggled. It was a sound Madeline had not thought she would hear again. "As I was saying before you made sport of my brother and his wife's names, Adam has many connections in Derbyshire, thusly through him, so do I. If and when we need to help you, he will know on whom we can rely. Thankfully, your husband-to-be is not at all liked anywhere in the country."

For the first time since the nightmare began, Elizabeth saw a sliver of hope. She threw her arms around her aunt and held onto her for many minutes.

'*I cannot tell Edward about what was done with Jane and Lizzy's letters yet,*' Madeline thought as she rubbed Lizzy's back. '*He would hie to Longbourn and pummel Bennet again, not that he does not deserve it, but I would rather not have Edward be arrested.*'

~~~~~~~/~~~~~~~

"What do you mean my fiancée is no longer at Longbourn? I will have the father killed if he let her escape!" the Duke thundered when Wickham returned with the ring to make his report.

"Your Grace, we know where she is, she did not escape, she is merely staying with an uncle and aunt, in fact, here in London," Wickham explained quickly in order to avoid being the next person the Duke permanently removed from this world.

"Why did you not say that to begin with? Sometimes I wonder if you are worth the trouble," the Duke drawled.

Wickham knew it would accomplish nothing were he to point out he had been telling the Duke all when the man had interrupted him. He had been working for His Grace long enough to know one did not gain anything by pointing out the master's errors.

"Well then take the ring to her," the Duke stated dismissively.

"Ahem, I tried Your Grace. Miss Elizabeth told me to tell you if you wish to present her with a ring, you need to present it yourself," Wickham elucidated.

"**WHAT!**" the Duke thundered. "Who does that chit think she is?"

"If you remember Your Grace, that is the precise reason you insisted on her being your wife," Wickham pointed out.

"I suppose it is," Hertfordshire allowed. "Where is this uncle's home, in Mayfair I hope?"

"No it is not, Your Grace," Wickham responded. "It is on Gracechurch Street near...Cheapside."

"**CHEAPSIDE!** Cheapside! Surely my intended is intelligent enough to know I would never go to *that* part of Town!" the Duke spat out.

"It is my opinion Miss Elizabeth is well aware of that fact. If I were to wager, I would say it is the precise reason she demanded you attend her there. That and..." Wickham trailed off.

"What are you not saying?" the Duke demanded.

"The uncle is in trade, Your Grace," Wickham revealed.

Wickham had, only that day, admitted to himself that he had become enamoured and impressed with the soon-to-be duchess. Never had he seen a woman as beautiful, even when he compared her to the blonde older sister. Her beauty was entwined with her indomitable spirit; she was far superior to any woman Wickham had ever met. She was scared of no one and all his employer wanted, after he had his precious heir, was to break her. Wickham did not think the Duke would succeed which would lead to him physically abusing the magnificent young lady to achieve his aims.

"Not only does she expect me to lower myself to go to Cheapside, but to the home of her tradesman uncle as well!" Hertfordshire barked in disgust.

Wickham refrained from pointing out a significant portion of the Duke's income was derived from the shipbuilding yards, so he was in fact in trade. One only pointed out unwanted information to the Duke if they did not value their lives.

"I believe it is her aim, Your Grace," Wickham opined.

"Wickham, return there with a letter of credit from my man of business and make sure my fiancée understands she needs to go to the best modistes and purchase the clothing she will need in her new station," the Duke commanded.

After a bow to his master, Wickham left the room to carry out the order.

Even though he did not appear in polite society, he still demanded his wife would look the part and not disgrace his name. He cared not how much it cost him.

On the one hand, Hertfordshire was irked by the insolence of his fiancée; she held no respect for him and his position at all. On the other hand, it was in fact the very reason he had chosen her. He supposed he should not be surprised she would challenge him at every turn.

Not for the first time, he repeated his hope to himself that she bear him an heir within the first year of marriage so he would be able to have his enjoyment with her soon enough.

To break her spirit would give him the ultimate

pleasure.

~~~~~~~/~~~~~~~

That evening the Duke of Hertfordshire called on the one peer in London who would receive him, albeit with extreme reluctance, the Earl of Colbath. The man had lost enough money in cards to Hertfordshire that he could have claimed his estate. It was the man's own fault, for he had never caught the Duke cheating.

In return for not calling in his debts, the price had been that Lord Kenneth McIntire, whose estate was on the Scottish Highlands, and his wife, would do anything Hertfordshire demanded of them.

Unfortunately, they had no unmarried daughter or it would have been the answer to the Duke's problem and given him a titled bride.

"Colbath, I need your wife to sponsor my new wife so she will be presented after we marry," Hertfordshire demanded.

"You had told me that the last *favour* you would ask of me was when you used my house in London to bed Lady Mowbray, and that you would return my vowels to me after that," the Earl stated with distaste.

"When your wife has mine presented, they will be yours," Hertfordshire promised.

"You will excuse me if I do not trust you, Your Grace," Colbath stated as evenly as he was able to in the face of the despicable man. "If you want this, then you will deliver the debt markers to my solicitor before my Morag assists your wife. As soon as the new Duchess is presented, he will release them to me."

Hertfordshire had wanted to keep his talons into Colbath, but he needed his wife presented more and there was not another noble's wife who would agree to do it.

"Agreed, give me your solicitor's direction, we will meet

SHANA GRANDERSON A LADY

there on the morrow and sign the agreement. Once signed, I will hand the man your vowels," the Duke agreed with no good cheer.

When the blackhearted man had been shown out of his house, the Earl felt a great weight lift from his shoulders. He would finally be free of Hertfordshire, as well as the threat to his estate and his son's inheritance.

With a lightness of step, Colbath sought out his beloved Morag to give her the excellent news. At least this time, the price of doing a *favour* for the damned Duke was not too high.

~~~~~~~/~~~~~~~

For the first time in her life, Fanny Bennet discovered what it was like to be on the receiving end of negative gossip. It had started at Sarah Lucas's house. Fanny had arrived to gleefully boast about her success in marrying off her second and least deserving daughter so well.

She was told Lady Lucas was not at home to her. Fanny had screeched at the housekeeper, the Lucases could not afford a butler, but the woman had closed the door in her face.

Rather than graciously retire, Fanny had banged on the door until none other than Sir William had answered it. He had told her the entire neighbourhood was aware of what she and Bennet had done to Eliza and neither she nor Bennet were welcome at Lucas Lodge again. To emphasise his point when Fanny had refused to leave without speaking to Sir William's wife, he had reminded her, he was the magistrate and as such he could have her arrested for trespassing.

From Lucas Lodge, Fanny had gone to the Longs, then the Gouldings, and lastly the Purvises. Her reception had been the same at each house.

After Purvis Lodge Fanny had instructed the coachman to take her to her sister's house in Meryton. The door had not been opened to her and all she received were looks of scorn from any townspeople who saw her.

Each one cut her.

By the time she had arrived back at Longbourn, Fanny had been in high dudgeon. She demanded her husband fix everything, but he had barely raised his eyes from his book as she fumed. He then returned to reading without a word.

Having convinced herself it was an aberration, after all, no one cared about what happened to Miss Lizzy, Fanny headed into Meryton the next day. She entered the milliner's store and every customer turned their backs on her. Worse than that, the proprietor told her Longbourn's account had been closed. She would, henceforth, have to use coin to purchase anything.

Reeling, Fanny went to four more shops, including the general emporium which used to belong to the Lucases. It was the same in each. Backs turned on her and no account, payment in full only.

This time when she returned home, because it would affect his ability to purchase books and port, Bennet roused himself from his study and rode into the town.

For once his wife had the right of it. Even his account at the bookseller was closed. He returned home after having received demands for payment of all accounts. It seemed the denizens of Meryton did not appreciate his way of trying to end the entail.

He remembered in her ranting his wife had suggested they apply to the Duke to set things to rights in the town for them.

Bennet sat and wrote a letter to the Duke of Hertfordshire requesting his help.

A terse reply, written by the Duke's secretary, was received the next day telling Bennet never to bother the Duke again.

~~~~~~~/~~~~~~~

On Saturday morning, the last one in April and only

three more days to the day Elizabeth dreaded, an enormous Hertfordshire coach came to a halt outside the Gardiners' house.

Not too long after, the butler announced the Duke of Hertfordshire and Mr. George Wickham.

Aunt Maddie, Jane, and herself had been sitting and working on embroidery when the corpulent old man was shown in. Elizabeth smirked as she watched her fiancé waddle into the room.

The three ladies stood and gave curtsies, the Duke inclined his head and Wickham bowed. "I am here to present my fiancée with an engagement ring and to inform her of the time of the wedding at St. Paul's," the Duke stated with no preamble.

He had taken a seat and pulled the ring from his waistcoat pocket. He handed it to Wickham to give to Miss Elizabeth.

"This is far too large for me, unless you mean for me to wear it on my thumb, Your Grace," Elizabeth noted impertinently.

"Wickham, measure my fiancée's finger," the Duke ordered.

Was she worth the trouble? He decided after a moment, she was. Or, at least, she would be after she bore him an heir. Regardless, it was too late now; the notice had appeared in all of the papers, both about the engagement and the date and time of the wedding at St. Paul's.

He would not allow the *Ton* to laugh at him for being jilted.

Wickham stepped forward and placed a length of twine around Miss Elizabeth's fourth finger of her left hand. He marked it and then withdrew after requesting she give him the ring.

"How soon?" the Duke enquired.

"The day before the wedding, Your Grace," Wickham replied.

"Who will give you away, your father or your uncle?" the Duke demanded.

"I have no father or mother. If you allow Mr. or Mrs. Bennet to attend, I will not walk up the aisle or recite my vows," Elizabeth promised.

As it was no hardship for him, the Duke agreed.

"My Uncle Edward will walk me up the aisle," Elizabeth informed the man.

Hertfordshire was about to make a comment about the degradation of a man in trade walking his new duchess to him, but for once he held his peace. He had no doubt his fiancée would use that as a reason not to arrive at the church.

"Be there a few minutes before ten," the Duke instructed. "Have you been purchasing your trousseau?"

As much as Elizabeth did not want to do anything *he* instructed her to, Aunt Maddie had convinced her it was necessary. Besides, Elizabeth had ordered garments for her sisters, Aunt Maddie, and Lilly as well.

"Yes, Your Grace, we are following your instructions regarding Lizzy's wardrobe," Madeline responded.

He stood to leave. He reached out for Elizabeth's hand but she put them behind her back. She did not want to be touched by this man any more than absolutely necessary.

As he rode back towards Mayfair in his coach, the Duke of Hertfordshire was conjuring up new ways he would break her spirit when the time came.

CHAPTER 10

As far as Elizabeth was concerned, the day of her wedding would be the worst day of her short life.

That evening Aunt Maddie had given Elizabeth the talk. While what she imparted was not quite as dire as the gleeful speech Mrs. Bennet had given where she concentrated on the pain and discomfort Elizabeth would experience, Aunt Maddie's had been far more gentle.

Aunt Maddie had given her strategies to try and mitigate the bulk of her soon-to-be husband. Also, her aunt had not made light of the probable pain given the man Elizabeth was marrying had a selfish disdain for the feelings of others. She explained that as such, the Duke would only care about taking his own pleasure. Hence she gave Elizabeth ways to *prepare* herself before the man came to her which would mitigate the pain each time.

As uncomfortable a subject it was for both of them, Elizabeth understood Aunt Maddie was attempting to make an untenable situation slightly more bearable.

Once Aunt Maddie left the bedchamber, Elizabeth's four sisters joined her. It was not lost on her that for the foreseeable future, she would not see them. It had been one of the conditions the old man had agreed to, her sisters would only be at one of their houses with her own express agreement.

Elizabeth simply did not trust the disgusting man around her sisters so she would not put them in a situation where he would have access to them. His condition to garner his agreement was she would only visit places, people, and write to those he approved of.

She hated having her freedoms restricted, but in order to protect Jane and her other sisters, Elizabeth had agreed.

"Lizzy, why are you not wearing your engagement ring?" Lydia asked when she spied it lying on the dresser.

The Duke's man, Mr. Wickham, had delivered it yester-afternoon.

"Because I will only keep it on my finger in *his* company," Elizabeth responded. "The fewer symbols I see to remind me of having to marry the despicable ancient man, the better!"

Slowly but surely Lydia had begun to understand the truth of her parents, especially her mother. The only person's welfare she was worried about was her own. Her daughters were pawns to be pushed around the board as she saw fit.

"I will miss you so very much," Mary stated as she hugged Elizabeth. Mary was not normally very demonstrative which made Elizabeth appreciate the gesture even more.

She returned Mary's hug in full measure. "As I will miss you, Mary, all of you." Elizabeth looked from sister to sister. "I do have a request of you three younger girls."

"Ask anything of us," Mary spoke for herself and her two younger sisters.

"Mary, forget all of the lies Mrs. Bennet told of you being plain. You are as pretty as any of us and that woman only said that because like me, you do not look like her. Kitty, you are your own person, you do not have to mimic another to warrant love and attention. What your mother tried to tell you about drawing and painting being a waste of time is a lie. Pursue it, you have talent.

"Lastly. Lyddie, you are a witty and intelligent girl. You are so much more than your looks and being lively which Mrs. Bennet would always harp on. Yes, those things are nice, as long as you know how to regulate your liveliness and do not act in an unrestrained way. A good reputation is hard to build and maintain, but can be destroyed in one unguarded moment. Further, do not forget—it would affect your sisters too. That was something your mother never understood because she was not raised as a gentleman's daughter. If you follow her advice regarding catching men, you will end up ruining yourself. You are but ten, treasure your childhood. None of you," Elizabeth looked at each of her younger sisters pointedly, "should be in a hurry to grow up and seek a man to marry."

"What Lizzy has told you is nothing but the truth. Heed her words well," Jane said in support. "Now you three go to your bedchamber, even if she does not think she does, Lizzy needs some sleep before tomorrow."

Starting with Mary the three youngest Bennet sisters kissed Elizabeth on one of her cheeks and then departed the bedchamber.

"Oh Janey," Elizabeth lamented once she heard the girls' chamber door close, "If only this was a nightmare from which I could wake. I have prayed so hard it was and I would awaken in our shared bed at Longbourn and none of this had occurred."

"I completely understand the sentiment. I wish I could wave a magic wand and it would be so, to my deep regret, it is not the case," Jane replied sorrowfully. "If only he would have chosen me, and not you..."

"Do not dare say that!" Elizabeth remonstrated more forcefully than she meant to. "If one of us had to be sacrificed, given my refusal to be intimidated, it is better it was me." The last was stated in a much more conciliatory tone of voice.

"Will you ever tell me why you changed your mind when he spoke to you without our pare...Mr. and Mrs. Bennet present?"

"Certainly not now, all I will commit to is to consider it one day in the future if and when this living hell is behind me."

"Knowing how stubborn you are, I will have to be happy with that reply." Jane hugged her sister. "You really must get some sleep, Lizzy. It will do you no good to make yourself sick."

Elizabeth knew what Jane said was nothing but the truth. In order to protect her sisters like she had vowed to do, she needed to be hale and healthy. She reminded herself although she detested the man who had forced her to engage herself to him, she was doing it for the deepest love.

"I will attempt to sleep, Janey, I promise you," she assured.

The two eldest Bennet sisters removed their robes and slid under the covers of the bed. It did not take long before Elizabeth heard Jane's breathing change as she succumbed to sleep.

Elizabeth remained awake for a few more hours, many thoughts running through her mind, although she eventually allowed herself to drift off to sleep.

~~~~~~~/~~~~~~~

Fanny Bennet was much discontented the morning of her wilful, disobedient daughter's wedding.

She had been so sure the Duke would welcome her, his soon-to-be mother-in-law, into his company with an invitation to his wedding. That, Fanny was sure, would rescue her from the social purgatory she found herself in all because of that ungrateful Miss Lizzy!

Her husband had refused to do his duty and write to their daughter's fiancé, so she had taken the task upon herself. The day after the brat left and her brother stole her other daughters, Fanny sent an express to Hertfordshire House in London.

So sure had she been of being invited to Town, she had packed all of her best gowns and any jewellery she owned in anticipation.

Soon all of those who disrespected her in the neighbourhood would be begging for her condescension. Knowing what a busy man he was, She had not been perturbed when there had been no immediate reply from the Duke.

Then yester-morning a letter had been delivered by none other than one of the Duke's couriers! Fanny had felt the compliment keenly, right up until she opened, and read the letter.

The offending missive was lying next to her chair, so she picked it up and read it again, hoping the words on the page would change.

28 April 1806

Hertfordshire House

Berkeley Square, London

Madam:

Do not send any further letters to me at <u>any</u> of my houses or estates! Any more from you will be consigned to the fire without being read. This applies to your husband as well, as he was told when he wrote to me for assistance!

Until such time as my fiancée, the future Her Grace, Lady Elizabeth Chamberlain, Duchess of Hertfordshire and Marchioness of Hertford Heights, agrees, you will not be welcome in my or her company.

There is nothing I will do to assist you in order to regain your daughters from your brother.

I send you no regards and no compliments.

M Jackson, secretary to His Grace the Duke of Hertfordshire, Marquess of Hertford Heights

How was it that daughter of hers had caused the Duke to acquiesce to her demand they would never be in company together again? On reading the note yesterday Fanny had gone directly to her husband's study.

As was his wont, he had been no help. The only thing he asked was what had she expected. He had shared—only because the letter had alluded to it—he too had written to His Grace and had been told to desist.

Now she would not be able to gain her re-entry to local society. Not only that, it would be worse. Thanks to that plain Charlotte Lucas corresponding with her wilful daughter, it would be known by everyone she had been excluded from the wedding as soon as Miss Lucas shared that nugget with her parents.

At least the entail would be broken as soon as that cursed girl bore her husband a son.

Fanny saw no contradiction between her insistence Elizabeth had been the reason she never bore a son and the fact she was counting on the self-same girl delivering one.

~~~~~~~/~~~~~~~

Elizabeth woke before the sun, after having had perhaps four hours of sleep. Next to her, Jane was still slumbering peacefully. Rather than exit the bed and wake her beloved sister, she remained as still as she was able as she counted the time until she would be the old man's wife.

Eventually, Elizabeth heard the sounds of the household waking up. The sun was up when one of the Gardiners' maids entered and told Miss Elizabeth her aunt was summoning her to her private sitting room.

Jane was awake by the time Elizabeth had secured her robe and left the chamber to go join her aunt.

On entering, Elizabeth did not miss the tray with her favourite strawberry pastries on the plate and a cup of hot chocolate, the steam still rising, next to it. As much as she loved both things, Elizabeth was not sure she would be able to eat or drink anything, especially on this day of all days.

Seeing her niece was about to protest, Madeline spoke first. "Lizzy, please trust me when I tell you it is in your best interest to break your fast now. Regardless of how much you do not want to be marrying the Duke, you will only hurt yourself if you are faint from hunger."

"I suppose," Elizabeth agreed with no good humour.

She threw herself onto the settee next to her aunt with resignation and took a bite of one of the pastries. As was common with many, as soon as she took the first bite, her body told her how hungry she was, and not long after both pastries were gone and the cup drained of all hot chocolate.

After scraping out the last drops of the decadent drink with the teaspoon and licking the remnants of the pastries from her fingers, it was time to make for the bath.

~~~~~~~/~~~~~~~

The Gardiner carriage arrived at St. Paul's just before the time the Duke had demanded they be there. Wickham had been posted outside and as soon as he saw them arrive, made his way into the cavernous church to inform his master.

The Duke had been sitting in one of the highbacked chairs on the side of the altar usually reserved for Bishops and above when Wickham drew his attention and nodded.

To his chagrin, the only peer present was the Earl of Colbath and his countess. In the back were a few people the Duke guessed were reporters for some of the gossip rags. He did not object to their presence as that way his wedding would garner some of the attention he felt was his right.

Less than five minutes after Wickham entered St. Paul's, the tradesman's wife and his bride's sisters, except for the blonde entered the nave of the church and took seats across the aisle from Colbath and his wife.

Per his agreement, the Duke had met at Colbath's solicitor's office handing the man the debt markers relating to Lord McEntire. He had signed a document stating once the Countess sponsored his wife and the new duchess was presented, the vowels were to be released to the Earl.

He lamented his shortsightedness; he should have made Colbath standing up with him part of the bargain. As it was, the Earl had refused thanks to the confidence of knowing the debt receipts were with his lawyer.

That had led to having Wickham stand up with him. How humiliating. At least it was better than having his valet do the duty.

As soon as he saw the blonde sister begin her walk up the aisle, Hertfordshire, with Wickham's assistance, stood and made his way to where he would await his magnificent bride.

He had ordered her to visit a modiste and acquire, at his expense, in addition to an appropriate wardrobe, a magnificent wedding gown so he was interested to see in what she would be bedecked. Also, he had sent some of the Hertfordshire jewels to the uncle's house for her to wear.

When the sister reached the place she was to stand opposite Wickham, the Bishop of St. Paul's—he had to be married by a bishop as he had his previous two weddings—indicated for the few people present to stand.

The uncle had entered with his niece on his arm. Even now she was defying him, which he had to admit still aroused him. She wore the same gown she had worn when he had met her at the assembly in Meryton and other than a garnet cross, the only other jewellery she wore was the engagement ring. It was on a finger on her right hand so there would be room to place the wedding ring.

Hertfordshire considered commenting on her dress and lack of jewels but decided against it. He was sure it was exactly what she expected.

~~~~~~~/~~~~~~~

All her prayers *he* would not be waiting for her in the church had gone unanswered. There he was in all of his old, corpulent glory.

Elizabeth walked as slowly as she was able in order

to delay the inevitable as long as possible. Eventually, Uncle Edward stopped at the head of the aisle where the old man stood waiting for her.

She wore a bonnet and Gardiner kissed each of her cheeks, delaying the moment he had to perform the distasteful task of handing his niece over to a brute. Once he did the duty, the last thing he wanted to do, Gardiner joined his wife and nieces in the front pew on the right.

The Bishop began the liturgy as prescribed by the *Book of Common Prayer*. When he asked if there were any who objected, Elizabeth had hoped there would be one who would speak. There was not. After no one raised an objection, Elizabeth stopped listening, trying to imagine something pleasant.

She noticed the Bishop and *he* both were looking at her expectantly. "I am waiting for your answer," the Bishop told her *sotto voce*.

"Please repeat the question, I was wool-gathering," Elizabeth responded.

"Wilt thou have this Man to thy wedded Husband, to live together after God's ordinance in the holy estate of Matrimony? Wilt thou obey him, and serve him, love, honour, and keep him in sickness and in health; and, forsaking all other, keep thee only unto him, so long as ye both shall live?" the Bishop repeated.

The Duke felt humiliated his bride was not paying attention. That made the small congregation a good thing, but it would be written about in the gossip columns. For a moment he thought she was about to refuse.

"I will," Elizabeth intoned. *'I mean hardly any of that, certainly, I will never love or honour him! And I will only obey when absolutely necessary! Hopefully, sickness will take him soon,"* Elizabeth promised herself silently.

From there things went according to plan, she even

managed to recite her vows without a look that was too sour.

Before she knew it, Elizabeth heard the Bishop recite the concluding prayers: "Those whom God hath joined together let no man put asunder.

"Forasmuch as Archibald and Elizabeth have consented together in holy Wedlock, and have witnessed the same before God and this company, and thereto have given and pledged their troth either to other, and have declared the same by giving and receiving of a ring, and by joining of hands; I pronounce that they be man and wife together. In the name of the Father, the Son, and of the Holy Ghost. Amen.

"God the Father, God the Son, God the Holy Ghost, bless, preserve, and keep you; the Lord mercifully with his favour look upon you; and so fill you with all spiritual benediction and grace, that ye may so live together in this life, that in the world to come ye may have life everlasting. Amen."

All that remained was the signing of the register. Given her dislike of her former parents, Elizabeth did not regret it would be the final time she signed her name with the family name Bennet.

It was irrevocable now. She was Lady Elizabeth Rose Chamberlain, Duchess of Hertfordshire, Marchioness of Hertford Heights. She tried not to think of the coming wedding night, but the contemplation of being touched by that repugnant old man was never far from her thoughts.

CHAPTER 11

L ady Elizabeth Rose Chamberlain, Duchess of Hertfordshire, Marchioness of Hertford Heights, looked around her suite at Hertfordshire House. There was no denying her husband was rich, but that made not a whit of difference to Elizabeth.

What she had seen of the house when they had arrived at his home—to her it was a prison, a gilded one, but a prison nonetheless—was ostentation, gaudiness, and uncomfortable furniture which was purchased for form and not function. She had been led up to her chambers by the housekeeper who had introduced Her Grace to the maid who would act as her lady's maid. If the Duchess did not approve of her, another could be employed in her place.

The maid's name was Loretta Jennings, and the housekeeper informed her in his households His Grace insisted personal servants be called by their family names. That of course meant Elizabeth would address her as Loretta whenever in private.

Knowing how her husband was, Elizabeth had no doubt he would punish the maid for being called by her familiar name. She wanted to show the Duke he would never rule over her, but that did not include innocents being blamed for decisions she made. The maid was barely twenty if she was a day and was rather timid. Based on what she knew of the man who had forced her to marry him, Elizabeth suspected all of his servants were cowed in this way.

The man had guided her into an ornate dining parlour where the midday meal, far too much food for just the two of them, had been served. Not only had there been an overabundance of food—to Elizabeth a waste—with each course, but there had been five of the latter. If the man was trying to impress her, he was failing spectacularly.

She had only pushed food around on her plate, not eating anything. At least she had sat at opposite ends of the long table to him so she had not been forced to be near him like she had been in the coach from St. Paul's to Berkeley Square.

All the way to his house—she would never think of it as her house—she had recited the mantra: she had subjected herself to this living hell to protect Janey, for a love which knew no limit.

She spent the afternoon in his library, a library where Elizabeth was sure he had not read any of the books on the shelves—based on the dust on the tomes. She also spent some time in the music room which boasted a Broadwood Grand pianoforte, a harp, and some sundry instruments.

At six, she found her way to her chambers to change for dinner. It was another meal with too much overly rich food, most of it drowning in sauces which did not appeal to her.

After the meal, at which if she had eaten a single bite it would have been a lot, the man told her he would come to her in an hour. She had requested an hour and a half, to which he had condescended.

Loretta had assisted her to undress and then she had soaked in the enormous—one of the few things Elizabeth liked in his house—bathtub in steaming water. Then her maid had assisted her to wash her hair. After Elizabeth had been dried with very large and warm towels, which was another luxury she quite enjoyed.

Once she was dry, she donned a plain, thick, cotton night rail. Then she had Loretta plait her hair. After that was done she dismissed the maid.

She knew what she needed to do, but even though Aunt

Maddie had explained how it would relieve some of the pain she would experience if she was not prepared for her husband to enter her, Elizabeth balked at the thought of actually doing the deed. She was in the privacy of her own suite, but that did not make it easier to do what she had been told to do.

'*Come now Elizabeth Rose, you are not a coward and your courage always rises at every turn when others would shrink back!*' Elizabeth remonstrated with herself silently. She laid back on her bed and began to prepare herself.

~~~~~~~/~~~~~~~

Not too long after she had completed what she needed to do; the disgusting brute entered her chambers from the door leading to the shared sitting room without so much as a knock.

Thankfully, Elizabeth remembered what Aunt Maddie had told her to do to mitigate his weight pushing down on her, and other than the pain when her maidenly barrier was breached, the instructions had borne fruit. She appreciated the fact the enormous and deplorable man lifted her nightgown and did not expect her to bare the whole of her body to him. She did as she had said she would, her eyes were tightly shut until he left the chamber.

Some minutes after he had left the same way he had entered; Elizabeth rang the bell for her maid. As soon as possible she was soaking in a freshly filled tub and Loretta was directing a chambermaid to change the sheets on the bed. Elizabeth scrubbed herself to remove any remaining odour of her husband which still clung to her.

An hour later, she was in bed, and cried herself to sleep, something she suspected would become regular in her life.

~~~~~~~/~~~~~~~

Normally the gossip sheets had no place at the Darcys' house, but there was a morbid interest regarding the young lady who had married the Duke of Hertfordshire the previous day. Lady Anne opened the rag and began to read the column.

The Tatler

1 May 1806

The D of H marries a girl young enough to be his granddaughter!

If this observer had not been there to see it herself, she would not have believed the depraved D of H would have sunk so low as to marry a girl, this reporter estimates is no more than 15 or 16 summers!

The new D'ess of H is a very pretty girl with striking emerald-green eyes. My question, however, is how could any decent person have agreed to marry a daughter to such a man regardless of his wealth and rank?

As would be expected, besides myself and some other purveyors of this kind of information, St. Paul's was all but empty.

The E and C of C were in attendance, why they continue to support the reviled D of H, is beyond my understanding.

As were some of Miss E B's family, it seemed she was attended by an uncle (who is a tradesman and gave her away), aunt, and 4 of her sisters including the one who was her bridesmaid. Of her parents there was no trace.

Most interesting of all was while she was still Miss E B, the new D'ess of H was not paying attention to the liturgy causing the Bishop to have to repeat part of the ceremony which required a response from her. The lady's 'I will' was not at all enthusiastic.

As no one in the Ton would stand up with him, the only one the D could get to be his witness was one of his lackeys who I have since learnt is a man named G W. He was rather young and handsome, but that did not change the fact the D needed to pay a man to stand up with him.

All we can do is pray the former Miss E of L in Hertfordshire will not suffer the same fate as his 2 former late wives.

"Surely not," Lady Anne exclaimed.

"What has disturbed your equanimity, Anne?" Darcy asked as he placed the broadsheet he was reading on the table.

Both William and Anna looked at their mother with concern.

"Read this Robert," Lady Anne instructed as she handed the gossip rag to her husband, the page open to the column regarding the new Duchess of Hertfordshire.

Darcy was aware why his wife, like many ladies in polite society this morning, was reading the smut in *The Tatler*. "Good gracious! A man of his age taking a bride of fifteen or sixteen. I always knew he was debauched, but even for him this is too far," Darcy spat out loudly in disgust as he threw the page down.

"His wife is barely four or five years older than Anna!" William spat out.

"That is bad enough, but read on husband, you will know what it is I want you to see as soon as you read it," Lady Anne insisted.

Not one to deny his wife anything it was in his power to give; he picked up the page again and continued to read.

"How can a young lady of that age agree to marry such a man?" William barked. "She must be quite a social climber and fortune hunter to agree to such."

"That is an extremely harsh judgement to make when you know not all the facts," Lady Anne admonished her son before her husband could speak. "It is more likely than not she was forced into the marriage by someone in her family."

"I hate to disagree with you Mother, but you know not that," William stated haughtily.

"Except, it is clearly intimated that the bride was not a willing participant!" Lady Anne pointed out. "What girl of fifteen or sixteen would want a husband of his age regardless of the incentives to marry him?"

"It is rather judgemental of you William," Darcy added. "How can you decide such without meeting the woman or knowing the circumstances of her marriage?"

"You are correct, Sir," William owned. "I had a vision of Anna in the same situation and it stoked my ire. As you and Mother said, without knowing all, I am making assumptions."

"Robert, did you see what I wanted you to read?" Lady Anne enquired.

"I did, but we know not if the GW they mention in the column is George Wickham," Darcy responded. "It is not like there is only one GW in the country."

"True, but surely the 'young' and 'handsome' point to our steward's son as the one working for the Duke," Lady Anne opined.

"May I?" William requested of his father who handed the gossip rag to his son.

"You are both correct," William stated once he had read the column. "Mother on two fronts. I made a rash judgement and if you can believe what is written, I am more than likely wrong. I think you both have some of the truth and although it may not be George, it could be."

"Was he really so very bad?" Anna asked innocently.

Before his son could respond to his sister and knowing William would think he was protecting Anna by not telling her the truth, Darcy replied, "Yes, Anna dear, he was. George Wickham is not a good man, in fact he is quite the opposite, and I can only thank goodness I woke up to that fact before it was too late."

"When you are a little older we will share more of the facts with you, but in the meanwhile do not forget that regardless of his ability to charm, George Wickham is not to be trusted," Lady Anne added.

~~~~~~~/~~~~~~~

When Hertfordshire was informed his wife had ordered a tray rather than coming to break her fast in the breakfast parlour, he allowed the disrespect to pass, for now at least.

As he sat and ate copious amounts of food, he began reading *The Times of London*. Other than the announcement of his wedding, there was nothing more on the subject. He thought it his right to have his marriage trumpeted for all to read about, but accepted it would not be so, unless he purchased the newspaper of course.

Wickham watched nervously as His Grace came to *The Tatler*. There was no doubt the reaction to the article in that and in other gossip rags would be an explosion of anger. He had predicted accurately.

When the Duke read the drivel in the gossip rag, he picked up his plate and flung it across the room.

As he had not anticipated this reaction, Wickham did not duck in time and the plate hit him on his lip, just below his nose. Blood started to pour out of his split upper lip, but for the moment all he could do was to dab it with his handkerchief. If he moved before His Grace gave him leave to do so, his punishment would be grave, especially in the mood the Duke was currently displaying.

"I will beat that impertinent wife of mine! No one makes me a laughing stock and survives to tell about it!" The Duke tried to stand up on his own—unsuccessfully.

As two footmen approached the raging man, Wickham knew he had to speak. "Your Grace, if you will allow me to remind you why you chose her and why, as you have stated many times, you need to wait for an heir before you take your pleasure with her," Wickham stated as clearly as he could with the blood still dripping from his wound.

The Duke waved the footmen away. He hated to admit it, but Wickham had the right of it. He reread the column and saw there was much more scorn heaped on his head besides his wife's inattentiveness.

He thought about possibly buying this and all the gossip rags. It was something to contemplate another time. As his fury receded, he noticed the blood on his man's face and clothing.

"Why would you stand before me like that?" Hertfordshire demanded.

Knowing reminding the Duke why he looked the way he did would gain him nothing other than possible punishment, Wickham held his peace on that subject. "By your leave, Your Grace, I will go wash up and change. Please accept my abject apologies."

With a dismissive wave of the Duke's hand, Wickham left for his room to fix himself up.

'At some point, the money will not be worth the abuse I have to put up with from this man,' Wickham thought as he climbed the servants' stairs to the sixth floor where his room was located.

CHAPTER 12

Lady Morag McIntire visited Hertfordshire House for the final practice session before Her Grace was to be presented to the Queen.

She had much sympathy for the very young Duchess. Without Lady Elizabeth saying so in words, Lady Morag was positive she had not married the horrible man by choice, but had somehow been forced into it.

Knowing how the Duke liked to leverage people to do his bidding, the Countess suspected it had been something along those lines that had led this young girl—for that is what she was—to marry such a man. Not for the first time Lady Morag gave thanks to on high for the fact her daughter was safely married. She was certain had Skye still been single, the Duke would have used the vowels he held to force a marriage to himself.

The Countess could not know if the leverage had been applied to the family or the girl herself. She would not be surprised if it were the latter because there were no depths to which the man would not sink.

There was no way to have a private conversation with the Duchess to confirm or refute the Countess's suspicions as they were never left alone. Either that Wickham man—as he was now—or one of the Duke's other lackeys were within hearing distance so the most the two would talk about were inconsequential subjects.

"You are ready, Your Grace," Lady Morag announced after the last practice was completed. The young girl learned fast and walked with a certain amount of confidence.

"Thank you for all of your assistance, your Ladyship," Elizabeth replied.

She relished these sessions each day as they allowed her contact with one who was not *him* or someone he employed. In their fortnight of marriage, much to her chagrin he had come to her, but not every night, so that was a small blessing. Elizabeth would take them where she could.

How Elizabeth missed Jane, her other three sisters, her aunts, and her uncles. Communication with Gracechurch Street was by letter. At first, *he* had wanted to read her incoming and even her outgoing letters.

At least she had won the concession—by reminding him of what he agreed to in the settlement. Her post would be delivered directly to her and no one else, including her hated husband.

There was a thick letter from Janey waiting for her in her chambers.

"Did you say your dress for the presentation was delivered yesterday?" Lady Morag asked in her Scottish brogue.

"Yes; what a waste. I will wear it for a few minutes and never again. Whatever was Her Majesty thinking to require such an ensemble?" Elizabeth huffed.

"You will be able to ask her yourself on the morrow when you are presented. You are a duchess and the Queen will have some conversation with you," Lady Morag pointed out, more in jest than seriousness regarding questioning the Queen. Court dress or one's objections to it would not be a subject looked upon with favour by the Queen.

For a moment, Elizabeth who claimed she never felt intimidated, felt intimidated. The Queen! She would have to have a sensible conversation with Queen Charlotte. She calmed, her courage rose, and told herself it was only a conversation with another person.

"Do I really need to wear the tiara and the other jewels my husband has made available to me?" Elizabeth enquired.

"The tiara you will wear indicates your rank and yes, it is expected you will be bejewelled when you are at court," Lady Morag clarified.

"Wearing the tiara is bad enough, but those peacock feathers as well! That is too much along with the hooped monstrosity I am to wear," Elizabeth sighed.

All Lady Morag could do was smile. It was no less than the objections she had made before her presentation. Like the Duchess, she would have been happy without it. It was something else she had in common with Her Grace. Before she had fallen in love with her Kenneth, she had been a happy lass living on a small estate near the estate of Colbath.

The only complaint she had ever had against her husband was his love of games of chance. Thankfully, since the Duke of Hertfordshire had won—he had cheated—so much, her husband had never so much as made a wager for a penny ever again.

Now, the leverage the Duke had held over their heads would be gone on the morrow. The solicitor would be present outside of St. James and as soon as the Duchess exited and confirmed she had been presented, the markers would be turned over to Kenneth. From that time on they would never again acknowledge the dastardly Duke, never mind be in his company again.

Knowing of the man's propensities, Morag would pray long and hard for Lady Elizabeth's protection from her husband.

~~~~~~~/~~~~~~~

Elizabeth made for her chambers to change out of the practice hooped dress as speedily as she was able. Her maid assisted her and soon, not soon enough for Elizabeth, she was dressed in a day dress.

She took Jane's letter with her into her private sitting room and after kicking her slippers off, sat down in a comfortable window seat, tucking her legs underneath herself.

She looked at Jane's thicker than normal letter longingly. How she wished she could see all her sisters and the rest of the family she was willing to acknowledge. Her selfish desires would not win out, they needed to be kept apart for the safety of her sisters, so apart they would remain. Elizabeth allowed her fingers to caress the Gardiner seal while imagining being at Gracechurch Street with them and not in this gilded prison she inhabited.

Elizabeth broke the seal. A second letter from Charlotte was contained within. Her old man husband would not allow letters from anyone but her close family hence when she wrote to Charlotte or vice versa, the letter would be contained within one to or from one of her sisters, or one time to Aunt Hattie.

Elizabeth began to read Jane's letter first.

15 May 1806

23 Gracechurch Street

My dearest sister and best friend, Lizzy,

How I miss you, Dearest. The enclosed letter from Charlotte arrived this morning. Knowing you would want to hear from her as soon as may be, I wrote to you as well.

It seems so strange to me that we are only a few miles apart, yet we could be at opposite ends of England. One day you will have to explain all to me. I know you said it is for my and our sisters' protection, but it does not mean I miss you any less.

Speaking of being close to you on Berkeley Square, on the morrow, the two older Gardiner children and we four Bennet sisters will have a picnic in Hyde Park and then we are to have some ices at the famous Gunter's.

How I wish you could bump into us just by chance but I

know that man has you watched at all times and under heavy escort when you are out of the house without him.

As I have told you in a previous letter, our sisters and I, and am sure it is true for Aunt Maddie and Uncle Edward as well, pray for your wellbeing and protection every night before we go to bed.

I hate that you are enslaved to that terrible man. I can only hope he is not as bad as we have heard even though I doubt that. You see Lizzy, I do not try and make everything in the world good any longer.

You will enjoy Charlotte's letter especially about Mr. and Mrs. Bennet.

Aunt Maddie is calling me so I will end here.

With all of my sisterly love,

Jane

"I miss you, all of you every minute of every day," Elizabeth told her sister's letter as she dashed some tears away from her cheeks which had fallen towards the end of her reading. She picked up the second letter, broke the seal, and smoothed the pages so she could read it.

14 May 1806

Lucas Lodge

My dear Eliza,

Or should I give a deep curtsy and say, Your Grace?

Elizabeth could see her friend's teasing face as she mockingly did just that. How she would love to see Charlotte again. Her gaoler would not allow her to have contact with someone with ties so close to trade. She returned to the page.

Much to her chagrin, Mrs. Bennet has discovered a fortnight would not make the residents of the area forget her crimes.

Yesterday, she had the temerity to call at Lucas Lodge as if nothing untoward had occurred. It did not take long before she was screeching at full volume, and using some expletives mind you, when she was not granted access to the house.

My father had once before threatened her with arrest for trespassing if she set foot on our land again. She obviously thought it was an idle threat. It was not! The woman who gave birth to you is in the town gaol and will remain there for 5 days.

Do you think she finally understood how serious my father was? I hear that no matter how much she screamed, screeched, and caterwauled for someone to have Mr. Bennet come and pay a fine so she could go home, he never did. I would wager he is relishing the temporary peace and quiet at Longbourn.

"Now that is something I would love to see! Fanny Bennet in a gaol cell," Elizabeth smiled widely. "If only it was for much longer and Mr. Bennet was in the cell next to hers!"

Although I understand you not being able to see us is not your choice, I do miss you so much. Each time I go for a walk and end up on Longbourn's lands, I almost expect, or more likely hope, you will come around a bend in the path singing and swinging your bonnet around in your hand as you walk.

Alas, it is not to be.

Before I forget, Mama and Papa, Franklin, John, and Maria all ask to be remembered to the Duchess. *John says he cannot imagine the girl who used to fight with him over a frog in the mud is now the Duchess of Hertfordshire and a marchioness as well.*

"John is not the only one who cannot believe it. I wish it were not true," Elizabeth said to her sitting room. "If only that was all I had to worry about, catching more frogs than Johnny Lucas."

You know Eliza, the Lord works in mysterious ways, so mayhap it will not be too long before I see you again.

Stay strong my friend. With warmest regards,

Charlotte

Elizabeth gave a long and loud sigh. It was almost time

to dress for dinner, the one meal of the day *he* insisted she join him.

~~~~~~~/~~~~~~~

Thankfully her husband was not welcome at St. James, or any other royal residence for that matter. It was a pleasure to be going to be presented without his objectionable company. His lackey, Mr. Wickham, would ride behind on a horse. Much to her approbation, he would not be allowed into St. James Palace either.

Elizabeth had been collected at Hertfordshire House by the Earl and Countess of Colbath. There was another man in the coach, who she quickly learnt was the man she would inform after her presentation was complete.

"Your Grace, we have never been away from your husband's men before, so excuse me if my question is impertinent," Lady Morag stated.

The Earl saw the Duchess give a questioning look towards his solicitor. "That is Mr. Crawley, my solicitor. He is the soul of discretion," the Earl assured Her Grace.

"In that case, please ask what you will," Elizabeth allowed.

"Am I correct being attached to that man was not your choice?" Lady Morag probed. "You of course are free to ignore any of my questions you feel have crossed a line."

"You will find I am rather outspoken with my opinions, so if I feel I do not choose to answer, I will tell you," Elizabeth informed the Countess. "No, it was most certainly not my choice." Elizabeth paused. "May I ask a question?"

"We will be as candid as you have been with us," Lady Morag responded.

"How is it you attend my husband when he is universally scorned by the *Ton*?" Elizabeth questioned.

"My husband was cheated..." Lady Morag told the

Duchess of their association with the Duke and all about how he had hung the vowels like the Sword of Damocles above their heads.

"That is why I must inform Mr. Crawley after I have been presented; it is the last thing you agreed..." Elizabeth was cut off by the Earl.

"We never agreed to anything with him, he always demanded using the threat of calling in my debts if I refused," Lord Kenneth revealed.

Each time she thought she had discovered the depths of her husband's depravity; she discovered a new low.

"I am so sorry he used you so ill for so long after he cheated you," Elizabeth averred.

"Your Grace, you are not the one who needs to apologise," Colbath insisted. "You are as much a victim of his machinations as I was, and I was supposed to be an intelligent man and yet I still fell into his spider web."

Just then they arrived at St. James Palace. If the ostentation Elizabeth saw outside was any indication, this was not her type of home.

She took a deep breath and when ready, nodded to the royal footman to open the door.

CHAPTER 13

Ladies Elaine and Anne were among the courtiers present at the Queen's drawing room the day the new Duchess of Hertfordshire was to be presented. Like others of their friends, specifically, Lady Rose Rhys-Davies and Lady Sarah De Melville, who were standing with them, they wanted to see for themselves if the debauched man truly had married one as young as had been reported in the gossip rags.

Standing just behind their wives in their full court regalia, including their ceremonial swords hanging at their sides, were the Duke of Bedford, the Earls of Matlock and Jersey, and Mr. Darcy.

The men would have willingly missed the spectacle, but their wives had told them they would be attending with them.

Darcy grinned as he remembered William begging off as he had to meet with Richard and their friend Bingley—without the latter's younger sister present—at White's. He was not one for court intrigue but his inability to deny his wife what she asked of him ensured his attendance.

"We will not have long to wait," Lady Elaine observed. "As a duchess, she will be one of, if not, the first to take her curtsy before Her Majesty."

Just then, the doors to the waiting room were opened by two royal footman. The palace's major domo who was standing off to the side of the doors spoke in a clear voice. "Her Grace, Lady Elizabeth Rose Chamberlain, Duchess of Hertfordshire and Marchioness of Hertford Heights presented by Lady Morag McIntire, Countess of Colbath."

The new duchess entered the presentation chamber. She was petite and extremely beautiful. It was obvious that what had been written about her age was not an exaggeration to make the story more salacious. If it were possible, the Duke of Hertfordshire's reputation sank even further in the eyes of the *Ton*.

Those watching had never seen a finer pair of emerald-green eyes that seemed to shine with intelligence and strength. Her hair was raven coloured, wavy, and done up in a fancy coiffure as expected for the Queen's drawing room. She wore the hooped dress mandated by her Majesty; it was not brightly coloured.

For jewellery, she wore an emerald studded tiara denoting her rank, a necklace, and a bracelet, all featuring large emeralds. On her one finger was a gold wedding ring and an engagement ring, also with an emerald. There were the feathers in her hair—placed behind the tiara—which were also prescribed—hers were from a peacock. She walked, her head held high, not looking at any of the courtiers gaping at her.

"Why do you think one with her obvious strength married that repugnant man?" Lady Anne asked after the new duchess had passed her and those standing with her. "She did not look at all intimidated by anything here."

"That is a question to which we will more than likely never know the answer," Lady Rose opined.

"My question," Lord Matlock said to the three men standing with him, "is what leverage the bastard holds over Colbath as he is the only one who will be in Hertfordshire's company."

"Does the Duke ever attend the Lords?" Darcy enquired.

"He does not," the Duke of Bedford responded. "Even though it is his right to attend, if he did, there would not be any sort of welcome, in fact, he would be cut."

"Enough nattering," Lady Elaine admonished playfully. "She is about to take her curtsy."

Conversation ceased as all eyes trained on the young lady as she prepared to bend her knee to the Queen.

~~~~~~~/~~~~~~~

As she walked past those present—who were standing on either side of the red carpet she was on, Elizabeth had not missed the way she was being stared at and evaluated by the courtiers. She was sure the first question in their minds was how was it that she had married the revolting old man.

The whole time she walked, which seemed like hours, but was in reality only a minute or so, Elizabeth kept her eyes forward, her chin up. They could stare all they wanted. She would not be intimidated.

Just like Lady Morag had taught her, Elizabeth reached the spot before her Majesty and made her deep curtsey. When she rose, the Queen indicated she should approach.

It was as she had been informed; the Queen would have some words with her being she was now a duchess. Elizabeth was sure her Majesty would have some inanities to impart fulfilling the expectation she would speak to one of her rank.

"Lady Elizabeth, you look very young to us," the Queen stated softly.

"I am but sixteen your Majesty," Elizabeth owned.

"Sixteen!" The Queen had almost made a loud exclamation, but she managed to maintain the low volume of her voice. "You are but a child. If you were forced into this, we will have our vicar annul your marriage."

Elizabeth had to school her features. She had not expected compassion and caring from Her Majesty. "It was not something I wanted, but it was my choice, Your Majesty. Besides, as I understand the law, it is too late," Elizabeth replied in *sotto voce*.

"Our vicar will do as we ask," the Queen insisted.

"This is my burden to bear, Your Majesty. For my own reasons, as much as I would love to be free of that man, I cannot be. For the good of others I love, I must remain married to him," Elizabeth averred. She had tried to stop herself, but a single tear rolled down her cheek.

The Queen wiped the tear coursing down the Duchess's cheek with her own handkerchief. Her heart went out to this beautiful girl before her. "If there is ever anything we may do for you, you will ask it of us, will you not?" Elizabeth understood it was not a question. She nodded her head.

~~~~~~~/~~~~~~~

Those watching were amazed at how long the Queen spoke to the Duchess of Hertfordshire in hushed tones. None missed when Her Majesty leaned forward and did something with the silk square she had retrieved from her sleeve.

Her Majesty kissed the Duchess's forehead—as was to be expected—and then she did something none who attended court had ever seen her do before. The Queen pulled the young Duchess into a hug, one which lasted for some moments.

All speaking in the chamber ceased as the courtiers looked on in wonderment, many with mouths hanging open.

The signal to the *Ton* was clear. Regardless of how ill the Duke of Hertfordshire was thought of, his wife had the approval and affection of the Queen of England. It would not do for any of them to try and paint her with the same brush as her husband.

The Countess of Colbath collected the train and handed it to Her Grace, who then backed out of the chamber without a single wobbly step.

Only once the door closed did the conversation in the chamber resume, somewhat louder than was normally acceptable. Those present had just witnessed something extraordinary. As much as they would have loved to have been privy to the conversation between the Queen and the Duchess, all the spectators could do was speculate.

~~~~~~~/~~~~~~~

"The sooner I can return to Hertfordshire House and remove this hooped monstrosity, the happier I will be," Elizabeth stated as soon as she and Lady Morag joined the Earl and his solicitor in the Colbath coach.

As he had been since Her Grace had entered the palace, Wickham sat atop the horse. As soon as the carriage began to move, he took up station a little behind it.

"May I assume you were presented, Your Grace," Crawley verified.

"Yes, Mr. Crawley, I was. The Countess discharged her duties as promised," Elizabeth confirmed.

The solicitor opened the case he was holding and withdrew some papers from it. "All of your debt markers," he announced as he handed them to the Earl.

Without a delay, Lord Colbath ripped them into tiny pieces. They would be consigned to a fire as soon as he and his countess gained Colbath House. His nightmare was over. The cheating Duke held no more leverage over him and if he never saw the blackguard again it would be too soon.

"May I ask what the Queen said to you, Your Grace?" Lady Morag queried.

Elizabeth related the substance of the conversation with Her Majesty. "I only wish I was able to accept her offer of help." She did not elaborate and the McIntires did not feel Her Grace had left any opening for them to ask what she meant.

"You could have no more powerful ally in polite society," Lady Morag observed.

For the rest of the relatively short ride back to Hertfordshire House, there was no more conversation in the coach. All that was heard was the clip-clop of the horses' hooves as they connected with the cobblestoned streets.

The door was opened by Wickham who had vaulted off his horse when the conveyance came to a stop at his master's house. He offered his hand to Her Grace, but she refused to take it and stepped out without his assistance. The Duchess stood and watched as the Colbath coach was pulled away by the two pairs of matched greys.

She had known this time was fast approaching. Now she was isolated once again, with only *him* and his lackeys for company.

At least she had Loretta, but she would need to continue to be circumspect in her treatment of her maid. The last thing Elizabeth wanted was for her husband to remove the maid if he felt his wife had become too close to her.

She took a deep breath. Then Elizabeth climbed the six stone steps which led to the small veranda and the front door of her prison.

~~~~~~~/~~~~~~~

The day of the presentation was the day Jane, Mary, Kitty, and Lydia, accompanied by the two eldest Gardiner children and the attendant nurse and footmen took a walk in Hyde Park before their picnic at the duckpond.

Jane looked longingly in the direction of where she believed Berkeley Square was. How she missed Lizzy. Based on her younger sister's last letter, today was the day Lizzy was to take her curtsey before the Queen, so mayhap she had not even returned to the Duke's house yet.

The two youngest Bennets were walking with Lilly and Eddy Gardiner a little ahead of Jane and Mary. One of the footmen was behind the latter pair, the other one and the nursemaid with the younger four. A footman and maid were organising the comestibles for the picnic.

It was then Jane noticed three young men. All were tall. The tallest had dark hair while the other two, an inch or two shorter than him had sandy-blond hair. One of the three was in the army as he was in uniform. Jane could not recognise rank or with what regiment the man was, but there was no mistaking the scarlet coat of the army.

The three were walking along the path towards her and Mary and seemingly deep in conversation.

~~~~~~~/~~~~~~~

Andrew Fitzwilliam, Viscount Hilldale had unexpectedly decided to join his brother and cousin to meet with Bingley at White's. On their return to Grosvenor Square, the three cousins had decided to take a stroll in Hyde Park. It was not close to the fashionable hour so both Andrew and William knew they would be able to ramble without being accosted.

The three had been in a deep discussion about Richard's regiment's upcoming move to the Peninsula. As such, they did not notice the group that left the path in front of them and headed for the picnic next to the duckpond nearby. Neither did they see the two young ladies walking towards them on the path.

The two Bennet sisters only realised the men were distracted at the last moment and hardly had any time to try and avoid the impending collision. The sisters attempted to get themselves over to the left side of the path. They did not succeed completely causing Jane to collide with the man on the left, while Mary managed to avoid the men altogether.

A collision with someone brought Andrew to awareness of his surroundings. He saw a young lady beginning to fall, and instinctively reached out to stop her from hitting the ground.

"And here we thought it was safe to amble in the park and not be accosted by fortune hunters," William barked. "Your machinations will not be gratified, Madam!"

"**William!**" Andrew and Richard called out in disgust at once. Both realised they had been in the wrong and the young ladies had tried to avoid them.

The footman had approached but stopped when he saw Miss Jane was well. He would keep watch and make sure the Misses Bennet were safe.

"How dare you impugn my sister's honour, Sir," Mary spat out. "You are no gentleman. You were walking and not paying attention and you and your friends walked into us! We tried to avoid you and your inattentiveness."

William was about to ask the young lady, who did not look much older than Anna, who she thought she was when he saw the warning looks from his two older cousins.

Until then, Andrew had not looked at the woman whom he had stopped from falling. Now he did and never had he seen a more beautiful creature. If Bingley was with them, he would be chasing her as his latest angel within seconds.

"What is wrong with you, William? You make judgements without thinking," Andrew admonished. "The young lady Miss...?"

"Miss Jane Bennet and Miss Mary Bennet," Jane supplied.

"Miss Bennet, Miss Mary, I am Lord Andrew Fitzwilliam, Viscount Hilldale. The one in uniform is my brother, Captain Richard Fitzwilliam, and the rude one is our cousin, Mr. William Darcy," Andrew responded. "You must excuse him; on occasion, he suffers from hessian in the mouth disease. As I was about to say, William, Miss Mary had the right of it. We were at fault, not them."

"Rather than try and have themselves compromised, they did everything they could to avoid us," Richard added.

"I am but fourteen, the last thing I am looking for is a husband," Mary stated disdainfully.

Realising he was very wrong; William did the only thing he could. "Miss Bennet, Miss Mary, please excuse my rude and untrue words to you both. It was very wrong and most ungentlemanlike of me." William bowed to the two.

After looking at Mary who nodded, Jane turned to the three men. "My sister and I pardon your behaviour, Mr. Darcy. In the future, we suggest you evaluate the situation before making assumptions." Jane paused and looked to where her sisters and cousins were blissfully feeding the ducks. "Now if you gentlemen will excuse us, we need to join our family members." Jane inclined her head towards the pond.

As much as he wanted to ask her where he could find her again, Andrew said nothing knowing he had no reason to do so without sounding extremely forward.

The cousins gave a bow to the ladies' curtsies. Jane and Mary, still followed by the footman, headed off the path towards the pond to join their sisters and cousins.

~~~~~~~/~~~~~~~

"What can you tell me about what occurred this morning, Wickham?" Hertfordshire demanded when his man reported his wife had been presented and was home.

"Given I was required to wait outside of the palace gates, nothing Your Grace." Wickham did not add what he would have liked to say: *'Like you, I am not allowed to attend.'*

"Damn Colbath not allowing you to ride in his coach so you were not able to report on what was said to, and by, my wife," the Duke huffed.

'Had I been within, they would have said nothing worth repeating,' Wickham told himself silently.

"And now I no longer have any leverage over that damned man!" Hertfordshire continued, not needing or wanting a response from his man. "At least she is presented, and it will not affect my future son." He paused. "Bring her to me," the Duke stated without looking up at his man.

Wickham bowed and made his way to Her Grace's chambers and knocked on the door. The lady's maid cracked the door open.

"His Grace has summoned Her Grace," Wickham relayed.

Elizabeth had heard the lackey. "Inform my husband I am changing. Once I have completed what I need to do, I will be there."

~~~~~~~/~~~~~~~

The Duke was not amused. It was over a half hour before his duchess joined him. "Tell me all!" he instructed.

"I am not sure what you would like to know and from when?" Elizabeth replied impertinently. "Do you mean for the whole of my life or a specific period?"

When motivated by anger as he was now, His Grace was able to stand from his chair with alacrity. He rounded on his wife and pulled his arm back.

She did not flinch and just stood there looking at him with extreme dislike. At the same time, Wickham cleared his throat and Hertfordshire remembered his need to wait until after an heir was born.

The corpulent man stepped back. "Get out of my sight," he hissed. "I will think of an appropriate punishment for your disrespect!"

'*With the greatest of pleasure*,' Elizabeth thought. She turned and made her way back towards the grand staircase and her chambers.

It was only when she reached her chambers that Elizabeth allowed the fear she had felt when he had been prepared to strike her to course through her body. She fell onto her bed, her body wracked by sobs.

Her maid sat on the bed saying not a word and rubbed Her Grace's back.

CHAPTER 14

Jane was in the sitting room at her aunt's and uncle's house working on some embroidery while her aunt sat and relaxed when the post was delivered. She was greatly excited to see one from Lizzy as it had been some weeks—before her presentation—since a letter had been received from her sister.

"Aunt Maddie, do you mind if I read my letter right away?" Jane requested.

"Why would I object Janey dear, go right ahead," Madeline allowed.

She broke the seal of the Dukes of Hertfordshire and opened up the pages of the thick missive. Unsurprisingly there was an enclosed letter addressed to Charlotte. Jane began to read as soon as the pages were smoothed out.

11 June 1806

Hertfordshire House

My dearest Janey,

You have my heartfelt apologies if I caused you any consternation by not having written to you since right before my presentation last month. As punishment for being disrespectful to him, *that man refused to allow me to send or receive letters until today.*

What a petty and vindictive man I am shackled to! I was prepared for the fact he is old, repugnant, and a brute, but I never imagined his small mindedness as well.

He did not react well when after I had changed out of the

hooped monstrosity I was forced to wear, I made sport of him. Would you believe the old man made as if he was about to strike me? Calm yourself, Janey, he did not, and to date has not harmed me physically.

Jane was distressed by what she had read. Thank goodness Lizzy had told her she was unharmed—at least her person was not hurt. Even though he had not hit her, the fact he threatened it, could not but make Jane even more worried for her younger sister. She continued to read.

As much as I disliked what I had to wear, there was a positive in being presented. I met and will greatly miss the company of Lady Morag McIntire, the Countess of Colbath who prepared and sponsored me. Without her visits, I am alone in my prison once more. At least when she was here for the practices, I had another lady to speak to—even though we had to be circumspect thanks to him *having one of his lapdogs always near.*

I was able to speak to her and her husband on the way to and back from the presentation at St. James Palace. One of the men employed by the old man rode behind the coach on a horse so he was unable to overhear us.

As much as I should have been surprised, I was not when they told me they had been forced to do my husband's bidding for some years now as he held the fate of their estate in Scotland over their heads. It was a debt of honour; one he stole by cheating! *Knowing how much my husband wanted me presented and that there were no others who would oblige him, the Earl demanded his debt markers returned to him. Unlike me, they are free of the man and never have to see him again.*

This being the first communication from me since I took my curtsey, I must tell you all!

St. James Palace is decorated as ostentatiously as you would imagine. Given my rank (one I would much prefer not to have) I was the first lady presented. The Queen spoke to me, and I do not mean some perfunctory inanities.

Lady Morag informed me Her Majesty would have a few words for me, but I was wholly unprepared for the reality.

Janey, she asked me if I wanted my marriage annulled by her vicar (the Archbishop of Canterbury)! Also, she let me know if I ever needed her assistance, it would be granted. As much as I wanted to accept her offer to end my marriage to him, *I cannot, so I did not.*

What her sister was not telling her, Jane could not imagine. She knew how stubborn Lizzy was and she had already made it clear—more than once—one day she would share her reasons for marrying the Duke. She suspected Aunt and Uncle knew, but had been sworn to secrecy. Hence they would not share it with her without Lizzy's permission.

At her compassion, I almost lost my composure. One or two tears escaped and would you believe the Queen used her own handkerchief to dry my cheek.

Since my return, I have only seen him *at dinner and some evenings. Not seeing him at all would still be too often for me.*

When you reply, please post your letter, and all subsequent ones to Falconwood. You can choose either Hertfordshire or Buckinghamshire as the estate straddles the border between said counties.

I was told we depart on the morrow. I will admit I am curious to see the estate. All I can do is hope there will be good paths for me to take my constitutionals again. How I have missed them while I have been languishing at his *house.*

If I enjoyed wagering I would take one on the fact I will have a shadow when I walk out. It is not that the man is worried I will run off—he is secure in his knowledge I will not—but he likes to control everything and having me watched so closely is another way he does that.

We leave Town on the morrow, Dearest. We will be at the estate by the afternoon.

Please give my warmest regards and love to our sisters, aunts, uncles, and cousins.

Your loving sister,

Lizzy

"Jane you do not look happy," Madeline observed as she spied the pensive look on Jane's countenance.

"Read this and you tell me," Jane thrust the letter forward into Aunt Maddie's hands.

As she read, the ire she felt towards His Grace rose significantly. If he had been nearby, Madeline would have been the one doing the striking.

Thankfully the despicable man had not physically beaten Lizzy. Madeline was sure had he done so, her Edward would have rushed to his home and tried to gain entry to revisit the favour upon the Duke's head ten times over. As well deserved as it would have been, she selfishly much preferred her husband alive and well.

"Lizzy will be well, she has to be," Madeline stated as she handed the letter back to her niece. "The letter to Charlotte will go in the post on the morrow."

~~~~~~~/~~~~~~~

Elizabeth had been told the coach ride to Falconwood would be about four hours, roughly the same length of time had they been travelling to Meryton. On the whole, she did not object to riding in a carriage. At least that had been true when the company was better, much better than the objectionable man sitting opposite her on the forward facing bench.

Even though it was the norm to allow the lady to face forward, the old man had used the excuse of his becoming sick if he faced the rear.

She cared not, as long as she did not have to sit next to him. Just the day before her monthly disposition had come, which was both a blessing and a curse. The former because

SHANA GRANDERSON A LADY

she would have almost a week without *his* sweaty, smelly, corpulent presence in her bedchamber, while the latter meant she was not with child and would have to suffer his coming to her some nights once her indisposition was over.

A prayer of thanks was offered for the fact her husband had fallen asleep soon after the coach passed the outskirts of London. His loud snoring was far preferable to having to converse with him.

At the almost two hour mark, they reached the same inn that had been used in the past travelling between Town and Meryton. It was about halfway between the two. Hertfordshire was just waking up when he noticed his wife had exited the conveyance and was entering the inn with her maid—who had been travelling in a following carriage—and Wickham as an escort.

While Elizabeth went to the necessary her maid stood outside the door and Wickham was standing at the end of the hallway.

"This way, Your Grace," Wickham stated once the Duchess exited the privy. "His Grace has a private parlour so you may enjoy some food and drink."

Knowing it would be cutting off her nose to spite her face to refuse as she needed some tea and perhaps something to eat, Elizabeth nodded and allowed her husband's guard dog to lead her to the designated room.

The landlord, who felt the compliment of a duke and duchess patronising his establishment keenly, was falling over himself to make sure the noble personages' needs were met.

There was an enormous platter, piled high with sandwiches on the table—far more than ten, never mind, two people could hope to eat. Some had been made with mutton and others with cheese. Elizabeth asked for a cup of tea and helped herself to a cheese sandwich.

"I trust you are comfortable, my dear," the Duke

drawled.

"Adequately," Elizabeth averred succinctly.

Seeing his wife was not in the mood to converse, Hertfordshire concentrated on his second mug of ale and the half dozen sandwiches he had placed on his plate.

Elizabeth sat silently as the man consumed sandwich after sandwich and then washed it all down with his third mug of ale. She knew not how he could eat so much after the enormous breakfast he had eaten.

Contrary to her wont of taking a tray in her chambers, she had been commanded to join her husband in the breakfast parlour that morning due to their impending travels. Watching him eat then reminded Elizabeth of the prize pig at Mr. Bennet's estate devouring everything it could find. Like the man sitting opposite her, it too could eat no matter how much food it had eaten before.

When the Duke had his fill, there were still many sandwiches on the platter. "Rather than allow the remaining sandwiches and the rest of the drinks to go to waste, can we not provide it to our servants who are accompanying us to your estate?" Elizabeth suggested.

"Do what you will with them, I care not," Hertfordshire responded dismissively.

"Mr. Wickham, please take for yourself, allow Jennings some, and then offer the rest to those of our servants who would like to eat and drink," Elizabeth instructed.

In the time he had worked for the Duke, not once had the man bothered about anyone's needs but his own. Wickham was amazed that this slip of a duchess had. He was sure she must hate him for being used to watch her by her husband, but yet, she still took his needs, and those of others into account.

The man did pay well, but that was all. Not for the first time it struck Wickham how easily he would be discarded, or disposed of, when the Duke decided he was no longer of use.

While His Grace went to the necessary, Wickham collected two footmen who, after he offered Her Grace's maid some, took the remaining food and drink to share among the servants waiting with the coaches outside. When he saw the shocked looks of the grateful, and hungry men, Wickham gave credit where credit was due naming the Duchess as their benefactor.

~~~~~~~/~~~~~~~

From the inn, rather than follow the road to the northwest which would have led to Meryton, the conveyances turned onto a road heading southwest.

This time Elizabeth feigned sleep to escape having to converse with her husband. If he suspected her of not truly being asleep, Hertfordshire did not attempt to rouse his wife as they rode on.

About an hour later, they were traversing a market town. Elizabeth sat up and looked out of the window.

"This is the market town of Chesham in Buckinghamshire. It is the closest town in this county to Falconwood," Hertfordshire explained without being prompted. He was proud of his primary estate and liked to talk about it and the area. He required no response from his wife. "We travel this way because although my estate sits both in this shire and Hertfordshire, the main entrance is in Buckinghamshire, three miles from where we sit now."

"Thank you," was all Elizabeth said in response.

As they rolled on towards the estate, Elizabeth could make out some hills in the distance, she guessed to the east, between them and London, but the land in the area was relatively flat, much like that around Longbourn where her beloved Oakham Mount stood out as the only eminence for miles around.

Eventually, the lead coach passed the large stone gate posts, each with a tall wrought iron gate attached. The gates were opened as far as they could be and the gatekeeper was present, next to his gatehouse, hat in hand, and bowing deeply as the Duke's equipage passed him by.

The drive was relatively level and someone had planted trees alongside it on both sides at some point creating an avenue. About a mile from the gates, much to her delight— although she kept her features schooled not wanting *him* to see her take pleasure in anything of his—Elizabeth saw a rather large, wooded area on the one side of the drive.

'*If I am allowed to ramble, I would like to explore the forest,*' Elizabeth told herself silently.

Almost two more miles were traversed before the mansion came into view. Never had Elizabeth seen a house half as big. Never mind Longbourn, it was five to six times larger than Netherfield Park's manor house if it was anything.

It was at least five storeys high from what she could see with large wings on the left and right of the front part of the structure. When she explored the area, she intended to find out if the wings extended to the rear as well, or only towards the front.

The coach followed the circular drive in front of the house—there was a large fountain with water spurting from the mouths of five cherubs in the centre of the circle—and came to a halt under an enormous portico.

On either side of the drive were formal gardens. They seemed vast. Elizabeth could see at least three gazebos, a topiary, and what seemed like an extensive rose garden. She was sure there was much more to see as the gardens disappeared from view behind the wings on either side of the house.

She was sure she would see the rest soon enough, besides, she much preferred untamed nature to a garden designed by the awkward tastes of man.

Lined up in front of the house were four neat rows

of servants behind two men and a woman, who Elizabeth assumed were the senior staff.

As much as she did not want to be helped down from the carriage by the man who repulsed her, Elizabeth knew in front of the staff and servants, she would have to maintain a façade of serenity. Thankfully, living her life with Jane had taught her how to apply that particular mask.

After handing her out, the Duke turned to those standing to welcome them home. "I present Her Grace, Lady Elizabeth Chamberlain, the Duchess of Hertfordshire and Marchioness of Hertford Heights," the Duke intoned.

A cheer rose from the assembled staff and servants. To Elizabeth's mind, it was not spontaneous, but what they thought the Duke wanted to hear.

Rather than lower himself to make the introductions, Hertfordshire nodded to Wickham who introduced Her Grace to Mr. and Mrs. Greaves, the butler and housekeeper, and to Mr. Hampstead, the steward.

"Your warm welcome of my husband and me is most appreciated," Elizabeth told the assembled servants while her husband had begun to walk into the house. "Please pardon me if it takes me time, but I will endeavour to learn all of your names."

Having been inured to the treatment from His Grace, there was a look of scepticism among the servants.

Elizabeth nodded to the housekeeper and butler who dismissed the servants. She took a deep breath and made her way into her new gaol. Yes, it was far larger than the house in London, but it was her prison nonetheless.

CHAPTER 15

"Andy, we have been walking the paths of Hyde Park at this time for close to a month and we have yet to see the young lady who caught your eye," William pointed out to his eldest cousin. "If this was Bingley chasing after the ghost of one of his willowy, blonde angels, then I would understand—but this is you, who I have always counted amongst the most sensible of men."

"Do you not think I realise how unlikely the chance is that I will encounter her again?" Andrew bit back. "I am fully aware my actions are illogical." He paused and added, "In that instant, when I stopped her from falling, I felt something. Something I have never felt before or, for that matter, since."

William admitted, shaking his head, "I need no reminder of my ungentlemanly conduct that day. I behaved more like Aunt Cat with my wild accusations, yet we were the ones in the wrong."

"Unlike our presumptuous aunt, you admit to your errors. When have you ever known her to do so?"

William bowed his head in thanks for his cousin's assessment of part of his character. "You are but six and twenty, surely you have time before you need to worry about taking a wife. Aunt and Uncle are not pressuring you are they?"

"No, they are not. Mother and Father want Rich and me to find what they and your parents have, a union based on mutual love and respect. Speaking of your puppy, Bingley, are you still ducking his younger sister? She is how old, nineteen now?"

"I believe so. I have never met a woman as obtuse as that one. My parents and I have all made it very clear she will never be my wife, but it seems she hears only that which she wants to hear—much like Aunt Cat."

"Does not the fact she has never been invited to Pemberley after she inserted herself uninvited when Bingley visited, or to Darcy House tell her something? Not to mention my parents and I will never permit the introduction to her. I am thinking you may want to make sure Bingley makes things clear to her." Andrew scrunched his nose up like there was a bad smell as he spoke about the fortune-hunting, social climbing, shrewish harridan.

"No, she does not see a connection between the lack of invitations and her not being desirable company. It does not help that Bingley refuses to tell her I will never offer for her under *any* circumstances. Mother and Father support me fully in this. If she tried to entrap me, the only one who would suffer would be her."

"And you know you will have the full support of the Fitzwilliams and our connections behind you if it ever comes to that, do you not William?"

"Speaking of only hearing what one wants to. Do you know that regardless of how many times my parents have refused her entreaties to engage me to Anne, Aunt Cat still writes to Mother every month or so demanding such? Her letters do seem to make good kindling for the fire."

"Lady Catty would be most gratified to hear that," Andrew grinned. William looked at his cousin quizzically. "You know how she likes to be of use, do you not? By the way, she writes to Father claiming me as her future son as well."

William let out a guffaw. "I am glad I am not her only *option*. It seems our aunt is even more obtuse than Miss Bingley!" William paused, his face changing to a more sombre mien. "I miss Richard every day. Have you or your parents heard from him since his departure to the Peninsula?"

"No, and I would not expect to hear for some weeks, if not months. It takes long enough for post from the continent when there is no war raging. Now it is ten times worse," Andrew opined.

"I suppose you have the right of it. I will keep praying for his safe return to us," William said as he lifted his eyes to the heavens.

The cousins arrived at the pond—as they did each day they walked together—where the Viscount had seen his angel on earth walk away from him to meet the younger group that day. As it had been every day after, she had not been seen.

Andrew and William turned and began the walk back towards the Grosvenor Gate and the square beyond it.

~~~~~~~/~~~~~~~

"Janey, was not that the man you bumped into some weeks ago?" Mary asked as she saw the two men turn and head away from the duck pond. "Also the rude one was with him, but not the officer."

The four Bennet sisters who resided with the Gardiners were walking in Hyde Park again that morning with the two eldest Gardiner children as well as an appropriate number of escorts.

This time, they had walked along the Serpentine first and then made for the pond so the younger among them could feed the waiting ducks.

When the man had saved her from falling Jane had felt a frisson at his touch which she could not explain. As soon as he had released her it was gone. Not for the first time since that day she admonished herself that a Viscount would not be interested in the poor daughter of a country squire who lived with her tradesman uncle on Gracechurch Street near Cheapside.

Besides, instant attraction and love at first sight were

the stuff of gothic romance novels, not real life. At least that is what Jane was trying to convince herself of to protect her heart.

"You may be correct, Mary," Jane acknowledged, "however, they seem to be walking away from where we will be."

"Lizzy should be at the Duke's estate now, should she not be?" Mary verified.

"Unless their plans changed, I believe so," Jane confirmed.

"How I wish we were able to visit her." Mary saw Jane was about to interject. "I know it is for our own protection, but that does not make me miss her any less."

"In that, we are in lockstep," Jane agreed.

"Jane," Mary stopped walking.

Jane noted that fact and returned to where Mary stood. "What is it, Mary?"

"Am I a bad person that I do not miss our parents? Does the bible not command us to honour our mother and father?" Mary worried her lip.

"It is a subject with which I too have struggled," Jane admitted. "Something Lizzy said makes much sense to me. As soon as our parents showed they were willing to barter one of us for their own selfish needs, they stopped being our parents. Mrs. Bennet only cares about her own future comfort and Mr. Bennet wants everything to come to him without stirring himself from his study."

"Brava Jane! That is the most unforgiving statement I have ever heard you utter, and it is all true." Jane playfully swatted at Mary's arm. "When I think of how our two youngest sisters," Mary inclined her head towards where Kitty and Lydia were assisting Lilly and Eddy feed the ducks, "had they been raised by our moth…Mrs. Bennet, they would have turned out very wild indeed, especially Lydia, I believe."

"As much as I wish Lizzy was not tied to that old man, there could be some positives to come out of our move away from the pernicious influence of our parents. All we need is Lizzy to be free for everything to be good."

"How do you like the expanded house?" Mary queried to change the subject to one less melancholy than them worrying about Lizzy.

Rather than completely break down the walls between the two houses altogether, a builder had suggested making a series of doorless entryways. Uncle Edward had agreed and the work had been completed within a fortnight and now there was plenty of room with bedchambers to spare at the Gardiners' house.

"Sharing with you was never a chore, but I must admit to enjoying having my own chamber, especially as it is next to yours and across from Kitty and Lyddie's."

"Lilly, Eddy, and May are enjoying the new nursery which is twice the size of the old one. I like that Uncle is converting the old nursery into rooms for the governess and nurses," Mary agreed.

The two linked arms and made their way towards where their sisters and cousins were feeding the quacking ducks trying to demand their attention and the pieces of bread being thrown.

As the sisters turned, neither saw the Viscount turn back and then freeze in his tracks.

Andrew's heart was convinced it was indeed Miss Bennet, but how could he be sure at the distance and what excuse would he have to suddenly make an about face and walk back from whence he had come.

He told himself he could only hope he would be given another chance to see her. Why had he not asked her direction at that first meeting?

~~~~~~~/~~~~~~~

 By the next morning, which was shaping up to be a gorgeous day, the story of how the Duchess had been concerned for the servants being able to eat had made its way to all those who worked below stairs like wildfire through dry brush.

Her words of greeting became all the more believable and the servants had begun to believe the new mistress would not treat them the way the master did. When Her Grace's lady's maid had reinforced her mistress's goodness and kindness, the prevailing sentiment was the new Duchess was someone who deserved their loyalty.

In the past when Wickham heard of negative sentiments regarding His Grace being expressed he would have reported what was being said and who was saying it. As he agreed with the expressed sentiments, not a word was repeated to his master.

As was her wont, especially when she was in the country, regardless of the fact he had wanted to importune her yester-night—only receding when he saw proof she was still indisposed, Elizabeth was up before the sun. Loretta attended her soon after the bell had been pulled.

Elizabeth dressed in a dark green day dress and laced up her favourite half boots for walking. She had Loretta pull her hair back into a simple chignon, took her lightweight pelisse, the same one she used to wear at Longbourn, and a bonnet, and then made for the front doors one floor below her.

Seeing two footmen in the hallway outside her apartment, Elizabeth greeted the men cheerfully, and just like she said she would, she asked each his name and then said it back to burn it into her memory.

She descended the grand staircase and found Mr. Wickham at the bottom in the entrance hall. Elizabeth was concerned he would stop her from taking a walk. Her husband had not forbidden the activity, but neither had he

150

countenanced it. First, Elizabeth greeted the four footmen on duty near the front doors and repeated the method she had used with the first two.

Next, she turned to Mr. Wickham with an arched eyebrow challenging him to stop her. "It is not my intention to curtail your desire to exercise Your Grace," Wickham bowed to the young Duchess. "However, walking out on your own, or riding, would not be looked upon with favour. I, and two footmen-guards, and when you ride, a groom will accompany you."

"It will be a walk. I do not ride," Elizabeth informed her husband's man. "As long as you allow me some space so at least I can imagine I have solitude, I will not object to being escorted," Elizabeth allowed.

"Most gracious of you, Your Grace," Wickham bowed again.

Detecting no mockery or condescension in his tone, Elizabeth accepted Mr. Wickham was being sincere. It confused her. The man had always been her husband's man in every way. Now was the time for walking, not contemplating Mr. Wickham and her husband.

One of the footmen assisted her into her selected pelisse, she thanked him recalling his name was Ralph, and then tied her bonnet's ties loosely under her chin, and they were off.

Not five minutes after being introduced to her enormous personal footmen-guards, John Biggs and Brian Johns, Her Grace began her walk, the servant's network had made it be known she had meant what she said which only added to the prevalent opinion stating she was the best mistress they could have hoped for.

~~~~~~~/~~~~~~~

Mr. Wickham kept to his word, he and the two guards walked behind her allowing the Duchess a little space.

The first thing Elizabeth did was circumnavigate the house. She discovered the wings did in fact extend out at the back of the structure so if one looked at the mansion—and it truly was that—from above it would look like an 'H' albeit a very large one.

The formal gardens were as extensive as Elizabeth had suspected, and everything was far too ordered for her liking. There was a mix of colours in flower beds, but like colours were in rows. The rose garden was very pleasant, especially the wonderful scent of the myriad of blooming roses. Much to her approbation, the rose garden was not nearly as organised as the rest.

At the rear of the house was a large hedge maze, something Elizabeth would puzzle out—it never took her long to solve them—another day.

From the one side of the house, Elizabeth could see the wooded area about a mile distant. She struck out in that direction at her normal blistering pace. She looked over her shoulder and could see she had surprised the men with her speed but they soon increased their pace and then kept up with her.

Just before she entered the treeline, Wickham instructed each of the guards to take up positions parallel to the Duchess while still maintaining the envelope of distance.

Walking among her friends—the trees—Elizabeth had not felt so relaxed since before she had met her husband and had no choice but to marry the pig of a man. The sun was still climbing into the eastern sky so thanks to its angle the forest was cool.

The one thing she had noticed on the drive into the estate—well of what she had seen of it—there was no equivalent to Oakham Mount for her to climb in order to watch the sunrise in the mornings. Of course, she could watch from anywhere with an unobstructed view of the east, but it was not the same.

Nothing was the same, nor had it been since *he* had disrupted her life. Until and unless she was rid of him, it would not be good again.

~~~~~~~/~~~~~~~

"Did I give permission for my wife to go tramping around my estate like a hoyden? What will people say when they hear my Duchess has such wild ways?" the Duke demanded. Wickham so much wanted to point out that no one ever visited his master but he bit his tongue. "At least you had the good sense to escort her, but why did you not stop her?"

"If Your Grace had left instructions Her Grace was not to leave the house, it would have been so," Wickham pointed out. "If I may, Your Grace."

Hertfordshire nodded.

Wickham thought quickly, it had to be the master's idea. "I have heard women who have regular exercise are able to become with child quicker than those who do not. I overheard two eminent London physicians discussing this some months ago."

"That is why I have decided to allow her to walk out in the mornings. As long as you and her guards continue to escort her, I will not rescind my permission," the Duke decided magnanimously.

"By your command, Your Grace," Wickham bowed to his master. "Her Grace does not ride, would you object if she were to learn? The head groom is an excellent teacher and that exercise is very good as well."

"I think the Duchess should learn to ride; arrange it with the head groom." The Duke waved Wickham away.

Once his back was turned to the Duke, Wickham grinned to himself at how easily he had manipulated His Grace.

CHAPTER 16

Hertfordshire was getting more and more frustrated. He had been married to the spitfire for more than seven months and she was not yet with child.

Of one thing he was certain, the failure was hers, it could not be his fault. Even though he had celebrated his seven and sixtieth birthday in January 1807, he was sure he was as virile as he had ever been.

He had come close to punishing her for her failure, but his desire for an heir had won out. If something occurred to end her life before he had an heir, Hertfordshire was sure no woman would ever again join herself with him. It was times like this the Duke wondered if the harpy of a mother—Mrs. Bennet—as his wife referred to her—had not been right and he should have chosen the older sister.

As he did whenever he had these thoughts, the Duke reminded himself he would not have enjoyed being married to the insipid one and as such, he would not have been able to rein in his proclivities until she bore him a son.

Even the fact the mother had birthed five daughters and no sons did not cause him to waiver from his determination that *when* his duchess bore him a child, it would be a son.

When he had considered taking away her privilege to send and receive letters via the post again—what cared he if the settlement stated she could, Wickham had suggested the chances of his wife becoming with child would be reduced if she was unhappy. That information had stayed his hand and Hertfordshire had allowed his wife to continue to communicate with her sisters unimpeded.

The nights he went to her, he had considered demanding she open her eyes when he was joining with her, but he had remembered what Wickham told him about the cause and effects of being unhappy, so he had not given the order.

He had hoped to be in London pursuing his preferred entertainment by now, but Hertfordshire had sworn to himself to remain with his wife until she was confirmed to be with child. His cravings to have his needs met were increasing daily. All he could hope was he would be able to continue to control them until his wife was in the family way.

The Duke tamped down his desires reminding himself he was doing this for the very survival of his name and line.

~~~~~~~/~~~~~~~

Aunt Maddie was with child again, and having a ⬛ of a time with sickness in the mornings, necessitating Jane's assistance. Hence the only park the Bennets and Gardiner offspring had visited for the past few months was the one opposite the Gardiners' house.

Three of the four Bennet sisters living at Gracechurch Street had become a year older since coming to live with their aunt and uncle. In July 1806, Lydia turned eleven. In October, Jane turned nineteen, and lastly, in November Kitty reached the age of thirteen. The only sister not to celebrate her birthday with the Gardiners was Mary who would be fifteen in April 1807, a little more than a month after Lizzy turned seventeen.

Jane was somewhat sorry she had not been able to return to Hyde Park and possibly spot the Viscount who had saved her from falling.

Even if she was socially too low for him to consider, Jane would have liked to see him again. It was something beyond her control so she decided not to expend energy dreaming of that which was impossible.

By December Aunt Maddie's morning illness had all but gone away, however, it was a particularly cold winter so walks in Hyde Park were out of the question. Even the pond in the park opposite had—much to Lilly and Eddy's consternation—frozen over. Both had been very concerned about their friends the ducks until Jane and Mary had explained how they would fly to the south of England where it was a little warmer.

So far, other than the month after her presentation, letters from Lizzy had not stopped coming. No matter how much she wanted to see her younger sister above all else, Jane was well aware it was in their best interests to be away from the old man's company.

It was a small consolation, but from what Jane could see, and in her letters received from Charlotte, her friend had agreed, it seemed there were parts of Lizzy's life which were not terrible for her.

Her husband had not restricted her from taking walks and Lizzy had learnt to ride at Falconwood.

That was something which had surprised Jane. Lizzy had been afraid of riding horses ever since she had fallen and broken her arm while learning to ride a pony when she was but ten. It was nothing the placid mount had done, Lizzy had simply lost her seat and fallen. That had led to, until now, her refusing to learn to ride.

Lizzy had written in one of her first letters after beginning her riding lessons about the extensive stables at her husband's estate. The stablemaster, and head groom—the one who had been her teacher—had introduced her to a perfectly docile white Arabian mare named *Jamil*, which Lizzy had been told was Arabic for beautiful. Evidently. rider and mare had adopted one another, so the horse was unofficially Lizzy's

According to Lizzy, the name was apropos as her mare

was truly beautiful. She had perfect lines and the longest eyelashes and perfectly coiffed main and tail. If she did not know better, Lizzy stated she would have sworn *Jamil* would preen when anyone looked at her, as if she knew how pretty she was.

The old man did not ride himself. Lizzy had opined it was his age, girth, or both which was the cause of his not partaking in the sport. Jane had smiled when Lizzy had written how her pleasure in riding had increased as soon as she discovered *he* did not ride.

She wrote that most days she saw him no more than once at dinner. Even when he imposed himself on her, she told Jane since the first time she had kept her eyes shut tightly so even though she was in his company—after a fashion—she did not see him. In her last letter, Lizzy had expressed frustration she was not with child yet.

Jane's thoughts meandered to her three sisters living with the Gardiners. All three had matured considerably. Mary no longer needed to hide her true self, her intelligence, or her beauty now Mrs. Bennet was no longer around to denigrate her.

Kitty—now called Kate—had been working with art masters who were developing her native talent for drawing, sketching, and painting. Subsequent to her past birthday, Kitty had decided she preferred Kate as it was a much more mature sounding name. She had become so accomplished at her art that Jane had requested she take a likeness of the Gardiners and Bennets in residence on Gracechurch Street which would be sent to Lizzy. The art master would add Kate to the portrait.

Lydia had grown the most. No longer was she the vapid, unmanageable, animal-spirited, and spoilt girl she was well on her way to becoming under Mrs. Bennet.

With her energy directed toward positive pursuits, Lydia had discovered her intelligence. She was now, more rather than not, seen reading a book. To her own shock as much as everyone else's, it was discovered that she had a talent for music! Lydia was now learning to play the pianoforte and the harp.

After the first few weeks living with the Gardiners, any mention of her mother and missing her had ceased. Lydia did not refer to them as Mr. and Mrs. Bennet like the rest of her sisters, she simply did not mention them at all.

~~~~~~~/~~~~~~~

Fanny Bennet could not believe it was more than seven months since that ungrateful, wilful girl married His Grace, and things had not improved for her in the Meryton area.

No one called on her and she was not welcome at anyone's house. Ever since the supposedly jovial Sir William had arrested her and caused her to languish in the town gaol for five days—a humiliation she was certain she would never live down—when she was told she was not welcome, Fanny took the person stating thus at their word.

The worst betrayal she felt, even more than her own sister turning on her, was the fact not one letter had been received from either Jane or Lydia.

Jane had begun to be influenced by that cursed Miss Lizzy, which was the obvious explanation for her defection. But Lydia, the girl who had been her unabashed favourite, to have abandoned her as well cut her to the quick.

There was nothing she could see she had ever done to cause this level of disloyalty from her favourite daughter. There was only one explanation, it must be Miss Lizzy's influence. That was it, she had turned Lydia against her own mother, just like she had done with Jane.

Writing to her illustrious son-in-law had produced no results. Not one letter had been received in reply, and that too Fanny had convinced herself was Miss Lizzy's doing. She conveniently forgot what the Duke had told her in the one and only reply he had sent.

Fanny could not remember the last time she had been in her husband's company for more than a few minutes at a time, not that she regretted it too much. He took all of his meals on trays in his infernal study and whatever estate business he needed to do was done in the early mornings before she rose from her warm bed.

Her only company was Mrs. Hill, her maid, and the other servants working at Longbourn's manor house. If it were not for them, Fanny Bennet would go weeks, or longer without conversing a word with another living soul.

~~~~~~~/~~~~~~~

Other than the fact he could no longer order his needs, mainly his books, port, and pipe tobacco on account, life had not changed too much for Thomas Bennet.

Without Lizzy there to perform his estate duties, he actually had to venture forth from his study to deal with estate issues—occasionally, not as much as was needed, but he made sure he did so when his wife was yet abed so she would not be able to accost him.

That he was drinking far more port than he used to did not worry him, nor the fact the more he imbibed, the more he seemed to need to dull his senses. To increase the effectiveness, Bennet had taken to substituting some of his glasses of port with at first, an occasional tumbler of whisky, gin, or brandy. Soon the volume of those spirits being imbibed increased, and they became the primary drinks for Bennet.

The one thing he missed was the stimulating conversation and games of chess he used to enjoy with Lizzy. There was a time, not long after Gardiner had hit him, when Bennet had felt a modicum of guilt for not protecting his daughter, but that was not a feeling he had indulged in for quite some time.

In his mind, the ends justified the means. The entail

would be broken and his daughters who were no longer his concern, would have dowries to rival those in the first circles. In addition to the monthly amount he sent to Gardiner, he missed the four hundred pounds per annum interest from the initial payment of the girls' dowries he had planned to use, but there was nothing to be done about that. He ignored the fact the settlement precluded him from using any of the interest.

The only way he was able to play chess now was either against himself or via the post. His some-time partner via the post was an old professor of Bennet's at Cambridge who was retired now and one who had evidently not heard about his local ostracization who would occasionally send a move by letter.

The best thing about the whole situation, besides the peace and quiet in his home, was the fact his wife had all but given up entering his study. At some point, Fanny had got it through her thick skull that no matter how many times she burst into his study to berate him, nothing would change. For the first fortnight after Gardiner took his daughters, it had been daily, sometimes more than once per day. A month later it had become every two or three days, then weekly, monthly, and eventually, as the futility of her actions sunk in, it became very rare; it had already been more than three months.

Financially there were less household expenses than there had been before Lizzy's wedding.

On the one hand, he paid forty pounds per month for his daughters' upkeep in London, but that was juxtaposed against no allowances for the girls, his wife not entertaining, and almost never buying new clothing.

Mrs. Hill made the orders for food and other goods needed from Meryton, and given how much more sensible than his wife she was, there was no extravagance there. The savings on their living expenses meant more books, port, and spirits. Bennet knew his spending on the latter three far outstripped the household savings, but it was not an issue as they gave him pleasure.

As much as he did not want to acknowledge it, the earnings from his estate had fallen precipitously. He had begun to use some of the principal from Fanny's settlement to make up what he needed. He intended to repay it all once things improved. He would make an effort to increase the estate's income only once the entail was broken.

When he looked at it objectively, Bennet decided his life was actually better than it had been before the Duke came into their lives.

~~~~~~~/~~~~~~~

Elizabeth still felt she was in a gilded prison, but at least with the painting Kate had made of the family which her uncle had sent her brightened her mood each time she looked at it. It was framed and occupied a place of honour on the wall opposite her bed. That way, it was the first thing she looked at when she got up in the morning, and the final thing she saw before the last candle was extinguished at night.

Over the months she had been the mistress of Falconwood, the staff and servants, including to a certain extent Mr. Wickham, had become fiercely loyal and protective of Her Grace.

After a few short weeks in residence, none of them were surprised she knew their names and a little about each of them. Several who worked for the Duke had been employed on other estates with different families. None of the servants, including those who had experienced working for others, had ever worked for a better mistress.

For Elizabeth's part, her interactions with the staff and servants, and soon enough the tenants, brightened her day.

After she raised a tenant issue the first time with her husband, he told her to speak to his steward. He did not believe in getting involved with his tenants, so Elizabeth had gone to Mr. Hampstead directly from that day on. For his part, the steward was more than pleased the Duchess was taking her duty to the tenants so seriously.

As much as Elizabeth had wanted to maintain a friendship with Lady Morag McIntire, the old man had forbidden it. It seemed he was still perturbed he had lost his leverage over the Earl of Colbath.

Elizabeth Chamberlain thought God had been playing a cruel trick on her. She had been shackled to *him* for more than seven months and her courses had come each month like clockwork, as they had from the time she had first experienced them.

"Please Lord, allow me to become with child and give me a son," Elizabeth beseeched in prayer as she lay in her bed one night after her husband had come to importune her again. "If You allow me to fall with child, then that man will no longer visit me. As long as it is a son, I will be safe from him."

At least her courses were due to begin in a day or two. That would—even though it would mean she was not with child—give her a week's respite from *his* disgusting attentions.

As she did every night, Elizabeth ended her prayer asking God and Jesus to watch over her sisters, aunts, uncles, cousins, and friends, and keep them safe. The warm bath Loretta had made sure was ready for her mistress, as she did every time her husband told her he would come to her in the evening—had been relaxing which helped Elizabeth slip away allowing sleep to claim her.

~~~~~~~/~~~~~~~

The next morning she was up early, as was her wont. It was a much colder winter than Elizabeth could remember. There had been much snow which had begun shortly before Christmas and since had fallen a few times. That fact did not stop Elizabeth from exercising as long as there was no precipitation.

On waking to a cup of hot chocolate her maid delivered,

Elizabeth had hoped it was not snowing or raining. Loretta had confirmed there was neither.

Warmly dressed in a thick wool riding habit, fur muffs over her ears, a fur-lined jacket and hood and wool-lined gloves, Elizabeth made her way to the stables—with Mr. Wickham, John, and Brian in tow—to greet *Jamil*. As she always did when she rode, she offered her mare an apple and carrot, both were munched gratefully which led to the horse nuzzling her mistress.

While the Duchess's horse was saddled, Wickham mounted the gelding he rode when at Falconwood, and by the time she was in her side-saddle, he, Biggs, and Johns were waiting with a groom, ready to escort Her Grace.

She was not sure when it had occurred, but Elizabeth no longer thought Mr. Wickham quite the most contemptable man who worked for her husband. He had begun to give her more space when they rode or walked and based on the lack of anger directed at her by her husband, Elizabeth was sure Mr. Wickham reported very little of what she said to his master.

It was not that she liked or trusted her husband's guard dog, but she no longer openly disdained him.

She had grown very close to her two guards, John Biggs and Brian Johns which was why she addressed them as John and Brian when not in *his* company. Elizabeth felt they were there to protect her, not spy on her for her vile husband.

This particular morning, they rode north into the part of the estate which was in Hertfordshire. The first ride they had made to the northern border of the estate, Mr. Wickham had informed Her Grace they were less than five miles from Meryton at that point.

Although she did not want to chance it, Elizabeth could not but imagine meeting her Aunt and Uncle Philips and Charlotte at the border of the estate. As much as she enjoyed Charlotte's letters, it was nothing to being able to see her again.

She did not want to strain the fragile détente with Mr. Wickham so it was something she thought about but never articulated.

All too soon she guided her mare towards the stables. It was time to break her fast.

CHAPTER 17

On her seventeenth birthday on the fifth day of March of 1807, Elizabeth felt like she had been given the greatest gift she had ever experienced in her short life.

It had begun in January when she, who had never done so since they had first begun, missed her courses. Even though it was not confirmed she was in fact with child yet, she had reported the fact of her missed indisposition to her husband. Thankfully the disgusting man believed it was dangerous to the child growing within her—if that in fact was occurring— for him to join with her, so he had ceased importuning her.

It was the first time Elizabeth had seen her husband seem genuinely happy as he pontificated on his certainty he would be gifted a son and heir.

A few weeks before missing her monthly indisposition, Elizabeth had noticed a tenderness in her breasts and then about three weeks after, the sickness in the morning had begun.

Thanks to one of Aunt Maddie's enclosed letters with the ones from Jane, Elizabeth had been warned of the signs to look for when she was with child. Her aunt had responded to a letter Elizabeth had sent telling of her missing her courses.

Hence, when she was ill for the first time, it had not been as worrying as it otherwise would have been. Aunt Maddie had warned her the illness, if she was afflicted—not all women suffered in the mornings when with child—could be mild or all the way to severe like she had experienced with her current time being with child.

Her aunt's advice was that if Elizabeth experienced morning illness to request dry toast and ginger tea. After the first time, Elizabeth had asked her maid to let Cook know the toast and tea would be required in the mornings.

Praise be, based on her aunt's information, Elizabeth had a mild case of the sickness.

In February, she had missed her second set of courses and after informing *him* of that fact, he had demanded the local physician be summoned.

The kindly man had examined Elizabeth with both Mrs. Greaves and her maid present. When she described her symptoms to the doctor, he had opined she had all of the early signs of being with child and had pronounced her to be in that state.

It was the best news so far in her forced marriage to the old, abominable man. As he had ceased to importune her from the first month's courses she missed, it was a dream come true for Elizabeth. She would put up with much worse morning illness than that which she was suffering from if it meant he did not come to her at night. She would be free of his attentions until many months after she gave birth, if ever again dependant on the sex of the babe.

This led to her birthday gift, one he had unintentionally provided. He did not know, and Elizabeth did not share, it was the anniversary of her birth. Elizabeth sat in her bedchamber while her maid, with some others assisting her, packed the trunks for the departure in the morning on the morrow. She could not but smile when she recalled the conversation in his study that afternoon.

Not long after the doctor's examination Elizabeth had been summoned to her husband's study.

On entering his inner sanctum Elizabeth fought to school her features. She had been informed about the specially

166

constructed chair to hold his girth, but she had never been in this room to see it before.

The Duke had mistaken the look on his wife's face as happiness for finally doing her duty to him and not that she was silently making sport of him. That was not something he could imagine as he was sure he commanded far too much deference for any to make him the subject of a jest, and certainly not to his face.

"Even though you should have been with child months earlier, I am well pleased about your finally doing your duty to me," the Duke had condescended. "I need to make for London to take care of business and other obligations and I am told Town is not a good place for a woman in your delicate condition."

'Yes,' *Elizabeth thought,* 'there are no women able to deliver their children in London. Does he think me a simpleton, he wants to run back to his mistress.'

"Does that mean I will remain here, Your Grace?" Elizabeth enquired. She was thinking about how to get him to agree to send her to the estate in Derbyshire as Aunt Maddie had advised her when her husband interrupted her thoughts.

"No, you are to be sent to one of my estates where you will be able to increase in peace without any distractions," he informed Elizabeth.

"Do you perhaps have an estate in Derbyshire?" Elizabeth enquired, seemingly innocuously. It seemed he was doing half her work for her.

"I do, what of it?" The Duke had been thinking of sending her to Ringdale in Wiltshire.

"I am a person who suffers greatly from the heat of the summer, and I am afraid it will be worse than normal as I increase. I am worried the heat will be dangerous for our child, so I suggest you send me to Derbyshire which is a cooler county from what I have read." Of course, Elizabeth had read no such thing, but she knew she needed to play on his need for an heir.

"There is Castlemere in Derbyshire," Hertfordshire stated

*thoughtfully. What cared he what estate she went to and with that particular estate being far from London, it was not a bad thing. "I have decided to send you to Derbyshire. **WICKHAM**!" he yelled.*

"Your Graces," Wickham bowed to the Duke and Duchess.

"My wife is to be sent to Castlemere to increase. Have my secretary write to the steward, butler, and housekeeper to expect her three days hence." The Duke waved Wickham away to carry out his orders. "You will depart first thing in the morning. You may have your maid, your guards, and any other servants you desire accompany you." He went back to reading what was on the desk effectively ending the one-sided interview.

It was hard to believe how easy it had been to direct the man so he did what she wanted. While her maid supervised the packing, which of course included the painting of her family, Elizabeth went to the escritoire in her chamber. She had some letters to write.

~~~~~~~~/~~~~~~~~

"Your Grace," Wickham bowed when his master called him to enter the study.

"You will accompany me to London in the morning and I expect you to acquire me wives of some of the peers who have tried to harm me and others who have rejected me when I am ready for that. We will begin with my mistresses so I may feel like myself again, then I will instruct you who will be my first lover," Hertfordshire told his man.

"As always, I am here to serve, Your Grace," Wickham bowed deferentially.

"Do not fail me or you know what will befall you," Hertfordshire threatened.

"I never do, Your Grace," Wickham averred.

"Since our arrival from Town, you spent every morning when there is no rain or snow with my impertinent wife and you tell me she never said anything which would be of interest to me?" the Duke demanded sceptically.

"Her Grace neither likes nor trusts me, hence when I am in her company on walks or rides, other than a curt greeting, she holds her peace," Wickham hedged. "If there had been something to report, it would have been done." Knowing how loyal Biggs and Johns were to the Duchess he added, "You may speak to the two guards, they will verify what I have told you."

Hertfordshire waved his man away. If he had not needed Wickham in London, he would have sent him north with the Duchess, but, in his opinion, his servants and guards were all supremely loyal to him so he was not concerned about his wishes not being adhered to at Castlemere.

~~~~~~~/~~~~~~~

The lead conveyance was the large, comfortable travelling coach she and her maid rode in, John was on the bench next to the coachman and Brian stood on the rear bench next to a footmen. There were two more carriages behind them, all escorted by a dozen outriders. A cart with her trunks followed when Elizabeth and her retinue departed before the sun broke above the eastern horizon.

Much to her joy, the stablemaster and head groom had made sure *Jamil* was being led by one of the outriders. Her husband had not been consulted. Being he never entered the stables no one was concerned about his discovering the horse was travelling north. The doctor had recommended she cease riding, but having her mare close by would be a comfort to Elizabeth.

With each mile the convoy placed between her and *his* primary estate, Elizabeth relaxed more. It was with a mixture of joy and trepidation she watched as they traversed Meryton on the way to the Great North Road. There were few people about as it was just barely after the sun had risen.

Elizabeth patted her reticule which contained her letters. She planned to post them at the first coaching inn they would stop at in about an hour. She did not want to take a chance her letters would have been pulled out of the post by *him* at Falconwood after her departure. After keeping her letters out of his hands since they married, Elizabeth did not want to rely on *him* not being vindictive.

Another reason she wanted to post her letters after leaving Falconwood was she had written letters to more than just her sisters. She was aware any letter not addressed to one of her sisters would not be posted from *his* estate.

She knew she had the loyalty of the staff and servants at Falconwood, but there was no reason to take such a chance with her letters. How she hoped the Gardiners, her sisters, the Philipses, and the Lucases would be able to do what she had suggested.

Time and replies to her letters would tell.

An hour later, they made the first scheduled stop. Elizabeth posted her letters, asking for them to be sent express and then with her maid accompanying her to wait at the door, and John watching in the hallway outside to make sure no one approached her, she made for the necessary.

When the landlady brought some refreshment to the private room the Duchess had secured, she was pleasantly surprised when Her Grace ordered food and drinks for all of the servants, guards, coachmen, and footmen travelling with her.

A little more than an hour later, they were on their way again.

~~~~~~~~/~~~~~~~~

"Charlotte, is that not a letter from Eliza?" Lady Lucas asked her daughter when she handed over the missive which had been delivered by an express rider. "I thought she was forbidden to send missives to you directly and this was delivered by express."

"Let me make sure all is well. I will tell you soon enough,

Mama," Charlotte stated worriedly as she broke the ornate seal. She began to read.

5 March 1807

Soon to be: Castlemere in Derbyshire

My best friend, Charlotte,

Do not be alarmed this arrived express or was posted to you directly. I am well, I promise you. I made sure to pay the express fees when I posted the letters so your family would not have to do so.

It has been confirmed, I am indeed with child. I have been free of that man's attentions since I missed my first courses in January. Today, what a present he unwittingly gifted me on my birthday. I am being sent to increase in Derbyshire at the above estate.

What a wonder. I will not see him *for a minimum of six months, and hopefully much longer than that. He is for London. I care not where he is or what he does as long as he is not near me! If only it could be I would never see him again. Rather than think about what could be, I will revel in what is: my travelling further and further away from the repulsive ancient man with each mile which passes.*

Do you think, perhaps there is a possibility you and some of your family could come visit Lambton in Derbyshire?

You can ask my Aunt Maddie for information about the inn or inns there as it is the market town where she grew up and where her brother, Mr. Adam Lambert is the rector of the local church.

If you are able to come, write to me first. I need to make sure it is safe to be in my company and word will not get back to him.

As much as I would love to see you and others, I cannot be selfish and will only confirm things if I am sure it will be completely safe to come. Given my husband is hated by his staff and servants, where I am not because I treat them with warmth and respect, I am hopeful it will be possible to spend time in your company.

That old man cannot spell respect, never mind give it.

Please give my regards to all of your family and my friends in the Meryton neighbourhood. Remind your father he is my personal hero for putting Mrs. Bennet in the town gaol.

As soon as I have evaluated the situation in Derbyshire, I will write to you, my friend. My prayer is it will be something which can be done without any possible harm to you or any of my family.

With the warmest regards of friendship and sisterhood,

Elizabeth (Eliza)

Charlotte handed the letter to her mother. How she hoped it would be advisable to travel north and see Eliza—Her Grace—again.

"What good news!" Lady Lucas exclaimed. "I am certain if Eliza says it is safe, your Papa will be the first one out of the door to take us to go see her."

Charlotte would add to her prayers not only for Eliza to be kept safe, but that they would see one another soon.

~~~~~~~/~~~~~~~

"Do you really think we will be able to see Lizzy in Derbyshire?" Jane asked her aunt and uncle excitedly after they had read the letters the express rider had just delivered.

"It is very good she was able to get her husband to send her to increase at Castlemere, it is but four or five miles from Lambton. I think I need to write to my brother and tell him it is time we took up his invitation to come visit him, Eve, and his children," Madeline asserted. "We can wait there until Lizzy feels it is safe to see us."

"How long would you want to be in the north, my Dear," Gardiner enquired.

"Until Lizzy delivers her child," Madeline averred. She saw the look on her husband's face. "I am well to travel, there are still more than two months before the time the midwife estimated I would begin my lying in. Giving birth in Lambton would not be such a bad thing."

"What if Lizzy judges it is not safe for us to be seen with her?" Jane worried.

"We will still be in the area if or when she can see us. If nothing else, I am sure she will be able to make forays into Lambton to shop. And I believe she will be able to attend church on Sundays," Madeline opined.

"I do not think I would be able to be away from the business for so long," Gardiner reminded his wife.

"Edward Gardiner, we both know you are able to take far more time away than you do," Madeline challenged. "Did you not tell me what a good manager Mr. Humphries is? And what of your head clerk, Captain Peacock and his assistant, young Mr. Grace? Surely they can run things effectively and will contact you by post when and if needed?"

"I suppose there is truth in your assertions," Gardiner admitted.

"Does that mean we are all to travel to Derbyshire?" Jane interjected excitedly.

"It seems we need to pack," Gardiner decided.

~~~~~~~/~~~~~~~

"Will you join us at Pemberley in time for Easter, Andrew?" Darcy asked his eldest nephew.

"I will be there the week before the holiday, Uncle Robert," Andrew averred. "There is not too much for me to do at Hilldale before I join you."

"As I am finding no enjoyment in the season, what say you I accompany you to Hilldale," William volunteered.

"If my aunt and uncle can spare you, I would enjoy the company," Andrew responded.

Neither Darcy parent had an objection. "We depart London on the morrow, when will you two head for Staffordshire?" Lady Anne queried.

"The day after," Andrew replied. "The same day as Mother and Father make for Snowhaven."

"It is wonderful Richard has returned in time for Easter," Lady Anne remarked. "I assume my sister and brother are waiting as that is when his leave from the army will begin?"

"You have the right of it, Aunt Anne," Andrew confirmed. "In fact, if he agrees, I will invite Rich to join William and me in travelling to my estate."

"Rich will be sorry he missed Anna's twelfth birthday, but I know he will be impressed at how much she has improved on the pianoforte since he has been away," Lady Anne guessed.

Those in the drawing room were treated to the sounds of the youngest Darcy practicing in the music room under the watchful eye of her governess, Miss Karen Younge.

CHAPTER 18

After almost three days of travel, the lead coach passed the old stone gateposts with a brass arch above them with big letters between the top and bottom bar of the arch proclaiming '*CASTLEMERE*' for one and all to see.

Much to Elizabeth's delight, there were hills aplenty here and not much flat land she could see. If the hills were not enough, some of the peaks of the Peak District rose majestically in the west. In the late afternoon with the sun already well past its zenith, the mountains took on a purple hue.

There was more to delight her: within a half mile of passing the gate, woods could be seen either side of the drive. The drive began to rise with an easy gradient and then turned towards the west just before the point the forested area ended.

The coachman was already familiar with the fact Her Grace loved nature and would be enamoured with the vista which came into view just after the drive began to slope down, so he pulled on the reins bringing the three matched pairs of bays and the carriage they were pulling to a halt.

With the bend in the drive, it gave a perfect view of the valley below and Elizabeth instantly understood what had inspired the name of the estate.

On the western side of the valley was, in fact, a castle. It was built with large grey and charcoal coloured stones. A more modern, and far larger wing, had been added on the eastern side of the castle on the banks of a lake, a fairly large one.

When she looked to the north, Elizabeth saw there was a river and a stream which both flowed into the lake. The southern end of the lake was rather narrow and a river and two streams, flowed onwards at various points towards the south and the hills which made up the one side of the valley. There was a stone bridge over the river, and smaller wooden ones over the streams.

As she looked around the castle and the newer wing, Elizabeth was well pleased to see the absence of any serious formal gardens. It seemed to her that previous generations of masters had allowed nature its head.

Before she departed Falconwood, Elizabeth had spoken to the Greaves who had replaced the butler's parents who had been the butler and housekeeper before himself and his wife. He and his parents had worked for the current duke's parents —who had been good people and nothing like their son. They had told her as far as they knew the current duke, unlike his parents used to, had never been to this or any of his smaller satellite estates, preferring London or Falconwood.

Elizabeth was happy *he* had never set foot on this estate which explained the lack of overly ordered formal gardens.

She knocked on the forward facing inside wall of the coach and the coachmen soon had his team moving again. She reminded herself to thank the driver for his consideration in stopping to allow her to see the place which would be her home for the next six to nine months.

Once she gave birth, as long as everything was well, she would remain here as long as she could, trying to defer her churching so she would not have to be in *his* company again too soon.

It took a little more than a quarter of an hour to arrive in front of the castle and the newer section of the house.

One of the footmen, with John and Brian looking on, assisted Elizabeth to alight, and then did the same for her maid. Elizabeth smiled knowing a footman would not have assisted Loretta with the Duke looking on. The staff and servants were lined up and waiting for her.

There were two lines of servants behind the three senior staff. The men gave deep bows while the ladies gave their curtsies to the Duchess.

"Welcome to Castlemere, Your Grace, I am your steward, Mr. Mason, may I present your butler and housekeeper?" the man who stepped forward requested.

"Please do, Mr. Mason," Elizabeth responded.

Thankfully the staff and servants who were employed at the estate had never had the displeasure of meeting His Grace. As was expected, the senior staff at each of the Duke's estates and houses did correspond and word that Her Grace was nothing like the Duke had reached Derbyshire as well. The praise for Her Grace had been flaming, and those standing before the Duchess had suspected it was exaggerated.

The respectful way she addressed the steward seemed to give truth to what they had been told.

"Your Grace, Mrs. Marrion Bannister, your housekeeper and Mr. Owen Toppin, your butler," Mason presented.

"I appreciate all of you being here to welcome me to what will be my home for many months," Elizabeth intoned. She told the servants she intended to learn their names, and unlike there had been at Falconwood, there was no scepticism as word had already filtered to the lowest of the servants about the Duchess doing exactly that at the largest of His Grace's estates.

The butler and housekeeper released those who worked for them to return to their posts. "If you will let me know your favourites Your Grace, I will impart the knowledge to Mrs. Black, your cook," the housekeeper requested.

"As I will be touring the house, which will include the kitchens, I will be happy to discuss my preferences with Mrs.

Black directly," Elizabeth asserted.

Mrs. Bannister was impressed. A duchess who did not eschew entering her kitchens. Yes, she was extremely young, but she seemed to possess a self-assuredness and had intelligence shining from her eyes.

"As you wish, Your Grace," the housekeeper averred. "May I show you and your maid to your apartments? Mr. Toppin will have his footmen bring your trunks up to you."

"Thank you, it will be good to wash the road dust off and change," Elizabeth accepted.

The main entrance of the manor house opened into the castle which in turn opened into a large hall lined with suits of armour and flags from wars past. They turned left through a doorway in the wall which led into the newer wing of the house.

"The great hall is used as a ballroom, except I understand the last ball held here was in the late duke's time," the housekeeper explained. "Everything else is in this wing. The first floor has the public rooms, including the breakfast and dining parlours. I would assume as it is only you, you would prefer to take your meals in your private sitting room which has a table for four to dine comfortably."

Mrs. Bannister led the Duchess and her maid up to the second floor which was the family floor. She opened a door and stood back allowing Her Grace to enter her chambers.

Elizabeth was pleased by what she saw. They had entered the bedchamber, which was a large airy room with an enormous four-poster bed against the wall facing the windows. There were bedside tables on either side of the bed and a pair of comfortable looking wingback chairs in one corner.

She was shown the walk-in closet, which was larger than the bedchamber she and Jane shared at Longbourn. Just past the closet was a door which led to the bathing room which contained a nice large brass tub.

When Elizabeth walked to the windows in the bedchamber, she was greeted with a view across the lake towards distant hills in the east. She noted there was a balcony running past the windows. She turned to the housekeeper with a questioning look. "The way to get to the balcony is from your sitting room, Your Grace," the housekeeper supplied.

Mrs. Bannister led the way through a door at one end of the chamber which led into the sitting room and small dining parlour. The table was next to the windows with the same view as from the bedchamber; there was a sideboard close by. Above the latter piece of furniture would be a good place to hang Kate's painting. In the sitting room itself, there were bookcases along the wall opposite the windows, a settee, two armchairs bracketing it and a low table in between them.

Where the windows ended, Elizabeth saw the door which led out onto the nice wide balcony. She used it.

There were benches and chairs to sit on if one so desired. A cool breeze was being blown off the lake which to Elizabeth felt heavenly. She turned to the housekeeper. "Do we have any neighbouring estates close by or towns in the area?" she enquired.

"The closest estate is Pemberley, to the east. The common border is only about two miles from here." The housekeeper pointed. "Chatsworth, the Duke of Devonshire's estate, is northwest of us, about twelve miles away. To the southeast is Snowhaven, the Earl of Matlock's estate, more than ten miles distant. As far as towns go, the closest are Kympton and Lambton. We are about equally distant from each. Lambton is much larger and has a greater variety of shops."

"Do they both have inns?" Elizabeth asked evenly.

"Yes, Your Grace, both do. Lambton's is a large well established inn, the Rose and Crown. The Charging Bull Inn is in Kympton, but it is far smaller and I would never recommend it over the Rose and Crown," Mrs. Bannister explained. "Your Grace, over the years some of the residents of Pemberley and the smaller estates in the area have been known to come fish in the lake. The late Duke used to welcome those who wanted to fish, and your husband has never changed that, mainly as I believe he is not aware of that fact given he has never been here."

"Is it possible for me to meet with the local midwife and physician, or is there only an apothecary hereabouts?" Elizabeth enquired.

"The Darcys at Pemberley have long kept a doctor in the area. Mr. Harrison, the elder is about to retire but his practice is being assumed by his son, Mr. Benjamin Harrison. They live in Lambton," the housekeeper averred. "Mr. Laraby is the apothecary and lives in Kympton. The midwife who serves both Pemberley and this estate, Mrs. Medford, works closely with both Mr. Harrisons. She has extremely high standards of cleanliness and as far as I know, has never lost a mother to childbed fever."

"Thank you greatly for all of the information. It seems you have a vast knowledge of the area," Elizabeth observed.

"I have lived in this neighbourhood for the whole of my life, Your Grace. Anything I am able to do to help, it will be my pleasure," the housekeeper stated as she bobbed a curtsey.

"Could we have hot water brought up for my bath, please," Elizabeth requested.

With another curtsey, the housekeeper bustled off to inform Mr. Toppin Her Grace required hot water.

~~~~~~~/~~~~~~~

"Welcome home your Ladyship," Mrs. Reynolds the housekeeper at Pemberley stated warmly. "And you, Sir, and it is good to see you, Miss Anna."

"It is good to be home," Georgiana exclaimed. "Mama

and Papa, may I go change and then practice on the pianoforte please?"

"I think you should rest and allow Miss Younge to do so as well. You will have plenty of time to practice later, Anna sweetling," Darcy replied.

Fighting her urge to pout, the youngest Darcy made for her chambers with a smiling governess following in her wake.

Lady Anne noticed Mrs. Reynolds was looking to see where William was. "It is good to see you, Mrs. Reynolds," Lady Anne returned. "Master William left London after us with his two Fitzwilliam cousins. They will join us anon after Lord Hilldale sees to some things at his estate. Is there any news in the neighbourhood of which you think I should be aware?"

"According to my friend Mrs. Bannister," the housekeeper saw the quizzical look on both the mistress and master's faces. "She is the housekeeper at Castlemere," she explained.

"Do not tell me the dastardly duke is finally coming to visit his estate," Darcy stated distastefully.

"Not the Duke," Mrs. Reynolds elucidated. "Her Grace is with child and while, according to my friend, the Duke is in London, he sent his wife to the country for peace and quiet so she can increase far away from the odours and bad air in London. If I understood correctly, she would have arrived today."

"Is there anything else of which we should be aware?" Darcy questioned.

"Nothing of import." Mrs. Reynolds turned to her mistress. "Will I meet you in your study in the morning on the morrow?"

"Please, after we break our fasts," Lady Anne informed her housekeeper. "It is good to see you again." Lady Anne gave Mrs. Reynolds's hand a light squeeze. They were mistress and housekeeper, but there was almost a bond of friendship between them.

"Anne, will you call on Her Grace?" Darcy enquired.

"I take it you do not approve if I were to do so?" Lady Anne challenged.

"We all saw her at her presentation, she seems like a nice sort of lady. My concern is if we reach out to her, how do we stop being in that libertine's company?" Darcy worried. "I care not he is a duke; he is the worst kind of man."

"That he is, but should his wife suffer for his crimes?" Lady Anne paused. "Because of the way my sister behaves, if my namesake was in the area would we shun her in case Catherine thinks it means we are accepting of her and her presumptuous behaviour?"

"You make a good point my love," Darcy conceded. "All I ask is we are circumspect. Also, it is not quite the same as it would be with Anne, who is our niece."

"I will see what unfolds, but I will discuss this with Elaine and Reggie as well," Lady Anne averred.

"We have been away from Pemberly for months, should we retire and reacquaint ourselves with our chambers," Darcy waggled his eyebrows suggestively at his wife.

"Robert Geroge Alexander Darcy, you are incorrigible. Do not change."

The dignified master and mistress were seen on their way up the grand stairs with huge smiles on their faces as they walked hand in hand.

~~~~~~~/~~~~~~~

On the fourth day after the express from Lizzy, the Gardiners departed Gracechurch Street; a rented carriage and a cart followed the Gardiner equipage. That evening on the Great North Road where the Gardiners and four Bennet sisters stopped to spend the night, they were met by the Lucas parents and daughters. With them were Frank and Hattie Philips.

Those travelling from Meryton had agreed to join the Gardiners and Bennet sisters and wait in Lambton until they were told it was safe to see Elizabeth. It had been far too long.

They were all determined. Somehow they would find a way to be in Lizzy's company.

CHAPTER 19

Due to the fact not only was the parsonage in Lambton a large one, but the home belonging to the Lamberts in the town had no tenant currently, there was more than enough space for those arriving from Meryton and London.

The Gardiners and the two youngest Bennets were hosted at the parsonage while the rest of the travellers found themselves at the house just the other side of the green from where the church and parsonage were situated.

Kate and Lydia had found it amusing when they were introduced to Aunt Maddie's younger brother, Uncle Adam, and his wife, Aunt Eve.

The two had two sons so far. "At least the boys are not named Cain and Abel," Lydia remarked to Kate, thinking she had spoken without being heard by others.

"We certainly did think of naming them thusly," Lambert jested, "but then Eve and I decided we did not want to chance history repeating itself with what had occurred in biblical times."

"Adam," his wife admonished him playfully. "Do not tell our nieces that, else they will think you serious."

"Aunt Maddie, may we cross the green to visit our sisters and those residing at Lambert House, please?" Kate requested. The Lambert boys, three and one respectively, were napping, meaning the noise in the house had to be regulated.

"I wanted to speak to Sir William, so come girls, I will escort you," Gardiner allowed.

Unlike Bennet, who Gardiner used to call his brother-in-law, Sir William had been secretly investing a small sum with Gardiner for some years now. He needed to tell the knight about a new and potentially lucrative investment opportunity he had discovered.

Once the front door clicked shut, Lambert turned to his sister. "In my ministering to my flock, I thought I had seen it all, but selling a child into marriage to a man older than her father for personal gain is something I could not have imagined before you told me of it."

"What sort of parent does that to their own flesh and blood?" Evangeline wondered.

"It is precisely the reason Lizzy decided they were no longer her parents. If she refers to them at all, she will only call them Mr. and Mrs. Bennet now," Madeline shared with her brother and sister-in-law. "The other sisters, except for Lydia call them the same as Lizzy. Lyddie does not refer to them at all. It hit her the hardest when she realised Fanny is incapable of loving any besides herself."

"Have you written to Lizzy to let her know you are all in Lambton?" Lambert enquired.

"I did first thing this morning, it is on the way to Castlemere with one of our footmen who accompanied us from London," Madeline responded.

"Did you know that estate is only second to Pemberley in size in Derbyshire?" Evangeline queried. "Chatsworth, the estate of the Duke of Devonshire has slightly less land than Castlemere. The Matlock estate, Snowhaven is about as large as Pemberley but part of it is in Nottinghamshire."

"I am sure Lizzy will love roaming about the estate where she is residing. It will have to be her legs now she has decided not to ride until after she delivers her child," Madeline opined.

~~~~~~~/~~~~~~~

The Hilldale coach in which the three cousins rode was traversing Lambton on the way to Pemberley when they passed the village green.

Andrew thought he was seeing things. There on a bench under the old chestnut tree in the centre of the green sat the woman who still inhabited his dreams. Not seeing her these many months had done nothing to chase her from his consciousness.

"Andy, at what are you staring?" Richard enquired.

His brother was sitting as if frozen on the forward facing bench staring intently out of the window facing the green.

As much as he wanted to strike the ceiling with his cane and have his coachman halt the conveyance, Andrew was well aware of how it would look and the last thing he wanted to do was frighten Miss Bennet.

"I-it is nothing, I thought I recognised someone, but I was in error," Andrew hedged.

"What say you to our riding to Castlemere and fishing in the lake on Monday?" William suggested. "The inhabitants have been undisturbed by me for far too long."

"The lake at that estate is far larger and deeper than the *pond* at Pemberley," Richard ribbed. He knew an easy way to discompose William was to give an implied insult to his father's much loved estate.

It was a long standing competition—albeit a friendly one—about which estate, Pemberley or Snowhaven, was the better. If Richard was honest, he would admit his uncle's estate was slightly superior, not only because it was a little larger, but it was much closer to the peaks and the view of said mountains from the hill behind Pemberley's manor house was unrivalled.

"What would you expect," William bit back peevishly. "The one at Castlemere is natural, ours is manmade. It is still better than the duckpond you have at Snowhaven."

Soon enough the coach made the turn onto Pemberley's land. They would arrive in less than a half hour.

~~~~~~~/~~~~~~~

"Are we agreed, we will take a wait and see attitude as far as the Duchess goes," Lady Matlock verified.

"What Darcy proposes is prudent, Elaine," Lord Matlock stated. "We know not what her situation is. Also, even though he may not be there now, Hertfordshire may arrive at his estate and I am with Robert on this. There is no reason to be connected to him at all."

"I do feel bad for her, she is so very young," Lady Anne lamented. "Everyone here saw her at the presentation."

"You could see she was aware the eyes of every courtier were upon her and she just raised her chin and walked, always looking directly ahead," Lady Matlock recalled. "What do you think her Majesty said to Her Grace?"

"I believe they are the only two ladies who would be able to answer that question," Darcy opined, "and given the lack of gossip about their conversation since the Duchess's presentation, it will not be something we will ever learn."

Further conversation about the residents of Castlemere was interrupted when the butler, Reynolds, informed the master a coach had entered the park.

Having promised Anna she would be notified when William and her cousins arrived, Lady Anne instructed the butler to inform Miss Darcy. The two sets of parents had just exited the door leading to the internal courtyard when, with blonde ringlets bouncing, Georgiana arrived breathlessly having obviously run from the music room in her excitement.

Anna launched herself into her brother's arms without thinking as soon as the three cousins alighted. She suddenly became rather shy as she remembered the lessons Miss Younge had been teaching about propriety and comportment. Anna blushed deeply at her lapse. "Please pardon my display,"

Georgiana stated contritely, her eyes directed at the ground.

"Although I have not been gone for so very long, I too missed you Sweetling," William soothed. "Rather than be upset, it warms my heart you were so happy to see me."

"Truly?" Georgiana lifted her head, a smile forming on her lips.

"You know how much I abhor disguise, so yes, your vivacious welcome was appreciated," William assured his much younger sister.

After greetings were exchanged, slightly more sedately than Anna's had been, the family group made their way back into the house.

In keeping with their decision, the parents did not mention the presence of the Duchess at Castlemere.

~~~~~~~/~~~~~~~

Elizabeth was sitting in the rose garden near the entrance to the castle when she thought she was seeing an apparition. If she did not know better she would swear she was looking at one of the Gardiner footmen.

As he drew nearer, she realised it was not a spectre, but a real flesh and blood man. "Peter! Surely my aunt and uncle did not send you all the way here from Gracechurch Street did they?" Elizabeth wondered.

"No Miss Lizzy...sorry, I mean Yer Grace, I comes from Lambton," the footman responded. "Mistress sent a letter for you."

"You may still call me Miss Lizzy when others are not near us," Elizabeth looked to where the two guards were stationed. She had seen them relax as soon as she indicated she knew the man. Also, they were well out of earshot. "How is it my aunt and uncle are so near? Is anyone else with them?"

The young man withdrew the missive from a pouch and handed it to the Duchess. "This 'ere will explain all. Should I wait for a reply?"

"Yes, please do, Peter." Elizabeth turned towards the one guard. "John, please show this young man to the kitchens so he may have some refreshment until I am ready for him."

"Aye Yer Grace," the guard bowed to the Duchess.

Elizabeth held onto the precious letter while she watched John lead Peter around the corner on their way to the kitchens. She hungrily broke the seal as soon as they were gone from her sight.

20 March 1807

The Parsonage, Lambton

My dearest niece, Lizzy,

Before you admonish us and remind us you said you would write when you thought it was safe, we could not stay away. 'We' in this case is more than your uncle, cousins, and sisters. Sir William, Lady Lucas, Charlotte, and Maria are here, as are your Aunt and Uncle Philips.

Before we departed, we read that dissipated man who forced you into marriage was in London. Also, you should know, if you are unaware, from what the locals tell he has never once been to the estate where you are.

In fact, under his late father, the Lambton living used to be in his gift, but it was taken away from him—the church did not think one of his character should be allowed to appoint a clergyman to a living—and given to my brother's patron's late father, Mr. George Alexander Darcy. I think if you check, you will see that none of his estates have livings tied to them.

I acknowledge your fears for our safety, especially that of Jane's, if we approach you openly before you deem it safe to do so. However, we have a plan.

If you have not been to church yet, tell your minders you will attend the Lambton Church starting this Sunday. If the men with you enter the church at all, they will remain at the rear of the nave. You will of course sit with us and they will not be able to see if we speak.

Also, if you have not met her yet, the midwife who will see to you is a Mrs. Medford. She and my sister-in-law are very close and she has agreed to take me on as her 'assistant' who will of course, need to examine you weekly, to make sure the growing ducal babe in your belly and you are well. I will, obviously, have a very pretty, blonde 'apprentice' accompany me when I come to 'examine' you.

When we visit under the guise of checking on your state, you can order any men far away from your chambers to maintain modesty so no one will be able to overhear our conversations.

You had mentioned how concerned your husband is about having a healthy heir. That means even if the frequent visits are reported back to him, he will not object.

Lizzy, is it possible you worry too much? Have you not told me, all of us, how loyal the staff and servants are to you?

It is not my aim to diminish your concerns as you unfortunately know that man's ways better than any of us. We will be careful I promise you. The very last thing we want is to cause that odious man to punish you in any way.

If he keeps to his reported proclivities, I would wager that you, what you are doing and who you are seeing, is the last thing on his mind. What he does is sickening to any right thinking and decent person, but in this case, I believe it works to our advantage.

I await your reply, my darling girl.

With all my love and regards,

Aunt Maddie

Tears of joy were streaming down her cheeks as she read the letter. Her beloved family and friends were but a few miles away from her at this very moment. Elizabeth stood and made for the castle.

She walked with purpose and climbed the stairs, making directly for her chambers. Poor Loretta was shaken by the door crashing against the wall as Elizabeth pushed it open.

The maid was concerned seeing the evidence Her Grace had been crying. "Are you well, Your Grace?" the maid asked.

"I have not felt better in some time." *'Since before I was tied to him!'* she added silently. Elizabeth realised she must have looked a fright having been crying. "Do not concern yourself Loretta, these are tears of joy."

With that, she sat at the table she had placed under the window in her bedchamber and began to write.

Less than an hour later, the Gardiner's footman, Peter, was on his way back to the parsonage at Lambton.

~~~~~~~/~~~~~~~

Hertfordshire had visited his three remaining mistresses and although he had initially found pleasure being able to treat them as he wanted to, he knew it was nothing to the absolute bliss he would experience when he was able to bring his spitfire of a wife to heel. If only it did not take so many months to deliver a babe.

He would do nothing to disturb her. She was carrying his future—insurance his name would live on—and that was all important. To make sure the babe was healthy, he would wait almost a year after his child was born before recalling her and his son from Derbyshire.

In his mind, if the child survived his first year of life, all would be well. Then, he would revel in taking his pleasure with her. She would be repaid tenfold for every insolent and impertinent remark and action. His thoughts were disrupted by Wickham's entry into the sitting room.

"You summoned me, Your Grace," Wickham bowed low the way he knew his master demanded.

The Duke had been debating who his first conquest would be. He most wanted to take the Duchess of Bedford. Not only did her husband dote on her, but the number of times he had been slighted by the *mighty* Bedford were too numerous to count.

The problem was the Rhys-Davies were wealthier than himself, far more powerful, and the trump was they were related to the Queen. No, he would have to give up on exacting his revenge by cuckolding Bedford. Instead, he would take his pleasure with the next one on the list. What a pity the two after her were no longer in London.

Wickham had informed him that the Darcys and Fitzwilliams had departed Town earlier than was their wont. Ladies Elaine and Anne would be plucked at another time.

"I have decided who the first *wife* to be bedded by me will be. You are to bring me Lady Jersey on Easter Sunday," the Duke ordered. "That bastard Jersey was one of the men who tried to get my titles and wealth stripped from me and he is a holier than thou, pious simpleton so his wife being violated on Easter will drive him insane."

Without a word, Wickham acknowledged the order and was dismissed by the Duke. He had about a fortnight to come up with a workable plan.

CHAPTER 20

N ever in the whole of her life had Elizabeth looked forward to attending church as much as she did that Sunday morning.

Elizabeth was in anticipation of seeing those she loved most in the world. She was filled with frenetic energy making Loretta's work in preparing her for the day that much harder. Every time she sat at the dresser, Elizabeth would jump up again and begin to pace.

"Your Grace, are you well?" Jennings inquired worriedly.

For the last few days, her mistress had been distracted like the maid had not seen in the months since she had begun to serve the Duchess. She would not normally be so forward as to ask her mistress the question she had, but with Her Grace being with child, she felt she must.

"Yes, indeed I am very well," Elizabeth responded distractedly. "I am in anticipation of attending church in Lambton, I have heard the rector delivers excellent sermons."

Elizabeth was not one who liked to prevaricate and she had had an internal debate about whether or not to take Loretta into her confidence.

In the end, for now at least, she had decided against it. She did not want to put the maid in the position of having to dissemble in order to protect her mistress if one of her vile husband's lap dogs questioned her. Loretta's loyalty was above reproach, it was that man and his lackeys she did not trust.

The maid made no further comment. She knew the mistress had not attended services the first Sunday they had been in Derbyshire and at Falconwood she had only been allowed to use the chapel at the estate. A curate from the church in Chesham came to deliver the service.

'*How fortunate,*' Elizabeth thought as she finally sat long enough for her maid to complete her work on her hair. '*It is John and Brian who will accompany me to the church today. They are completely loyal to me.*'

One day at Falconwood she had overheard the two men discussing the hardships of their families and how what the Duke paid them was not enough. Elizabeth had begun to use some of her vast amounts of pin money to begin to augment the wages of John Biggs and Brian Johns. She had not done it to purchase their loyalty, but the result had been the two, who her delusional husband thought were his men, would do anything to protect Her Grace.

Yester-afternoon Elizabeth had requested they wait outside of the church as she was sure she would be perfectly safe inside with the worshipers.

Neither man had questioned her motives and agreed without hesitation. For the same reason she had not shared with her maid, Elizabeth had decided not to tell John and Brian the truth at this point.

"I think you are ready, Your Grace," Jennings stated.

The maid had piled most of the hair on top of her head, held in place with pearl-tipped pins. Elizabeth was dressed in one of the myriad of new gowns she had been supplied with after the days of shopping in London.

It was certainly not the most ostentatious of her gowns. Even though she cared not, she guessed it would be finer than what most were wearing.

At the door, the butler was holding her bonnet and light pelisse her lady's maid had provided him. The day was not cold, and with her body heat increased because of being with child, Elizabeth had chosen the lightest of her pelisses. She tied her bonnet in place and then exited via the great hall.

On the large stone veranda, John and Brian were waiting for her. The former offered his arm to his mistress to guide her to the waiting coach.

~~~~~~~/~~~~~~~

Andrew was frustrated. They had been busy since their arrival and he had not found an excuse or time to go into Lambton to see if he would be able to discover the whereabouts of Miss Bennet.

If that were not bad enough, the family were to attend the church at Kympton this week. As the gifts of both that church and Lambton were his uncle's to bestow, the Darcy's alternated between the two churches each week.

He could have asked Uncle Robert for them to attend Lambton's church, but that would have engendered too many questions Andrew was not yet ready to answer.

Monday they would be in Lambton. William had suggested they go fishing at Castlemere in the morning that day and return via Lambton where they would have their midday meal at the Rose and Crown Inn. Like his own family did in Matlock and he did in Hilldale, the Darcys patronised the local businesses as much as possible when they were in residence.

He enjoyed fishing, but he would have been willing to eschew the activity on Monday if it meant spending more time seeking out Miss Bennet. The longer he could escape Richard's inevitable, relentless teasing once his brother discovered he was seeking out a young lady, the better.

The Earl and Countess were meeting with their brother and sister in the Darcy's private sitting room. "What will we do if the Duchess attends Kympton?" Lady Anne asked her husband. "We cannot ignore her because we all disdain the man she is shackled to."

"From what Wickham, he and the steward at

Castlemere are very good friends, told me, she did not attend either Lambton or Kympton churches last week," Darcy informed his family.

"It is no wonder," Lord Matlock spat out. "From what is known of the dastard, I would not be surprised if he had her locked away at that estate of his."

"It is all speculation," Lady Matlock stated. "I, like Anne, do not think we should be shunning her because of *that* man. Do not forget the approval of her the Queen demonstrated so very clearly."

"It could be I am being overly cautious," Darcy admitted. "Anne and Elaine, mayhap you can call on her during the next fortnight?"

"We have plans on Monday, but both Tuesday and Wednesday are available for calls," Lady Anne averred.

"Do you not want to wait until the following week, after Easter?" Darcy suggested.

"I think not, Robert," Lady Anne replied firmly, "We have allowed for enough time to pass already."

Robert Darcy knew when to withdraw from the field of battle, and the look his beloved wife was giving him informed him that the time was now. He simply raised his hands in surrender.

~~~~~~~/~~~~~~~

Those congregants who had not taken up their seats in their pews inside yet were standing about speaking to one another in front of the Lambton church. All were greatly surprised to see the large coach with a coat of arms on the door none recognised pulled to a halt.

As the Darcys and Fitzwilliams had attended the week before, it was known it would not be them, and besides, their coats of arms were known by the locals.

Those watching observed two mountainous men alight,

one from the bench next to the driver, and the other from the back bench, one of whom opened the door. He handed a young lady out, one who was perhaps fifteen or so years of age. She was followed by a maid. Based on the quality of her clothing, she was clearly wealthy.

The enormous man who had offered the young lady his arm, guided her to the outer vestibule door and then stepped back. The maid followed her mistress inside while one of the men stood on one side of the doors leading into the vestibule and the nave of the church beyond. The other seemed to be walking around the church for some reason.

Elizabeth had to remind herself to breathe. She turned to Loretta and nodded to a pew near the rear of the church. The maid slid in and took her seat. She faced forward again allowing her eyes to sweep left to right to spot her family and friends.

The first she noticed in the second pew from the front on the left of the aisle was the balding head of Sir William, next to him was Lady Lucas, and then, Elizabeth had to fight to keep her equanimity, was Charlotte. Aunt Hattie was next to her best friend with Uncle Frank just beyond her.

Her eyes looked to the first pew. There was a lady Elizabeth did not recognise in the first seat of the front pew. Next to her was Jane, then an open place, followed by Aunt Maddie, Uncle Edward, her three younger sisters, Maria Lucas, and Lilly. She assumed at five years of age, Eddy, was at the parsonage where the Gardiners were being hosted.

She fought her inclination to run up the aisle and fling herself into the arms of her loved ones. Rather, Elizabeth walked sedately and as she approached the front pew, the lady she knew not, stood to allow her to enter.

Like all of those there to see Lizzy, Jane had kept her eyes trained steadfastly on the pulpit where Uncle Adam was waiting. They did not want to give the impression they were waiting for Lizzy in case one of his watchers was present.

As soon as Jane saw Lizzy, her first instinct was to jump up and wrap her much loved sister in her arms. She tamped down the burning inclination and when Aunt Eve stood to allow Lizzy to join them in the pew, Jane stood as well, still looking to the front.

The three youngest Bennets wanted nothing more than to pull Lizzy into hugs, but the necessity of not showing any emotion and recognition had been impressed upon them, a lesson they had taken to heart. All three kept their eyes forward—for the most part—stealing sideways glances as Lizzy entered the pew. Maria and Lilly followed their lead.

No sooner had Elizabeth sat than her hand on each side sought that of Jane and Aunt Maddie. Hard squeezes were exchanged while all three looked, as nonchalantly as they were able, to where Adam stood.

It did not take long before opinion the unknown young lady was none other than the new Duchess of Hertfordshire began to circulate among those seated in the nave of the church. It was only the parson's clearing of his throat and his signal for everyone to stand that quelled the talk and blatant staring.

After the opening prayer, the clergyman signalled his congregation to be seated. As soon as she sat, Elizabeth's hands again sought those of her sister and aunt. All three ladies had a few tears rolling down their cheeks, but due to where they were seated and the bonnets they were wearing, that fact was not visible to the rest of the congregation.

Jane lifted her prayer book to shield her mouth. "The lady you do not know is Uncle Adam's wife, Evangeline, we all call her Eve," Jane told her younger sister in *sotto voce*.

At the thought of the couple being known as Adam and Eve, Elizabeth had to fight not to giggle.

"It is beyond the best thing to see all of you again,"

Elizabeth responded softly so only Jane and their aunt could hear.

"You are looking well, Lizzy," Aunt Maddie quietly added as she assiduously *concentrated* on her prayer book. "You have not been harmed, at least not physically, have you?"

"No, Aunt, not physically," Elizabeth confirmed.

When they next stood, Elizabeth felt some pressure on her arm from behind her. Charlotte wanted to speak to and hug her friend, but she had to be satisfied with some brief comfort as everyone stood.

For the rest of the service Elizabeth revelled in the closeness of those she loved and who loved her in return.

She felt strong pangs of regret when the concluding hymn had been sung as she had no excuse to remain at the church for longer than it would take her to walk to her coach. When she exited out of the vestibule into the bright sunlight she could have kissed Uncle Adam.

"Excuse me for asking, but are you Her Grace, the Duchess of Hertfordshire?" he asked innocently.

"I am," Elizabeth averred. "I was most taken with the lesson you preached in your sermon, Mr. Lambert if I heard correctly."

A murmur went up from the crowd milling about outside of the church as the speculation she was the Duchess was confirmed. None would walk home until Her Grace departed.

"Indeed Your Grace. Would you allow me to introduce you to my family and some friends?" Lambert requested.

Lambert made a show of introducing his family— instead of Bennet, he used the family name of Gardiner—and friends. All Elizabeth could do was incline her head to each. If she extended her hand, it would have raised too many questions, and if there was a watcher loyal to the old man, she did not want to provide any morsels to be reported to him.

Biggs and Johns noted Her Grace was happy to be introduced and was not being importuned against her wishes. Hence they kept in the background, ever vigilant, ready to pounce if needs be.

Mrs. Medford the midwife, who had examined Elizabeth the same day the doctor had earlier in the week, approached.

After conveying sabbath wishes, the midwife spoke at a volume easily heard. "I see you have met my assistant Mrs. Gardiner and her apprentice, Miss Jane. They will be calling on you at Castlemere on Tuesday for your next examination, if that meets your approval, Your Grace."

"Yes, thank you, Mrs. Medford, that is entirely acceptable to me," Elizabeth agreed.

To not make it seem as if he was especially singling out certain people to meet Her Grace, Lambert introduced some of the leading denizens of Lambton to the Duchess before one of her giant-sized men handed her into the coach, and it departed in the direction of Castlemere.

~~~~~~~/~~~~~~~

That afternoon, subsequent to the post church meal, the Darcy and Fitzwilliam parents were seated in the former's private sitting room in the master suite.

"You will not believe what Mrs. Reynolds told me," Lady Anne articulated.

"What is it?" Lady Matlock enquired.

"The young Duchess attended Lambton's church, and those who met her, say she is open and friendly," Lady Anne reported. "Evidently, she sat with the rector's family."

"That is particular," Lord Matlock opined. "I would wager she sat among the populace because her husband is far away in London. Let us hope he remains there when word of his wife mixing with the *unwashed masses* reaches him."

"That she was willing to mix with all at the church

speaks well of her character, I think," Lady Anne postulated.

"I look forward to meeting her, if she is home to callers on Tuesday," Lady Matlock stated.

"You and me both, Elaine," Lady Anne agreed.

CHAPTER 21

Come Monday morning, Elizabeth was feeling rather melancholic. She had been ecstatic to see her family and friends, even if she had been unable to acknowledge them as such at the church.

The cause of her sadness was knowing that for as long as *he* was alive, she would have to keep a distance between herself and those she loved best in the world.

Yes, Jane and Aunt Maddie would be seeing her once a week, but it was covert and they would have to be so very circumspect to guard against word of the subterfuge reaching the heinous old man in London.

It was nothing she would ever say to Jane and the rest of her family and friends, but in a way, it was cruel seeing them but not being able to be free in her interactions with them. She openly admitted it was her own suggestion they join her in Derbyshire, all they had done was advance the date of their arrival. That knowledge did not lighten the burden she felt in knowing that she could not be free in her interactions with those she loved most as long as she was tied to *him*. For their own protection, Elizabeth would have to keep her distance from her loved ones.

She had married a monster to protect Jane and she would not allow anything to redound on Jane, their younger sisters, or any of her other loved ones.

That morning she felt nauseous as she had for some time now, but at least she had not vomited. Loretta had her ginger tea and two slices of dry toast ready for her as soon as she was dressed.

Elizabeth sat at the table in the sitting room looking out over the lake. It was a vista which usually brought cheer to her, but not today. For so long she had put up a brave front, even convincing herself her life could be far worse. The truth was she was enslaved to the worst man she had ever met, or could imagine. She believed it was cliché to call every bad man evil, but in the man she had been coerced to marry Elizabeth believed he was in fact, pure evil. The ████ incarnate.

She remembered when she had asked him why he chose her, both in front of Mr. Bennet and when he had revealed his plan to give her a choice, her or Jane, he had said he had his reasons. To date, he had not told her what they were, and she doubted he ever would.

The more she thought about her lot, the more the sadness crushed her soul. Elizabeth could not understand what she had ever done to offend God that He would see fit to punish her to this degree.

Acknowledging she might never know His plan, her faith was as strong as it ever was, but she wished she knew why she had been chosen to suffer so.

Despite her inclination to sit and cry in her chambers, she decided to go for a walk. She drank most of her tea and consumed only one slice of toast. Elizabeth made for her bedchamber, removed her slippers, and laced up her sturdy half boots.

Plastering a smile on her face, she turned to her maid who was working on tidying the implements on the dressing table. "Loretta, please have John and Brian informed I intend to walk out soon," Elizabeth requested. "I will meet them at the front entrance in ten minutes or so."

Jennings could tell Her Grace was upset about something, but unless the mistress confided in her, it was not her place to ask.

She curtsied to the Duchess and exited the chambers to convey the request to the guards. When she spoke to them she debated whether she should mention her suspicion about Her Grace being maudlin, but she decided against sharing anything so personal with the two huge men. On her way back to the master apartments the maid passed her mistress on the stairs. Jennings did not miss the put-on smile displayed for her as soon as Her Grace had seen her coming up the stairs towards her.

She hoped the mistress would feel more like herself again soon. The Duchess was the kindest and nicest person she had ever worked for, hence Jennings hated to see the sadness she detected in Her Grace's eyes.

~~~~~~~/~~~~~~~

"Well Wickham, have you succeeded where your predecessor failed me?" the Duke demanded.

The man who used to procure what Hertfordshire wanted as far as married women went, had failed in his charge to bring Lady Jersey to him. He hoped Wickham was more resourceful. It would be a pity if he had to pay for him to be dispatched, but if he failed, he would join the others who had not done what he needed.

"I have charmed her lady's maid..." Wickham began.

"What care I about her lady's maid?" the Duke returned derisively.

"As such, I know Lady Jersey will be at home alone after church. Her husband will be away from Jersey House for at least four hours. I can have the maid suggest a walk to her Ladyship," Wickham related.

The Duke's face twisted in an evil smile. "No! Much better would be to take her in his house, on his bed," Hertfordshire decided gleefully. "You will use this maid to ensure there are no footmen in my way when I enter the house and that Sarah De Melville will be in her husband's bedchamber when I arrive."

This would be a perfect revenge for the ages. Not only would he bed her, but in the hated man's own bed. It would break Jersey's spirit and he would never say a word publicly or call him out because it would unleash a scandal to dwarf all scandals.

If things went according to plan, as he was sure they would, Hertfordshire could see the ultimate ending would be Jersey taking his own life over the despondency of failing to protect his wife.

It was a great pity the man had an heir, otherwise he may have ended the line.

Wickham showed no emotion as he watched his master revel in his planned revenge. He would have to make sure that everything went according to plan otherwise his life would be forfeit.

"There will be a large bonus in this for you when I have taken my vengeance," the Duke promised his man.

"If I am to make sure you will be unmolested at Jersey House some funds will be needed to bribe the footmen. The maid will not have the kind of influence we need. That means the men who *fail* in their duties will be sacked. They will need enough so they will be able to leave without a character and live well," Wickham stated thoughtfully.

"How much do you need?" Hertfordshire enquired.

"I would estimate at least two thousand pounds," Wickham responded.

The Duke rang for his secretary. "Prepare a bank draft in Wickham's favour in the amount of four thousand pounds for me to sign," he commanded. "Also a letter to my banker to verify I have authorised him to withdraw banknotes for the amount." He waved the man away.

"It is far more than I will need, Your Grace," Wickham informed his master.

"Rather you have more, than not enough. I will need a complete accounting of how you expended the funds and any balance is to be returned to me," Hertfordshire ordered. "You know what will happen if I even suspect you are cheating me out of a single penny, do you not?"

"That is not something I would ever do, Your Grace." Wickham bowed to show his deference.

Hertfordshire waved the man away. He was confident in his power to make anyone fearful enough never to cross him.

~~~~~~~/~~~~~~~

The three cousins allowed their horses their heads as they easily jumped the boundary fence between Pemberley and Castlemere.

As the youngest of the group, William at four and twenty, was beyond the age where his parents needed to know where he was at all times. Hence they had not enquired as to where he and his cousins were riding to that morning.

In addition, his mother would not have thought to ask as she was too busy preparing for the Portnoys and Barringtons, who would arrive on Wednesday.

From the fence it was a little less than two miles to the eastern bank of the lake, and a place to fish, which had always been generous in surrendering the residents of the lake to be caught on previous fishing expeditions. The cousins looked forward to providing the fish course for dinner that evening.

With a little more than a mile to go, they slowed their horses down to a canter, then a trot, and eventually a walk. They all loved their stallions too much to gallop for the miles they had without allowing them to cool down correctly.

The cousins dismounted close to the shore of the lake. All three horses were trained to the extent they did not need to be secured to something to stop them wandering away.

Leaving their horses munching the long grasses

growing around the lake and with an unlimited supply of water when they wanted it, the two Fitzwilliams and a Darcy removed their fishing rods which had been secured to the one side of their saddles. Next they removed the rest of what they needed from their saddlebags. Each man also had a canvass bag with him to hold the bounty he expected to catch.

Being rather competitive, they had elected separate bags to be able to tell who caught the most.

While his cousins were attaching their reels to their rods, William walked along the bank to the south for a little distance. He was trying to remember the spot which had yielded many fish when he had fished here on his last visit almost a year past. As he wanted to win, he had said nothing to his cousins.

He walked a little towards the south and then William froze. Then he listened again. He could have sworn he heard someone crying. Just when he convinced himself it was his imagination, he heard someone blow their nose.

~~~~~~~/~~~~~~~

Elizabeth had begged John and Brian's indulgence to allow her a big distance ahead of them. She knew she needed to release her pent up emotions and did not want to explain why she was crying to her guards, or anyone who worked for *him*.

They crossed the stone and two wooden bridges over the river and streams which ran out of the lake at its narrow, southern end. The two huge men agreed to remain there as long as they could see her.

She walked on the path which ran next to the shore of the lake until she was a few hundred yards distant from her guards. Elizabeth found a relatively flat boulder and sat on it with her back to the two men.

Once she was assured of her relative privacy, she allowed the floodgates to open. She regulated the shaking of her shoulders not wanting John and Brian to guess what she was doing.

Once she had cried all she needed, Elizabeth blew her nose, rather noisily. When in company she would give a dainty wipe of that organ, never emulate a trumpet as she had now. Before she could react, the most handsome man she had ever beheld entered her field of vision walking along the bank of the lake from the north.

"Who gives you the right to be on the Duke's land?" William demanded. It was a young lady, not much more than a girl, sitting alone unescorted so he was sure she did not belong here. He did not pay attention to the quality of her dress.

The two guards started to run towards Her Grace as soon as they saw the man approach her.

"Just who do you think you are? I am a resident of this estate while you are trespassing!" Elizabeth spat back with anger. She was standing now, her fists balled up at her sides while figuratively fire was shooting from her eyes.

It was at that moment he saw the beauty before him, the finest eyes of any colour he had ever beheld. Before he could respond, Andrew and Richard arrived at his side, and it was then he saw the giant men bearing down on them.

"Excuse me madam, has my *younger* cousin inserted his hessian into his mouth again?" Andrew enquired.

"If you call asking me what I am doing at an estate where I am legally a resident, then yes, I suppose he has," Elizabeth replied with only slightly less asperity.

Just then the guards reach Her Grace. "Your Grace," Biggs called out as he looked at the three men malevolently. "Are you well?"

When he heard the manner in which she was addressed, William felt so small he would have crawled under the nearest pebble had he been able to. The shame burnt deeply.

"Well done William, I think you just insulted the mistress of this estate, the Duchess of Hertfordshire," Richard interjected.

"I am well John. If you and Brian remain close by, I am certain we can determine who is, and is not, authorised to be here." Elizabeth turned to the slightly taller of the two sandy blond men. "As you have ascertained who I am, will you share who you are, including your rude cousin and what your purpose is here."

William was about to defend himself but he decided discretion was the better part of valour, and there was no defence for his behaviour, which had been rude in the extreme. If the young duchess unleashed her men, he would be pummelled to a pulp.

Elizabeth arched her eyebrow as she waited for a response.

"Your Grace, please allow me to apologise for my cousin, at times he speaks before he engages his vast intellect." Elizabeth inclined her head. "I am Lord Andrew Fitzwilliam, Viscount Hilldale. Next to me is my brother, the Honourable Captain Richard Fitzwilliam, and our cousin who misspoke is Master Fitzwilliam Darcy of Pemberley, the estate which borders yours to the east."

"If that is the case, my housekeeper has informed me my late father-in-law authorised members of your family to fish here, which I assume was your purpose today." All three men nodded. "Permission which the current duke has never rescinded. As long as no one insults me or anyone who is employed here." Elizabeth looked at the dark haired one pointedly, "then I will not change the permission you have to visit the lake."

"You are most magnanimous, Your Grace," William bowed to the emerald green-eyed beauty before him. "Please accept my abject apologies for my ungentlemanlike conduct. As a visitor here myself, I had no justification to question your presence."

It was easy to see the handsome man was entirely sincere. As such, there was only one thing Elizabeth could do. "I pardon you unreservedly, Master Darcy." She turned to her two guards who had visibly relaxed seeing their mistress was not in any sort of danger. "You may give us a little space, but not as far away as I had requested you wait before."

"Aye, Your Grace," Johns responded for the two men. "We will wait some twenty yards away."

Once the two men had retreated, William looked into the beautiful eyes deeply. "If I am not too forward, Your Grace, are you well?" he asked.

Elizabeth was about to deny she was anything but well when she realised it was the sound of her crying which had more than likely brought Master Darcy to her.

"If you would like to unburden yourself, Your Grace," William offered. "My cousins and I will be the souls of discretion and there are times when a problem shared is one halved."

Elizabeth looked from man to man and saw nothing but compassion reflected in their eyes. She did not know why, but she instinctively knew she could trust them. What the young man, Darcy, said about unburdening herself rang true. Until this moment she did not realise how much she needed to do so.

"How much time do you have?" she enquired.

"As much as you need, Your Grace," Andrew stated for all three.

"It is a long story," Elizabeth related as she sat back down on her boulder. "It all begins one night in April of last year at the assembly in the town near the estate where I grew up…"

When she was done, all three men's eyes were suspiciously moist. "You love your sister so deeply you married a man you detest to protect…Jane?" Andrew verified in wonder.

Before the Duchess responded, William needed to make another amends. "Please pardon me once again. When I heard the Duke of Hertfordshire had found another wife, I made the assumption she—you—were a social climber and fortune hunter. I could not have been more wrong if I had attempted to do so. The bravery and nobility of sacrificing your own comfort and happiness to protect your sister, is beyond anything I have ever heard of in my life."

"As I told my aunt, I always swore to marry for the deepest love, and I did so, for the love of Janey," Elizabeth stated wistfully.

"And your parents..." Richard began before he was cut off by an angry retort.

"Mr. and Mrs. Bennet are *not* my parents, I have none!" Elizabeth barked.

"Bennet," Andrew repeated, "Do you have a younger sister Miss Mary?"

"Yes, I do, how would you know that?" Elizabeth puzzled.

"My goodness, it is my day for apologies," William stated. "He then proceeded to tell the Duchess about the meeting in Hyde Park and his ill-advised accusations.

A tinkling laugh, like a glass bell being rung, issued forth from Her Grace.

"Mary may be slower to forgive, but I am sure Jane will forgive you, if she has not already," Elizabeth stated.

"He apologised to your sisters right away, Your Grace, and they forgave him, Miss Mary too," Andrew related.

"And I was there to see our William's performance, it was a few days before my regiment departed for the Peninsula," Richard revealed.

"You have been candid with us, Your Grace, may we be the same with you?" Andrew requested.

Elizabeth inclined her head in permission.

"It may sound fantastical, but I felt a connection with Miss Bennet and have been seeking her out since then. I saw her in Lambton the day we three arrived from my estate," Andrew reported.

"Your Grace, do we have your leave to talk to our parents about what you have revealed?" William questioned. "They have no more love for your husband than you or we do and they may have an idea how to affect a meeting between you, your family, and friends away from prying eyes."

The chance of seeing her loved ones and being able to be open with them was too great an attraction to Elizabeth. "You may. I would like nothing more than to see them openly."

"If that be the case, we need to return to Pemberley. One of us, or one of our parents will be in touch, Your Grace," William stated.

The three men bowed and then made for where they had left their horses. Elizabeth turned and walked towards where her guards waited and as soon as she passed them, they fell in behind her as she struck out towards the mansion.

CHAPTER 22

"We *must* assist her!" Lady Anne exclaimed, tears running down her cheeks. "I feel so guilty we did not call on her as soon as we became aware Her Grace was resident at Castlemere."

Darcy wrapped his tender hearted wife in his arms. "Do not take on yourself the guilt which belongs to me. It was me and my damnable Darcy pride which insisted we be circumspect in approaching the Duchess," Darcy acknowledged. "I have never heard of such an act of selfless love before. To sacrifice her own happiness and freedom to protect a most loved sister—all of her sisters—is also the bravest action to which I have ever been privy. If she can be so brave, we can fend off the dastardly man if he tries to exploit the connection."

"Well said, Darcy, I could not agree with you more," Lord Matlock stated.

"None of you mentioned her presence to us," Andrew noted. "It would have been good information to have before William admonished her for being where he thought she had no right to be."

"William, you omitted that from your telling," Lord Matlock pointed out with raised eyebrows.

"I suppose I suffer from the same improper pride as my father," William stated, his eyes downcast. He would not have hidden the truth from his parents; he had only hoped to make that particular disclosure in private.

SHANA GRANDERSON A LADY

"That is neither here nor there," Lady Matlock interjected. "How are we to assist Lady Elizabeth?"

"We will first invite Her Grace, and then her family and friends to spend time here at Pemberley as our guests and to celebrate Easter with us," Lady Anne decided.

"It is a good plan, Anne. Even with our sisters and their families arriving on Wednesday, we have more than enough room to house everyone," Darcy interjected.

Lady Anne squeezed her husband's hand. After, she turned to her sister. "Elaine, you and I will make for Castlemere today and make ourselves known to Her Grace. We will invite her to be here as well and any of her servants other than her lady's maid will not be allowed anywhere but the servants' areas."

"The two guards we saw today may have something to say about that," Richard opined. "By their bearing I would guess they are former soldiers and the most enormous men I have ever seen. Their size notwithstanding, I believe they have catlike reflexes."

Richard still wanted to question his brother about his having sought out Miss Bennet after the time they had almost knocked her to the ground. That would wait.

"When we see her, I will hand her a written invitation and add a page with our intentions with it," Lady Anne stated. "If she is as intelligent as you three give her credit for, the Duchess will find the note. Come Elaine, let us prepare to depart."

"May I join you Mama?" Georgiana who had been silent so far requested. "Her Grace is but a few years older than me and she may enjoy someone who is closer to some of her younger sisters' age being present."

Ladies Matlock and Anne looked at one another and nodded. "That depends on your Papa, Anna dear, I have no objection if he agrees," Lady Anne responded.

Anna turned her face to her father with her best begging look on her countenance, with her deep blue eyes opened as widely as she was able.

Even had he been of a mind to refuse his daughter—which he was not—the puppy dog look would have convinced him to give into her entreaty. Anna looked so very much like her mother so refusing her was almost like refusing his beloved Anne.

"You may accompany Mama and Aunt Elaine, sweetling," Darcy granted. He was rewarded by a hug and kiss on his cheek from his excited and grateful daughter.

It was a matter of minutes until the Darcy coach was on its way to Castlemere with two ladies and a young girl within.

~~~~~~~/~~~~~~~

Elizabeth took a deep breath as she was about to take a great risk with her personal freedom by confiding in John and Brian. The two men had been summoned to meet with her in her private sitting room off her bedchamber. She was assured of Loretta's discretion and loyalty. She felt like she could count on the two guards, but it was a chance—as any unknown was—anyway.

"You asked to see us Your Grace," Biggs bowed to the Duchess, as did Johns next to him.

"Do you two know of any of the other servants who are reporting on my activities to the Duke?" Elizabeth began.

"The only ones 'oo sends reports to Mr. Wickham is one of us," Johns informed the mistress. "'Owever, there be nothing in our reports which would raise any suspicions."

"Your Grace, our loyalty is yours completely," Biggs insisted. "There is nothing your 'usband could do to convince us to 'urt you in any way. We said nothing about the people you met at the church."

Elizabeth was not surprised that the ever vigilant and

observant men had noted something in the church. They were tall enough to see in the windows which had been open on the one side and as she suspected, their aim was to protect her, not report on her activities to that man.

"Ya gotta know, Your Grace, the staff, servants, and guards 'ere all know if they ever did anything to 'arm you, they will answer to us," Biggs assured the Duchess.

Tears of relief were released to course down her cheeks. It was safe to see her family and friends. She saw the looks of concern on the two men at her crying.

"These are good tears, not of sadness," she reassured the two guards.

There was a knock on her sitting room door. Elizabeth nodded to John who opened the door to reveal the butler. "Your Grace are you at home to Lady Elaine Fitzwilliam, the Countess of Matlock, Lady Anne Darcy, the mistress of Pemberley, and Miss Darcy?" Toppin enquired.

Elizabeth remembered the conversation from earlier that day and how the three men had asserted they would be speaking to their parents to see what assistance they would be able to offer.

"I am, thank you Mr. Toppin. Please have them wait in the large drawing room which faces the lake and have Mrs. Bannister deliver tea in a quarter of an hour. As soon as my maid repairs my coiffure, I will join them," Elizabeth imparted.

Mr. Timmons returned to the great hall of the castle where the two ladies and the young girl waited. "Your Ladyships, Miss Darcy, if you will follow me I will show you to the lakeside drawing room," the butler intoned.

The three visitors had barely entered the room when the door was opened by the footman on duty in the hall, the same one who had done so for them, and in walked the young duchess followed by her butler. The two older ladies had recognised her from when they had seen her presented those months ago.

The Duchess nodded to her butler. "Lady Matlock, Lady Anne, and Miss Darcy, it is my honour to introduce you to Lady Elizabeth Chamberlain, Her Grace, the Duchess of Hertfordshire and Marchioness of Hertford Heights. Your Grace, I present to you Lady Elaine Fitzwilliam, the Countess of Matlock, Lady Anne Darcy, the mistress of Pemberley, and Miss Georgiana Darcy." The butler performed his duty with aplomb. Once he had completed the introductions, with another quick nod from Her Grace, he bowed to the ladies and exited the room pulling the door closed after him.

The Countess and Lady Anne were surprised they were left alone, they had expected one of the Duke's men to be present to hear whatever was being said.

Elizabeth smiled when she saw the ladies looking around the room and immediately understood why. "We are quite alone here my Ladies. If you are uncomfortable with me, I can have one of my guards summoned." She arched an eyebrow as she teased the ladies.

"That is most unexpected, and welcome, Your Grace," Lady Anne began to say when the door opened and the housekeeper directed two footmen where to place the tea service.

There was a plate of seasonal and some exotic fruits, including slices of pineapple next to a platter of teacakes and pastries.

"Is that pineapple?" Georgiana blurted out before she clapped her hand over her mouth and blushed deeply at her ignoring etiquette. She should have waited for the Duchess to address her.

"Please Miss Darcy, do not make yourself uneasy," Elizabeth soothed. "I had almost the same reaction when I discovered there were a few growing in the conservatory attached to the rear of the castle. If you would like, I will send one home with you today so you may share it with all of your family."

Anna lit up with pleasure. "That would be very kind, and greatly appreciated Your Grace," she responded in relief.

Elizabeth poured the tea to the specifications each lady provided. They enjoyed some of the provided comestibles, Miss Darcy enjoying two slices of pineapple. When everyone had completed their tea, Elizabeth pulled the bell cord and soon the tea service had been cleared away and they were left alone once again, the door firmly closed.

"I assume your sons related to you what I shared with them?" Elizabeth began. All three ladies nodded. "As you know I am not here of my own choice and I never sought the title this nightmarish marriage has brought me, please call me Elizabeth, or at the very least Lady Elizabeth when we are alone."

"In that case Lady Elizabeth, please call me Lady Elaine, my sister-in-law is Lady Anne, and her daughter answers to Anna," Lady Matlock responded. "If I may, how come you are left without any of your husband's men making sure you say or do nothing impolitic?"

"Unlike *him* I treat the staff and servants with respect and consideration..." Elizabeth explained how she related to those who worked for her husband.

"We too believe in treating those employed on our estates and in our houses thusly," Lady Matlock agreed.

"As we have privacy, I would like to invite you to spend the days before Easter, and as long as you desire after, with us at Pemberley," Lady Anne proposed. "Is our information you are increasing correct?"

"It is, I have been seen by both Mr. Harrisons and Mrs. Medford, and all of them have opined I am proceeding as would be expected," Elizabeth confirmed. "I should give birth in September or October of this year. As much as I would love to accept your invitation, my aunt and dearest sister will be here on the morrow under the guise of working with Mrs. Medford."

"How old are your younger sisters?" Georgiana interjected. She was about to admonish herself for speaking out of turn again when she saw Lady Elizabeth smile warmly.

"Mary is fourteen, she will be fifteen next month, Kate is thirteen, and the youngest, Lydia recently turned eleven," Elizabeth related.

"I turned twelve in March," Georgiana enthused.

"My birthday was also in March, I reached the *ripe old age* of seventeen," Elizabeth responded.

Just when they did not think they could think worse of him and with confirmation she had been but sixteen when the dissipated duke married her, Ladies Matlock and Anne felt even more disgust for the repellent man.

"You would not have to eschew seeing your family and friends. In fact, you would be able to see them all openly," Lady Anne explained. Seeing the hopeful and questioning look Lady Anne elucidated. "On our way back to Pemberley, Elaine, Anna, and I will stop at the parsonage in Lambton. It is my intention to invite all of your family and friends to be our guests at Pemberley for as long as they desire to be with us. That way, rather than take the risk someone would perhaps see you with them in Lambton and decide to send a letter to your husband, the interactions will all be hidden from prying eyes."

For the second time that day, Elizabeth cried tears of gratitude. Without thinking, Lady Anne stood and seated herself next to the young duchess and pulled her into a motherly hug.

As she felt the warm and genuine motherly affection, something which had been denied her for the whole of her life by Mrs. Bennet, Elizabeth's crying turned into great big wracking sobs. Lady Anne said nothing; she held Elizabeth and allowed her to release her pent up emotions all the while rubbing her back.

Seeing how distressed her niece was feeling, Lady Matlock leaned over towards her. "This is healthy for her Anna. She has been beyond brave and I believe this is the first time she has felt she has support and she does not need to ignore it for her and others' protection."

It took some minutes for the storm of tears to pass. When she was cried out, Elizabeth did not want to break the contact with the woman sitting next to her. This kind of affection from a mother figure was very rare for her, and something she did not want to lose anytime soon.

She had only received warmth and love from Aunt Maddie during the short stays at Gracechurch Street, and to a certain extent from Aunt Hattie, but this was somehow inexplicably different.

"In that case, I gladly accept your invitation to Pemberley," Elizabeth stated. "One thing, in case your sons," she looked at Anna, "and your brother did not relate it clearly, not a word of my reasons for marrying *him* is to be breathed to Jane or my other sisters. One day, if or when, I am free of the old man, I will tell Jane the truth."

"I swear I will say nothing," Georgiana vowed.

"We will honour your wishes Lady Elizabeth, as will our husbands and sons," Lady Matlock added.

"What time should I arrive on the morrow?" Elizabeth enquired. "I will have my lady's maid and two guards with me. None of them will report anything untoward to my husband."

"Any time comfortable for you," Lady Anne replied. "If you will excuse us, we have a stop to make at the parsonage on our return to Pemberley."

"Before you depart I have one request. When we are at your home can I be just plain Elizabeth or Lizzy?" she requested.

Agreement was given with alacrity. The two ladies and

one girl hugged Elizabeth and then took their leave. Tomorrow would be a very good day.

Anna was delighted to find a pineapple had been placed in the Darcy coach.

~~~~~~~/~~~~~~~

"Welcome to the parsonage, Lady Matlock, Lady Anne, and Miss Darcy," Evangeline stated surprisedly. There were times she had met with the mistress of Pemberley regarding parish business or charities, but that was normally a call to Pemberley, where she was received in Lady Anne's study, or at the church.

Only once, shortly after she married Adam had Lady Anne visited at the parsonage. She led the highborn ladies into the drawing room where Maddie, Lady Lucas, and Hattie Philips were seated. The men and children were taking a walk around the town.

The three ladies stood when Eve entered with two ladies and a girl, all wearing very expensive and fine dresses denoting their wealth and rank. Madeline recognised Lady Anne from the time she used to live in Lambton.

"Mrs. Lambert, would you introduce us to your friends please," Lady Matlock, as the highest ranking person present, requested.

Eve made the requested introductions. While she had, she had noted how Lady Anne had been looking at her sister-in-law questioningly.

"You may remember Maddie as Maddie Lambert, my husband's older sister. Some years back before her father passed away, she moved away when she married Mr. Gardiner," Evangeline explained to Lady Anne.

"Why of course. I remember you would accompany your mother to Pemberley sometimes," Lady Anne recalled. "We—my sister, my daughter, and I—have a very specific purpose in mind by calling on you this afternoon. Before coming here, we visited with Lady Elizabeth. She will be visiting us at Pemberley from the morning on the morrow..." Lady Anne did not miss the looks of great shock on all four ladies' faces. She related an edited version of the visit at Castlemere making no illusion to her knowing the true reason Lady Elizabeth married the brute. "Which leads me to inviting all of you, the Gardiners, Bennet sisters, Philipses, Lucases, and Lamberts to be our guests at Pemberley for as long as you choose."

Madeline was the first to recover her voice. "You say it is safe for Lizzy to come to your home and remain there for some days?" she verified.

"Yes, perfectly so..." Lady Matlock related what Lady Elizabeth had shared regarding her staff, servants, and guards.

"Of course we will..." Hattie began to respond enthusiastically. She stopped when Madeline placed a restraining hand on her arm.

"We will speak with our husbands and of course Lizzy's sisters and send you a note with our decision as soon as may be," Madeline completed what her sister-in-law had begun to say.

"For us, my husband cannot be away from the parish, but I will visit most days, and he will when he is able," Evangeline stated.

With that understanding, the two Darcys and one Fitzwilliam lady took their leave.

~~~~~~~/~~~~~~~

Less than two hours later a note of acceptance detailing all who would be in their party was received at Pemberley.

CHAPTER 23

Hertfordshire summoned his man demanding an update on the progress of his mission to get him into Jersey House.

"Well Wickham, what news is there?" he demanded.

"The maid I have charmed has been most helpful. I am sure that by Thursday at the latest we will have every man who we need to execute the plan agreeing to accept your funds. Each will be willing to make sure you will not see anyone from the time you enter the house until you reach the master suite," Wickham reported.

"I am certain all the banknotes I have provided you are helping." The Duke could not conceive of servants and peasants not having a purchase price to gain their cooperation.

"Your money is and will be spent well Your Grace, a worthy investment to further your aims," Wickham stated. His words had the intended effect of inflating the master's ego.

"That is why I suggested you have money to assist with my plan," the Duke stated assuredly.

Knowing it would only engender anger, Wickham said nothing about whose plan it was and who had suggested the need for funds to make the plan work. "I have the latest report from Biggs in Derbyshire, Your Grace," Wickham changed the subject.

"What has that big lunkhead to tell about my impertinent wife's behaviour?" Hertfordshire demanded.

"There is nothing of note, Your Grace," Wickham read. "Her Grace remains at your estate, has had no callers—other than the doctor and midwife, and has called on no one. She is yet to receive any letters and has only posted one to her sister."

"It pleases me she is under the care of the physician and midwife. It shows she is taking her duty to me seriously," the Duke decided, "even if she took too long to become with child."

Wickham kept his features schooled and allowed His Grace to rant on, as he was wont to do, spewing nonsense. As was the way of things, once the Duke had spewed his vitriol, he waved dismissively releasing Wickham.

~~~~~~~/~~~~~~~

Elizabeth felt the excitement building as her coach rolled over the rise in the drive and began its descent on the other side. Her anticipation had kept her blind to the forests her coachman was driving past.

The previous night she had managed very little sleep. Each time she had felt herself slipping into Morpheus's arms, her exhilaration at seeing her sisters, family, and friends openly and without fear on the morrow woke her all over again. It had been the wee hours of the night before she had finally slipped off to sleep. Then, less than three hours later, as dawn was fighting to assert itself, she had woken.

Loretta was sitting opposite her and as they always were when she travelled anywhere, John was next to the coachman and Brian on the rear bench.

She was unsurprised when she was met by a large group. Brian handed her out. Except for the two older men, she recognised everyone. The men seemed to be waiting and Elizabeth realised as the highest ranking person there, it was up to her to request an introduction.

William could not believe this beauty was at his house. Since he had met the fiery duchess he had been having rather inappropriate thoughts about a married woman. Yes, she had been coerced into matrimony, but it did not change the facts. She was, in fact, someone's wife, regardless of how deplorable the man was. William cared not for the Duke, but he did care about the vows the man and his wife had taken before God and he would not dishonour the Duchess in any way.

"Lady Elaine, would you introduce your husband and brother to me, please," Elizabeth requested.

"Lady Elizabeth, it is my pleasure to introduce Lord Reginald Fitzwilliam, the Earl of Matlock, my husband, and Mr. Robert Darcy the master of this estate, and my brother-in-law. Reggie and Robert, Lady Elizabeth Chamberlain, Her Grace, the Duchess of Hertfordshire and Marchioness of Hertford Heights," Lady Matlock performed the duty.

There were bows and curtsies exchanged, even though Elizabeth was aware as a duchess she was not required to curtsey to those of lower rank. If *he* had been present, it would have disturbed *his* equanimity. Even though her husband was absent, she felt it was an act of freedom to defy him in any way she was able.

"Quite a mouthful is it not," Elizabeth jested.

Both men smiled. "It is, Your Grace," Darcy intoned. "Welcome to Pemberley."

"As I requested of your wives and Anna, please address me as Lady Elizabeth if you will not use my familiar name," Elizabeth responded. "And thank you for inviting me, and especially for inviting my family to your estate."

"May I suggest we enter the house, *Elizabeth*," Lady Anne stated. She did not miss the glow of happiness the young duchess demonstrated to be addressed without any title.

"Thank you for your note informing me of your exceedingly kind invitation to my family and friends had been accepted," Elizabeth told Lady Anne as they walked down the hallway, arms linked, towards the large foyer near the main front doors. "When did they say they would be here?"

Lady Anne squeezed the younger lady's hand in reassurance, not at all surprised Lady Elizabeth...Elizabeth was keen for information on the pending arrival of her loved ones. "According to what your Aunt Madeline wrote, they will be here after eleven this morning," Lady Anne shared. "As it is not yet ten, you have over an hour to wash, change, and if you choose to, have a rest."

The housekeeper was waiting for her mistress at the base of the wide, white marble grand staircase. Lady Anne made the introductions.

Mrs. Reynolds looked like a very pleasant woman to Elizabeth. Before the housekeeper could lead her away, the youngest Darcy spoke up. "Mama, may I show Lizzy...Lady Elizabeth to her suite?"

Elizabeth gave Lady Anne a nod when the latter looked at Elizabeth to gauge her feelings on the subject. Lady Anne smiled and gave an almost imperceptible nod. "Go ahead, Anna. You know which suite Elizabeth is in, do you not?" Lady Anne verified.

"Yes, Mama. The Rose Suite if I understood correctly," Georgiana confirmed.

"That is the one. Off you go sweet girl." Lady Anne turned to Elizabeth. "I assume you will be with us in an hour before our *other* guests arrive."

"If not sooner, yes I will be downstairs," Elizabeth enthused.

"Your maid is already in your suite unpacking, Your Grace," Mrs. Reynolds informed the Duchess. "If you require anything else, please ring your bell."

While the rest of the party made for a drawing room, Elizabeth followed the bubbly Anna up the stairs.

~~~~~~~/~~~~~~~

As they approached the biggest mansion Jane had ever beheld, she was sitting on the edge of her seat willing the carriage to speed up so she could be in Lizzy's company already. Yes, she had seen and even touched her sister at the church, but now they were about to have unrestricted and open contact with Lizzy.

The Gardiner conveyance was in the lead, followed by the rented one, which in turn was followed by the Lucas equipage, and lastly the conveyance bearing the Philipses. The Lamberts would come to call on the morrow as both had parish work this day.

Jane and Mary were riding with their aunt and uncle, the two youngest Bennets were in the rented carriage following along with the three Gardiner children and their nursemaid.

She did not realise she was holding her breath until the conveyance made a turn from the drive into an internal courtyard. Several people were waiting to welcome them, but Jane only saw one. She finally exhaled when she saw Lizzy standing between two older ladies with a blonde girl.

The footman had barely opened the door when Jane, followed closely by Mary, exploded out of the carriage.

Elizabeth dropped Anna's hand and ran forward her arms open to receive two of her sisters. Before the rented carriage stopped, the three sisters were already crying tears of joy. No sooner had the carriage they were in come to a halt, if not before it did, Kate and Lydia were running to join the group of their sisters hugging and crying unashamedly in the middle of the courtyard.

The five sisters were all speaking at once which came out as a garbled mess of words, but they were together, and that was all any of them cared about.

The Gardiners stood back to allow the sisters their time.

Soon enough the other two conveyances had come to a stop and those riding within alighted with slightly more dignity. Charlotte wanted nothing more than to hug Eliza as well, but she held back, knowing her time would come.

The Lucas parents, Maria, and the Philipses joined the

Gardiner parents who were standing with their children at that point.

The Bennet sisters, all trying to dry their eyes, stepped back from one another. There followed a stream of family and friends who wanted to greet Elizabeth and hug her to assure themselves she was as well as she looked.

Aunt Hattie tried to apologise for her sister and Elizabeth would not hear it. She held her aunt blameless and informed her aunt her only request was there would be no talk of Mr. and Mrs. Bennet. It was something with which her aunt and all others from Meryton were more than happy to comply.

There were many happy tears shed as Elizabeth was embraced and kissed, even by Sir William.

The last was Charlotte who had stood and waited until everyone else had their turn. Just when Elizabeth thought she had cried all of her happy tears for that day, she fell into her friend's arms and cried all over again.

"Should we enter the house? My housekeeper will show everyone to their chambers." Lady Anne suggested.

"Before we do, I would like to introduce everyone," Elizabeth stated.

"Go ahead, Elizabeth," Lady Anne agreed.

It took some minutes, but Elizabeth made the introductions. As they all began to move towards the entryway, Elizabeth leaned towards Jane. "Your bedchamber is the second one in the suite where I am. We will only have a sitting room between us."

"Are the Darcys really able to accommodate all of us?" Jane enquired worriedly.

William turned as he heard the tinkling laugh that had captivated him at the lake. How much more beautiful the Duchess was while she glowed with happiness.

"Jane, this house is enormous, even larger than the

one at Castlemere, which is three to four times larger than Netherfield Park's manor house," Elizabeth giggled. "Anna told me..." Elizabeth trailed off when she saw Jane's questioning look. "Anna is Miss Darcy. She told me there are three floors of guest chambers, and a full floor of family apartments. Two families, Mr. Darcy's sisters and their families, arrive on the morrow, and even with them added to the rest of us, only about a quarter of the available chambers will be filled." Elizabeth paused. "The only house I have seen to rival this one in size is *his* at Falconwood."

There was no missing the moue of distaste whenever Lizzy referred to *him*. Jane shuddered as she imagined what her sister had to endure to become with child. She still had her maidenly sensibilities, but until recently, she had lived on a working farm all of her life.

Charlotte was walking with the two eldest Bennet sisters but was content to just listen to Eliza's happy babbling. This was the Eliza she knew and loved, not the one who had written to her while in the Duke's house.

Unsurprisingly, Anna led the three youngest Bennets and Maria Lucas to their chambers. Mary and Kate shared a suite while Maria and Lydia another.

Across the corridor from the suite Jane and Elizabeth were in, was Charlotte's bedchamber. The Gardiner parents, Philipses, and Lucas parents all had suites close by the girls on the same floor. The Gardiner's was very close to the guest nursery where Lilly, Eddy, and May would be.

While the maid Jane had been assigned was unpacking her trunk, she made her way into Lizzy's bedchamber. Just to make sure it was not a dream, the sisters hugged one more time.

Seeing Loretta carrying some gowns to her walk-in closet, Elizabeth called her over and introduced her maid to her beloved sister. After the maid curtsied, and went back to her work, Elizabeth turned back to Jane. "She is completely loyal to me, as are the two huge guards, John and Brian, who you will see whenever we venture out of the house."

"You are sure none of them will report back to the vile old man?"

Elizabeth explained why the staff and servants were loyal to her. Jane was amazed the Duke owned so many estates and business interests, and took no care of the dependants or took the time to manage them himself, not even visiting any of his satellite estates.

"Your husband is extremely wealthy, but he seems to be as indolent as Mr. Bennet."

"As distasteful as I find it to speak of Mr. Bennet, I tend to agree with you." Elizabeth shook her head.

"How does it feel to be with child?" Jane asked to move them away from the subject Lizzy disdained.

"Other than some mild morning illness, I do not feel very different yet," Elizabeth averred. "Well," she blushed, "my breasts have been tender."

"Have you felt the quickening yet?"

"Not yet. Mrs. Medford, the midwife you met, says I should feel it in early to the middle of May."

"You do not know how long your husband will allow you to remain in Derbyshire in peace, do you?"

Elizabeth shook her head and decided to change the subject. "Janey, you recognise some of the young men, three of them do you not?" Elizabeth asked after they had thrown themselves onto the enormous four-poster bed.

"How would you know that?" Jane wondered.

Elizabeth related her meeting the three cousins at Castlemere. Jane began to giggle when she came to the part about Master Darcy's insulting words. "He told me he made some wild accusations against you when they were not minding where they walked," Elizabeth recalled.

"Yes, he did, although he was quick to apologise. But Lizzy, that does not explain your question."

"What do you think of the Viscount?" Elizabeth asked a seemingly incongruous question.

"I hardly know him Lizzy, however..." Jane's voice faded.

"Yes?"

"You will think me a romantic fool."

"Janey, I think you romantic, but a fool? Never! Is it possible you felt a connection to him?" Jane nodded. "He has been seeking you out because he felt something similar for you."

Jane sat upright. Her mouth opened and closed a few times and no sound came forth, but she did blush deeply. "But I am the daughter of an insignificant country squire who lives with her uncle who is in trade."

"You are also the sister of a duchess and marchioness. Keep in mind that after I birth a son, you will be in possession of a large dowry." Elizabeth sat up as well and took Jane's hands in her own. "If he or any other man only sees your connections, fortune, and beauty at the exclusion of your character, then he, or they, do not deserve you. I have not been much in Lord Hilldale's company, but I do not believe he is such a man."

"I do not want to court expectations which may come to nought. First, before we speak of anything like that, he and I need to get to know one another and see if we suit. Before that, I want to spend time with my younger sister, not with a duchess or *his* wife."

Soon they were joined by the other three Bennet sisters. No one in the house thought them rude that they spent the next two hours talking among themselves before they joined the rest of the residents in the largest drawing room, where among other treats served with tea, was some of the pineapple Elizabeth had sent home with Anna.

CHAPTER 24

As planned, the Portnoy and Barrington families arrived at Pemberley on Wednesday afternoon past. To say they were surprised at the number of guests in residence was an understatement, and then to learn one of them was the Duchess of Hertfordshire had flabbergasted them.

Once the shock had worn off, everyone mixed well with new connections made and friendships begun. Missing was the one Portnoy daughter who had married and resigned that family name some four months previously. The other female cousin missing was Retta on the Barrington side, she had been married for over a year and was increasing, causing her and her husband to choose to remain at their estate in Devonshire.

As her eldest daughter would only enter her lying-in in two to three months, Darcy's younger sister, Leticia, had joined her husband, son, and youngest daughter in travelling to her brother's estate for Easter.

It was the Saturday before Easter and, as they had each day since the day after they arrived at Pemberley, Jane, Elizabeth, and Charlotte were taking a stroll around the manmade lake in front of the manor house.

Since she had been openly reunited with her family and friends, practically other than when she slept, Elizabeth was in the company of one or more of them. As they walked, Elizabeth kept a reasonable pace knowing that neither Charlotte nor Jane walked as fast as was her wont. As always, they were followed at a distance by John and Brian.

What *he* had almost done that day when he stopped himself from striking her was not amusing, but Elizabeth could not but smile at Uncle Edward's reaction when she had shared that detail with him the evening they arrived. He had been ready to charge back to London to find the deplorable old man and thrash him. Failing that, he wanted to go to Longbourn to punish Mr. Bennet for not protecting his daughters as he should have. However, between herself and Aunt Maddie, they had sufficiently calmed Uncle Edward by assuring him that the man had never actually struck her and since then, had not threatened to do so.

Once his equanimity had been restored, Elizabeth had explained how she had begged Aunt Maddie not to share that with him until he was far away from London.

"What makes you smile like that, Eliza?" Charlotte asked.

"I was thinking of Uncle Edward's reaction when he was told about the day of my presentation," Elizabeth revealed.

"He would not have been alone in returning to London had that man actually physically harmed you," Charlotte surmised. "In fact, I think he would have been joined by most of the men here."

"Unfortunately while he still lives, I am considered his property so he would say he is allowed to do what he will with something which belongs to him," Elizabeth mused. "Enough about him. Is it my imagination or is Lawrence Portnoy interested in you Charlotte?"

Charlotte blushed and looked away. "Come Charlotte, do not be coy, it has only been a few days, but he always seeks you out," Jane observed.

"You mean like Lord Andrew does with you?" Charlotte responded. Now it was Jane's turn to blush deeply.

"And Janey met Lord Hilldale many months ago," Elizabeth pointed out.

She could not be with the man she wanted to be with, but she would do what she could to make sure those she loved were able to find men of their choice.

Elizabeth stopped in her tracks. At the instant she thought about Jane and Charlotte being able to make free choices about who, if anyone, they ever married; a handsome face invaded her thoughts. It was the face of the man she had been dreaming of since meeting him, regardless of his insulting her.

"Lizzy, are you well? Should we return to the manor house?" Jane asked concernedly.

"Excuse me, I was wool-gathering," Elizabeth hedged.

Neither her sister nor her friend thought that was what had caused Elizabeth to freeze, but they would not press her until she was ready to share with them—that is if ever she was able. She already had too many choices stolen from her and they would not do anything to force her into a confidence.

Although she was walking again, Elizabeth was thinking of the interactions she had with Master Darcy —William. The times she sat in Pemberley's magnificent library, usually with Mary, and sometimes others as well, accompanying her, the Darcy heir seemed to find his way there as well. So far they had debated one of Shakespeare's histories and a volume of poetry by Lord Byron.

He never discounted her opinions because of her sex. In fact, he treated her with respect for her intellect. As often as she conceded his point was correct, he did the same with what she had been arguing.

Whenever, and it had not been many days from the time they first met, she was in his company, it just felt right. Unfortunately, they could never be more than friends. Neither of them would think of flouting propriety or contravening her marriage vows, at least the one to keep herself unto her husband and none other.

'*If only...*' Elizabeth began to think, but then she stopped herself. She reminded herself how she had told Janey about seeing the world as it was, not how she wanted it to be.

She had to take her own advice. Who knew what would happen to her loathsome husband or how long it would be before he went to where he belonged? Hell!

And if she was freed from the bondage which was her marriage, would William still be available then? It was not like she could expect him to wait for her for an undeterminable amount of time. Besides this, she did not know his feelings on the subject. Even if she were free now, would he want to pursue her?

Surely he, like all men, would want his wife to come to him pure on their wedding night. Elizabeth was positive William would not want a wife who was sullied, as she was. As always occurred when she reached this conclusion, she felt an overarching sadness descend over her.

Jane looked at Charlotte questioningly. Charlotte shrugged. Neither of them knew why Lizzy looked like she had been gripped by melancholy all of a sudden. As hard as it was, they stuck to their resolve not to press her. Since they were almost at the house anyway, Jane decided she would talk to Aunt Maddie to see if her aunt had any idea what caused Lizzy's mood to change so suddenly.

~~~~~~~/~~~~~~~

Fitzwilliam Darcy was well aware he was losing his heart. The problem was not only that she was a duchess, but she was married, to the most worthless, vile man in the realm, but married nonetheless.

When they were together it felt like his heart was whole. How was it his heart had gone and settled on one who could never be his?

As much as he knew no other woman would ever measure up to Lady Elizabeth, he was certain that for the continuation of the Darcy line, he would have to take a wife one day. It would be a difficult search as everyone would be measured against *Elizabeth*, and he was sure they would all be found wanting.

Yes, he had only turned four and twenty in January past, so he was still relatively young and had time. Would time erase the ache of not being able to be with the woman with whom he was falling in love?

Until he had to cross that particular bridge, he revelled in spending time with her and was amazed by her intelligence. Not only was she well read, but she played chess as well. Her skills were far from rudimentary. In the days since she had been in residence, they had played four games and each of them had won one with two ending in draws.

He had been a chess champion at Cambridge which made her playing that much more impressive.

She was one of the most compassionate people he knew to the extent that she had agreed to meet with Pemberley's steward, Mr. Lucas Wickham, and tell him all about his son and what she knew of his employment with the Duke.

During the meeting in his father's study, she had related how she had seen some subtle, although small, shifts in George Wickham's behaviour as it related to his treatment of her. She could not be sure, but based on her husband not ringing a peel over her head, she believed his man no longer reported anything the Duke would find objectionable about herself.

If her goodness and intellect were not enough, he knew of no more beautiful young lady. Her extremely fine, emerald-green eyes, radiated intelligence, flashing when she was angered, absolutely bewitched him.

On several occasions, he had heard her say her older sister was far better looking than herself. William could not agree with that assessment, Lady Elizabeth was, by far, the most handsome woman of his acquaintance.

He did not begrudge either of his cousins the burgeoning friendships Andrew and Lawrence had with Jane Bennet and Miss Lucas respectively.

'If only she was not married to that corpulent bastard,' William thought to himself. He did not wish the damned Duke dead, but he knew he would not complain if the man did them all a favour and shuffled off the mortal coil.

~~~~~~~/~~~~~~~

"You have told me all is planned for the morrow, but I want you to go over everything again," the Duke demanded when Wickham stood before him.

"As you wish, Your Grace," Wickham bowed. If his master needed to hear the plans again, then so be it.

"I am waiting," Hertfordshire interjected petulantly.

"It is confirmed Lord Jersey will convey his son and daughter to his brother-in-law's estate outside of London directly from St. George's after the Easter services on the morrow," Wickham began. "Lady Jersey will be returning to Jersey House to confirm all the arrangements for the dinner she has planned, and to be held there on the morrow are satisfactory.

"As the brother's estate is a little under two hours away, with time to spend with his family, Lord Jersey will be away for upwards of five hours giving you more than enough time for what you plan to do."

"Have you used my money wisely bribing all of the footmen who would normally be on duty in the house?" Hertfordshire asked the same question he had asked earlier.

"Yes, I most certainly have, Your Grace. I showed you the accounting did I not? They will all leave the house as soon as Lady Jersey enters her bedchamber to change. We will be in your nondescript carriage near the house and we will see her arrive home and then before you enter the house, you will see the footmen departing," Wickham explained. "Before he leaves, one of the men will unlock a door on the side of the house which leads into the ballroom. From there we will enter the house and take the stairs up to the master suite. Are you certain you do not want to take the servants' stairs for added security?"

"Of course not, do not suggest that again or it will not go well for you," the Duke spat out. "There is no world in which I would use the servants' anything!"

"As you wish, Your Grace. The entrance hall, stairs, and upstairs hallways will all be devoid of the footmen we would have seen abandoning the house. I will lead you to Lord Jersey's bedchamber. It is there the maid I bedded told me her Ladyship will be to take a rest after church." Wickham paused. "Do you require me to enter the bedchamber with you?"

"Of course I do not, you simpleton," the Duke stated disdainfully. "I will bring her to heel, and if she resists me, my pistol will be with me! It is not the first time I have forced a reluctant woman to have me, and it will not be the last."

"In that case, Your Grace, I will wait for you outside the door. As soon as you are satisfied, I will lead you safely out of the house," Wickham related. "It is a pity you will not be able to see the look on your enemy's face when he discovers you have violated his wife."

"He will come to call me out and then I will see the anguish I will have caused him. When I threaten to release all of the information to the gossip sheets, he will leave my house with his tail between his legs. My revenge will be complete!" The Duke looked gleeful as he spoke. "Even if he does not end his own miserable life, he will be a broken man."

Finally happy the plans were in place and they met with his approval, the Duke waived Wickham away.

~~~~~~~/~~~~~~~

After dinner on Saturday evening, the residents of Pemberley sat in the drawing room, with the movable wall between it and the music room pushed back. They had been treated to the pleasure of Lady Anne exhibiting on the pianoforte. She was a true proficient.

Mary and Anna had played a duet, and then they had been followed by Olive Portnoy on the harp while her cousin Marjorie Barrington accompanied her in song.

There had been card tables set up as well with whist at one table and loo at another.

Given the early hour of the Easter services, no one lingered past an hour or so in the drawing room, everyone making for their bedchambers. They would all be attending the Lambton church and then Adam, Eve, and their two boys would join them at Pemberley for the Easter meal.

When they reached the first guest floor where they were being housed, Aunt Maddie invited Lizzy into the suite's private sitting room.

"Lizzy, are you well?" Madeline asked her niece once they were comfortably seated facing one another across the low coffee table.

"What do you mean, Aunt? I have never been happier."

"Then Lizzy dear, explain why you have periods of great sadness disconnected from anything we know about?"

"Did Jane mention this?"

"No Lizzy, she did not have to, I have seen it for myself."

"Now and again, it hits me that regardless of the pleasure of being with all of you now, I am still in the prison which is my marriage. Yes, I know, I am free right now, surrounded by love and acceptance, but at some point after I give birth," Elizabeth placed her hands on the slight bump in her belly, "A time will come when I will be back living with *him*. In many ways after experiencing the complete bliss of being with everyone, having to go back to *him* could very well break my spirit. I think I am strong enough for that not to happen, but I will only know then."

Madeline pulled her niece into a hug. "We will find a way so you will not be cut off from us again. I know not how, but we will. That I swear to you. Also, it is quite possible you may hardly be in that man's company if the babe growing inside of you is an heir." All the talk of babes cause Madeline to place her hands on her large belly where her new daughter or son was making her or his presence known.

"It must be! I cannot have *him* importune me ever again!" Elizabeth knew she was omitting the reason for a major part of her melancholy, however, there was nothing she said that was not true.

"Go and prepare for bed, Lizzy. I need to go join your uncle in our bedchamber." Madeline kissed her niece on the forehead.

Elizabeth watched wistfully as her aunt entered the bedchamber. As long as she was married to *him* she would never know a love like the one her aunt and uncle shared.

CHAPTER 25

S tarting with the first row, six rows of pews on the lefthand side of Lambton's church were filled for the Easter service by the party from Pemberley. With the added visitors at the estate, there was standing room only to hear Reverend Lambert deliver his Easter lesson.

The novelty of a duchess attending their church had worn off to a certain extent for the parishioners. Besides the Duchess, for those enamoured with nobility, there was additionally an earl, a countess, and a viscount attending the service as well.

Even though they were unrestrained in showing affection between them at Pemberley, at the church Elizabeth's friends—a group which was considerably larger than before she had been residing at the Darcy estate—and family were circumspect in the way they related to her in public.

Notwithstanding the fact John and Brian had assured Her Grace there were none working for her husband who would report back to him about her activities in the area, other than the information they sent—which they allowed the Duchess to read beforehand—Elizabeth had decided to err on the side of caution. Something all the adults residing at Pemberley agreed with whole heartedly.

Elizabeth was seated in the front pew—as befit one of her rank—between Lady Matlock and Jane. Her Uncle Adam had just asked the congregation to recite some silent prayers.

'Lord God Who art in Heaven, please save me from this hellish marriage I am in. Since I came to Derbyshire and have not seen him, *my life has at least been tolerable. I thank You for enabling me to spend time with those I love and for allowing me to meet my new friends. Surely I have paid enough penance having had* him *importune me until I fell with child.*

'On that subject, could You have not granted my falling in that state some months earlier? It would have saved me many times the disgraceful man lay with me. But I suppose You had a plan for me all along. Had it happened sooner, the Darcys and Fitzwilliams would have been in London and there is a chance I would not have met them. Please pardon me Lord if I am questioning Your plan. It is not my place to do so.

'I am not sure what I am asking regarding my husband, but one thing I do know, which I am sure You know all too well, he is the least godly man I have ever encountered. Of one thing I am certain, when You decide it is his time, he will not be going to Heaven.

'Please God, keep protecting my sisters, aunts, uncles, cousins, and friends. They have all been so very good to me and they deserve every good thing You decide to bestow on them. In Jesus's name I send you my prayer.'*

The whole time she had been beseeching God, Elizabeth's eyes had been pointed to the heavens.

~~~~~~~/~~~~~~~

It was no surprise to Wickham that His Grace did not attend church services that morning. In all of the time he had been employed by the Duke, he could not remember a single instance his master had attended church.

Even at Falconwood when the curate came to deliver the Sunday service at the chapel, Her Grace attended along with the servants; His Grace never did.

At that moment Wickham and the Duke of Hertfordshire were sitting in the old, unmarked carriage a little distance from St. George's church. Rather than wait near Jersey House, the Duke had decided he wanted to see Jersey and his children depart while Lady Sarah De Melville was conveyed home on her own.

They had been there for about half an hour when the church bells began to peal indicating the end of the Easter service.

"You see Your Grace, two coaches with Jersey markings have been pulled forward to the front of the church," Wickham stated as he pointed to the conveyances.

"So far things are going according to my plan," Hertfordshire returned.

As the two men watched, they saw the Earl of Jersey hand his wife into the lead carriage. He, his son, and his daughter stood and waved as the coach pulled away. The three then boarded the second conveyance. Unlike the one which had departed in the direction of Jersey House, the second coach turned onto a street which led away from Mayfair in the direction expected for the reported destination.

"I used the last of your funds you gave me to bribe Lord Jersey's coachman. He will turn a two hour journey into more than three hours each way, so you will have even more time than we had originally planned," Wickham reported.

"Excellent, I am well pleased I instructed you to do that," the Duke claimed.

After a nod from His Grace, Wickham struck the ceiling with his cane and they began to move in the direction of Jersey House. They arrived at Portman Square just in time to observe Lady Jersey being handed out of the coach by one of her footmen.

The driver of the Duke's carriage halted the equipage in the position Wickham had instructed him, which gave them an unobstructed view of the front façade of Jersey House.

Within a half hour first one, then two, and then soon several more men slipped out of the house. The last one came out of the ballroom side of the house and nodded towards the carriage before he too melted away like the rest of the men had.

Given the Duke did not want to walk too far, Wickham signalled the coachman to approach Jersey House. Per his instructions, the carriage stopped in a place where the view of other houses—more importantly their view of Jersey House—was obscured by trees.

Wickham alighted and then assisted his large master to do the same. He looked left and right and saw no one. As he had promised the Duke, there were no footmen on duty in front of the entrance door of the house.

"There is no one about, Your Grace. We can proceed," Wickham told his master.

Hertfordshire lumbered after his man. They reached the side of the house where there were three stone steps leading to a door that was cracked open. Although he was out of breath after climbing the stairs, the Duke was well pleased when he and his man entered Jersey House's ballroom.

He had attended a ball here during his brief marriage to his first wife. It had been the last time he had been invited to any social event at this house, and then soon after his second wife passed away, any invitations from members of the *Ton* dried up altogether.

What he considered his ill-usage was part of what drove Hertfordshire to dally with married women, and he loved taking that which was not available to him. Given what Jersey had tried to take away from him, had marked him for a particularly hard lesson, one Hertfordshire would dispense this day, in a matter of minutes in fact.

They reached the doors at the other end of the ballroom which led into the main part of the house. "Please wait here, Your Grace, and allow me to verify there is no one between us and the stairs," Wickham requested respectfully.

The Duke waved Wickham forward. He was happy for the respite to catch his breath before he had to climb the stairs to the family floor.

It took Wickham less than five minutes to confirm there were no obstacles leading to the stairs. After informing his master of this, he led the Duke out of the ballroom, along a corridor to the main entrance hall and the grand staircase.

Even though he had already checked to make sure their way was clear, Wickham looked around to double check there was no one about. He nodded and the two men began a slow climb up the main stairs. Rather than ask the Duke what speed to go, Wickham knew to take his time. That way their speed of climbing the stairs would be because of the pace he set and not the corpulent Duke needing to slow down and rest.

They arrived on the second floor and again Wickham looked around and saw no one. He pulled a piece of paper from his pocket with the directions to reach the master suite, which he told the master was provided by the maid he had seduced.

It took longer than it should have because Wickham walked very slowly to accommodate the huffing and puffing of the Duke as he attempted to bring his breathing rate back to normal levels.

"This is the door, Your Grace," Wickham whispered. "The maid suggested her Ladyship recline on the bed in the Earl's bedchamber. Are you sure you do not require my presence with you?"

"As I already told you, no, I do not. Wait here," the Duke averred with asperity.

Hertfordshire turned the door handle and then pushed it open. He advanced inside of the room. The chamber was darkened and there was a form he could make out on the bed. It seemed his enemy's wife was resting just like he had planned. This would be easier than he expected.

He pushed the door closed which plunged the room into almost total darkness. He was frustrated Wickham had not provided a candle for him. The damned man should have known she liked the room dark when resting.

The problem was he did not know where the door was and it would have been too humiliating to call out to Wickham to open the door. He felt along the wall and eventually found the window and pulled the curtains aside as hard as he was able.

"What are you doing in my bedchamber," a voice called out. From the times he had spoken to Jersey, he recognised the voice as his. But how could he be here?

Slowly he turned back towards the voice of his enemy. There standing, all with pistols trained on him was Jersey, his son, some other men, and Wickham!

Ignoring the fact he had been caught in Lord Jersey's bedchamber, he looked at Wickham indignantly. "What is the meaning of this betrayal, Wickham?" he demanded. "You will be dead before this day is out!"

"Did you really think I would allow you to harm Her Grace like you planned to after she bore you an heir? And as you are about to die, how would you be able to order anyone to do anything?" Wickham laughed derisively.

"Of what do you speak?" Hertfordshire asked nervously not feeling nearly as confident as he had before. Then he convinced himself none of them would harm a duke.

He reached into his coat pocket and pulled his pistol out intending to end Wickham himself. The last thing Lord Archibald Winston Chamberlain did in the mortal world before he was sent to hell was to cock his small pistol.

As soon as he saw the Duke cock his weapon, Lord Jersey, who was a crack shot, fired his pistol striking the dissolute duke between his eyes, killing him instantly.

The corpulent body fell face forward onto the floor.

~~~~~~~/~~~~~~~

A few days after the Duke told Wickham what he desired:

The Earl of Jersey was in his study with his son and heir, Wesley, Viscount Westmore when the butler knocked on the door and entered when bade to do so.

"There is a Mr. Wickham who works for His Grace the Duke of Hertfordshire here to see you, my Lord," the butler intoned.

"I want nothing to do with anyone associated with that man," the Earl spat out with distaste.

"That is what the man said you would say, my Lord, he urged me to give this note to you." The butler extended his salver.

His curiosity aroused; Lord Jersey nodded to his son who retrieved the missive. The Viscount handed it to his father.

The Earl unfolded the note. It was not long.

My master plans to do great harm to your wife and through her to you and to your name.

"Send him in Smithington," Lord Jersey barked.

"What did it say, Father?" Lord Westmore enquired. His father handed him the note.

Before the Viscount could say anything, the butler showed the man into the study.

"My Lords," Wickham bowed to the two men.

"Tell me what this is about or be on your way, I have no time for Hertfordshire's games," Lord Jersey insisted.

"This is as serious as can be, my Lord," Wickham assured the Earl. "You have no doubt heard whispers of the Duke's predilection for imposing himself on married women, and in most cases forcing himself on them."

"Yes, I have. It is one of the many reasons I and others tried to have him defanged," Lord Jersey acknowledged.

"It is because you and the Duke of Bedford led that effort that he has marked your wife to be his next victim. He knows Lord Bedford is too powerful and well connected to attempt something, but he feels you..." Wickham related the Duke's instructions to him

to the Earl and his son.

By the time he was done with his telling, Lord Jersey had to restrain his son from seeking the Duke out that day and calling him out.

"Why are you turning on your master, and what do you expect from me? Some sort of reward?" the Earl questioned.

"I am doing this for the protection of the new Duchess," Wickham averred simply. Seeing the disbelieving looks on the two men, he told them all how he had assisted the Duke to find the information which had forced his choice of wife to accept him. He related all up to, and including, the Duke's plans for her once he had an heir. "I am not proud of what I have done in service of His Grace, but I will not stand by and allow him to harm Lady Elizabeth. She is someone who treats everyone with respect and cares about the welfare of her staff and servants, something the Duke knows not how to do. Furthermore, she is only seventeen years old." Wickham paused. "I will not lie, I would like to leave England and have some money saved, so if you decided to offer me a reward, I would happily accept it, but it is not something I will demand."

"What do you propose?" Lord Jersey enquired.

Wickham laid out what he wanted to tell the Duke about Easter Sunday. "If you agree, we will allow him to see you depart St. George's—I will suggest we wait near your house, but he will want to see you at the church—with your children while the Countess makes for Jersey House on her own. You will go to the back of the house entering via the servants' door. His Grace would never imagine a peer would enter his house via a door servants use.

"He must see Lady Jersey enter the house, but she will continue through the house and exit the way you and the Viscount enter and join her daughter in the coach. When the 'bribed' footmen supposedly abandon the house, they too will go around to the back of the house as soon as they are able and can no longer be seen from the carriage in which we will travel. I will lead him to

your bedchamber, given his desire to do his deed on your bed. He will be armed and as such, when one of your men shoot an armed intruder, it will be discovered after the fact he is a duke."

"Father, I believe the plan Mr. Wickham proposes is sound and will work," Lord Westmore opined.

"How do we know this is not a ruse?" Lord Jersey demanded.

"Do you have a trusted man?" Wickham asked.

"I do, why do you ask?" the Earl averred.

"Send him back with me," Wickham urged. "I will place him in the servant's corridor which runs next to the master's study. There is a hole in the panelling to allow him to watch and listen. I will tell His Grace all is planned and suggest I need money with which to bribe your footmen. He will be able to report back to you on the veracity of my claims."

The Earl had agreed to that. A few hours later his man returned and reported that which Mr. Wickham had told them was, unfortunately, accurate.

~~~~~~~/~~~~~~~

"It is your intention to seek your fortune in the former colonies, is it not?" Lord Jersey verified with Wickham.

The Earl was not a violent man, but he had felt nothing but pleasure when he had aimed his shot at the Duke and pulled the trigger. He had watched dispassionately as the ball hit its mark and the bastard fell over, dead even before he hit the floor.

"With the money I saved and the four thousand pounds the late duke *contributed*, I will be seeking passage to the Americas as soon as may be," Wickham confirmed. "I ask only you allow me a little time to write two letters. One to Her Grace and the other to my father, and then I will leave your house."

"In anticipation of your choice to depart for the colonies, I have arranged a first class passage on a Dennington Lines ship from Liverpool. You have a sennight to arrive and embark on time," Lord Jersey told the surprised man. "And for the service you did my family, I have five thousand pounds in banknotes for you." The Earl paused. "Try and live an honourable life from now on."

Wickham was taken aback and a little choked up. He had not expected anything, but it was most welcome. Least of all he had not anticipated words of kindness from the Earl. He was shown to a room and sat at an escritoire to write his letters. The butler took them from him and was told he had been instructed to send them express.

With well over ten thousand pounds to his name, Wickham left Jersey House to begin his long journey to his new life. Another shock awaited him outside. The Earl had one of his spare coaches waiting to convey Wickham to Liverpool.

Once Wickham had departed, Lord Jersey sent for a doctor and the magistrate to report an unknown intruder had been shot in his house.

CHAPTER 26

On the afternoon of the Tuesday after Easter, the younger set was having a picnic in the park. As was usual, both men took the opportunity to be close to his lady, Andrew was sitting next to Jane and Lawrence Portnoy was attending to Charlotte.

At the same time, William found himself inexorably pulled to sit next to Lady Elizabeth. As had become their usual practice, they were in a deep discussion about a book. This time, one he was currently reading, and Elizabeth had read some weeks ago. Although he suspected Lady Elizabeth had taken a position she did not hold which was contrary to his own to spark debate, William enjoyed debating with the beauty far too much to let her know he was aware of what she was doing.

"William," Lydia called out. "Is it true you have fished in the lake at Lizzy's estate many times before the day you met Lizzy there?"

"It is, why do you ask? Are you like your Uncle Edward who loves to fish?" William responded with a smile."

"No, I have never attempted to fish. It is just unfair you have seen Lizzy's estate and we have not," Lydia pouted.

"Lyddie, it is *not* my estate," Elizabeth corrected. "It is one of *his* estates."

"He is not here so surely we can go and see the castle and the lake. I have never seen a castle before," Lydia complained.

"One day, sooner rather than later, I hope, I will be able to show you the estate," Elizabeth placated.

Before she could return to her debate with William, a footman from the house approached. "Your Grace," he bowed deeply. "The master instructed me to inform you an express has arrived for you, which has been redirected from Castlemere."

"Smithers, thank you for relaying the message to Her Grace. We will be right behind you," William stated. He turned to Lady Elizabeth. "I assume you would like to see who sent you an express."

"I hope it is not from *him*," Elizabeth responded, "but yes, I think I must."

He stood and extended his hands to assist Lady Elizabeth in standing. As neither was wearing gloves, William felt a frisson of pleasure when he held her dainty hands in his much larger ones.

"Would you like me to accompany you, Dearest?" Jane enquired.

"You remain where you are," Elizabeth looked between Jane and Andrew while the former blushed becomingly. "I am sure this big, brave, gallant man can escort me all the way to the house. If he suffers from hessian in the mouth again, John will be close by." Elizabeth inclined her head to Biggs who was watching over her.

With a dimple-revealing smile, William offered his arm to Elizabeth. It was less than two hundred yards to the manor house.

Mr. Reynolds informed Her Grace and Master William that those who had remained in the house were in the green drawing room and the express was there as well. They thanked the butler and made their way to the indicated drawing room.

After greeting those seated in the room, Elizabeth looked around for her express and spied a silver salver on the sideboard with a missive thereon. She picked it up and her eyebrows shot up in surprise when she saw the name of the sender.

"What is it, Lizzy?" Madeline asked concernedly.

"If this is accurate," Elizabeth pointed to the name on the outside of the letter, "it was sent to me by Mr. Wickham. I cannot imagine why he would write to me."

"At least you know your husband has no idea you are at Pemberley," Lady Anne stated. "The letter was directed to Castlemere."

"That is the same conclusion I reached," Lord Matlock agreed with his younger sister.

"The only way you will know why that man wrote to you is to open and read it," Gardiner told his niece.

Elizabeth sat on an unoccupied settee. No one missed how William stood and watched Elizabeth protectively. She opened the letter, smoothed it out, and then began to read.

29 March 1807

London (By the time you read this I will no longer be in Town)

Your Grace,

Please excuse my presumption in writing to you, but I think you will agree when you read what I have to say, it had to be done.

It gives me the greatest pleasure to inform you that your husband is no longer alive.

Elizabeth sat frozen in place. She read and reread that line five times before it registered. As soon as it did, she began to sob uncontrollably as she felt a millstone lift from around her neck. Could it be true? She so wanted it to be true.

Without thinking, William sat next to Lady Elizabeth and pulled her into his arms as she sobbed. He watched as the offending letter fell from her hand and floated down to the rug. "What did he say that upset you so much?" William asked, trying to control his anger at the steward's son.

The rest of the occupants of the room were all standing with concerned looks. No one mentioned the impropriety of William embracing an unrelated married woman.

"Please...read...it...aloud," Elizabeth managed between sobs.

William stood and picked up the missive and skimmed it before he read it as she asked. "This upset you?"

"Cannot...believe...it...true," Elizabeth averred as she fought to control her emotions.

William understood. She was not mourning him; they were tears of relief.

"William, read!" Darcy instructed. William stood and cleared his throat and began to read from the most salient sentence onward.

It gives me the greatest pleasure to inform you that your husband is no longer alive.

As much as everyone wanted to speak at once, those in the drawing room controlled their urge. Madeline sat down on one side of Lizzy while Lady Anne took the other side and each took one of her hands in their own.

My motivation for making sure your husband met his end was simple. To make amends for finding the information he used to force you to accept him and knowing what his plan for you was once he had an heir.

Your Grace, he chose you because of your spirit, strength, and impertinence. He wanted someone who would be a challenge when, after he had an heir, he would then break like one would a green horse. Each time you challenged him you only increased his anticipation of future pleasure.

At first, I would, and did, do anything and everything the late Duke asked of me. The money was good and to my shame, I cared not who got hurt as long as I was well paid. That all began to change when I was witness to your kindness, grace, and thoughtfulness to everyone around you.

No one was below your notice and you treated everyone with respect and compassion regardless of who they were or what their position was. That included myself, as much as I did not deserve your condescension.

I am well aware Biggs and Johns are not the only servants you have assisted with whatever help you were able to give. It did not go unnoticed how you used your own allowance to have repairs made to the tenants' cottages when your late husband refused. It was never for others to see you doing good, it is just who you are.

I have been a selfish, uncaring, and even a criminal being for much of my life. Such I would have still been had I not met you. The way you treated me and others was the genesis of my determination to begin to try to repair some of which I had helped to cause.

When we arrived in London after you were sent to Castlemere, the late Duke spent time with his mistresses (3 of them!) When he was tired of abusing them (he quickly found no enjoyment in the activities as they were paid to be compliant and he only took true enjoyment when there was genuine resistance), he called me into his study and instructed me to get him into Jersey House so he could defile Lady Jersey as a way to exact revenge on the Earl.

He lamented the fact Lady Matlock and Lady Anne Darcy were away from London as he would have liked to have had his way with them as well.

"If he was not already dead, I would kill the bastard!" Lord Matlock boomed.

"You would be in a queue behind me!" Darcy insisted.

"Please tell me Sarah was not harmed," Lady Matlock pleaded.

"He was so much worse than we imagined, and we knew he was terrible," Edith Portnoy stated.

SHANA GRANDERSON A LADY

William returned to the pages in his hand.

I went directly to Lord Jersey... The whole plan was laid out and explained in detail how the trap for the vile man was made ready.

To maximise the pain to Lord Jersey, the late Duke demanded his plan be carried out on Easter Sunday. The plan explained above worked to perfection and Lord Jersey shot the intruder *dead when said man tried to cock his pistol.*

Hence, Your Grace, you are free. All I can do is beg your pardon for the part I played in causing you to be married to such a man. I cannot change the past, but in the future, I will try to be a better man.

To that end, I will make my way to the Americas and seek my fortune (honestly) in the United States.

I know of the provisions you had placed in the settlement thanks to your intelligence, so I worry not for your security. Your sisters are safe and their futures assured, Your Grace. At this point, I will relate a conversation I had with the late duke soon after the settlements were signed.

When I asked him how he could agree to all you demanded, he simply said: I will make sure she does not survive me. *He had to die.*

I ask you for nothing regardless of how wealthy you are as of the day the scourge which was the late Duke was washed from the earth. I did not do this to seek a reward from you. I will keep the £4,000 your late husband was simple enough to hand me.

The last thing I need to do, is to wish you a happy life now you are free.

Sincerely,

George Wickham

No one spoke for some minutes after the reading was completed.

"Lizzy, what did young Wickham mean about the terms

you had inserted into your settlement?" Gardiner enquired.

"As happy as I am, until we see the reports in the Times of London, I want to reserve my celebration, just in case," Elizabeth responded. "If all is as Mr. Wickham has reported, I will free Uncle Frank from his promise of confidentiality to tell you all."

"Robert, when will Monday's papers arrive here?" Lady Anne queried.

"On the morrow," Darcy averred.

"In that case, I will plan a celebratory dinner for the morrow," Lady Anne decided.

"I suppose this means Lydia will get to see the castle," William stated in an attempt to ease the tension in the room.

In that moment, Elizabeth's and William's eyes locked as each was starting to consider what this news may portend for a shared future.

"Yes, she most certainly will," Elizabeth agreed. Seeing the looks from those who knew not to what they were referring, Elizabeth elucidated.

"If, as I believe it will be, it is confirmed, how long will you mourn him?" Lady Matlock questioned.

"Not one single day," Elizabeth replied firmly. "When I was presented, Her Majesty and I had a conversation."

"We were present," Lady Anne shared. "We always wondered what the Queen said to you, but never felt it was our place to enquire once we met you."

Elizabeth related a condensed version of the conversation. "I intend to request a royal decree stating due to his crimes, no mourning is required. There is one more thing I intend to ask. I will share that if and when Her Majesty grants my request."

"He will not be buried in consecrated ground," Hubert Barrington, the barrister informed everyone. "When his past and intended crimes come to light, I am sure the Archbishop, with the royals' encouragement, will excommunicate him."

"I always thought he would go to hell when he died, now I am certain," Elizabeth reported.

"Lizzy, shall we wait until the morrow, before I share what you authorised me to do?" Philips verified.

"That seems best, Uncle Frank," Elizabeth responded.

She smiled as she noted the look on Aunt Hattie's face. Elizabeth was sure she would do everything in her power—unsuccessfully—to learn about the clauses before the rest of the party.

"Will you share the news of the Duke's demise with everyone else?" Maddie asked.

"I see no reason why not. I will be sure to tell them we are waiting for the papers to be completely sure," Elizabeth averred.

"And Jane?" Gardiner added.

There was no doubt in her mind what her uncle was referring to. "As soon as I see it in the papers, I will have a long, private conversation with Janey," Elizabeth decided.

CHAPTER 27

Mr. Reynolds had never seen such anticipation for the London papers as he had when he delivered them to the large breakfast parlour that Wednesday morning.

At that time of the morning, it was usually the master, Master William, and sometimes Her Grace who would be breaking their fasts. This morning, however, the whole of the party resident at the estate were present, and not one of them had food in front of them.

As he always did, the butler was about to lay *the Times of London* in front of the master to read. "Please hand the broadsheets to Her Grace," Darcy instructed.

The butler carried out his master's instruction without question, laying the folded paper face down in front of the Duchess.

"Mr. Reynolds, please remove the two footmen and close the door on the way out. I will ring when they may return and the doors be opened again," Lady Anne instructed. The butler bowed to the mistress, and then led his two footmen out of the breakfast parlour before pulling the doors closed behind him.

Elizabeth looked at the folded newspaper in front of her. She so much wanted to see if what the letter told was the truth, while at the same time, she was fearful her hopes of freedom would be dashed.

'Come now Lizzy,' she told herself silently, '*are you not the one who tells how your courage rises when faced with adversity?*' Elizabeth took a deep breath. She stood so she would be able to see the whole of the page, picked up the folded sheets, unfolded them, and then turned them over to display the first page.

As soon as she saw the headline on the front page her face lit up with joy as she smiled with the warmth of the rising sun. The clear signal to everyone in the parlour was that which she had hoped for had been confirmed.

There was no thought of society's mores that one did not revel in the death of another. Elizabeth was rather sure hers was not the first, nor would it be the last merriment expressed at *his* demise. If there had been even the smallest measure of goodness in her late husband, it would have been different. There was not and Elizabeth was as certain as she could be his eternal soul was now discovering how hot the fires of hell were.

After her thoughts, Elizabeth lifted her eyes to the heavens to say a prayer of thanks for her deliverance out of bondage. She added thanks for her Easter prayers being granted.

With her thanks to God on high completed, she placed the unfolded edition of the newspaper back on the table allowing everyone to see the large, bold headline which went from one side of the page to the other.

THE DUKE OF HERTFORDSHIRE SHOT DEAD!

William had been closest to her and before either knew what they were about they were hugging. When they realised what they were doing, in front of everyone present no less, Elizabeth and William stepped back from one another.

It was clear the rest of the party wanted their share of

wishing Elizabeth well on her freedom. After William stepped back, Elizabeth was surrounded by her four sisters. None was more gleeful than Lydia, and not only because she would be able to see the Castle. Lizzy was free and would never have to see *him* again.

"I know we are not supposed to feel jubilation at the death of any person, but I find I care not," Lydia insisted. "That man deserved what he got."

There was not a single voice in the room that said a word in disagreement with the sentiments Lydia expressed. In fact, Lord Matlock and Darcy separately were sorry he was gone for one reason only. Each of them would have liked to have been the man who ended the stain on humanity the late Duke represented.

"Lizzy, you are free!" Jane exclaimed.

"Yes, yes! I most certainly am," Elizabeth gushed as she accepted a joint hug from Mary—who would turn fifteen on the morrow—and Kate.

"This being the first day of April, rather than someone pranking our Lizzy, she has been given the best gift anyone could ever conceive," Gardiner remarked. Those who heard him nodded their emphatic agreement.

While Lady Elizabeth was being hugged by her sisters who were soon replaced by her aunts and uncles, William picked up the paper and read the article accompanying the headline. "What George Wickham informed us of in his letter was nothing but the truth. The reporter's writing corroborates what he wrote," William stated to no one in particular once he had completed reading the words on the broadsheet.

"My steward received a letter from his son telling of his intention to leave England in which the son begged his father's pardon for his past misdeeds," Darcy revealed after they had heard what William said was revealed in the article.

"I am happy for Mr. Wickham," Lady Anne commented.

"At long last he can feel proud about his son's actions." She turned to her son. "William, it does not mention anything regarding my friend being harmed does it?"

"She was not harmed, Mother. According to this Lady Sarah was away from the house with her daughter when her husband, son, and some of their men detected the intruder. They only discovered who it was after he had been shot to stop him from shooting one of them," William averred.

The Darcy father and son, who normally found disguise abhorrent, shared a look which told of their being sanguine with it in this case.

"I wonder if Bennet has seen this yet?" Philips said to his brother. "He will not be happy as he knows what the added clauses to the settlement are and how the Duke's death before the birth of an heir will affect his big plan for the entail to be broken."

"Who cares what Bennet thinks," Gardiner spat out. His anger over Bennet not protecting his daughter had not diminished. "However, I am in anticipation of knowing the details of the provisions Lizzy had added," Gardiner stated.

"Once the celebration calms, I will do as Lizzy asked and reveal all," Philips assured his brother.

~~~~~~~/~~~~~~~

Thomas Bennet was not feeling very well. He was sure it had nothing to do with the volume of spirits he was drinking. It had been some months now since he had ceased bothering with port as it had become like drinking water and had no dulling effect on him at all.

For a few days now his skin felt very clammy, he would lose consciousness at various times, at other times he felt rather confused, and he had been nauseous not a few times each day. He practically lived in his study, and even though he had his manservant keep the fire in his study built high, of late he had begun to feel cold all the time. Also, the few times he got out of his chair, he felt rather light-headed.

Bennet had for nigh on four months drank whisky, brandy, and gin exclusively. For more than two months now, he had been consuming at least two bottles of the cheapest drink he could find each day.

To support his habits and prop up the estate—given for some time now their income did not meet the expenses any longer—Bennet had withdrawn more and more funds from the principal which made up Fanny's dowry of five thousand pounds. His intention to replace the money was long forgotten.

In his state of confusion, he had paid for things multiple times and had indulged in purchasing some very expensive sets of first editions. Between all of his mismanagement and indulgences, there was less than one thousand pounds of his wife's fortune remaining. As he cared not for her present or her future, he never for one moment considered the impact on his wife of what he had done.

He had no idea what the malaise he was suffering from was. To dull his senses, Bennet consumed more and more of the spirits to try and make himself feel better. On the other hand, he was eating very little solid food. He could not remember the last time he had bathed, and his beard and whiskers were evidence of the fact he had not been shaved for weeks.

Given his and his wife's ostracization from local society and the fact no one would deign to call on them, the only way news of the outside world was made known to him was when he chose to read the newspaper. The *Times of London* was delivered each day it was printed, but he did not read the news as diligently as he had in the past.

Reaching over to the pile of unread newspapers, Bennet happened to pull this past Monday's edition from the four editions that lay untidily on his desk.

He unfolded the paper and saw the large print headline staring back at him. It took him much effort to focus and be able to read what it said. Even after reading it several times, it took some minutes before his brain communicated the meaning of the information before him in a way he was able to understand.

He rang the bell for Hill. The man looked greatly surprised when he entered the study as it had been some considerable time since the master had summoned him thither. "Hill," Bennet slurred, "bring my wife."

Hill gave a curt bow and went to summon the mistress who was ensconced in her bedchamber. It had been some months since she had taken to her chambers and remained there.

"The master requires you attend him in the study," Hill conveyed.

Fanny had thought to refuse, but it had been so long since she had been invited into her husband's sanctuary, she decided to see what it was he wanted. She had her maid assist her to dress and put her hair up in a simple coiffure— something she had not done in many weeks.

"You summoned me," Fanny stated on entering his inner sanctum.

Bennet handed her the paper, "Read this," he managed.

"What do I care if the man who refused to acknowledge his own parents-in-law is dead?" Fanny demanded nastily once she had read the article.

"You should, with him dead, Lizzy has all of the power now."

"What nonsense do you speak of?" Fanny screeched.

He pulled open the centre drawer in his desk and withdrew a document, opened it to one of the last few pages, and handed it to his wife.

Fanny began to read:

Addendum to the marriage contract between Lord Archibald Winston Chamberlain, the Duke of Hertfordshire and Marquess of Hertford Heights and Miss Elizabeth Rose Bennet of Longbourn.

The terms hereunder are binding unless both parties jointly agree to dissolve any or all of them. They can be changed by one of the parties, only if that person survives the other.

    i.   *The entail on the Longbourn Estate in Hertfordshire will only be broken with both the Duke's and the Duchess's agreement. If one of them predeceases the other, then the surviving party can decide on his or her own.*

    ii.   *His Grace hereby agrees to not approach the Duchess's sisters in any way without her written permission.*

    iii.   *The Duchess will not be forced to give up a connection with her sisters, and is free to write to, and receive letters from them.*

    iv.   *The Duke must agree on any non-family connections.*

    v.   *The Duke agrees to sever any connection to or with Mr. Thomas and Mrs. Frances Bennet of Longbourn, Hertfordshire.*

    vi.   *Mr. Thomas Bennet is to sign the agreement on the last page revoking his parental rights on Miss Jane Bennet, Miss Mary Bennet, Miss Catherine Bennet, and Miss Lydia Bennet. If both the Duke and Duchess jointly call for the named sisters to live with them, they will be sent without delay. In the event either the Duke or Duchess predecease each other, the surviving party will be the full legal guardian of the four named Bennet sisters.*

    vii.   *None of the promised dowries or interest thereon will be permitted to be used by either, or both, Mr. Thomas Bennet or Mrs. Frances Bennet.*

    viii.   *If the Duke predeceases his Duchess, then Her Grace, Lady Elizabeth Rose, Duchess of Hertfordshire and Marchioness of Hertford Heights is the sole beneficiary of all of the Duke's unentailed houses, estates, business interests, and fortune. The only estate and income thereof which is entailed to the dukedom is Falconwood which is in both Buckinghamshire and Hertfordshire. Likewise, Hertfordshire House is the only house that is tied to the dukedom.*

    ix.   *In the case the eventuality in clause viii above comes to pass before the Duchess attains the age of 21, Mr. Edward Gardiner of London and Mr. Frank Philips of Meryton will be the Duchess's guardians until such time as she either remarries or reaches her majority, whichever occurs first.*

    x.   *Unless agreed to by both the Duke and Duchess, or in the event one of them predeceases the other, clause viii is held inviolate and supersedes any last Will and Testament of Lord Archibald Winston Chamberlain, the Duke of Hertfordshire and Marquess of Hertford Heights even if said will is dated after the day the marriage settlement was signed.*

    xi.   *If a son is born after the Duke's death, he would inherit all entailed property plus whatever Her Grace conveys him from the unentailed properties and fortune.*

    xii.   *If a daughter and no son is born and the Duke*

is not living to produce a male heir, then as laid out in the patents of the dukedom, the title will be bestowed on said daughter's first-born male child.

"This means Miss Lizzy is rich beyond our wildest dreams and all of our concerns are over," Fanny asserted.

"Mrs. Bennet, are you addlepated?" Bennet managed to say derisively. "The Duchess hates us. She had these clauses added to ensure if her husband passed before her, we would receive nothing."

"**HOW COULD YOU AGREE TO SUCH A THING**?" Fanny screamed. She launched into a vitriol and expletive-laced tirade aimed at her useless husband.

To assist in drowning out the sound of his wife's voice, Bennet unstopped a new bottle of whiskey and while his wife berated him, he drained the entirety of the bottle's contents. No sooner had he put the bottle down when he began to be violently sick as what he had just guzzled down came back up.

He suddenly had trouble breathing as his dulled responses did not protect his ability to draw breath and swallow. Much of what remained in his mouth ran down his throat and ended up blocking his ability to breathe.

Fanny was still screeching when she noticed her husband was slumped over his desk in a pool of his vomit and was not moving. She promptly fainted at the view before her.

The Hills entered the study and found the mistress lying on the floor, fainted dead away. While Mrs. Hill opened the bottle of salts, which was always in her pocket, Mr. Hill went to check on the master; he found no signs of life.

Hill dispatched the single footman to first go to Mr. Jones and request he attend Longbourn post-haste. Next, the lad was to go to Mr. Long who was the substitute magistrate while Sir William was away. Lastly, Mr. Philips's clerk would have to be told as there was a record on file which told how to contact the heir to Longbourn.

He was thankful it was his wife who had escorted the mistress to her chambers. Although she was in a daze, it was only a matter of time before the caterwauling would commence.

CHAPTER 28

After Philips related the special clauses Elizabeth had demanded to be added to her settlement, there was silence from those who had been told.

"Lizzy, do you have any idea how wealthy you are?" Gardiner asked once he recovered the power of speech.

"Not really. I know *he* settled a large amount on me, but according to the younger Mr. Wickham, everything he agreed to was done believing he would murder me before any of the clauses would be enforced," Elizabeth responded.

"That makes the one about the guardianship of your sisters very risky," Madeline pointed out.

"When I demanded that specific clause, I knew not what he planned to do once he had an heir, and being that I am fifty years younger than he was, I never imagined a scenario where he would have survived me," Elizabeth explained. "With the advantage of the knowledge I have now, I can see why he agreed to all of what I demanded without hesitation."

"What may have been is neither here nor there, he is the one in hell and by God's providence Lady Elizabeth is very much well and alive," William stated warmly as he looked at Elizabeth.

Elizabeth's heart swelled at William's desire to defend her. There was much to do now, but soon she would be able to think about her future.

"Lizzy, you need to travel to London," Philips opined. "Everything needs to be formalised and all of the deeds to your estates need to be changed to reflect your name as owner in the Court of Chancery. We must, I believe, call on the late Duke's solicitor in Town." He turned to his brother. "Believing Lizzy would be disposed of before *he* passed away explains why he agreed to the added terms so quickly."

"Now I am aware of his dastardly plans for me, his agreeing to you and Uncle Edward as possible guardians when he had a complete disdain for anyone in trade is understandable," Elizabeth stated.

"Hopefully he will be burning in hell when he realises his Duchess is now the ward of two tradesmen," Philips grinned.

"Yes," Gardiner looked at William Darcy, "unless she marries before her majority."

Elizabeth was about to protest she would never marry again when she realised it would be a lie. If William proposed after she had Her Majesty's permission to forgo any mourning, she would accept and this time it would be for love. Her love of him, not her love for Jane.

"Lady Lucas and I will return to Lucas Lodge," Sir William decided after conferring with his wife. "However, after missing Eliza for so long, I know Charlotte is loath to be separated from her so soon. If agreeable to Eliza and Charlotte desires to, she is welcome to remain."

"Of course Charlotte should remain with us," Elizabeth enthused. "It seems I have a few homes in Town, so accommodation will not be an issue."

"The Darcys will accompany you to Town," Darcy stated after a nod from his wife.

"As will the Fitzwilliams," Lord Matlock added. He was fully aware regardless of what he decided to do that Andrew would be going to London if Miss Bennet was as well.

"I will be in London after a stop at Rivington," Barrington informed the family.

"We will make for our estate," Edith Portnoy stated, "however, it seems Lawrence has decided to join the group making for Town."

"In that case, all of us need to see to our packing as I assume we will depart on the morrow with the first light," Lady Anne guessed.

"Will I only see the castle when we return to Derbyshire?" Lydia asked disappointedly.

"No Lyddie, you will see it today," Elizabeth responded. "I need to speak to the senior staff and apprise them of the change in ownership and regarding our travel plans."

It was decided that in addition to Elizabeth and her sisters, Charlotte, Anna, Maria, Andrew, Lawrence, Richard, and William would join her for the short ride to Castlemere. John Biggs and Brian Johns would be part of the party as wherever Her Grace went, so did they.

"Jane," Elizabeth placed her hand on her older sister's arm to hold her back as the rest of those travelling to her estate went to make themselves ready. Jane turned to face her sister. "You remember I promised I would one day tell you what made me change my mind and marry *him*?" Jane nodded. "Once I have spoken to my senior staff, I would like you to join me in my chambers at Castlemere so we may speak."

Jane nodded again.

~~~~~~~/~~~~~~~

"It really is a castle!" Lydia exclaimed, bouncing up and down on the coach's seat when the structure came into view.

The coach they were riding in was, thankfully, large enough for all eight ladies, none of whom were very large, riding within while the men were on horses alongside. Of course, Biggs and Johns were in their usual places.

"Did you think all of us were imagining it?" Elizabeth smiled at her youngest sister's enthusiasm.

"My goodness Eliza, it is exactly as you described it in the one letter that I received from you while you were here," Charlotte remarked.

"Why are any of you surprised my descriptions were accurate?" Elizabeth teased.

Not two minutes later they arrived at the entrance. By the time the carriage halted, the butler and several of his footmen were waiting. The riders dismounted from their horses before the coach came to a halt.

Once the door was opened, the butler signalled to the footman to stand back when he noticed the one gentleman reaching in to hand out the Duchess. Two other men handed two unknown ladies out, and then the other gentleman did the same for five more young ladies of varying ages.

Elizabeth introduced her guests to the butler. "Mr. Toppin, I would like my sisters and friends to have a tour of the castle and the new wing, but before we do, please have Mr. Mason and Mrs. Bannister summoned and then all three of you please attend me in the study as soon as may be."

The butler bowed and went to execute Her Grace's orders.

Elizabeth led everyone into the castle. "It is one big room," Kate noted.

"Yes, some of the Chamberlain ancestors restored the castle and kept it as a great hall when they built the wing you saw between it and the lake. I am told it functions as a ballroom, although I know not when it was used to host one previously," Elizabeth related. "There is one tower remaining to be explored."

Mr. Toppin entered the great hall after some minutes and nodded to the Duchess. "Jane, will you join me?" Elizabeth requested. "We will speak after the meeting which will be brief." Jane nodded her agreement. She turned to the rest of her guests. "Please explore in here; Mrs. Bannister will join you shortly and conduct a tour."

Jane followed Elizabeth towards what she assumed was the study in the newer wing. She noticed that one of Lizzy's huge guards followed behind them. She thought it was the one named Brian Johns. Even in her home, Elizabeth was never far from someone willing to protect her.

The sisters entered the study where the three senior staff members were standing in front of the desk. Johns pulled the door closed behind them and took up station in the hallway. Elizabeth introduced her dearest sister to the housekeeper and steward.

"Thank you for meeting with me," Elizabeth began. "There is no easy way to say this, so I will not beat around the bush. The Duke is dead." None of the three showed any emotion having never met the man, only knowing him by his terrible reputation. Elizabeth gave a brief recounting of how the late duke had been killed when he had been caught trying to harm a lady in her own home. "Under the terms of the marriage settlement, all non-ducal properties are mine. I have two uncles who will act as guardians until I reach my majority.

"As I am very happy with all of you, as well as those below you, I will not be making any changes unless you feel I need to consider some." Elizabeth looked at all three in turn. She received three shaken heads. "In that case, we will continue as you have before. The main difference is I will not be an absentee landlord. Mr. Mason."

"Yes, Your Grace," the steward responded.

"I will make funds available to you for any repairs and improvements you deem needed to the tenants' homes and any other structures on the estate. The same is true for you two as well. Anything you feel is needed to repair or improve, please inform me. Before you ask, this house and estate *will not* go into mourning. We depart for London on the morrow and I will be requesting a decree from the Monarchs stating that due to his evil, there will be no mourning for the late Duke."

Not a word was said in question of Her Grace's statement. "What do you require of us right now?" Mason asked.

"Nothing, other than your regular duties" Elizabeth replied. "Mrs. Bannister, I do have a request for you. You will find a group of my family and friends in the great hall, please conduct a tour of the house for them."

With a curtsy and two bows, the senior staff departed the study. Elizabeth stood and took Jane by the hand to lead her to the bedchamber.

~~~~~~~/~~~~~~~

"Lizzy, what a magnificent view from your bedchamber and sitting room," Jane enthused. "May I go out on the balcony?"

"Of course you may, silly. You are my sister, you can do anything you want here without my say so," Elizabeth returned playfully.

How much lighter Elizabeth felt in one of *his* former properties now she was free of him. There was no more putting off the conversation to come. Nevertheless, she would try to gain a few minutes. Having Jane come to the bedchamber had the intended effect of relaxing her sister.

"Jane, should I ring for some refreshments?"

"Lizzy! I have waited many long months to know why you changed your mind. Please do not procrastinate now."

"It was me who told you of your need to see the world as it is, but I am not sure I enjoy this new tough Jane," Elizabeth jested. "Come let us take a seat on the chairs there." Elizabeth pointed to a few chairs positioned on the balcony which allowed a glorious view across the lakes and the hills in the distance.

Elizabeth took a deep breath. "Janey, I did not marry

him because I loved him, not even like, but I did marry for the deepest, truest love."

"What do you...Lizzy, did you marry him to protect me?"

"Primarily you, but our younger sisters as well. You remember that afternoon Mr. and Mrs. Bennet forced me to meet with him, do you not?" Jane nodded. "His offer of dowries for you and my sisters, as well as to break the entail—I know it may sound selfish—did not move me to change my mind. When I still refused, *he* wanted to speak to me without Mr. and Mrs. Bennet present. They both stood and left the room with no thought for me remaining alone with that lecherous, ancient man." Elizabeth paused and took a series of very deep breaths. "He made me an offer I could not refuse..." Elizabeth told Jane all.

The more Elizabeth reported what had been said, the more the tears fell from Jane's eyes. "It is all my fault!" Jane wailed.

"**NO**! No Jane, it was *his* fault, and only his. He was the vile one who made the threat and at that point, he was aware I would do *anything* to protect you, as you would have done for me if the roles were reversed. As much as I detest Mr. and Mrs. Bennet for not upholding their duty as parents, it was not in their power to force me to marry. It had to be, and was, my decision alone." Elizabeth paused and handed Jane a large silk handkerchief. "Did I not tell you I married for the deepest love?"

"I know in my heart it is that dastardly man's fault. I am angry at Mr. Wickham for discovering your Achilles' heel and then telling that evil man. Even though in the end, he did move to protect you. None of that mitigates the feelings of guilt I have that it was your love for me which was exploited."

"If it were not for him being the architect of my freedom, I too would feel that way about Mr. George Wickham.

I do, however, believe in the power of redemption, as all of us Christians must. Still, I hope he finds a good life far from us and across the other side of the Atlantic Ocean." Elizabeth hugged her Janey. "I understand the feelings you are having. As long as you do not allow them to overpower you."

Elizabeth rang and had a maid summoned—Loretta was at Pemberley supervising her mistress's packing—to help Jane set herself to rights.

A quarter of an hour later, arm in arm the sisters made their way downstairs to find the group touring the house with Mrs. Bannister.

~~~~~~~/~~~~~~~

Lord Jersey had been true to his word.

Wickham had ridden to Liverpool in style. How he had enjoyed the comfort of one of the Earl's travelling coaches! The rooms at the inns were reserved ahead of time with the cost for board and lodging having been paid by the Earl of Jersey.

He had arrived in Liverpool with two days to spare, again sleeping at a comfortable inn, paid for by the largess of the Earl.

On the morning of the sailing, Wickham, with his valise and the special pouches containing his banknotes sewn into the inside lining of his coat, was one of the first passengers to board.

The Dennington Line ship, *the Rose IX*, was to set sail from Liverpool on the tide that day. Not long before midday, the ship had slipped its moorings and they were shortly under sail travelling west. Wickham waited, leaning against the railing, until the coastline had become barely distinguishable. He then made his way to his first class accommodations to rest for a while before their first meal on board the ship.

~~~~~~~/~~~~~~~

Hill found himself having to make all of the arrangements for the late master's funeral. Mr. Bennet had no family who would acknowledge him, and even had they been willing to, Hill was aware the Philipses were away from Meryton.

Mr. Philips's clerk had assured Hill he would send an express to Mr. Philips and Mr. Gardiner to notify them of Mr. Bennet's passing. That was in addition to the one he sent to Clem Collins.

From there Hill had made his way to the church at Longbourn village and met with Mr. Pierce. As it was a warm spring and none were interested in condoling with the mistress—she was heavily dosed with laudanum—the interment would be the day after the death.

Other than the rector, Hill, and the one male servant from Longbourn no one else was present for the service and subsequent interment.

Thomas Bennet was buried much like he lived—almost alone.

~~~~~~~/~~~~~~~

By the time the expresses reached Lambton, those headed for London had been gone for a day. The missives were redirected to Town.

CHAPTER 29

Kingsford Marylebone looked over his late client's will as well as the marriage articles the late Duke had signed.

Everything was in order. As to clauses viii, ix, x, and xi in the addendum to the marriage contract, the solicitor had tried to advise his client that if he passed, as had now occurred, the Duchess would inherit almost everything.

Yes, the Duke had been a rogue, but Marylebone had earned much money from him over the years. He was aware one of the uncles who was to be her guardian was, in fact, a lawyer. He was concerned if the Duchess moved all of her custom to another solicitor, it would leave a rather large hole in his annual income. All he could do was show Her Grace he carried out his duties in a professional manner and that duty included adhering to the letter of the law. He hoped Her Grace would continue to retain his services.

"Here is the documentary evidence you will require to file the petitions with the court of Chancery to have the deeds made over in Her Grace's name. If you do not have the name of a barrister, I know of a few," Marylebone told Philips. "This is what you will need for the banks, along with this list of banks where accounts are held. The clear profits from Falconwood, which are around fourteen thousand pounds per annum, will be accumulated in a trust account for the future Duke's use. Both that estate as well as Hertfordshire House are available for the Duchess's use, but as they are both tied to the dukedom and per the agreement, they will be held in trust until there is a duke who reaches his majority.

"The ownership of the shipbuilding yards in Southampton, Liverpool, and near Glasgow will be recorded in Her Grace's name in the next day, or two days at the most. You should know the Duke of Bedford, who has shipbuilding concerns as well as a shipping line, has in the past expressed interest in purchasing these three yards. His final offer was six hundred and fifty thousand pounds."

With an uncle, each one a guardian, seated on either side of her, Elizabeth was dumbfounded. She knew the man was purported to be wealthy, but the numbers just mentioned were far beyond anything she had imagined.

"J-just how much have I inherited?" Elizabeth asked tentatively.

"From the seven estates which now belong to you, the combined income is around fifty thousand pounds per annum," Marylebone began to explain. "The shipbuilding yards primarily, but the other business concerns as well, earn a similar amount each year. You have close to two million pounds in the various banks, most of which is in the four percents earning a little less than eighty thousand pounds per annum. Then there is the collection of gold and jewels which is rather extensive. Some belong to the dukedom, but most do not. Your late husband refused to have the collection valued for some years now, but if I were to guess I would say you own more than three hundred thousand pounds in gold and jewels."

It was not only Elizabeth who was stupefied. An uncle sitting on each side of her had his mouth hanging open as well.

"Now I understand why he settled two hundred thousand pounds on Lizzy as if it was nothing to him," Philips managed once he recovered the power of speech. "As far as a barrister is concerned, we are known to Mr. Hubert Barrington."

"A very good man who is excellent at what he does,"

Marylebone commented.

"He agreed to that amount as he believed Lizzy would not live to spend it," Gardiner added harshly.

"Is any of this money the proceeds of illegal activity?" Elizabeth questioned.

"No, Your Grace, it is not. Your late husband held one small account for gambling and as I am sure you have heard, he cheated to win," Marylebone articulated. "It was never about the money, but rather a way for the late Duke to gain leverage over those he wanted to control. It is one of the reasons the late Duke was never challenged by anyone whose wife he had forced himself on, until Lord Jersey ended his life."

"Where are those debt markers held?" Elizabeth demanded.

"In a safe in the study at Hertfordshire House. The key was always on his person. It was returned to me with his other effects he had with him the day justice found him." Marylebone opened a drawer in his desk and handed Her Grace the key.

Elizabeth handed the key to Uncle Edward. "I want every single debt marker returned to the victims as soon as may be."

Gardiner took the key and nodded. "It will be a great pleasure to release the markers back to those on whom he used to prey." He turned to Marylebone. "Is there anything else other than signing these documents now? My niece has an appointment at Buckingham House."

The solicitor indicated there was not. The two guardians signed the documents making Lizzy the richest woman in the realm, in fact one of the richest people who was not a royal.

"Mr. Marylebone, although I intended to cut ties with anyone who used to enable my late husband's repulsive behaviour, I can see you were not one of those, so I will be happy to retain your services for any work in London," Elizabeth told the relieved man. "You will of course work through my Uncle Philips who will be my primary representative."

The two uncles shook hands with the solicitor and Elizabeth inclined her head to him. Her uncles led her out of the office.

"How am I to explain to my sisters and the rest of the family just how wealthy I am?" Elizabeth wondered after they sat in the Hertfordshire town coach.

When they had arrived in London, Elizabeth, her sisters, one aunt, an uncle, and Charlotte had taken up residence at Hertfordshire House. Aunt Maddie and Uncle Edward had returned to Gracechurch Street to prepare for the impending lying-in. The first thing Elizabeth had ordered was for any sign of mourning to be removed from the doors or anywhere else in the house.

It had been obvious none of the staff or servants were upset at the Duke's passing nor at the order regarding there was to be no mourning.

"What say you we sell the shipyards to the Duke of Bedford?" Elizabeth proposed as the coachman got his team of six moving. "Although what I will do with the money I already have, I know not. There will be charities I support and my sister's dowries will be increased significantly."

"There is much time to make those decisions, Lizzy. Nothing needs to be decided today." Gardiner pointed out. "As you requested, the Fitzwilliams and Darcys will meet you and accompany you into Buckingham House."

"I wish you and Uncle Frank would be welcomed there as well," Elizabeth lamented. "Such nonsense that because you are both in trade…"

"It is the society of which we are a part," Philips took one of his niece's hands. "Who knows, one day there may come a time when those in trade are welcomed everywhere. Until that time, we conform with the conventions of the day."

"It does not mean I need to like it," Elizabeth pouted.

Both her uncles grinned. It was easy to forget she was but seventeen years old.

~~~~~~~/~~~~~~~

After an unforeseen delay along the route, the expresses for Gardiner and Philips arrived at the former's house around the time they and Elizabeth were on the way to Buckingham House. The rider delivered the two missives to the Gardiners' butler. Knowing where his master was for the day, and where the Philipses were residing, and after gaining the mistress's agreement, he instructed a groom to ride to Berkeley Square and deliver them to Hertfordshire House.

Less than a half hour later, the butler at Hertfordshire House took possession of the two letters and delivered them to Mrs. Philips who was in the main drawing room with some of her nieces and their friends.

Hattie returned them to the butler telling him to provide them to her husband and brother when they returned with Lizzy from Buckingham House.

~~~~~~~/~~~~~~~

Elizabeth and those who accompanied her were led into an ornate drawing room at Buckingham House. The Queen was seated on one of the two large chairs in the centre of the room. The Crown Prince was seated to her left.

"We welcome you to our house, Lady Elizabeth," the Queen inclined her head as Elizabeth and those with her gave deep curtsies and bows. "We are pleased to see Lord and Lady Matlock, Lord Hilldale, and Captain Fitzwilliam as well as Lady Anne, Mr. Darcy, and their son with you." The Queen turned to her eldest son. "Why has your father not bestowed a title on Mr. Darcy?"

"Because like all Darcys before him, he will turn down

the honour," the Prince of Wales drawled. "Father decided not to be politely refused, so he did not make an offer to the current Mr. Darcy."

If the Queen objected to Elizabeth not wearing mourning clothing, she said not a word about it.

"We are pleased to see you Lady Elizabeth, especially as you are freed from that millstone which had been tied about your neck. How may we help you?" the Queen enquired.

"There are two things for which I beg your indulgence, Your Majesty. The first is regarding the mourning period, or more to the point, the lack thereof, for that man," Elizabeth began. "I assume the true facts of his death are known to you." The Queen and Crown Prince agreed it was so. "I thank goodness Lady Jersey was not hurt by that depraved man, but there were others, and not a few, who were. I request that a royal decree be published stating due to his wickedness, no mourning, official or otherwise, will be observed for him."

"That is easy to allow. We agree it would not do to honour a man who had no honour," the Queen granted. "As it is, we have spoken to our vicar to investigate whether posthumous excommunication is warranted; we think it is. Is the other request as easy to allow?"

Elizabeth had to stop herself smiling at the way the Queen referred to the Archbishop of Canterbury as her vicar.

"If Your Majesty is not aware, I am carrying his child," Elizabeth's hand unconsciously went to the slight swell in her belly. "With all the evil he encompassed, I do not think his name should live on. I am well aware the late Duke's father was a man of honour, as were those before him, but the son sullied the name to such a degree anyone bearing that name will be tainted by association."

"We find your request reasonable," the Queen agreed. "Do you have a name in mind, Lady Elizabeth?"

"Given my former parents' behaviour, I do not want the

name Bennet to be used." A picture of a man she was fast falling in love with formed in her mind. She looked at William as she spoke. "*If* I marry again, what think you if my son or daughter bear his surname? Until then, I would like to adopt the surname Gardiner, that way if I am not married before the birth, the babe will not have a reviled family name."

The Queen looked to her son who nodded. "His Majesty will grant that boon. It may take some weeks, but as soon as he does, we will have a royal decree published." The Queen smiled playfully. "We understand you are now a lady of some means. We *do* have a *few* unmarried sons, you know."

Elizabeth could not help but smile. She knew the Queen would never try and push her to marry where she was not inclined; once was far more than enough.

"*If* I decide to marry again, I will keep that in mind, Your Majesty," Elizabeth jested back.

"Where will you live until that occurs?" the Queen questioned.

"It is not something I have thought on, but I suppose I would prefer Castlemere," Elizabeth related. "I found the area and the people to be much to my liking."

The Queen looked to Ladies Matlock and Anne. "Are not your husband's estates close to the one the Duchess mentioned?" the Queen wondered.

"Pemberley is but two miles away, Your Majesty. We share a boundary fence with Her Grace's estate," Lady Anne confirmed.

"And Snowhaven is a little more than ten miles distant," Lady Matlock added.

The Queen looked at the Darcy heir. She had not missed the tender way he and the Duchess looked at one another from time to time. "It is well you have made good friends," the Queen turned back to Elizabeth. "We are well pleased you and your sisters are all safe from that man."

"As am I, Your Majesty, as am I," Elizabeth responded.

The Queen ordered some tea and cakes. As would be expected there was enough to feed an army. Once tea was drunk and some slices of cake consumed, the Queen and the Prince of Wales stood, received their bows and curtsies, and then exited the drawing room.

~~~~~~~/~~~~~~~

That afternoon one Clem William Collins presented himself at Mr. Philips's law offices in Meryton.

"I thought you would be older," the clerk stated when he saw the man who was barely twenty sitting before him.

"My honoured father passed away a little over a year past. It is only my mother and me now," Collins informed the clerk. "As much as I appreciate my inheritance, I know not how to manage an estate."

"There are many in the neighbourhood who would assist you," the clerk replied. "I do have a question. The only Bennet remaining at Longbourn is the former mistress, Mrs. Frances Bennet, what will you do regarding her?"

"My mother will be the mistress for now. I will decide what the best course of action is regarding Mrs. Bennet after I have met her," Collins mused. "Is not one of my distant cousins a duchess?"

"Yes, the second daughter of the late Thomas Bennet is the Duchess of Hertfordshire, and if you have read the news recently, you will know her husband is lately deceased," the clerk responded.

"Does that mean I am her and her sisters' guardian?" The idea of being the protector of a duchess appealed to Collins.

"It does not. That was all spelled out in the articles of the marriage settlement. She and her four sisters are, for now at least, under the guardianship of their two uncles." The clerk quickly dispelled the notion Collins would have any authority over the Duchess or her sisters.

There was no missing the way Collins's face fell at learning the last. "I suppose I should go and introduce myself as the new master at my estate...how do I get there?" Collins wondered.

The clerk imparted the information Collins needed to reach Longbourn. Soon he was on his way in the gig in which he and his mother had arrived.

~~~~~~~/~~~~~~~

"Charles!" Caroline Bingley shrieked. "I hear the Darcys have returned to London. When will we see our friends?"

Bingley knew telling Caroline how disinclined the Darcys and their family were to be in her company was not worth the tantrum which would follow. "Mayhap we will see them at Drury Lane this evening. *Much Ado About Nothing* is being performed and I know it is one of Darcy's favourites."

"Then you must go and acquire tickets right now," Miss Bingley commanded. "As soon as he sees us he will invite us to the Darcy box, of course."

Bingley obediently ordered his coach to go to the box office to acquire the tickets his sister demanded. Anything was better than her whinging.

CHAPTER 30

"You are gifting us dowries of *how much*!" Jane exclaimed with the volume of her voice rising. It was hard enough to comprehend her sister's wealth, but this was far too much.

"Was I not clear? You will each have one hundred thousand pounds," Elizabeth repeated. "Once word gets out, every fortune hunter in the land will be after you…"

"And you, Lizzy," Madeline interjected. "You know it is true."

"I suppose it is," Elizabeth mused. "Do not forget, I will always be with John, Brian, and Albert when I am not at home, and I have asked them to find more men of their quality to guard not only me but my sisters as well." She paused as she remembered what they had been discussing. "Uncle Frank is having the conditions of the release of the dowries written in such a way that a fortune hunter will not benefit from even one penny. Moreover, if some man is dishonourable enough to convince one of you to elope, other than the one thousand pounds you would have received from Mrs. Bennet's portion, you will receive nothing."

"I for one would never elope," Lydia insisted.

"Lyddie, I am happy to hear that. Also Janey, did you not hear how much the Duke of Bedford will be paying for the shipyards?" Jane nodded. "Even after your dowries are deducted and invested, I will still have a vast amount remaining, and when you add that to what is in the various bank accounts already…" Elizabeth trailed off not saying what she was about to. She still felt uncomfortable with the amount of her vast wealth.

"If you put it like that, then I suppose all I can do is thank you for your generosity," Jane responded. "I do not want to feel like I am taking advantage of you, Lizzy. We are living with you, you are giving us a quarterly allowance which makes what we received in the past at Longbourn in a year a mere pittance, and you will be purchasing new wardrobes for all of us. Need I go on?"

"Do you not understand what a pleasure it is for me to be able to do this for all of you?" Elizabeth challenged. "The fact it was *his* money, and I am able to lavish it on you, whom he threatened to gain my compliance makes it even sweeter for me to do."

"I understand your desire to turn what was once used for evil to good. Thank you for loving and caring for us as you do, Lizzy." Jane averred.

There was a chorus of appreciation from the three youngest Bennet sisters.

"When are Lord Hilldale and Lawrence Portnoy supposed to call?" Elizabeth asked, causing her older sister and Charlotte to blush with pleasure.

"By the way, Charlotte, I intend to speak to your father about dowering you and Maria as well," Elizabeth whispered in her friend's ear.

"Eliza!" Charlotte admonished.

"Why not? I have more than I, more than all of us, would be able to spend before the Second Coming," Elizabeth stated quietly. "What is it all for if I am not able to gain pleasure from being generous to those I love?"

"Maria and I are not blood; it would not be the same," Charlotte protested.

"Would you gainsay a duchess?" Elizabeth teased. "To me, you and your family *are* my family," Elizabeth said with conviction.

"I know how hard it is to divert you once your mind is made up. Speak to Papa; I will leave it up to him," Charlotte capitulated.

Just then the butler entered carrying his silver salver. "Mr. Gardiner and Mr. Philips, please pardon me, these arrived while you were out with Her Grace. I had handed them to Mrs. Philips and she requested I give them to you on your return. I was caught up in my duties until now," the butler stated contritely.

"No harm done," Gardiner said as he removed the two missives. He kept the one addressed to himself and handed the other to Philips.

"It is in my clerk's hand," Philips shared. "I wonder why Jackson sent me an express. By the direction, it was posted to Lambton and then forwarded to Gracechurch Street."

Gardiner was the first one to break the seal. He read the note quickly which caused his eyebrows to climb up to his hairline. "I think I need to read this to you all."

Philips had just read his letter. "I agree with Gardiner," he added.

Gardiner cleared his throat and began to read.

1 April 1807

Law Office, Meryton, Hertfordshire

Mr. Gardiner:

I know you had permanently broken with Mr. and Mrs. Thomas Bennet but you need to know that Mr. Bennet passed away today.

Ever since Her Grace and her sisters left Longbourn, the remaining Bennets were ostracised by the locals hereabout. It had been some time since either Mr. or Mrs. Bennet had been seen in the town (not since Mrs. Bennet spent her time in the town gaol).

From what the Hills have shared, Mrs. Bennet kept to her

chambers for the most part while Mr. Bennet lived within his study. It is reported he drank larger and larger quantities each day. In the last few months of his life, he was finishing at least two bottles of brandy, whiskey, or gin every day and had given up port as it was not strong enough.

I have sent a letter to the last known address of the heir and will notify you and Mr Philips when Mr Collins makes contact.

I do need to inform you from what I can tell, Mr. Bennet has been using the money from Mrs. Bennet's settlement to pay for his and the estate's expenses. There is barely £800 left.

Until I receive instructions from Mr. Philips, I am his and your servant.

L. Jackson

Head Clerk

Philips and Gardiner traded letters; in essentials they were the same.

"Will we have to mourn him?" Kate asked.

"That will be up to each of you. You know I will not," Elizabeth responded. She turned to her Uncle Frank. "Will you write to your clerk and inform him I would like to meet with the heir as soon as may be?"

"I will, but would you like to share why?" Philips averred.

"Let us see if the heir is willing to meet with a member of the fairer sex, and then I will reveal what I have in mind," Elizabeth returned.

Even though she had not wished this on the man who had been her father, Elizabeth found she felt no sorrow at his passing. He had been complicit in selling her into slavery, making her a brood mare for a disgusting old man.

She was well aware it was her Christian duty to forgive, but not yet. Perhaps one day in the future, but she was not close to being ready to do so at present. Even if she was able to eventually forgive him, she would never be able to forget.

"We are for the Drury Lane with the Darcys and Fitzwilliams to see *Much Ado About Nothing* this evening," Hattie reminded everyone. "Those who need to, what say you we make for Meryton in the morning?" There was general agreement.

Gardiner took his leave to return to his wife.

A few minutes later the butler showed the Fitzwilliam brothers, Lawrence Portnoy, and William Darcy into the drawing room. Elizabeth found herself blushing with pleasure at the men's arrival—just like Jane and Charlotte were doing.

~~~~~~~/~~~~~~~

A light dinner was held at Darcy House that evening for the group who would be attending the theatre. It was a fairly large group, but with the Fitzwilliam box right next to the Darcy box, there would be more than enough seats between the two.

Everyone would return to Hertfordshire House for supper after the performance.

When Lady Elizabeth entered the drawing room at his father's house, William felt his breath hitch on seeing her. She was already beautiful. This night, however, she was resplendent in a hunter-green silk gown. Her jewels were chosen tastefully, rather than as a demonstration of wealth as so many in the upper ten thousand were wont to do.

Her raven, wavy hair—how he longed to run his fingers through her silky tresses—was piled up on top of her head with some curls loosely framing her face and cascading down her neck in back.

Andrew had a similar reaction to Jane with whom he was rapidly falling in love. In fact, he planned to find a moment to request a courtship that night. As soon as Jane entered the room, Andrew was at her side to lead her to a seat next to him, of course.

Lawrence Portnoy was convinced his future happiness lay with Miss Lucas, he intended to request a private interview from her soon. He suspected she had tender feelings for him, but he wanted a few more days to be sure.

Killion, Darcy House's butler announced dinner.

William led Elizabeth into the dining room and seated her next to himself. His cousins Andrew and Lawrence did the same with the lady who held each of their interests.

The four younger girls—Anna, Mary, Kate, and Lydia— would remain at Darcy House for the night under the care of Miss Younge and some of the Darcy and Hertfordshire footmen and guards. As they all understood their time would come one day, none of the younger girls complained about having to remain at home.

~~~~~~~/~~~~~~~

The edict regarding no mourning for the late dastardly Duke of Hertfordshire had appeared in all the newspapers that morning. In addition was one from His Grace, Charles Manners-Sutton, The Most Reverend Willowmere, by Divine Providence Lord Archbishop of Canterbury, Her Majesty's *vicar*, which announced that Archibald Chamberlain had been posthumously excommunicated.

Other than the few who briefly saw her at her presentation, no one other than the Duchess of Bedford and Lady Jersey recognised the newly widowed Duchess of Hertfordshire when she entered the theatre with a large group.

Both ladies kept their knowledge of the Duchess's presence to themselves, informing only their husbands. They resolved to visit the Fitzwilliams and Darcys at the first intermission to garner introductions. All the while, the gossip-hungry attendees at the Drury Lane that evening clamoured to discover who the two unknown beauties were.

That the dark-haired beauty was on the Darcy heir's arm and the blonde was being escorted by Viscount Hilldale only increased the *Ton's* desire to know who they were. Another lady, not as pretty as the first two, was on the arm of the Portnoy heir. Although he had impeccable connections, their presence was not as interesting as his family was not nearly as wealthy as the Darcys.

The group did not stop to speak with anyone in the foyer, nodding to some acquaintances, and made their way directly up to the Fitzwilliam and Darcy boxes. Elizabeth, Gardiner—his wife had insisted he attend, and Charlotte were seated in the Darcy box while Jane and the Philipses joined the four Fitzwilliams.

Elizabeth was enchanted; the view of the stage was excellent from the Darcy box. She loved Shakespeare and especially his comedies. For her, the one they were to see that evening was second only to *A Midsummer Night's Dream*. Now that she had limitless funds, seeing all of the Bard's plays from her own box would not be a problem for her.

~~~~~~~/~~~~~~~

As was her wont, Caroline Bingley chose to arrive anywhere at a time she deemed to be fashionably late. In this instance, it was after the final bell signalling the commencement of the first act, so rather than crowds in the foyer looking at her admiringly—as she felt was her due, there were only the retreating backs of some patrons making their way to their seats.

Thanks to the late hour Bingley had purchased his two tickets, the seats he and his sister found themselves in were almost at the end of the second to last row, and there was a column which half obscured their view of the stage.

Caroline Bingley did not care that she could not see the stage as there was one advantage to the terrible seats. With the use of her Galilean binoculars, she had a clear view of the Darcy and Fitzwilliam boxes.

She trained her opera glasses on the Matlock's box first.

The Viscount was seated next to his mother and next to him was a very pretty young lady. Her dress, however, was a few seasons out of fashion and there were no jewels of which to speak. Caroline guessed she was about her own age. Next to the woman was the second son. In addition, there were two unknown people in the box, an older couple who were very unfashionably dressed.

Then she swung her glasses to peer into the Darcy box. There were Mr. Darcy and Lady Anne with an unfashionable man next to them. There was a young lady, rather plain in Caroline's opinion, sitting next to one of the Darcy cousins.

She frowned when she did not at first see the man she intended to marry. Then she noticed on the other side of the couple she had just seen was the Darcy heir, deep in conversation with, and smiling at—he never smiled at her in that way—a very pretty young lady. Unlike the one in the Fitzwilliam box, this one was wearing a current and fashionable evening gown. She wore jewellery which was far too understated.

Seeing the lack of jewels assured Caroline the woman would have a small dowry, nothing like *her* twenty thousand pounds.

The lights dimmed and the performance commenced so try as she might, Miss Bingley could no longer see the occupants of the Darcy box.

~~~~~~~/~~~~~~~

As soon as the lights burned bright at the end of the first act, Miss Bingley again trained her glasses on the Darcy box. The interloper and her intended practically had their heads together.

"Charles, do you know who those people in the Darcy box are?" she demanded.

Bingley trained his Galilean binoculars in the direction his sister was looking. As he moved his glasses he saw a flash of blonde and immediately traversed back the way he had been moving.

There sitting and speaking to Lord Hilldale was the most perfect blonde angel he had ever seen.

Seeing her brother was fixated on the blonde, Miss Bingley elbowed him in his ribs. Bingley reluctantly swung his vision to the Darcy box. "I only know one of the men. He is Mr. Edward Gardiner, the owner of an import-export company our late father had some dealings with."

"How can the Darcy's entertain a tradesman?" Miss Bingley hissed.

Not wanting to cause an argument, Bingley did not point out his sister's hypocrisy by reminding her, they were the children of a tradesman and the money for her oft boasted-about dowry was all from trade. Additionally, Bingley did not want to tell his sister he knew Mr. Gardiner because he was himself still active in trade. What he had said about his father, had basically been the truth.

Miss Bingley stood up to begin her way up to the Darcy box. She stopped when her brother placed a restraining hand on her arm.

"More than half of the intermission is over, we will not reach them before the lights go down again," Bingley stated, "The intermission after the second act is longer, so as soon as the next act ends, I will accompany you." He had to meet the angel.

~~~~~~~/~~~~~~~

Andrew and Jane were the only two left in the box as Lord Matlock, Mr. Philips, and Richard had gone to find refreshments while Lady Matlock and Mrs. Philips had joined those in the Darcy box.

"Miss Bennet, Jane, my attentions to you have been too marked for you not to recognise my interest in you, which is completely honourable. If you grant it, I would like to enter a formal courtship with you," Andrew stated as he looked directly into her cerulean blue eyes. "During the time we have been together, I have developed extremely tender feelings for you, teetering on the precipice of love. I have never been drawn to another woman before you, and I am quite sure there can never be any other than you for me."

"As I do not feel quite the same for you," Jane did not miss how Andrew's face fell a little, "in fact, I may already be in love with you," her suitor's face was beaming now, "I would like nothing better than to be courted by you," Jane responded as she glowed with pleasure. "You will have to speak first to Lizzy though, and then with her agreement, to my uncles. Is it not strange my younger sister is technically my guardian?"

Before Andrew could respond, the rest of those seated with them in the box returned. No one commented on the look of bliss shared by Andrew and Jane.

~~~~~~~/~~~~~~~

At the next intermission, before all the lights were lit, Miss Bingley was dragging her brother towards the nearest stairs, not giving a whit on whose toes she stepped in her haste.

When they arrived at the Darcy box, she did not wait to be invited to enter, she simply barged in. From close-up she could see the intimacy between her intended and the raven-haired beauty and that drove any discretion from her mind.

"I suppose you are connected to the tradesman who wheedled his way into my friends, the Darcys' box," Miss Bingley sneered at the dark-haired young lady next to the Darcy heir.

If she had taken the trouble to look, she would have seen the Duke and Duchess of Bedford, the Earls of Jersey and Matlock along with their Countesses looking at her as if she was fit for Bedlam. All Miss Bingley saw, however, was the person standing too close to the one she counted as her own.

Elizabeth shook her head so all the men and women who were about to spring to her defence restrained themselves. "Even though we have not been introduced, I am proud to say the *tradesman,* as you called him, is a much-loved uncle," Elizabeth responded sweetly.

"How did one with ties to trade force herself on the younger Mr. Darcy?" Miss Bingley spat. "Some may think you prettyish, but you have no style, no jewellery to speak of, I am sure you do not have close to my twenty thousand pound dowry, and your complexion is so brown. I suppose that is from working as a shopgirl somewhere."

Bingley was doing his best to fade into the background hoping he could simply go to the neighbouring box to meet the angel when Gardiner recognised him. "I assume that person is your sister?" Gardiner barked at Bingley.

"Yes, she is," Bingley admitted with great chagrin. "Miss Caroline Bingley."

"Miss Bingley, your father was in trade, your brother *is* in trade, and you dare to disdain others for the same background as yourself?" Gardiner pointed out.

Before she could respond, her pallor turned a deep shade of puce. There was nothing Caroline Bingley hated more than having her roots pointed out, especially in front of those whom she was trying to impress. The young lady next to her Mr. Darcy stood.

"Lady Anne, will you please introduce this person who has invaded our pleasant time without invitation?" Elizabeth requested with a twinkle in her eye.

Caroline was about to berate the person for daring to ask to be introduced to one so far above her as Caroline knew she was. Lady Anne spoke first.

"It will be my displeasure before we rid ourselves of this blight forever, *Your Grace,*" Lady Anne averred.

Caroline's world came to a sudden halt. She must have

misheard. Lady Anne responded as if the one before her was a...duchess! No, it could not be she had just verbally attacked a duchess with so many members of the *Ton* looking on.

If only she could have disappeared. Instead, she had to stand there and try to salvage some dignity. "Lady Elizabeth, this pretentious harpy is Miss Caroline Bingley of Scarborough, the daughter of an honourable *tradesman*. Miss Bingley, *Her Grace*, Lady Elizabeth Chamberlain, Duchess of Hertfordshire and Marchioness of Hertford Heights."

While Caroline Bingley was wishing herself away—anywhere but where she was—the identity of the beauty on the Darcy heir's arm was soon spread to the farthest corners of the theatre.

"Bingley, how many times have you been told your sister is not welcome among us?" William shook his head as he spoke to his friend. "Until and unless you are willing and able to exert control over your sister, who has most certainly ruined herself tonight, I will not know you."

Both Bingleys left the Darcy box in shock. They made for the exit and called for their carriage. One saw all her dreams disappear as wisps of smoke in the wind while her brother was finally asking himself if the cost of placating his younger sister was too high a price to bear. He also realised that he never met the blonde angel!

Back in the box, Elizabeth was introduced to the Rhys-Davies and De Melvilles. Both couples along with their sons and daughters who had accompanied them to the Drury Lane were invited back to Hertfordshire House for supper, an invitation that was gladly accepted.

CHAPTER 31

A t supper, which was thoroughly enjoyed by all, Elizabeth had the Duke of Bedford on her left hand side and William to her right.

Uncle Edward, who had not felt comfortable attending the performance without his wife, had said his farewells and left for home directly from the theatre. Thankfully, if the subject of the sale of the shipyards was broached, Uncle Frank was present.

No business had been discussed during the meal and the Duke had taken no offence if his hostess had awarded the young Darcy most of her attention. Being one who had married for love, Bedford recognised the signs in the two.

There was a brief separation of the sexes and when the men rejoined the ladies, Bedford approached Lady Elizabeth who was seated with her older sister, Hilldale, and William Darcy.

"If you will pardon this old man, may I have a few words with the Duchess?" Bedford requested. No one objected. The Duke assisted Lady Elizabeth to stand and led her to a settee which was unoccupied. "As one of your guardians is present, would you object if I ask Mr. Philips to join us?" Bedford enquired.

"Please do. If this is regarding the shipyards, it will be for the best for Uncle Frank to be a party to our discussion," Elizabeth agreed.

Bedford and Philips returned within a minute to where Elizabeth was seated. "My solicitor received a note

SHANA GRANDERSON A LADY

from Mr. Marylebone regarding your willingness to sell your shipbuilding interests, is that accurate?" Bedford verified.

"Your information is correct," Elizabeth confirmed. "My uncles and I discussed the price Mr. Marylebone related, and we think it is a fair price for the three yards."

Philips nodded his agreement. "If that is still the amount you are offering we see no need for delay," Philips added.

"If only all negotiation were so easy. Should my solicitor send the proposed agreement to you or the offices of Marylebone and Scrooge?" Bedford enquired as he extended his hand to Philips who shook it.

"I will review the contracts with him, but as Marylebone is more familiar with my niece's holdings, send the documents to him," Philips stated.

"It will be so." Bedford turned to Lady Elizabeth. "May I tell you how happy we are you are free of that blackguard?"

"Please do. Although, no one can possibly feel more relief over his being sent to ███████ fires than myself," Elizabeth inclined her head. "The mortal world is a far better place for his not being part of it."

The Earl and Countess of Jersey were preparing to depart so they approached Lady Elizabeth to make their farewells.

"Lord Jersey you must allow me to thank you for the service you did me, and many others, by dispatching that man," Elizabeth stood and curtseyed to the Earl.

"As much as I abhor violence, in this instance, it was the right thing to do," Lord Jersey responded. "You of course know we were prepared for him thanks to Mr. Wickham, do you not?"

"Yes, I am fully aware of George Wickham's part in all of this. I am well pleased Lady Sarah was never in harm's way at any point," Elizabeth stated as she looked at the Countess.

300

"My daughter, Alicia," Lady Jersey cocked her head to her daughter who was sitting with Lady Marie Rhys-Davies and her brother, Viscount Westmore, "and I were far from Jersey House when he met his end," Lady Jersey related. "I had been willing to act as bait in the trap, but my Cyril would hear none of it." Lady Jersey looked at her husband lovingly. She smiled and turned back to the Duchess. "That Miss Bingley who you encountered this evening has been trying to gain a voucher for Almack's for some years now. Even before she ruined herself at the Drury Lane tonight she would have never been gratified."

"It was only a matter of time before Miss Bingley caused her expulsion from society," Lady Anne added as she arrived with her husband and son to convey thanks and farewells. "Sarah, it surprises me how she kept applying to you and the other patronesses regardless of how many times she had been refused."

"Her pursuit of my person proves she is unable to take no for an answer when it is stated as clearly as can be," William opined.

"Are you pained it cost you a friendship with Mr. Bingley?" Elizabeth enquired concernedly. "I understand from your Fitzwilliam cousins it was a friendship of some years."

Her worrying about others regardless of what was happening to her was one of the many things which attracted William to Lady Elizabeth. "My hope is he will mature and grow a spine. If that occurs, we may be friends again at some point."

Within a few minutes, all the guests took their leave which left Elizabeth, her sisters and the Philipses to make for their bedchambers.

~~~~~~~/~~~~~~~

Even though he had volunteered to join them to journey into Hertfordshire, Edward Gardiner had been excused by all of his family members and told to remain in London with his wife and three children as they waited for the fourth to be born.

Rather than make for Longbourn, the coaches arrived at Lucas Lodge. Elizabeth, as did her sisters—all of whom had decided to follow Elizabeth's lead regarding mourning Mr. Bennet, had no desire to see Mrs. Bennet as she was still living at the former Bennet estate. The four Lucases who were at home—Johnny had returned to Oxford where he was in is first year—were waiting for the travellers to alight.

"Eliza it is so good to see you back in the neighbourhood again," Sir William enthused as he pulled her into a hug.

"Father," Franklin chuckled, "do not squeeze all of Her Grace's air out."

"Franklin Lucas, you have known me from the time I was born, you will call me Eliza like the rest of your family does, or," Elizabeth raised her nose with mock haughtier, "I will have you sent to the tower where you will lose your head."

"Yes, Your Grace," Franklin teased playfully. "It is good to see you again, *Eliza*."

"Sir William, would you object if we invite the new master of Longbourn to join us here?" Elizabeth requested. She had received an affirmative response via her uncle's offices. "I am sure you know there is an objectionable person residing at Longbourn. One who I choose not to see."

"Eliza, you are like a third daughter to me, so of course you may," Sir William averred.

"Lotte where is this *mythical* suitor of yours?" Franklin jested with his sister who he had been missing.

"Lawrence Portnoy is no spectre," Jane spoke up. "I would not be surprised if he asks for her hand soon."

"Our Jane is being courted," Lydia informed everyone as they entered the manor house. Lydia's revelation caused her eldest sister to blush a deeper shade of scarlet.

Blessings from Lizzy and the uncles for the courtship had been granted without delay.

"Did Lord Hilldale finally get around to making it official?" Lady Lucas smiled.

"Yes, he did, at the theatre yester-evening," Elizabeth related gleefully.

"How long do you think it will be before William Darcy has a question for you, sister dearest," Jane responded with raised eyebrows.

"Jane Bennet!" Now it was Elizabeth's turn to blush deeply. "May I sit and write a note to be sent to Longbourn? I need to inform the heir we are here." Elizabeth changed the subject most decidedly. "What is he like?"

"He and his mother, Mrs. Ophelia Collins, who is the new mistress of the estate, much to Mrs. Bennet's protests, seem like pleasant people," Lady Lucas revealed. "He is not the most intelligent person you will meet, but his mother mitigates much of his silliness, and even better yet, will tolerate no nonsense from Mrs. Bennet. He also happens to be awed by titles."

"In that case, I will invite both of them, not just Mr. Collins, to attend us here as soon as may be today, if that is convenient with you and Sir William," Elizabeth responded.

"We have nothing we must do today," Sir William confirmed after his wife nodded to him.

Elizabeth sat at Sir William's desk to write the note. Seeing Charlotte's father was about to leave the study, Elizabeth requested he remain. It took very little time to scribe the invitation. Sir William rang for the housekeeper and told her to send a groom with the note to Longbourn and that it should only be put into either Mr. Collins or his mother's hands.

"You asked me to remain?" Sir William pointed out when the housekeeper was on her way to carry out his orders.

"Sir William, since that man's death, I find I have more wealth than I know with what to do..." Elizabeth shared the essentials without giving specific amounts. "I tell you this not to boast, but so you will understand what I am about to offer will not in any way affect me or the following generations in the least. I have spoken to my uncles and if you agree, they do as well. It is my desire to dower Charlotte and Maria with five and twenty thousand pounds each. In addition, as he is a second son and must shift for himself, I will establish a legacy in the same amount for Johnny. As the heir, Franklin would receive ten thousand pounds."

The normally garrulous Sir William had been robbed of the power of speech. On the one hand, he did not want Eliza to use her wealth on his family, but how could he refuse such a gift which would give his children choices like they had never had before, even with the small amount he had been earning from Gardiner.

Elizabeth hoped she had not insulted Sir William with her offer. She saw the emotions playing over his face. "Before you make your decision know that this money will not even come from the vast accounts in the banks. I am in the process of selling the ship building yards. After what I am giving to each of my sisters for a dowry, and the total I would like to gift to your children, there will still be a significant portion of the money remaining which I will receive for the sale. In addition, I am sure you know the man who was my husband used his power and wealth to hurt others." Sir William nodded it was so. "I am determined to do the exact opposite and this is but the beginning."

After weighing her words and realising he could not rob his children of such a future, Sir William reached a decision. "In that case, Eliza, with my and Lady Lucas's undying gratitude, we accept your overly generous gift."

For the second time that day, Sir William pulled Eliza into a warm hug. At his request, Elizabeth sent Lady Lucas in to see her husband in his study.

"Your father accepted my gift," Elizabeth whispered to Charlotte on sitting next to her in the drawing room.

Having promised to accept her father's decision, Charlotte said nothing except shared her heartfelt thanks.

To say Lady Lucas was shocked when her husband related what Eliza was gifting her children would have been rather a gross understatement. Like her husband, as soon as she got past the idea of accepting such a thing from Eliza, she saw the choices which would be open to her children.

Lady Lucas smiled to herself as she was fairly sure Charlotte's dowry would not remain with her for long and would soon be part of her marriage settlement with Lawrence Portnoy.

~~~~~~~/~~~~~~~

"Where are you and your mother off to, again without me," Fanny whined.

"We have been invited to Lucas Lodge by the Duchess of Hertfordshire," Collins preened.

"Then I *must* accompany you," Fanny insisted.

"No, Mrs. Bennet, you will not," Ophelia Collins interjected. She knew the woman may be able to browbeat her son, but she was no wilting flower. "Unless you would like to be arrested for arriving at Lucas Lodge uninvited." Ophelia challenged and did not miss how the nasty woman blanched. She turned to her son and with a much softer voice asked, "Clem, did Her Grace not write for us not to bother to arrive if we bring Mrs. Bennet with us?"

"Yes Mother, you have the right of it. Come Mother, we must away." Collins led his mother out of the drawing room and to the waiting carriage.

Ophelia was determined that Mrs. Bennet's sojourn at their estate would be of short duration. It was still only days since her husband's death and Ophelia did not want to be heartless and turn the widow out quite yet, regardless of how much Fanny Bennet was disdained in the area.

Fanny was more scared than disappointed she would not be in her high and mighty daughter's company. If the spiteful girl convinced the Collinses to turn her out into the hedgerows, how would she survive? Her awful husband had died leaving her just over eight hundred pounds of her dowry remaining. She could not live on about thirty pounds per annum.

But she had no one to whom she could turn. Her brother and sister both refused to see her and they were her only family in the world. This was all that damned Lizzy's fault!

~~~~~~~/~~~~~~~

Even being warned Mr. Collins was fascinated by people of rank, seeing him genuflect before her as if she was a queen made Elizabeth want to burst into laughter. She had to fight to maintain her equanimity.

"Sir William, will you introduce our distant cousins to us please?" Elizabeth requested.

The Collinses were introduced to Her Grace, the four other Bennet sisters, and the Philipses. "It is such a great honour you bestow on us, Your Grace..." Collins began to bow again.

"Clem dear," Ophelia placed a restraining hand on her son's arm before he could bow low repeatedly. "Why do we not allow Her Grace to inform us why she invited us here today."

"You are so wise, Mother," Collins agreed. "Please pardon me, Your Grace."

"Mr. Collins, Mrs. Collins, please be seated," Elizabeth invited.

Before her son could unleash another speech, Ophelia sat and made sure he sat next to her without a further word.

"We are at your disposal, Your Grace," Ophelia stated and then waited, a restraining hand remaining on her son's forearm.

"Mr. Collins, am I correct you were not brought up to manage an estate?" Elizabeth began.

Before Collins could launch into a long soliloquy, his mother spoke first. "That is true, Your Grace."

"We are family, please address me as Lady Elizabeth." She paused and looked from mother to son. "In that case, as the entail ended with you, Mr. Collins, I would like to purchase Longbourn. I am willing to pay you sixty thousand pounds, which you will find based on the income having fallen to well below two thousand per annum, and the profit a fraction of that, is a very generous price."

Before her son could say anything, Ophelia did. "Clem, you have always wanted to study and become a clergyman, have you not?" Collins nodded. "We have never had the funds for you to study at university before. If you agree to sell the estate to Her Grace, not only will you have more than enough money to study, but we will be able to purchase a nice house in Wiltshire near where we used to live in that rented cottage and have a very comfortable life."

Collins thought about things for a while and the more he did, the more attractive the offer became. He was intimidated by estate management, even with his mother to assist him. He did want to study and take orders, and Mother would never have to worry about money again. Not only that, they would be able to afford servants and so much more. At the estate's current income, it would take him well over fifty years to earn as much as Her Grace was offering.

"Mother is correct, I will sell Longbourn to you for the amount you offered, Your...Lady Elizabeth," Collins decided.

"Perfect, my Uncle Philips will have the papers drawn up. As soon as the bill of sale is signed by both of us, you will have your money," Elizabeth stated happily.

"What of Mrs. Bennet who is still, for now at least, at Longbourn?" Ophelia enquired.

"Uncle Philips will go and see Mrs. Bennet and explain her options for her future to her," Elizabeth stated without emotion.

She had a plan for Longbourn which did not include Fanny Bennet remaining at the estate.

CHAPTER 32

F anny Bennet sniffed with disdain as her traitorous sister's husband entered the small parlour at Longbourn.

At first, she had refused to meet with Frank Philips but had changed her mind with alacrity when Mrs. Collins told her if she refused to do what was being asked of her, Fanny would be evicted from the house that very day.

"Mrs. Bennet, you have not been informed of this fact yet, but Her Grace is purchasing Longbourn from Mr. Collins and as such will be the new owner in a matter of days," Philips stated in a very businesslike tone. "You must comprehend Her Grace will not allow you to remain here once the estate is hers."

"That ungrateful, disobedient, wilful girl," Fanny wailed. "She is to throw me into the hedgerows!"

"Before you put on a performance which would be appreciated in any theatre in London, as much as you deserve it, Her Grace does not desire to see you turned out into the street with nothing to your name," Philips informed the avaricious woman.

"My Lydia or Jane must have convinced Miss Lizzy to do her duty to me," Fanny squealed. She thought this was to be her last day living in comfort, however, she now believed that surely Miss Lizzy would place her at one of her estates, or better yet one of the houses in London or Bath.

"This was the Duchess's decision alone. You had better pay attention, Mrs. Bennet," Philips admonished. "You have two choices and two choices only. One, you will have a small cottage in Lerwick, which is on the largest of the Shetland Islands and your five thousand pounds will be restored to you. Two, you will leave this house on the morrow with the remainder of your dowry and be left to shift for yourself."

All visions of her living in luxury came crashing down around her head. She knew she had no choice. "Where is this Lerwick?" she asked defeatedly.

"Lerwick is on one of the almost one hundred islands which make up the Shetland Islands. It happens to be the largest island in the chain. Where you will be living is approximately one hundred miles off the northeast coast of Scotland," Philips explained.

"That uppity girl is sending me to purgatory!" Fanny screeched.

"As I said, you have a choice. What will it be?" Philips insisted dispassionately.

Fanny began to cry crocodile tears. She seemed to forget her put on tears had never affected her sister's husband before. Even had she remembered, it would have not stopped her trying it now.

"Surely you do not desire to see me sent to the other side of the world?" Fanny leaned forward suggestively making sure her bosom was on full display. Fanny looked at Philips fetchingly, batting her eyelids, so there was no doubt of what she was offering him.

"You disgust me!" Philips barked out at the woman with undisguised asperity. "If it were not for Her Grace's insistence you not be turned out into your beloved *hedgerows* without a choice, I would have you ejected from this house this very day! Your sister, who I love dearly, has something you will never have—character." Philips paused as he reined in his anger. "Now choose! There are no other options than the two I enumerated."

Fanny shrank back at her brother-in-law's fury. How

was it he did not fall for her feminine wiles? Seeing the implacable resentment in his eyes, she came to the realisation she in fact had no choice but to accept the banishment. Without her full dowry, she would have no way to live or eat.

"The first option is what I choose," Fanny Bennet stated almost softly.

Yes, none of her former friends would see her, but she had still remained at Longbourn, in the neighbourhood she had grown up in. It was only at that moment Fanny had her first, albeit fleeting, doubts regarding the way she had treated her second daughter.

"In that case, be ready to depart at first light on the morrow. You will be transported to Aberdeen in Scotland. From there you will board a ship which will convey you to Lerwick." Philips drew a breath. "The principal of five thousand pounds will be invested with Mr. Gardiner. What is left after your rent is paid from the interest on that sum will be handed to you each quarter. Do not even think you can return to the mainland. You will be watched and if you attempt such, the money Her Grace has added will be withdrawn and you will be left to shift for yourself with very little money. Do you understand Mrs. Bennet?"

Miss Lizzy had always been too clever and now the girl had thought of a way to well and truly imprison her in this far-flung place. Fanny nodded her head.

Philips departed and left Fanny to begin her packing. She was about to call for Hill when she remembered the new mistress of the estate demanded Fanny request any assistance she wanted from a Longbourn servant from Mrs. Collins first.

As much as she hated having to humble herself before the interloper, Fanny knew she needed help, so she went to seek out Mrs. Collins.

~~~~~~~/~~~~~~~

Up until the carriage pulled away from the house she

had lived in since her marriage, Fanny Bennet had been expecting a reprieve of some sort. None had come and other than the servants who had loaded her worldly possessions onto the conveyance, not a single person had come to see her off.

As the equipage turned out of the estate's gateposts, Fanny looked back longingly. She knew she would never see this place again.

During the drive through Meryton Fanny kept herself pushed back against the squabs. She did not want her last memory of the town to be the disdainful looks she would receive, if she was seen, from any of those who were already up and about.

Soon, the town she had spent her life in was behind her. Like Longbourn, she was certain she would never see Meryton again.

As she settled down for what she had been told would be a six day carriage ride, her thoughts were about the one who had been the bane of her existence: Miss Lizzy! If only the Duke had chosen Jane like he had been supposed to do! Everything would have been as it should be, and she would not be on her way to some godforsaken place in the middle of the sea.

Fanny never noticed the self-same daughter, accompanied by two of her massive guards, standing and watching the conveyance as it passed the Red Lion Inn, where she had taken all of the rooms for her sojourn in Meryton.

John Biggs had found a good group of men who had been employed as guards, more than enough for two men to be assigned to each of her sisters, the four men who would be living in Lerwick to make sure Mrs. Bennet never attempted to return to England, and some additional men to be placed as needed.

Two of the men had departed as soon as Mrs. Bennet accepted her fate, the other two were travelling with her.

Elizabeth watched until she could no longer see the back of the carriage. Mrs. Bennet was out of their life forever. The money Elizabeth had added to restore the woman's dowry had been well spent.

Knowing how extravagant Mrs. Bennet tended to be, she had insisted the woman not have access to the principal. If she wanted to waste her money each quarter and not have enough to live on, that would he her choice and problem.

She smiled as she thought of the upcoming meeting at Uncle Frank's offices. The purchase of Longbourn would be final. A few days after that, Netherfield Park would be hers as well. Her intention was to reunite the two largest parts which had been one before a dissolute ancestor had lost so much of the Bennets' land. The Gouldings, Lucases, and Purvises had no interest in selling their estates, which would have restored all historical Bennet lands.

The enlarged Longbourn would be presented to Mary as part of her dowry. Mary had the most emotional ties to the Meryton area. Only on her marriage to one she loved and respected, and who felt the same for her, would the estate be signed over to Mary.

The same was true for her other sisters. Castlemere would of course be Lydia's. Jane and Kate would be allowed to choose from the other six estates when they married.

Knowing Jane's future husband had a large estate, and would one day have all those which belonged to the Matlock earldom made it less urgent to inform Jane. Elizabeth was sure Jane would turn down the estate, and she would not try and press too hard if that indeed happened to be the case.

With John Biggs and Brian Johns escorting her, Elizabeth made her way to Oakham Mount. The sun was already above the horizon when she arrived, but that was no matter to her.

John had gone up the path to verify no one was on

the summit. On his return, Elizabeth had walked up to the flattened top of the hill. Everything was as it was the last time she had been here. That was before *he* had caused her to leave the neighbourhood.

She twirled around laughing with pleasure at being back in a place she had believed she would never see again. The stand of four oak trees, the benches below them, and the boulders at various points were all exactly as she recalled. She touched the boulder in the eastern corner of the summit reverently.

How many times had she escaped from Mrs. Bennet and sat in this very spot to contemplate her life and watch the sun greet the new day. In a few hours, with some signatures and money paid, it would all be hers. Oakham Mount was on Longbourn's land.

As Elizabeth sat there, she realised the only thing which would have made her enjoyment complete was if William had been here with her. She missed him when they were apart. In fact, it was as if a part of her heart was not in her chest. She knew where the missing piece resided—it was with William.

For a little while, even while acknowledging she loved him, Elizabeth had thought about never again placing herself at the mercy of a man.

She had quickly realised if she allowed the bitterness of being married to *him* to govern her future choices, then *he* would still be controlling her. That was something she would never allow! The best and total repudiation of *that man* would be for her to marry. Not just to remarry, but to marry a man she loved and respected and who felt the same way about her.

William was that man. As she sat and looked out over the rolling land to the east, Elizabeth knew one thing for certain. If William asked her to marry him, she would accept without a moment's hesitation. That she would gain a wonderful mother and father only added to her desire to marry the man she loved. It did not hurt she would be gaining a fifth sister she already loved dearly as well.

All she needed was for William to propose. She already knew William was a very careful man and more than likely would not do anything unless he was sure she was receptive. In that case she would need to give him a subtle hint, if subtlety did not work, she would be a little more direct in her approach.

As soon as the decision was made, Elizabeth felt a lightness she had not experienced since before meeting the vile old man. If things went according to the way she thought they would, she would be gaining two more brothers soon enough and Charlotte would become her cousin.

With a renewed spring in her step, Elizabeth made her way down the path to where John and Brian awaited her.

~~~~~~~/~~~~~~~

William Darcy felt like he was in a daze. He could not concentrate on anything. How was it he had become such a mooncalf of a man? All over a slip of a woman who he was missing terribly.

Why had he not thought to ask if she wanted him to join those travelling into Hertfordshire? If he had, he would not have been missing Elizabeth the way he was.

He missed smelling her delightful lavender scent, the gleam in her eyes when she knew she was about to win a debate, her wit, her intelligence, her compassion—he missed everything about her. It was as if she held his heart in the palm of her delicate hand. His heart was with her in Hertfordshire, and William had no desire for her to return it to him...ever.

He did not know if he possessed her heart the way she owned his. He hoped it would not be many more days before Elizabeth returned to London. When he was in her company he felt pulled to her as if by some invisible force.

If she did not desire to have him as her husband, his heart would forever be lost in a wilderness of sadness, but above all else, he wanted her to be happy—even if that meant her happiness rested with another or not marrying again. After her experience with her first marriage, he would have been able to understand her never wanting to once again be someone's wife. With her having been blackmailed into marrying the bastard, he never wanted her to feel pressured to accept him—or any other—if that was not her free will.

Based on her request that her unborn child could take the name of the man she married—if she remarried, William had hope that is what she wanted. The fact she had looked at him as she had said that was encouraging. And if she did, his prayer was he would be the man she desired to have as her husband.

As soon as he knew Elizabeth was back in London, he needed to see her and try and divine her feelings for him. Perhaps he would receive some sort of sign.

He was shaken out of his musings by the arrival of three of his cousins. Two of them were as forlorn as he that the lady of his choice was not in Town. At least Andrew had been granted a courtship by Jane Bennet. All that was needed now was to find a way so Richard would not need to remain an officer in His Majesty's army. That was a problem for another day. After greetings were exchanged, the four young men made their way to the billiards room.

~~~~~~~/~~~~~~~

Given Longbourn became her property on the tenth day of April (the same day Mary turned fifteen) for the first time since the day the Gardiners had taken them away from the estate, all five sisters were together in the house of their birth to celebrate the dual milestone.

The two Collinses had been ready to depart that morning, but they had been invited to remain to honour Mary's birthday. They had gladly accepted with Mrs. Collins restricting her son's effusions and making sure he did not toady up to Lady Elizabeth.

Mrs. Hill and the female servants had cried tears of happiness to have the girls they loved back in their childhood home. Even the stoic Mr. Hill's eyes were suspiciously moist.

An impromptu birthday party was soon planned. The Lucases and Philipses were present, as would be expected. As word that the sisters were at Longbourn spread, callers streamed in to come see them. Very soon, the celebration of Mary's birth became a party to also mark the return of the sisters to the area.

Pleasure was expressed by the many neighbours who called at Longbourn regarding Elizabeth's freedom and the fact none in the neighbourhood would ever have to encounter Mrs. Bennet again. No words of sorrow for Mr. Bennet's passing were mentioned either.

If anyone from the area noticed or disagreed with none of the sisters wearing mourning garb, not one word was said.

During the celebration, Mr. Hill brought Miss Lizzy the newspaper. It contained the royal decree naming her family name to be Gardiner and stating that the name of Chamberlain would not continue regardless of whether Her Grace delivered a son or a daughter.

Her final outward connection to *him* had been severed. Never would his name be mentioned again and the child she was carrying would not know about him.

Lady Elizabeth Rose Gardiner was contented.

CHAPTER 33

In the coach on the return to London the morning after the party, Elizabeth could see Lydia mulling something over. A few times her youngest sister seemed like she was on the verge of asking a question, but each time she seemed to think better of it.

"Lyddie, you know there is no embargo on asking questions," Elizabeth told her sister gently. "If you have a query, go ahead and ask it. If it is not something I am able to, or choose not to answer, I will inform you."

"It is the change of your name and the ending of the Chamberlain line which has had me cogitating," Lydia shared.

"Let me guess, you are wondering why I asked Her Majesty to remove that name from the line, are you not?" Elizabeth conjectured.

"Yes, it is. I know how evil your late husband was," Lydia responded, "however, did I not hear that his parents and those before him were honourable and good, Godly people?"

Elizabeth considered her sister's words. Lydia was but eleven but was showing much thoughtfulness in what she said. "It is something which was canvassed with Her Majesty," Elizabeth began to explain. "What you alluded to is true about all those who came *before him* being good people." Elizabeth paused to consider how to explain it to Lydia. "You like to ride, do you not Lyddie?"

"Very much," Lydia responded confusedly.

"Let us suppose there was a bloodline which had produced good animals who were much sought after to ride."

Lydia nodded still not quite sure where Lizzy was headed with her analogy. "Something happens to corrupt the line producing unrideable horses who only desire to hurt their riders. Due to the corruption, regardless of the past, the line must be ended and a new one begun."

Understanding dawned for Lydia as well as the other three sisters who had been listening intently. "Your late husband is the corruption of the line, and starting anew does not negate the goodness of those who came before him."

"That is it exactly! Even though *he* is with the ▮▮▮▮ where he richly deserves to be, I am denying him the fondest wish he had." Elizabeth further explained, "the main objective by enslaving me and making me *his* brood mare was so that his line, his *name* would continue on after him. With the royals' help, it will be made known in the realm that the change of name in no way sullies those who came before the deplorable ancient man."

"I am happy Lyddie asked you this Lizzy," Jane stated. "I too wondered about the same thing, but I did not want to raise something you may have found distasteful."

Mary and Kate nodded indicating they were of similar minds.

"Please take what I said to Lyddie about asking what you desire to heart. You are my dearest sisters, my closest family, my flesh and blood. I will never be upset at a question from any of you," Elizabeth stated. "You should know if I bear a female child, I will, thankfully, not be the dowager duchess any longer. The title will transfer to my daughter and her son will be the next duke. In the case I am blessed with a son, I will have to keep the title, little that I want it."

"If you marry again. Let us say the son of a gentleman farmer," Mary smiled at her sister slyly, "the most you will be called is Lady Elizabeth unless the occasion is extremely formal."

Mary was lucky she was sitting across the coach from Elizabeth else the latter would have swatted her, albeit playfully.

"It will be your time to look at men as more than big brothers in two or three years, Mary," Kate pointed out.

"It is a long time off," Mary waved her younger sister's comment away. As she did the visions of a certain captain danced in her mind.

For the remainder of the ride to London, less weighty subjects were discussed. When they were not occupied with their younger sisters, the two eldest sisters' minds would contemplate the virtues and visages of the man each loved.

~~~~~~~/~~~~~~~

Not an hour after arriving at Hertfordshire House, Peter, the Gardiner footman (the same one who had delivered the letter to Elizabeth at Castlemere), arrived to deliver a note informing the residents that Madeline Gardiner had been taken to bed for her lying-in.

The coaches were ordered made ready again and soon the newly arrived residents of the house were on their way to Gracechurch Street.

On arriving, Philips went to keep his brother company, the four maiden Bennet sisters went to entertain their cousins, and Aunt Hattie with Elizabeth made their way up to the birthing chamber.

"Lizzy dear, as one who is no longer a maiden, you are welcome here, but are you sure you want to witness the travails of childbirth before it is your time?" Madeline asked between pains.

"Yes, Aunt Maddie. It will help prepare me," Elizabeth replied firmly. "And I remember what Mrs. Medford told me, no two births are quite the same."

"In that case..." Madeline winced as another, bigger pain

than those before, hit. "As I was saying, you are welcome to remain."

Even though Hattie Philips had never been blessed with a child of her own, she had attended all five lying-ins of her younger sister as well as being present when Maddie birthed Lilly. Hence, she was a great help to the midwife.

As was often the case for a lady who had borne more than one child previously, the labours were not very long and two hours later, the squalling of a newborn babe was heard.

Elizabeth had the pleasure of assisting the housekeeper to clean and swaddle the newborn. In the meanwhile, a maid was changing the bedding and another helping the mistress to change.

The housekeeper handed the precious bundle to the Duchess. "You hand him to his mother, Your Grace."

She gingerly took the babe who was asleep, and handed him to his proud mamma. "Have you and Uncle Edward considered names yet?" Elizabeth asked as she placed the slumbering babe in his mother's welcoming arms.

The newest Gardiner squirmed a little when he was transferred, but soon settled, with his little lips making a sucking noise. "We did select both a girl's and a boy's name. If it had been a girl, she would have been named Bethany after her brave cousin, but this little one is Peter for my late father," Madeline revealed. "Lizzy, will you please go tell Edward to come meet his son."

Elizabeth did not need to be asked twice. She found her uncles in the drawing room with her sisters and young cousins. Everyone was looking at her expectantly.

"It is a boy, both mother and Peter are doing very well," Elizabeth reported.

Gardiner sprang out of his chair like a young man, kissed his niece on her forehead and was up the stairs before anyone could move.

It was rather late that night when the coaches returned to Hertfordshire House. The only one who was missing was Hattie Philips who would remain with her sister for a few days.

~~~~~~~/~~~~~~~

Even though she had not had many hours of sleep, Elizabeth was up and dressed not long after dawn. As was her habit, she did not ring for Loretta, but her maid had an uncanny knack for knowing when she was needed. Hence, she had been ready to assist Her Grace to change into a walking dress. Now that the morning illness had abated, rather than ginger tea, a steaming cup of hot chocolate was waiting for Elizabeth.

As much as she missed *Jamil*, not being able to ride until after she delivered, Elizabeth had decided to leave her beloved mare—she was truly her mare now—in Derbyshire.

After her drink, Elizabeth made her way downstairs where the butler was ready with her gloves, light pelisse, and bonnet.

Unsurprisingly, Brian and John were waiting for her as well. Being that they were in London and not the country John had suggested, and Elizabeth had agreed that a third man join them when she walked out in Town.

The newer man, Albert Smith, was waiting for them on the steps just past the front door of the house. Brian Johns walked ahead of her—she had accepted her guards needed to be aware of where she wanted to walk ahead of time—John Biggs to one side of her and, Albert behind.

In less than a half mile they entered the park and headed for the wide end of the Serpentine.

~~~~~~~/~~~~~~~

William had debated whether to walk or ride in Hyde Park that morning. With the excitement of seeing Elizabeth later in the day, he had woken even earlier than was his wont. In the end, he decided to take Zeus out for a ride.

By the time he reached the stables in the mews, word had reached the grooms he wanted to ride so his stallion was saddled and waiting for him when he arrived. He pulled a large, red apple from his pocket and placed it on his palm to offer to the horse. Zeus nickered in anticipation of his treat. The apple was soon no more.

Once mounted, William headed to the park and entered via the Grosvenor Gate. First, he gave his horse his head as he galloped along Rotten Row. At that time of the morning it was practically deserted. As soon as he judged Zeus had been worked out sufficiently, William slowed to a canter and headed to the narrow end of the Serpentine to ride along the path paralleling its banks to the other end.

About half way along, he slowed to a trot. When he looked up, he thought his eyes were playing tricks on him. There ahead of him, about a hundred yards away was Elizabeth, walking toward him. He did not miss the two giant guards as well as it seemed one more.

The added security made good sense to William. He was not sure if word of her wealth was known in broader society yet, but rather safe than sorry.

He dismounted and began walking with Zeus trailing him towards the lady he loved. She was a vision in the early morning light, even before the sun had risen. If it were not for her guards, looking at her, one would not know she was a person of rank, especially not a duchess, and an extremely wealthy one at that.

She never dressed in too fine a dress, and unless it was a special occasion, the only jewellery she wore was a garnet cross her late grandmother had gifted her.

~~~~~~~/~~~~~~~

Elizabeth had seen the man on the horse riding towards them. She had wished it would be William and when he was close enough to see, she could see her wish had been granted.

Her heart sped up and she missed a breath at the excitement generated by seeing his handsome form as he vaulted from his horse's back and began to walk towards her, beaming a smile which although she could not see at the distance, Elizabeth was sure displayed his dimples in full.

Biggs and Johns knew exactly who the man approaching Her Grace was so they relaxed. Biggs gave a signal to Albert Smith to let him know all was well.

"Good morning, Lady Elizabeth," William greeted. He took one of her dainty hands, bowed over it, and kissed it.

Even though she was wearing gloves—thankfully light ones for the warmer weather—Elizabeth felt a frisson of pleasure when William kissed her hand. She could not help wishing it was not only her hand he was kissing.

"Master William," Elizabeth returned. "I did not think I would meet someone I knew so early in the morning."

"Neither did I," William averred. "However, I hope our meeting by chance like this is not unpleasant."

"Anything but," Elizabeth responded with a becoming blush.

"Would you mind if Zeus and I join you on your walk?" William requested.

"You are both most welcome Sir," Elizabeth granted. "Do one of the men need to lead your horse?"

"No, thank you, Lady Elizabeth," William replied. "He will follow me unless I tell him otherwise." He offered his arm and she rested her hand on it gently.

"Mayhap one day he will meet *Jamil*," Elizabeth said shyly knowing full well what she was implying.

"*Jamil*?" William questioned.

"You did not meet my mare at Castlemere as I was already with child and chose not to ride until after I deliver," Elizabeth explained. "She is an Arabian and her name means beautiful in that language."

"I doubt she is close to as beautiful as you," William stated with a rasp in his voice.

William heard the tinkling laugh he so much loved. "My mare may have something to say about that. Before her, I have never seen a horse preen the way she does."

"Elizabeth, I would like to speak to you privately more than anything, but I will remain silent if you think it is too soon."

He did not notice he had used her familiar name and she did not object at all.

"No William, it is not too soon," Elizabeth stated as she blushed scarlet from the roots of her hair to where her body was covered by her clothing.

"In that case, may I call on you at Hertfordshire House at eleven?"

"You may, I will be very pleased to see you."

William knew he was grinning like a fool, but he could not help himself. He had hoped for a subtle sign she was receptive to hear what he wanted to say, but the message in her response had been as clear as day.

The first question he would ask during the interview was if she desired him to request a courtship or engagement.

He knew her situation was more complicated than most men would expect in the woman they hoped to marry. William however, was sensitive to the challenges of her carrying a child of a man she reviled. He cared not she was not a maiden, or that she was in the family way. Above all, he wanted to support her through the months ahead and for the rest of her life. All he cared about was he would be able to call her his.

Elizabeth was glad she was holding onto William's arm. She felt positively giddy.

She had her choice stolen from her when she married

before, but this time, it was, and would be her decision. As long as William did not care she was no longer considered pure, she could see no impediment to their union.

Her free hand went to her belly as one of them always did when she talked about or thought about the child—the life growing within her—she was carrying.

From her conversations with the Greaves at Falconwood, she had learnt through the anecdotes the butler's father and mother had related what the big mistake the previous master and mistress had made. It had been to relentlessly indulge and spoil their son. He had been an only child and after waiting many years to conceive, his mother had had a very hard, almost life ending, birth.

Were William to propose, she was sure he would agree with her that, son or daughter, this child would be raised with limits and never spoilt. Rather, he or she would have a loving father in William and would be raised to be honourable.

Revelling in one another's company, there was not much more conversation until they returned to Hertfordshire House. "Until eleven," William stated as he bowed over her hand and then kissed it.

"Until eleven," Elizabeth repeated dreamily.

She stood and watched until William rode out of her field of vision and then floated into her house passing a bemused butler who had been holding the front door open for some minutes.

CHAPTER 34

As the clock in the hall struck eleven, Hertfordshire House's butler answered the front door, and like the Duchess had told him to expect, the younger Mr. Darcy was the one waiting to enter the house.

"I believe Her Grace is expecting me," William stated as the butler took his hat and gloves.

"She is Mr. Darcy, however before announcing you to the mistress, her guardians would like to meet with you in the study," the butler informed the guest.

On her return from the park, Elizabeth had informed her Uncle Frank of what had transpired and the fact she had agreed to a private interview with William Darcy. Philips sent a note to Gardiner, who had arrived a half hour before William's visit.

William had been somewhat nervous at having to see her guardians prior to his interview. Afterwards, he had fully expected to approach them. When he entered the study and took note of the fact both men looked like they always did and he could detect no anger in them, William relaxed.

"We would not be doing our duty as Lizzy's guardians if we did not speak with you prior to your seeing her," Gardiner began. "Let me preface this by telling you we are not here to question your honour and nor do we believe, even for the smallest measure of time, your interest in Lizzy is sparked by her vast, and for a lady, unprecedented wealth."

At Gardiner's words, with Philips nodding his

agreement, any tension William felt was banished.

"The reason we wanted to speak to you is to tell you we will not approve an engagement today..." Philips took over.

All of his tension returned. Did the two men before him think he was not good enough for their niece? Thankfully William said nothing.

"...what we want is for you to request only a courtship," Philips completed.

"We think ultimately you and Lizzy will be the ideal pairing, but you know her history and the way she was forced to marry that...sorry excuse for a man!" It was a statement not a question. Gardiner was aware William knew all regarding Lizzy's relationship and reason for marrying the man who had been below contempt. "From what our niece has related to us, you and she met only a few days prior to Easter, is that accurate?"

"It is," William acknowledged.

"That is the reason for our request. We would like you to court her for three months, to really get to know one another. We do not want her to feel she must marry now only to eradicate the stain of that man; we want her to choose to marry for positive reasons." Gardiner paused. "We are not saying that if you two marry now it will not be for the right motivations, but after what she has experienced over the past almost year, we do not want to take any chances with her future happiness."

"At the end of that time, if you offer a proposal of marriage, and she accepts, we will bestow our permission and blessing unreservedly," Philips added.

William cogitated on the uncles' words for some minutes. The more he did so, the more he began to see flaws in their plan.

"On one condition will I agree to your restrictions," William responded. "Have you spoken to Lady Elizabeth and explained why you feel the way you do?"

"We decided to have the conversation with you first," Gardiner admitted.

"Then are you not doing the very thing you are trying to guard against? Taking away her choices?" William pushed.

Both uncles looked sheepish. There was no denying the logic of William's words. "You want us all to speak to Elizabeth first, do you not?" Gardiner realised.

"You have the right of it. If Lady Elizabeth agrees then I am happy to comply," William informed the two men. "However, if she convinces you she knows her own mind and her choice is not the one you prefer, do both of you give your word of honour you will respect her choice?"

"I agree," Gardiner stated.

"As do I," Philips added.

"In wanting to make sure she is able to make her own choices, we almost deprived her of one," Gardiner said stoically.

"Unlike her former parents, never mind the terrible, criminal man she was married to, you both only had her best interests at heart," William stated.

Gardiner and Philips found their opinions of the Darcy heir—which had been very good before—improving. It seemed he understood their niece very well already.

~~~~~~~/~~~~~~~

When Elizabeth entered the study, she had been gloriously happy to see William. Her happiness diminished when she saw her uncles were also with him, and then when her uncles began to speak, she had wanted to lash out at them, all three of them.

Elizabeth's building emotion had been fury that three men had sat around making decisions for her. The more her uncles spoke, the quicker she came to realise William had done

SHANA GRANDERSON A LADY

the opposite while Uncles Edward and Frank had only wanted to protect her right to choose, even if they had put the cart before the horse.

When William had first met her at Castlemere and been rude, he had witnessed the look of fiery anger in her eyes. He had been convinced she would lump him in with her uncles as—he assumed—her righteous anger built at decisions being made without her input.

He had seen the moment she had allowed herself to hear the words and understand it was not what was occurring, and certainly not what he had endorsed.

"You have my thanks for involving me in this discussion about my future," Elizabeth responded evenly. "Although I understand your reasoning uncles, you have to trust that after having my free will subjugated, never will I allow that to happen again. Whatever I agree to or not with regard to my future will be done because it *is* my choice. You both know my financial position." Both uncles allowed it was so. "As such, you know better than anyone the main factor which drives so many ladies in our society to marry—security—is not one of my needs."

The truth of her wealth was unknown to William, but he was aware she had inherited much. He fully intended to suggest—if she accepted him as her husband—the settlement would leave what she brought into the marriage under her control.

"We do know that Lizzy," Philips agreed.

"Then you must trust that whatever decision I make about my future will be my free choice," Elizabeth told her uncles. "There is nothing anyone can do to right the wrongs of the late Mr. Bennet, and being over protective does not balance out his lack of protection."

Gardiner looked at Philips who shrugged his shoulders and then nodded. "You are a very wise lady, Lizzy," Gardiner owned. "We will trust that whatever decision you make will be made because it is what you choose and not because you feel pressured."

"If someone tried to compromise me for my fortune, assuming he survived the encounter with John, Brian, and Albert, I would still not marry him, so I can categorically tell you whatever I accept or deny will not be forced," Elizabeth assured her uncles.

She understood her uncles were motivated by the unwarranted guilt they felt at not having been able to save her before it had been too late. Even had they known ahead of time, she would have done the same thing she had done to protect Jane and all her sisters. Although she had ultimately been blackmailed, it had in the end been a choice.

"Then I suppose Gardiner and I will leave you to it." Philips turned to William. "You two will have ten minutes, the door will not be closed all the way, and bear in mind Biggs and Johns are positioned in the hallway."

A shudder travelled down William's spine. Elizabeth's guards were not men of whom he would ever run afoul. He had no doubt they would do *anything* to protect her.

"Alone at last," Elizabeth smiled at her suitor.

"Lady Elizabeth..." William stopped at her raised hand.

"Elizabeth please, and I will call you William," she commanded with the teasing affectation of imperiousness.

"Yes, *Your Grace*," William gave a low bow in jest. Elizabeth rolled her eyes at his silliness. "As I was about to say, I would like to suggest we do, in fact, begin with a courtship. Perhaps not three months as they wanted, rather a month or less," William recommended. "Before you tell me why I am wrong, allow me to state my reasons." Elizabeth nodded. "We have, in fact, known one another for a few weeks. I am sure I am falling, if not already, in love with you. I suggest this for ourselves and for no one else's opinion. I think spending more time to get to know one another will not be harmful. What think you?"

"Never have I been in love before, but I am almost certain I am in love with you. Your suggestion for a month or *less* for a courtship does make sense." Elizabeth smiled teasingly. "Fitzwilliam Darcy, will you court me officially?"

She thought William had taken offence at her forwardness, so she decided to explain herself to him.

"When *he* proposed, it was an order. I did not want to overstep, I know the asking of the question is in the province of men, but I just wanted to feel like it was truly my free decision this time."

"Elizabeth, if I gave the impression I was anything but charmed at your asking me, I must beg your pardon," William responded with a huge dimple-revealing grin. "I would like nothing more than to court you, Elizabeth Gardiner. Do you have a middle name?"

"It is Rose."

"Yes, Elizabeth Rose Gardiner, yes, as many times as you need to hear it. Yes."

William approached Elizabeth and took each of her dainty hands in one of his. All the while looking into her mesmerising emerald-green eyes, while his own sought permission, which he found there, he gently turned her hands over to expose the underside of her wrists. He placed a lingering kiss first on one and then the other. His lips on the pulse of each wrist sent her heart racing off at a roaring pace. Elizabeth swore she could hear it beating in her ears and it sounded like galloping horses. She knew this was not the time, but how she wished for him to kiss her lips. At least that would be one first they would share. She realised there would be many other firsts.

Once they were married, in her mind it *would* occur, she would never close her eyes when he came to her and she would never have to *prepare* herself. If she knew nothing else, she knew William would always make sure they both experienced pleasure.

She was brought back to the present as she heard William's voice pierce the fog of her dream of future felicity with him.

"Should I invite your uncles to join us?" William grinned. It was the second time he had asked her the same thing.

"Yes, I suppose so," Elizabeth managed.

Permission and blessings for the courtship were bestowed without delay and when informed they would court for a month or less, neither Gardiner nor Philips said a word in opposition.

"Elizabeth, do you object to us making the short drive to Darcy House so we may inform my parents and Anna of our news?" William requested. "I used the curricle to come to your house so it is ready in front of the house. It is just little more than a quarter of a mile."

"My three *small* guards will follow on horses," Elizabeth stated.

So it was a few minutes later, with William driving, that Elizabeth found herself seated on the high bench next to him. Biggs rode alongside while Johns and Smith were positioned a little behind the small carriage.

~~~~~~~/~~~~~~~

"Lizzy! I will have you as a sister. Oh! Even better, I will gain five sisters," Georgiana gushed.

For once Miss Younge did nothing to correct her charge knowing how excited the girl of twelve was.

"We have not agreed to marry yet, Anna," William corrected with an indulgent smile.

"But you will," Lady Anne stated with surety as she

pulled the young lady who she knew would be her daughter before too long into her arms.

Like it always did when she was in Lady Anne's arms, Elizabeth felt the kind of motherly love she had never experienced before meeting her. Neither Elizabeth nor William refuted the claim.

"Would you object if I call you Mama like Anna does," Elizabeth turned to William's father, "and you Papa?"

"Nothing would please me more my dear girl. I always wanted more sons and daughters, it seems that dream is about to come true," Lady Anne responded as some tears of joy rolled down her cheeks.

With suspiciously moist eyes and a voice gruff with emotion, Darcy also happily agreed to Elizabeth's request.

"Lizzy dear, will you not need to notify Her Majesty of your intention to marry again?" Lady Anne enquired.

"I suppose I will." Elizabeth looked at William with love in her eyes. "You will have to accompany me as you did on our last visit, Her Majesty will need to interrogate you to see if you are good enough for me," she teased.

Lady Anne sent a note across the square and soon the Fitzwilliams joined those celebrating the good news. There was no missing Andrew's disappointment that Jane was not present, but that did not inhibit his wishing the newly acknowledged couple happy.

~~~~~~~/~~~~~~~

Lady Catherine was desperate to marry Anne to one of her two cousins who were heirs. In just over two months Anne would reach her majority and then Rosings Park and everything else Sir Lewis had owned would be her daughter's. She was at her wit's end as to what to do to force the issue.

Not normally one to read the society pages, she had just seen information one of her targets was courting some unknown woman while Fitzwilliam had been seen in the company of some widow. She missed the part about the widow's rank.

Lady Catherine decided the only thing for it was to hie to London and make sure she would be gratified. That no one had ever given into her whims before did not discourage her in her plans.

In the morning, she would set off for Town with Anne and her parson in tow. She would not take no for an answer!

CHAPTER 35

Lady Catherine began her London odyssey at Hilldale House on Portman Square. The butler informed her the master was not in residence, but would tell her no more, no matter how many times she asked him if he knew who she was.

Finding no gratification at her eldest nephew's house, Lady Catherine ordered her coachman to Grosvenor Square and Matlock House. Much to her frustration, her brother was not home to receive her and the insolent butler would not allow her entrance without his master or mistress being present.

Thankfully her sister's house was just across the green from her brother's, so she ordered her man to drive them around the green to the other side of the square.

Anne de Bourgh was fighting to keep the mirth she was feeling from bubbling over into full-blown laughter at her mother's futile attempts to marry her off to one of her cousins. Regardless of her mother's lies that Rosings Park was her own until her death, Anne had seen her father's will. She was well aware on the second day of June; all would be hers.

She did not desire to marry one of her cousins any more than either of them wanted to marry her. In fact, she was resolved she would never marry. So here she sat in the barouche as it was driven to the other side of the square when walking would have reached Darcy House in less than half of the time.

Her mother was grumbling about the blatant disrespect

of her family not being at home to receive her. The sycophantic parson, Mr. Hopkinson, was doing what he always did, agreeing with every ridiculous word which flowed from her mother's mouth.

She knew appointments were for life, but Anne was sure once the bishop was informed of all of the improprieties—by her mother's command—of the rector of Hunsford, he would be dismissed and then Anne would be able to appoint a man who deserved the title of clergyman.

A Darcy footman placed the step and opened the door of the de Bourgh coach. Lady Catherine alighted and made her way up to the front door on which she rapped with the handle of her walking stick.

Killion opened the door. "May I be of assistance?" he asked, with a stance which subtly blocked the door. With his hand, he signalled to the two footmen in the hall.

The previous time the termagant before him had appeared at the house, she had pushed her way in. The mistress and master had then bestowed their permission to keep the woman out of the house by any means necessary if she arrived, as she had now, without their express permission.

"Move aside," Lady Catherine shrieked. "Do you know who I am?"

"Yes, Lady Catherine I know who you are, however, I am following orders to not allow you entrance without Mr. Darcy or Lady Anne permitting me to do so."

"I will see you are sacked with no character!" Lady Catherine yelled.

~~~~~~~/~~~~~~~

The Darcy's, Fitzwilliams, and the five Bennet sisters were all in the largest of the drawing rooms at Darcy House when they heard the caterwauling from the front door.

"Anne's majority is approaching, my sister must be hunting for a husband for my namesake," Lady Anne shook her head.

Seeing the questioning looks from the sisters who had never had the *pleasure* of meeting Lady Catherine, the Darcys and Fitzwilliams explained all about her and her demands either Andrew or William marry her daughter.

"I suppose we will have to go and expel her from our property," Darcy huffed.

"Robert, allow her to enter so she can make a fool of herself away from our neighbours' prying eyes. Perhaps she will finally understand none of us are fooled by the façade she tries to present," Lady Anne suggested.

Darcy looked around the room. Andrew was seated next to Jane and William and Lizzy were next to one another. "Are you sure, Anne," Darcy verified, "you know she will release her vitriol as soon as she notes the ladies sitting next to Andrew and William."

"Papa, do not be uneasy on our account, and for myself, I do dearly like to laugh," Elizabeth stated. "From what you have all said, it should be a rather amusing performance."

Seeing nods from the other four sisters, Darcy made his way down to the entrance hall.

When he arrived, his sister-in-law was still screeching like a fishmonger's wife hawking her wares in the market.

"Catherine, desist immediately!" Darcy thundered. "What is the meaning of this display of ill-breeding on my doorstep?"

"You need to sack this man; he denied me entry..." Lady Catherine tried to say before Darcy interjected.

"He was following direct orders from Anne and me," Darcy bellowed. "The only reason I would have sacked him was if he had ignored our instructions and allowed you to force your way into our house uninvited."

"Well I never! How dare you speak to me in that way, I

am the daughter of..." Lady Catherine attempted to bluster.

Rather than continue to have the woman provide entertainment for his neighbours, Darcy nodded to his butler. Seeing his master's permission, Killion motioned for the two large footmen to take a few steps back, and then he stood aside himself.

As soon as the door was closed, Darcy rounded on his sister-in-law. "Catherine, just like me you are a commoner. You have a courtesy title and we all know your late husband was only knighted because you could not accept being married to a man without some sort of title." Seeing she wanted to interrupt him, Darcy raised his hand. "You will either behave with decorum in my house or you will be evicted and never allowed to enter again. Do I make myself clear?"

Being aware Robert Darcy never issued idle threats, Lady Catherine gave a tight nod of acceptance.

Before Darcy could speak again, there was the sound of the knocker striking the door. He nodded to Killion who opened it to reveal his niece. "Good afternoon, Uncle Robert," Anne stated cheerily as she entered the house. "I waited for a little while as I did not want anyone who witnessed my mother's performance to think I endorsed that kind of behaviour."

"Anne! How could you?" Lady Catherine raised her hand to slap her daughter but found her wrist clamped in a large hand.

"You will not harm your daughter!" Darcy snarled.

The footman who had caught Lady Catherine's wrist looked to the master who nodded, so the man released his hold on the woman. Those in the entrance hall ignored the woman's outraged look at being manhandled.

"The man who masquerades as a parson, Mr. Hopkinson, is in the carriage because my mother ordered him to wait," Anne informed her uncle.

"Why would your parson..." Darcy paused as it hit him what the delusional woman had hoped to achieve. "You thought bringing him along would somehow make that which we have all refused over and over again to come to pass? Besides the fact we would never gratify you, both Andrew and William have entered into courtships."

"We had read about Andrew, but I look forward to congratulating William," Anne stated before her mother could start up again.

"Let us to the drawing room where everyone awaits us," Darcy commanded. "I would prefer to have this discussion in a more private setting."

As much as she wanted to release her fury, Lady Catherine bit her tongue as she followed her disrespectful daughter and brother-in-law up the stairs, closely shadowed by the two footmen.

Her resolution to remain silent did not survive the drawing room doors being closed. In front of her sat her nephew, Andrew, and next to him—far too close for her liking—sat a very pretty blonde woman. If that was not bad enough, the other nephew who would suit as a husband for Anne was seated next to a stunningly beautiful young lady with raven hair and emerald-green eyes.

"Who are these lowborn hussies of no rank or fortune who are using their arts and allurements on my nephews?" Lady Catherine shrieked. "Move away from them now, you inconsequential nothings!"

"And just who are you to order me away from William, or for that matter, Jane away from Andrew?" Elizabeth enquired amusedly.

"I am Lady Catherine de Bourgh, a peer of the realm and their nearest relation. One of them is to marry my daughter!" she screeched as she puffed up her chest with self-importance.

"So, you care not which one marries your daughter.

Does she have any say in the matter? Also, it is a most extraordinary claim you make about being their nearest relation when their parents and siblings are in this room with them." Elizabeth shot back rapidly before Lady Catherine could gather her wits. She turned to Lady Anne. "Mama, you did not tell me your sister is a peer."

"That is only in Catherine's mind, Lizzy. She was married to a knight so she holds the same rank as Lady Lucas. She is called Lady Catherine, and not Lady de Bourgh, only because like me, she received a courtesy title from our late father being an earl," Lady Anne averred.

Ignoring everything which did not fit with her desires, Lady Catherine latched onto one thing the dark-haired beauty had said. "How dare you address my sister thusly? Mama indeed!"

"What can the way I address Mama be to you? We agreed on the form of address between us with no reference to one so wholly unconnected to myself," Elizabeth returned.

"As I outrank you, you will treat me with the respect I deserve," Lady Catherine blustered.

"So, you believe in the distinction of rank?" Elizabeth asked innocently.

"Of course, I am most attentive to such things," Lady Catherine responded.

"Uncle Reggie, as it seems your sister knows not who she is addressing, please introduce her to me," Elizabeth smiled at the Earl.

Before Lady Catherine could point out the temerity of the young lady asking to be introduced to one so far above her and from an earl who was by far the highest-ranking person in the room, her brother stood.

"It would be my pleasure." Lord Matlock turned to his wayward sister. "Catherine the lady you called lowborn, of no rank, and no fortune *is, in fact,* unlike you, a peer of the realm.

This is Her Grace, Lady Elizabeth Rose Gardiner, *Duchess* of Hertfordshire and *Marchioness* of Hertford Heights. She is the owner of seven estates and has more wealth than you could imagine, and if that were not enough, she is greatly favoured by the Queen. William is courting her. The other lady you insulted is Miss Jane Bennet, sister to said duchess who is being courted by Andrew with the blessing of his true closest relations. Not that it should matter, but my future daughter is anything but without fortune."

Lady Catherine did not know which way to look. The slip of a woman next to her Darcy nephew was a duchess, and if that were not bad enough, a marchioness as well.

"Anne, was what I witnessed the first time your mother had attempted to strike you?" Darcy asked.

"It was, Uncle Robert," Anne assured her uncle. "It was the first time I allowed my mother to see I am not the weak, compliant daughter she thinks I am." Anne turned to her mother. "Mother, I have seen my father's will and I am well aware on my birthday upcoming all of my father's property and wealth become mine. It has been many years I have known your only reason for trying to marry me to one of my cousins was so they would take me away from Rosings Park and leave you to continue to mismanage it."

As if being confronted with the fact one of her nephews was courting a duchess and the other her sister was not enough, Anne's revelation was too much. Lady Catherine got a crazed look in her eye and was looking around the room for an outlet for her ire. She settled on the upstart duchess. She should have been a duchess, not this girl.

With nails bared Lady Catherine started towards the pretender. She took two steps before she was on the flat of her back. Biggs had been standing just inside the servants' door and as soon as he heard the way the woman had verbally assaulted Her Grace, he had unobtrusively moved into the room standing in a corner where it would be easy to reach the

Duchess if needs be.

On seeing the crazed woman move threateningly towards Her Grace, Biggs had jumped over a settee and reached the woman before she had been able to get close to Lady Elizabeth.

"It seems Catherine has lost her sanity; we need to have her committed to an asylum for her own protection and the protection of others." Darcy shook his head as the lady was bound and gagged.

"Thank you for saving me from this insane woman, John," Elizabeth stated appreciatively.

"It were me duty, Yer Grace," Biggs bowed.

"Just like I said," Richard added, "catlike reflexes."

"There is a private asylum on Stornoway on the Island of Lewis in the Outer Hebrides. When Sir Lewis was alive, I assisted with some research in case Catherine ever slipped the bounds of reason," Lord Matlock stated pensively.

"It would be best, Uncle Reggie," Anne agreed. "Other than the rector still waiting in the barouche, I am afraid to say she will not be missed by anyone."

"Who will live with you at Rosings Park until your birthday?" Richard enquired.

"I think you should resign from the army and come learn how to manage Rosings Park," Anne responded. "I am feeling better than I have in a long time, but I have no desire to marry and I know I will never be able to bear a child."

When she had thought Miss de Bourgh was in essence proposing to Richard Fitzwilliam, Mary had felt inexplicably sad. Although she was not happy regarding what Miss de Bourgh said about not being able to birth a child, hearing that she never wanted to marry, lightened Mary's mood.

While her cousin sat with his mouth open and no sound issuing forth, Anne turned to the Duchess. "Your Grace..." She stopped when the beauty raised her hand.

"We are to be cousins, please call me Elizabeth or Lizzy, and I will call you Anne," Elizabeth interjected.

"Lizzy, please accept my contrition for my mother's…" Anne held what she was about to say as Elizabeth raised her hand again.

"I do not hold you as responsible for the actions of a clearly insane woman as I would not for the weather being bad, or any other thing you are unable to control," Elizabeth stated firmly. "You only control your own actions, not those of your mother. You bear no fault for her behaviour."

"I think I will like having you as a cousin, your sister as well," Anne smiled.

"There are three more…" Elizabeth introduced the three youngest Bennets.

"The papers had much to report about your late husband, are you well?" Anne queried.

"As you can see, I am. He was sent to hell before he could physically hurt me or any of those I love. If it is all the same to you, it is not a subject I desire to speak about," Elizabeth requested.

After what she had read about the things attributed to the man, Anne could understand why Lizzy would not want to canvass that subject.

"Anne, what do you mean I should come to learn how to run your estate?" Richard finally managed.

"Richard, I am not someone who wants to manage an estate," Anne responded. "Unlike my mother, I know my limitations. As such, the day the estate becomes mine, I will have documents drawn up transferring the estate to you once you are ready. In the meanwhile, I will need help to undo all of my mother's mismanagement."

When Elizabeth had proposed gifting him one of her

estates, Richard had refused and allowed his pride to rule. Anne and Rosings Park were different. Anne said she would never marry so it would be his duty to keep it in the family. That meant he had to learn how to manage it, and make the estate thrive again."

Lord and Lady Matlock were holding their breath as they waited for Richard's decision. They both hated seeing him go off to the war and had worried about him each day he was away. If the Matlock Earldom did not have such an ironclad entail, they would have made one of the estates Richard's long before he went into the army.

"In that case, I will see Lieutenant-Colonel Atherton on the morrow and begin the process of resigning from the army," Richard decided.

There were many effusions of joy from those present. Mary Bennet said a silent prayer Richard would never return to war again. Contrary to her previous feelings on the matter, she had begun to wish the two to three years until she came out would speed by quickly.

CHAPTER 36

Shortly after Lady Catherine had begun her journey north which would take her to her new home in Stornoway in the Outer Hebrides, Uncles Philips and Gardiner had informed Elizabeth all the transfers of the deeds for her estates had been completed, as well as the sale of the shipbuilding yards to the Duke of Bedford. By that time the number of estates included Longbourn and Netherfield Park and Elizabeth had issued orders for the latter two estates to be merged.

The two manor houses would remain as they were and any servants who desired to, would keep their jobs. All the servants at both estates elected to keep their current employment. One day, when Mary took possession of the much-enlarged Longbourn, she would decide which would be the main house and which the dower house.

Although his regimental commander had been sorry to lose Richard, he had accepted his resignation. As soon as he had sold out, Richard made his way to Rosings Park, where he would meet Mr. Lucas Wickham who had been spared from his duties at Pemberley for as long as he was needed in Kent. With Mr. Wickham's vast experience and his excellent teaching ability, Richard would rapidly learn the duties of estate master and management. In Mr. Wickham's absence, two excellent under-stewards would fulfil his duties at Pemberley while he was away.

As soon as all business was concluded, the residents of Hertfordshire, Darcy House, and Matlock House travelled away from London.

One of the motivations to depart London had been the fact rumours of her vast wealth had begun to spread among the *Ton*. The number being bandied about was a fraction of the reality, but it was still far more than any woman in polite society had. Hence, the line of men who wanted to call on Elizabeth was endless.

In an attempt to discourage these men, with the Queen's hearty blessing, a notice of the official courtship between the Duchess of Hertfordshire and the Darcy heir had been placed in the papers.

It had slowed the stream of callers, but many still called deciding they had a chance until the Duchess was married. Any man who may have considered a compromise was discouraged as soon as he entered the drawing room where the callers were received. A little behind but right next to the seat where Her Grace was seated, was one giant man who would give a fearsome scowl to any man who attempted to approach beyond where he had been told to sit. If that was not enough, there was another almost as big and intimidating, just behind where the callers were to sit. It did not help there were two rather fearsome men posted in the hallway at the entry to the drawing room—one on either side of the door.

~~~~~~~/~~~~~~~

Much to Lydia's delight she and her sisters were residing at the estate with the fascinating castle—she had no knowledge Castlemere would be hers one day. Given Elizabeth and William were courting, she could not be hosted at Pemberley, so the sisters and their escorts were at Elizabeth's Derbyshire estate.

Andrew had accepted an invitation to Pemberley so he would be able to visit his fiancée each day—he had proposed to Jane and been accepted the day before the departure from London. There was only a short distance between the estates making it a quick ride to reach Castlemere. He was of course accompanied by William. Jane and Andrew had decided to marry on the penultimate day of May, a Saturday.

They would marry from Castlemere with Jane's Uncle Adam performing the marriage rite in the chapel at her sister's estate. Elizabeth was seeking a clergyman to take the estate's living.

The Queen had spoken to her *vicar* and all the livings which had been stripped from the late duke's gift would be returned. The final switch of each preferment would occur when the incumbent at each left or retired. To start with, Elizabeth would begin to offer livings at each of her larger estates which had a church or chapel without a rector.

~~~~~~~/~~~~~~~

The third couple was ensconced in Hertfordshire. Lawrence Portnoy was being hosted at Longbourn. He had proposed to Charlotte the day he had arrived in the neighbourhood and been promptly accepted. They would marry on the eighteenth day of June from St. Albert's in Meryton.

The Portnoys and Barringtons would all meet in Hertfordshire soon after Jane and Andrew's wedding. The two families would be joined by the Lucases, Philipses, Longs, and Gouldings returning to Hertfordshire as they would be in Derbyshire to witness Jane marry her viscount. The Darcys and four sisters would arrive a few days before the Lucas-Portnoy wedding.

The residents of Castlemere visited Pemberley and Snowhaven as much as the Darcys and Fitzwilliams visited them at Elizabeth's estate.

Anna, who was counted a very close friend by the three youngest Bennets was being hosted at Elizabeth's estate. After Jane's wedding, the four girls would be at Pemberley until everyone travelled to Meryton for the Lucas-Portnoy wedding.

~~~~~~~/~~~~~~~

With Biggs and Johns ten yards behind them, Elizabeth and William were walking at Castlemere along the shore of the lake in mid-May when she stopped suddenly, and her hands shot down to the growing bulge in her belly.

"Are you well, Elizabeth? Do we need to return to the house?" William asked concernedly.

"No all is well, William," Elizabeth averred her face wreathed in smiles. "I just felt the quickening. It was just like Mrs. Medford, Mama, and other ladies told me it would be, like a butterfly fluttering in my belly."

The two walkers and their escorts crossed the bridges on the southern, narrow end of the lake and continued walking on the eastern shore. Soon enough, they reached the boulder where William had first encountered Elizabeth and promptly inserted his hessian into his mouth.

The couple stopped, looked at the boulder, then one another, and began to smile widely. Soon the smiles changed to giggles and chortles, and finally to a tinkling laugh and a full-throated belly guffaw.

Both had tears of mirth running down their cheeks as their first meeting and their subsequent behaviour towards one another was conjured in their minds.

"We have come so very far since that day, have we not?" Elizabeth stated once she had ceased her giggles and dried her eyes.

"We most certainly have," William agreed. All mirth disappeared from his deep blue eyes and was replaced by a look which conveyed love and passion. "Elizabeth, there is a question I would very much like to ask you, but if you are not ready for me to ask that now, let me know, and I will remain silent until you are prepared for me to articulate what is in my heart."

"If it is the question I am hoping it is, then I am more than willing to hear it, and in my opinion, this is the perfect place to ask it," Elizabeth replied her eyes telling William of her deep and abiding love for him.

William inclined his head to the spot Elizabeth had been sitting the fateful day they had met. Elizabeth took a seat on the edge of the rock. William sunk down onto one knee in the sand in front of her taking her small hands into his large ones.

"Elizabeth Rose Gardiner, until I met you, I never knew it was possible to love someone the way I do you, with the power of a thousand suns. You not only have my love but my total and complete respect as well. Had I tried, never would I have been able to imagine a woman who is more perfect for me than you are. You are brave, selfless, compassionate, caring, intelligent, witty, and the strongest woman I have ever met.

"I know you come to me with a child growing inside of you and I swear," William released her one hand and after silently seeking and receiving permission to do so, placed his hand gently over where her son or daughter was growing, "I will be a father to this babe as I would if he or she was of my own blood.

"There is nothing I can do to erase the past, but I can offer you a life where we will be partners and you will never have your choices taken away from you."

William retook her other hand in the one which had rested over her—soon-to-be their—child. "Elizabeth, will you make me the happiest man in the world and agree to be my wife?"

"When I first met you at this spot, I thought you an arrogant horse's hind quarters. However, it did not take me long to see you were the best of men and one who, if I had been free, would be an ideal husband for me.

"There is no doubt in me that you are my perfect match in every way. I love and respect you in a way I never knew was possible. Therefore, I could never regret, even in the smallest measure, accepting your proposal of marriage. Yes, William, I will absolutely marry you...the sooner the better."

He wanted nothing more than to kiss his fiancée, but William was aware her two guards were not far off and were, as usual watching over her intently.

Elizabeth read the desire in William's eyes, a desire which matched her own. Now she was engaged to a man she loved; she was impatient to experience her first kiss.

She turned and signalled her two guards who understood what she wanted from the way she was making a circle in the air with her one finger. Elizabeth was well pleased when she saw John and Brian turn their backs on her and William.

In the meantime, William had stood up. As soon as he saw the guards turn, he gently pulled Elizabeth up off her perch on the boulder until they were standing with no more than an inch or two between them. With their eyes locked onto each other, William lowered his head slowly until his lips brushed against hers.

Even though the kiss had been brief and chaste, Elizabeth felt a bolt of electricity travelling throughout the whole of her body from the crown of her head to the very tips of her toes.

William drew his head back a little to make sure Elizabeth was well. What he saw was not concern in her eyes but instead, he saw a roiling passion. He lowered his head again, capturing her lips with his own. This time it was no brush of their lips, but a hungry demanding kiss, followed by more and more kisses.

Her arms snaked around William's neck while his went around her waist as they deepened the kisses. At some point, Elizabeth felt his tongue licking her lips. She instinctively opened her mouth to allow him entry. As their tongues danced, tasting one another, Elizabeth felt her heart racing as her breathing became rapid as well.

The bliss Elizabeth was experiencing with this man she loved beyond all reason had been worth the wait.

For his part, not even in his imagination had William been able to conjure up just how sweet her lips were. They had never discussed her past in so many words, but William believed from what Elizabeth had related she was experiencing her first kisses with him.

As they pressed together, he could feel her taut nipples pressing against his chest through her thin, summer walking dress and his waistcoat and shirt. His jacket had been left at the house.

He could feel the hardened swell in her belly, the new life growing within her, pressing against his waist. He cared not any longer who had caused her to be in this state. All that counted was he was the one who would be the babe's father. This child—and any others with whom they may be blessed—would be raised in love.

After some minutes, neither knew how many, the clearing of a throat snapped them out of the passionate haze. They jumped back, one from the other, as John Biggs and Brian Johns stood grinning.

"We need to return to the house and share our happiness with our sisters. A call to Pemberley would then be in order," Elizabeth stated when she stopped blushing so deeply.

When both John and Brian wished them happy, Elizabeth conveyed her thanks but could not look either man in the eye.

"I need to ride to London and Meryton," William decided. "I would wish for our engagement to become official sooner rather than later."

"That will only gain us a few days and you will be away for about a sennight. You would return the middle of next week and they will be here early the following week." Elizabeth did not miss the disappointment on William's face. "When we reach the house, you and I will scribe expresses to Uncles Edward and Frank. That way there will be no question this is absolutely my choice."

"I knew you could not be so intelligent for nothing my dearest, loveliest Elizabeth," William kissed her hand. "There is a chance we will have their replies by Saturday."

"That and we will not be separated."

William looked at the fourth finger on her left hand which was resting on his arm as they made their way back to the castle and added wing. As soon as the news of her husband's demise had been confirmed, she had removed *his* wedding ring. The engagement ring was in a drawer, as it always was when not in *his* company. Having heard the story of how the bastard had not given her choice in anything, he was determined not to do that to her ever, including the choice of an engagement ring.

Once he had his father's permission, he would open the vault hidden in the study and show her the two drawers where the rings were kept and allow Elizabeth to choose.

They discovered their combined five sisters sitting in the lakeside drawing room—a favourite of theirs—with, as would be expected, Andrew seated next to Jane. With the four younger girls present there was no shortage of chaperones.

Elizabeth cleared her throat garnering the attention of those seated in the drawing room. "William and I have an announcement..." Elizabeth began.

"You are engaged!" Jane blurted out excitedly.

She had not told Lizzy this, but ever since her younger sister had shared the true reason for her decision to marry the blackhearted old man, Jane had felt much guilt. Andrew had assisted her in beginning to move past it. Then, when Lizzy had accepted the courtship with William, her guilt had been partly assuaged. So, if her sister was in fact engaged, it would remove the last vestiges of her self-imposed blame.

"Jane has the right of it! William proposed while we were out walking and I accepted him with alacrity, before he could change his mind," Elizabeth shared gleefully.

While Andrew slapped William on the back and then shook his hand, Elizabeth was surrounded by her sisters and future sister, each one vying to wish her happy first. Jane allowed the younger girls to congratulate Lizzy first before she pulled her sister into a hug, telling her she was almost as happy for her as she had been the day Andrew asked for her hand. It took some minutes, but eventually everyone had conveyed their approbation to the newly engaged couple.

"William and I need to write a letter each. As soon as we have done so, I think we need to call on Pemberley," Elizabeth related. "Jane, be a dear and tell Mr. Toppin we need a coach made ready."

~~~~~~~/~~~~~~~

Lady Anne and Robert Darcy were standing in the courtyard by the time the coach, with Andrew and William riding alongside, came to a halt.

"You are most welcome, but we did not expect to see you girls today…" Lady Anne stopped as she saw the way Anna and the two youngest Bennets were rocking on the balls of their feet, evidently trying their best not to blurt out something.

Then she looked at Lizzy and William. As soon as she saw them, she knew. "William, you have proposed, and Lizzy accepted you!" Both nodded. "How wonderful, it is the best news," Lady Anne enthused.

She hugged Elizabeth to herself while her husband shook his son's hand vigorously. "Should we go inside?" Darcy suggested.

Lady Anne stopped outside the drawing room. "Will you all remain for dinner? If you say yes, I will send a groom to Snowhaven so Elaine and Reggie can join us to celebrate."

"I see no reason we cannot remain, Mama," Elizabeth agreed. "I just need to send a note to Mrs. Bannister. I will instruct her to use what would have been our dinner as a celebratory meal for the staff and servants instead."

"One groom will ride to your estate the other one to Snowhaven," Lady Anne told her future daughter.

"I was sure you two would marry. I am well pleased to be proved correct," Darcy stated after he kissed both of Elizabeth's cheeks. "I, we, could not be happier in gaining you as a daughter. We will consider your sisters our daughters as well."

Her Papa's words warmed Elizabeth's heart. She could not wait for the contingent from London and Meryton to arrive to share her joy with them as well. In the meantime, the letters she had sent with the courier would have to suffice.

CHAPTER 37

Just as Elizabeth had predicted, the couriers returned within three days with the replies from both uncles giving their consent and blessing for her to marry William. Both agreed with her assertion there was no reason to delay the wedding.

With her uncles' permission in hand, Elizabeth had a discussion with William where she made a suggestion. He agreed as long as those involved had no objections.

Hence she asked for her fiancé, his parents, Jane, Andrew, and his parents to meet with her in the lakeside drawing room the Monday after the engagements were announced, a few days before the family and friends from London and Meryton were due to arrive at Castlemere and Pemberley.

"William and I have discussed when we should marry, and we are of like minds with the uncles that there is no imperative to have a long engagement. It is not like anyone can accuse us of anticipating our wedding vows as it is known throughout society I was with child before *he* was sent to Hades," Elizabeth revealed.

"If that is the case, then why do you and William not marry the same day as us?" Jane suggested.

"You would not object, Janey?" Elizabeth enquired. "We do not want to detract from your day."

"No silly, other than marrying Andrew, I can think of nothing which I would like more," Jane insisted. "It will be like we dreamed as little girls, a double wedding. Besides with our family and friends all to arrive to attend our wedding, what could be better?"

"Andrew, do you agree as well?" William verified.

"Why would I object? Of course I approve," Andrew confirmed.

"Mama and Papa? Aunt Elaine and Uncle Reggie? Do any of you have an objection?" Elizabeth questioned.

"Robert and I do not," Lady Anne stated happily. "The sooner you become our daughter, the happier we will be."

"Neither do Reggie and myself," Lady Matlock added. "Jane is already counted as a daughter and you and your younger sisters nieces. You and William marrying the same day will only enhance the celebration."

"In that case, I will apply to your Uncle Adam for a common licence," William decided.

"Soon to be your Uncle Adam too," Jane pointed out teasingly.

"I suppose we should tell the four younger girls," Lady Anne suggested.

The four were taking a ride around the lake. Mary was riding *Jamil*; Anna had her own pony with her, Miss Younge was on the mare Mr. Darcy had made available for her to ride. Kate and Lydia each rode a pony from the estate's stables. They were protected by six guards and two grooms.

"They should return in an hour," Elizabeth estimated.

~~~~~~~/~~~~~~~

The four younger girls could not have been more excited if it were one of them marrying in a little more than a sennight. The main reason was all four of them would perform the duties of bridesmaids. Before the double wedding, Lizzy was to be Jane's matron of honour, now Mary and Lydia would stand up with Jane while Kate and Anna would be Elizabeth's attendants.

Andrew had asked Richard to stand up with him before the decision regarding the double wedding had been taken.

Richard and Anne were on their way and expected to arrive on Wednesday. The two grooms decided if Richard agreed, he would do duty to both of them. Even though it was a double wedding, Mr. Lambert would solemnise the ceremony for Jane and Andrew completely (Elizabeth had insisted Jane be married first regardless of her own rank) so Richard would be able to attend both grooms without a problem.

Given the departure from London the day after Andrew proposed, Jane had not purchased her trousseau in Town. Instead she had been giving her custom to the dressmaker in Lambton, which had endeared her to the lady and her seamstresses who had never had so much work at one time.

Anything she felt was not attainable in Lambton would be ordered in Town after their wedding trip.

Elizabeth had a rather extensive wardrobe, so all she ordered in Lambton was a wedding gown. She refused to marry the man she loved in an ensemble *he* had ordered purchased.

With the wedding breakfast being held at Castlemere, Mrs. Reynolds, Pemberley's cook, and some of the kitchen maids had the pleasure of working closely with Mrs. Bannister, the cook, and the rest of the servants at the Duchess's estate to make sure everything would be perfect on the day.

~~~~~~~/~~~~~~~

Anne and Richard, along with Mrs. Jenkinson—Anne's longtime companion—arrived at Pemberley as planned. Richard accepted the request to stand up for William as well as Andrew without a moment's hesitation.

Two days after the three from Rosings Park arrived, the convoy from London and Meryton reached Pemberley and Castlemere. As would be expected, the Portnoys and Barringtons were to be hosted at the former estate. With young Peter not having reached two months yet, the group from Hertfordshire—who had met the Gardiners on the Great North Road—had taken a day longer to travel than normal to facilitate shorter distances between stops.

The Longs and Gouldings who had not seen Lizzy's estate previously were awed by what they saw. They had heard about the castle and the large lake, but until they saw it with their own eyes, it had not been real for them.

Except for the Gardiner children, after they had refreshed themselves, an hour later, everyone met in the lakeside drawing room.

Elizabeth stood and waited until the hum of conversation ceased. "As I am sure you have heard, I am to marry William Darcy." All those who had arrived that day nodded they were aware of the recent engagement. "What you do not know is on the thirtieth, you will attend not one but two weddings."

It took a few moments for the import of her words to sink in. "Jane and Lizzy, you are marrying in a double ceremony!" Madeline exclaimed happily.

"We are," Jane and Elizabeth chorused.

It took a while for the expressions of approbation and congratulations to die down.

Charlotte sat next to her friend and took her hand with much pleasure. "Eliza, this is the best news. I see you did not want to wait until after I wed my Lawrence," Charlotte teased.

"If I had my choice we would be married already," Elizabeth stated seriously. "Marrying a man I love with my whole heart, a man *I* have chosen with my free will and who I accept whole-heartedly, will eradicate the last vestiges of the memories of *him*. I cannot wait until my family name becomes Darcy. When this one is born," Elizabeth touched her belly, "he or she will be a Darcy. That man will have failed in everything he tried to do by blackmailing me into marrying him. As part of his punishment in purgatory, I hope he is able to understand the depth of his failures."

"He deserves no less than that," Charlotte averred. She decided to change the subject to something more palatable. "I am well pleased you are still able to travel and will attend my wedding in Meryton. All of those who love you and your sisters will be gratified to see you again. Have you and your fiancé spoken of a wedding trip yet? And what of a settlement or were you waiting for your Uncle Frank to arrive?"

"With my increasing, we will remain here at Castlemere while Jane is on her honeymoon. Just being together alone will be the best sort of wedding trip for us," Elizabeth related. "Our sisters will be at Pemberley with Anna. As to the other, William and I will sit and discuss things with Uncles Edward and Frank on the morrow."

Charlotte remembered how Eliza had written to inform her she would be involved in all decisions which affected her. Hence, she made no comment.

~~~~~~~/~~~~~~~

William and his father arrived at Castlemere at the appointed hour in the morning to meet with Elizabeth and her guardians. As the master of all Darcy holdings, Robert Darcy's signature was needed on any document which could affect his holdings, like a marriage settlement.

Philips had contacted the local solicitor in Lambton who had agreed to allow his clerk to scribe the settlement once all parties were in agreement.

"Welcome Papa and William," Elizabeth enthused as Timmons showed father and son into the study.

Darcy kissed his soon to be daughter on her cheek. As much as she and William wanted to kiss one another, they refrained with his father and her uncles in the room. Elizabeth sat between her uncles on one of the two facing settees in the study. William and his father were on the one opposite on the other side of a low table. The clerk was at the desk ready to make notes of the salient points agreed upon.

"Before we begin, I am adamant on one clause in the settlement," William stated. "Anything which belongs to Elizabeth, will remain under her control after we wed."

A document was passed by Darcy to Philips. "I noted the stipulation William enumerated as well as the amount William would like to settle on Elizabeth."

Philips handed the document to Elizabeth who read it dispassionately. Once she finished reading it, she gave it to Uncle Edward.

"As much as I appreciate the gesture, I would not know what to do with the fifty thousand you are settling on me, especially as you demand my wealth and properties I own now remain with me," Elizabeth stated gratefully. "Please do not mistake my reaction for ingratitude." Elizabeth turned to Uncle Frank. "Please hand the summary document to Papa and William."

Philips did as his niece requested.

Father and son put their heads together so they could both see what was listed on the document at the same time. At first the looks were ones of incredulity, as if someone was making sport of them. Seeing a nod from Philips confirming this was no jest, both men lost some of their colour.

Elizabeth's income from her estates and investments, even after the sale of the ship building yards, was more than double the Darcys' income. The massive amounts she had in the banks made the more than half a million pounds the Darcys had on hand look insignificant.

"I had no idea..." William managed before he faltered after he had absorbed the numbers on the page in front of him.

"Even had we not known your upstanding character, we were certain it was not Lizzy's fortune which drew you to her," Gardiner stated.

"You never mentioned just how wealthy you are," Darcy exclaimed.

"You never asked Papa," Elizabeth replied simply. "It was not a secret, but I never thought about it or found a reason to discuss the particulars."

"As you are now aware of her wealth, here are some things Elizabeth intends for its use," Philips read from a document he had picked up off the low table. "At least fifteen percent of the liquid wealth and annual income will be made available for charities. If Lizzy bears a son, he will be gifted a quarter of the wealth along with Falconwood and Hertfordshire House. If she bears a daughter, she will receive a dowry of two hundred thousand pounds and her first son will be given that which would have gone to a son. Falconwood and Hertfordshire House will be managed by Lizzy until her son or daughter is of age, and if a daughter is born, they would become the property of her son in the future.

"Any daughters begot from your union will be dowered with the same amount Lizzy gave to her sisters." Philips could see from the looks the two Darcys were not aware of the amount, only that Lizzy had dowered them. "It is one hundred thousand pounds. If there is more than one son born, they will receive one of the remaining estates after Lizzy's sisters are given one each."

"We have three satellite estates too, if there are a bevy of sons, there should be enough estates to go around," Darcy added.

"In addition, from the second son born of Lizzy and William's union onward, in addition to an estate, they will receive a legacy of five and seventy thousand pounds," Philips summed up.

"That is fair as the first son, if they are blessed with a son, will inherit Pemberley and all the Darcy holdings one day," Darcy agreed.

"Then are we agreed that settling an amount on me would be superfluous? Also, as you are determined to leave what I own under my purview, with the income I have can we agree I will not need an allowance from Pemberley?" Elizabeth clarified. "One last item, as my wealth will be under my control, I will be free to transfer, if I choose to, any amount to be added to the Darcy holdings."

Darcy and William looked at one another. William knew how stubborn Elizabeth could be if she was determined, as he could see she was now. He nodded to his father.

"We agree. If you will have the clerk write up the contract we will sign it," Darcy stated.

"As much as it is not done, I want a place for Elizabeth to sign as well," William insisted as his eyes locked onto his fiancée's.

If it was possible, Elizabeth felt her love for William grow. He truly wanted her as a partner in everything. Legally her signature was meaningless, but it symbolised so much for Elizabeth so she cared nothing about the legal insignificance.

Thanks to Zeus being led behind the coach when the Darcys arrived at Castlemere, William remained when his father departed.

With Brian Johns and Albert Smith—John Biggs had the day off—as escorts, the engaged couple set out for a walk along the shore of the lake. If they arrived at their special boulder, neither remarked on that fact. Each time they walked on the shore, they were inexorably pulled to that spot.

CHAPTER 38

Although she had received the 'talk' before her wedding to *him*, Elizabeth was pleased to be included the night before their double wedding when Aunt Maddie came to speak to Jane. Elizabeth could have had her Mama give her the talk that evening, but as she was about to marry Mama's son, it would have been too awkward for that subject to have been canvased between them.

As her aunt was speaking, Elizabeth looked at the engagement ring she had chosen glinting in the candlelight on her finger. It had a gold band with alternating small diamonds and emeralds leading to the two stones in the centre, a diamond and emerald set side by side. There were delicate roses engraved on the band between the stones, which given her middle name had drawn Elizabeth to this particular ring. Unlike the one from *him* which she had only worn in *his* company, this one she never wanted to take off. It was from William, and she had been the one to choose it.

The wedding ring William would slip onto her finger on the morrow was part of a set of which the ring she was wearing belonged to. There were no stones on the wedding ring, but there were raised roses all the way around it. Elizabeth pulled her attention back to her aunt and away from the ring.

With both sisters marrying men they loved, what Aunt Maddie shared with them was centred around that fact, the giving and receiving of pleasure, never being afraid to tell what they enjoyed, or did not enjoy, and making sure they discovered the same about their husbands.

Once Aunt Maddie's talk was complete, she remained

with Elizabeth after Jane had departed to her own chambers.

"Lizzy, you heard what I told Jane about having relations with her husband even after she falls with child, did you not?" Madeline verified.

Elizabeth could have kissed Jane when she had raised that particular question as it was one she really wanted the answer to and did not feel comfortable asking it in front of Jane who was, after all, still a maiden.

"Yes, I did," Elizabeth responded with only a slight blush. "If Janey had not asked it, I would have done so now once we were alone. Even after I have felt the quickening it is safe to be with William?"

It had been the one thing which had concerned Elizabeth. She wanted to banish any memory of *him* importuning her and she had been praying it would not be only after she gave birth.

"It is quite safe. Your body will tell you when it becomes too uncomfortable to join with your husband," Madeline informed her niece. "That should not be much time before you begin your lying in, but you never know, everyone is different."

"I am marrying for the deepest love again," Elizabeth mused. "Last time it was my love for Janey, this time it is because I adore William and love him so very ardently."

"On another subject, did I see a letter from the Shetland Islands today?" Madeline enquired.

"The man in command of the watchers sent a report. Although she hates it, Mrs. Bennet is in her small cottage. Evidently, she complains to any who will listen about her wilful, disobliging daughter." Elizabeth smiled. Unlike Mrs. Bennet who it seemed thought about Elizabeth constantly, Elizabeth never spared the woman a thought if she was not reading one of the reports.

Thankfully, from that point on, the man in charge would only post a letter if there was something of significance to report.

"I am sure her whinging will not endear her to her neighbours," Madeline stated.

"Your perspicacity does you proud. According to what I read; she is already being shunned by the locals." Elizabeth took a deep breath. "Enough about that woman. I want to thank you and Uncle Edward for your love and support. I do not know if I would have been able to remain strong without knowing you would be there for me if I ever needed it."

"We could not have done less," Madeline replied as she wiped an errant tear which had begun to roll down her cheek. "Knowing how strong you are Lizzy; you would have been able to endure far more. I am well pleased that man was dispatched before he could ever put his dastardly plan to break you into action."

"From this point forward, I choose to think of the past only as it gives me pleasure!" Elizabeth insisted.

"When the notices of Jane's and your engagements appeared in the London papers, especially yours with royal sanction, there were many disappointed men and young ladies, and I am sure much gnashing of teeth. There were not a few who wanted to marry you for your wealth and ladies who fancied themselves the future Countess of Matlock."

"Did I tell you that hopeful men kept calling at Hertfordshire House even after our departure? I could not be happier knowing the next time I am in London I will be a *happily* married woman."

"I think it is time for you to get some sleep," Madeline opined

"I would not want to walk up the aisle to William looking haggard now would I?" Elizabeth nodded. She threw her arms around her aunt. "Thank you Aunt Maddie, for everything."

The ceremony had been moved to the Lambton church.

Since the decision to have a double wedding, and the expanded number of guests, the chapel did not have enough seating for all of those in the family and the Fitzwilliam connections who had accepted the invitations, let alone people from neighbouring estates, and the servants from the three family estates who would be present.

As soon as she had a clergyman in place for the Castlemere living, consulting with him, Elizabeth planned to enlarge the chapel to a full sized church. Her Uncle Adam had given her a list of names of estimable men seeking a living.

The Falconwood steward had forwarded her the information on three possible men for that estate's living. She intended to discuss the men with William in a few days.

Madeline fought to keep her emotions in check as she kissed Lizzy on both cheeks and her forehead. "Sleep well Lizzy dear."

With her aunt's departure from the master sitting room, Elizabeth made her way into the bedchamber where Loretta was waiting to prepare her for bed. She was determined it would be the last night she would sleep alone in her bed.

~~~~~~~/~~~~~~~

William woke the morning of his wedding far earlier than he had planned. With the excitement he felt at marrying the love of his life in a few hours, he was more surprised he had been able to sleep at all rather than at his waking early.

He still felt some embarrassment at the conversation he had with Father yester-night. Unlike Elizabeth, William was an innocent. He understood the irony at the role reversal of the sexes. It was the man who would usually come to a marriage having experienced the pleasures of the flesh while the lady would be the innocent.

From conversations they had on the subject, Elizabeth had made it clear she had never experienced pleasure from the couplings she had been forced to endure. She had told him that although she was no longer a maiden, there would be many firsts for them both. One of the many important firsts they would share was her welcoming him to her bed willingly. Before she had no choice, now it was completely her decision and she chose him.

Who was and was not an innocent was immaterial. All that mattered was the love they shared.

Once he was dressed in a shirt, breaches, and riding boots, William made his way down to the small breakfast parlour where he knew there would be coffee, warm rolls, and muffins on hand.

Surprisingly, he was not the first one to reach the parlour. Andrew, Richard, and Lawrence were all sitting and sipping steaming mugs of coffee.

"Did I not tell you William would be along within minutes?" Richard drawled.

Andrew and Lawrence nodded their heads.

William drank some coffee and munched on two muffins. "Do any of you desire to join me for a ride?" he enquired. All three cousins responded in the affirmative.

They exited the house via the kitchen where each man found a treat for his horse. Word had been sent to the stables as all four mounts were tacked, saddled and waiting for their riders when the four young men arrived. Each horse happily munched the proffered treat before their riders mounted.

The horses were allowed to walk until the cousins rode through a gate, being held open by one of the grooms, which led into a field. Within seconds all four horses were thundering across the field in full gallop.

Thankfully the four were riding abreast so none of them were treated to the clods of earth and grass being thrown up by the hooves as they propelled the horses forward.

After an hour and a half of punishing exercise, the four

returned to the mansion, more than ready to bathe and dress.

~~~~~~~/~~~~~~~

As the coach was brought to a halt outside of the church in Lambton, Edward Gardiner looked at his nieces seated on the forward facing bench opposite him with as much fatherly pride as he would have felt had they been daughters of his blood.

Atop the conveyance, looking as proud as if he were the man walking Her Grace up the aisle was Biggs. Johns, who felt no less pride in the Duchess finding her happiness, was on the back bench with Smith. This day, they would not be waiting outside of the church, but would be in one of the rear pews watching the woman they would give their lives to protect marry a man of her own free choice.

Johns placed the step himself and then handed Miss Bennet out. He stood aside and allowed Biggs the honour of handing down Her Grace.

Elizabeth smiled at John, Brian, and Albert. When she had asked if they wished to continue with her and be employed by the Darcys, there had been not even a moment's hesitation before accepting the offer of continued employment.

With Jane on one arm and Elizabeth on the other—being followed by their attendants who had ridden in a separate carriage, Gardiner led his nieces into the vestibule of the church where his wife waited with Lilly and Eddy. The former was the flower girl, to whit she had a large basket of rose petals while Eddy was the ring bearer. He did not care that the rings were sewn onto the pillow or that they were not the ones which would be used in the ceremony, as long as he could be part of his two favourite cousins' weddings.

Andrew and William were both impatient to marry their respective sister. When they saw the inner vestibule door open and their new aunt enter after giving her brother a nod, they knew their wait was almost over.

Lilly entered first. She was a poised girl of almost nine. She took handfuls of the colourful petals—from roses of Pemberley, Snowhaven, and Castlemere—and dropped them on the aisle's carpet as she walked. Soon, Eddy, who was six followed her. He was extremely proud and walked with his head up. When they reached the head of the aisle, the two eldest Gardiner children slipped into the pew past Aunt Eve to take their seats beyond their mother, leaving an open seat next to her for their father.

Soon Mary and Lydia were walking up the aisle, the latter a few steps behind the former. Both were holding bouquets of flowers picked that morning from the conservatory at Castlemere.

Next, once Mary and Lydia took their positions on the side where Jane would stand, it was Kate and Anna's turn, also with bouquets of fresh flowers, to enter the nave of the church. After they were in position opposite their sisters, the inner vestibule door was closed and Reverand Lambert signalled the congregation to stand.

Both inner doors were opened and much to the grooms' pleasure, Gardiner with Jane on one arm and Elizabeth on the other entered the nave.

Jane was dressed in an ivory silk gown, with an empire waist. The shoulders were puffed and the sleeves ended a few inches above her elbows. Her ivory satin gloves did not quite reach her elbows. Jane had elected to wear a veil instead of a wedding bonnet. It was made of very fine Belgium lace.

Elizabeth had allowed Jane to choose whatever she desired to wear from the Jewels which had been sent from London. She had chosen a delicate set of sapphire earrings and her hairpins were also sapphire tipped. Instead of a matching sapphire necklace, Jane was wearing her simple gold cross.

Andrew had to restrain himself when he saw Jane walking towards him. His desire was to run down the aisle and

He was about to

sweep her up into his arms, but he regulated himself.

When William saw the beauty he loved walking up the aisle, his mouth fell open. She wore a simple hunter green empire waisted silk gown, matching elbow length gloves, and a white wedding bonnet.

She had selected the earrings, necklace, bracelet, and hairpins which had the same rose design as her rings.

As Elizabeth walked, her eyes locked with William's and that was the impetus for him to close his mouth. By the time Gardiner and his nieces reached the spot near the head of the aisle, each groom was waiting impatiently for his bride.

Gardiner lifted Jane's veil, kissed her cheek and placed her hand on Andrew's forearm. He kissed Lizzy on her cheek and repeated the action of placing her hand on her fiancé's arm as he had Jane's.

With Elizabeth on his arm, William smiled at his parents sitting in the front pew across the aisle from the Gardiners and Lucases. He led Elizabeth to their spot and waited.

As was planned, Lambert performed the ceremony for Jane and Andrew first. It was not too long before they were married. While the newly married Fitzwilliams had recited their vows, Elizabeth and William, lost in one another's eyes, had mouthed the vows one to the other.

Next it was their turn while Jane and Andrew stood to the side as spectators. There were no objections expressed to their marriage and when it came to the vows, there had been one small, almost unnoticeable change. William had asked his soon-to-be uncle to omit the word 'obey' from Elizabeth's vows. He had done so.

Soon the wedding ring with the roses was slipped into place. Just before the ceremony, she had, albeit reluctantly, removed the engagement ring and placed it on the corresponding finger on her right hand. Before they made for the wedding breakfast, it would be back in its rightful place.

As Elizabeth signed the register, she wistfully looked at the name she had just signed: *Elizabeth Rose Gardiner*. The family name had not been hers for long, but it had fit until now.

'*Elizabeth Rose Darcy,*' she tried out in her thoughts. '*How very well that sounds.*'

As there were two couples, they did not tarry in the registry. "You are My Grace now," William whispered as they walked back into the nave of the church behind Jane and Andrew.

"I *am* my beloved's and my beloved *is* mine," Elizabeth whispered back.

After a round of hearty congratulations from their family and close friends, with Biggs, Johns, and Smith in their regular positions, the coach which had brought the two brides to Lambton now made its way back to Castlemere; two newly wed couples within.

CHAPTER 39

It took a few hours but eventually all the guests and family departed leaving Elizabeth and William alone at Castlemere—save only the necessary staff and servants.

The wedding breakfast had been celebrated in the great hall of the castle, something which had been both fascinating and enjoyable for all of the guests. The younger men and women who were present had especially enjoyed exploring the castle, most of all, the one remaining intact, and safe to enter, tower.

Those who were returning to Meryton would be hosted at Pemberley until their departure on Monday morning, the first day of June. The Lucases needed to return to plan Charlotte's upcoming wedding.

Jane and Andrew were on their way to the Lakes where they would spend their honeymoon at Lakeside House; a house owned by the Fitzwilliams which overlooked Lakes Windermere and Coniston on its eastern side, with views of some of the smaller waters and lakes to the west.

Anne de Bourgh and Richard would remain at Pemberley for some days before departing for Kent. The Portnoys and Barringtons would soon depart for Hertfordshire where they would remain until Charlotte and Lawrence's wedding.

Elizabeth and William would have a fortnight of wedded bliss before having to venture out into the world again. Their plan was to travel with the Darcys and their sisters into Hertfordshire departing on the third Monday in June.

"Elizabeth, would you like to wait until after dinner, or would you like to retire to the master suite now?" William asked his wife after the final guests had departed her estate.

"Now William, now," Elizabeth insisted. "I am not of a mind to wait for us to become true husband and wife."

He extended his hand, which his wife took and the two made their way upstairs, no more conversation was required. When they reached the door to the bedchamber Elizabeth had used, which would now be theirs as they had decided to share a bed and do away with separate bedchambers, William took both of his wife's hands and leaned over and kissed her languidly.

"How much time do you need?" he asked his breathless love.

"No more than half an hour," Elizabeth, her legs feeling rather wobbly, managed.

It was not often he discomposed her, but William was happy to have been able to do so now. "I will see you soon my love."

William made for the smaller bedchamber in the suite which was being used as his dressing and bathing room, although he was not averse, if Elizabeth desired the same, to sharing a bathtub from time to time. He found his valet, Carstens, waiting for him.

Her maid had to school her features when she saw the dreamy look on Her Grace's face when she entered the bedchamber. She assisted her mistress to change into a thin, practically translucent, night gown. Jennings helped the Duchess into the matching robe.

With her mistress seated in front of her dresser, the maid removed all of the pins from the coiffure and then began to brush the long, raven coloured, silky tresses out.

There was a slight pause, but before Elizabeth could ask

Loretta if all was well, the relaxing brush strokes resumed. She soon opened her eyes and looked into the dresser's mirror and rather than Loretta, it was her beloved husband running the brush through her tresses.

"I hope you are not angry that I dismissed your maid. She will return when you ring for her," William stated. "You have no idea how long I have dreamed of being able to see you with your hair down, and even more, being able to touch your locks."

"How could I be angry with you, Husband. However, I must concede as a lady's maid, you may be lacking just a little."

"Minx!" William growled. "Before we proceed, did you enquire about us joining when you are with child?"

"I did, and there is no danger to the babe," Elizabeth responded breathlessly.

William ran the brush through her hair one more time and then slowly replaced it on the dresser.

Elizabeth stood and looked at her handsome husband. He was wearing a lawn shirt, not tucked into his breeches, which was open down to the fourth button revealing the downy looking dark hair on his chest. Her heart sped up as she saw the strong chest muscles below the shirt.

Her eyes travelled down his form and she was delighted to see he was sans stockings and boots. She stepped towards William and began to unbutton his shirt. There were two more buttons to open and then he pulled it over his head and allowed it to drop onto the floor.

Elizabeth's breath hitched as she was able to see his muscular chest, washboard stomach, and broad shoulders. There was a trail of dark hair which tapered and disappeared into his breeches. There was no missing the distinct bulge in said breeches.

William gently slipped the robe off her shoulders and allowed it to fall to the ground and pool around her feet. Now it was his turn to have his breath taken away when he saw his wife's body revealed through her transparent night gown. Her pert breasts were on the large size, her nipples were hard and pushing against the thin layer of fabric.

Seeing her like this made his member throb with anticipation. His eyes travelled down to the dark triangle between her legs.

She stepped forward again and released the buttons keeping his breeches up. They fell to the floor as the rest of him was revealed to her. His arousal was large and looked very hard. His legs were as muscular as one would expect of one who rode his horse as much as he did.

He bent down a little, took hold of the hem of the nightgown and slowly lifted it up and over Elizabeth's head. Once it was clear, he tossed it aside.

They moved toward one another as if they had silently agreed to do so. William placed his hands on her cheeks as his head dipped and he captured her lips with his own. Elizabeth let out a moan of pleasure into his mouth as they kissed, their bodies rubbing against each other's.

William swept Elizabeth into his arms as if she were weightless and gently lowered her onto the enormous bed. He climbed onto the bed and their lips hungrily sought each other's.

As Elizabeth watched him intently, William kissed her neck, behind her ears, and then made his way down until his lips found one of her breasts.

The frisson of pleasure which shot through her body was like nothing she had ever felt before, causing her to arch her back. Then when his hand found her most private of places, her pleasure only increased.

"Make me your wife, William," Elizabeth managed in a husky, passion filled voice.

Being the gentleman he was, William could not refuse

his wife anything she asked for. It was the first of seven couplings they would enjoy before the sun rose the next day.

They did not sleep much, but waking with William holding her in his arms was almost as thrilling as the marital relations they had enjoyed. The babe began to move more than it had until now.

William said a prayer of thanks for the information—regardless of how embarrassing it had been—his father had imparted the previous night, coupled with the various books he had read on the subject. Without it, he would have acted like the innocent he had been before their first coupling.

When her stomach growled embarrassingly, Elizabeth remembered they had not had dinner. As soon as they were both covered, the bell was pulled and in due course a mountain of food was awaiting them on the sideboard in the sitting room next door.

They spent most of the time while they ate lost in one another's eyes, although they did glance at the view across the lake towards their boulder once or twice.

~~~~~~~/~~~~~~~

Fanny Bennet had taken to reading the London papers as her way of feeling connected to the world from which that unfeeling, ungrateful, wilful girl had banished her. The papers were about a sennight old when they arrived in Lerwick.

She opened the one dated the first day of June.

Duchess of Hertfordshire re-marries

Her Grace Lady Elizabeth Rose Gardiner, with the blessing of their Majesties the King and Queen, married William Alexander Darcy of Pemberley in Derbyshire on the 30th day of May 1807.

> From the time of the wedding forward, the Duchess will be Lady Elizabeth Darcy and the child she carries will bear the last name of Darcy as well.
>
> At the same ceremony, Her Grace's older sister, Miss Jane Esmeralda Bennet of London married Lord Andrew Reginald Harrison Fitzwilliam, Viscount Hilldale.
>
> The new Viscountess Hilldale was very close to as beautiful on the day of her wedding as her younger sister was.

Fanny threw the paper down in disgust. How dare they say that Miss Lizzy was prettier than Jane. Jane resembled herself and there was no way Miss Lizzy was better looking than Fanny Bennet.

How disgusting that Miss Lizzy married during the mourning period for her late husband. It did not surprise Fanny that the hoyden would do something so very improper. She of course ignored the part about Their Majesties' approval.

What was this Gardiner nonsense? The late Duke had been a Chamberlain. Fanny had missed the royal decrees regarding the names and the one before that about no mourning. Nor had she seen the announcements about the engagements.

Jane was a viscountess now. She would write to Jane and of course Jane would rescue her from this purgatory and invite Fanny to live with her. If that occurred, as Fanny was sure it would, then she would not need the additional funds Miss Lizzy had added to her dowry.

Fanny wrote many letters, addressed to Jane via the Gardiners, Philipses, and to the estate she assumed was the Viscount's, Hilldale, although she knew not what county it was in.

Towards the end of June Fanny read a column which did

not please her at all.

Wedding of Miss Charlotte Lucas to Mr. Lawrence Portnoy

Miss Charlotte Lucas of Lucas Lodge in Hertfordshire was joined in marriage to Mr. Lawrence Portnoy, heir to Portnoy Run in Nottinghamshire, on the 20th day of June, 1807.

The wedding was attended by Her Grace the Duchess of Hertfordshire, Marchioness of Hertford Heights and her husband. The recently married couple could not have looked happier.

Mr. Portnoy's mother is sister to Mr. Robert Darcy, master of Pemberley in Derbyshire which makes the new Mrs. Charlotte Portnoy cousin to Her Grace.

Her rival Sarah Lucas had not only married off her plain daughter, but she was connected to all sorts of wealthy people including Miss Lizzy who was still a duchess.

Fanny tore the paper to shreds and consigned it to the fire.

In October of that year, the cruellest blow of all was struck. It was delivered by something Fanny read in the latest paper she saw.

New Duke of Hertfordshire Born

On the 16th day of October, 1807 Lord William Robert Alexander Darcy, the Duke of Hertfordshire, Marquess of Hertford Heights was born.

Her Grace, Lady Elizabeth Darcy and the new duke are both well.

Her Majesty the Queen…

Fanny threw the paper into the fire without reading more. How could this be. She had never born a son, and Miss Lizzy did with her first child.

It was the day Fanny gave up reading the newspapers. There was too much bad news delivered in them. Here she was in this godforsaken place, October not even over yet, and it was colder than the height of winter in Meryton!

Jane had not replied to one of her many letters. Fanny was sure it was Miss Lizzy who made sure her sister ignored her mother. If she ever got off this island which was a living hell, she would exact her revenge on that wilful, disobliging girl!

She still blamed everyone else for her situation, rather than the person who was actually responsible—herself.

~~~~~~~/~~~~~~~

William was in one of the chairs in their private sitting room overlooking the lake watching his wife providing sustenance to their son.

He had not said a word of opposition when Elizabeth had insisted she would feed Will during the day. At least they had reached a compromise and had a wetnurse for the nights so Elizabeth was able to sleep without being disturbed.

The proud Grandmama and Grandpapa had been to visit earlier. They could not have loved the babe, named after his father, grandfather, and great-grandfather, more if he had been of Darcy blood.

Once Will was fed and sated, William took him while Elizabeth closed the front of her dress. He placed a napkin over his shoulder and rested his son there, gently patting his back until he emitted a healthy belch.

Will's eyes were soon closed and the bell was pulled to summon the nursemaid.

"William, if you are not too tired, what say you to us walking on the shore of the lake for a while?" Elizabeth invited.

"You know I love to walk there with you, even if the weather is getting colder," William responded.

Soon enough, they were crossing the bridges at the southern end of the lake and headed for their boulder. As Her Grace was walking with her husband, only Biggs was following them at a respectful distance.

When they reached their boulder, William placed a blanket he had brought with them. As the temperatures cooled it was becoming too cold to sit on the rock without one. With the blanket in place, they sat side by side, their hands linked.

"That day we met for the first time in April of this year, even though I insulted you, you kept your equanimity," William stated as Elizabeth rested her head on his shoulder.

"Neither of us were on their best behaviour that day," she owned.

"True, but my beloved Elizabeth, you showed your grace that day, as you have many times since then, and it had nothing to do with your rank," William asserted.

"I have always tried to be more than my rank, a level of society I never wanted, and would have gladly given up had I borne a daughter," Elizabeth mused. "We will make sure that Will understands his responsibilities to those who are dependent on him, and educate him so he shows grace to all and understands it is more than a way to address him."

"Like his mother always has, and always will; her grace is unlimited."

Elizabeth turned her head and kissed her husband

silencing him. Some fifteen to twenty yards away, Biggs turned around and found the birds on the wing very interesting.

EPILOGUE

T he vast extended family had come together for the wedding of His Grace, Lord William Robert Alexander Darcy to Miss Edith Sarah Portnoy, eldest daughter of Charlotte and Lawrence Portnoy.

"If Mrs. Bennet had been alive, Charlotte's daughter about to become the next Duchess of Hertfordshire would have surely caused her an apoplexy," Lady Jane Fitzwilliam, the Countess of Matlock said quietly next to her sister, the Dowager Duchess of Hertfordshire.

~~~~~~~/~~~~~~~

The afore mentioned lady had taken a walk in October 1807 to try and burn off her anger at reading of Lady Elizabeth Darcy's success of birthing a son. As the weather was rather foul, unbeknownst to her a snow storm was blowing in, none of the watchers thought she would venture out of doors.

When she was not seen for a few days, one of the men watching over her braved the frigid temperatures and entered her cottage. He had seen no sign of her there and also the bed had not been slept in for some time. A search had been mounted and after a day of searching, her frozen body had been discovered in a shallow gully. Evidently, she had tripped or slipped and more than likely become unconscious. The cold had done the rest.

When the final report from the man in charge of the watchers had reached Elizabeth, she had passed the information on to her sisters, but like her, none of them chose to mourn the woman.

~~~~~~~/~~~~~~~

"I dare say you would be correct," Elizabeth agreed.

"We are all much better off for her not being in our lives," Jane stated.

Jane and Andrew had moved to Snowhaven when Lord Reginald Fitzwilliam had passed away peacefully in his sleep some six years previously. Lady Elaine, the Dowager Countess had joined him in heaven just over a year ago. Just as Elizabeth had predicted, Jane had refused the gift of an estate in addition to the massive dowry Elizabeth had bestowed on her. Per her vow to herself, Elizabeth had not argued to convince Jane to change her mind.

Elizabeth looked to her side where her beloved husband sat. At almost fifty a fair amount of his hair was grey, but he was as handsome as he had been that first day she met him near the lake. Next to her husband sat her Mama. Lady Anne, just into her seventh decade, was rather spry for one of her age. Her beloved Robert, close to eighty by then, had gone to his final reward just on five years after his brother and best friend, Reggie. As sad as she had been to carry on without the other half of her heart, on her Robert's deathbed, Lady Anne had promised him she would not give up on life and their bevy of grandchildren.

As the adopted mother of the other four Bennet sisters, when added to William and Anna's children, she had over thirty grandchildren.

Taking her husband's hand as she looked at her firstborn with pride as he recited his vows, Elizabeth felt nothing but contentment in the life God had granted her. Ben, the first child born to her and William, was standing up with his older brother.

~~~~~~~/~~~~~~~

Benjamin Robert Darcy had been born in July 1809.

Edward William had arrived in February 1812, then the twins, Annabeth and Joshua were next in January 1815. Almost four years had passed and Elizabeth had thought she would not be blessed with another child when she started missing her courses and then felt the quickening before the end of 1819. Mary-Jane was born in May 1820. The youngest Darcy, Alexander Frank, joined the family in December 1822.

Since Alex's birth, Elizabeth had never conceived again. She and William agreed seven were more than enough.

The Darcy offspring not involved with the wedding, were interspersed among their many cousins. Edward was sitting between two beautiful blonde haired, blue eyed Fitzwilliams. Elaine Madeline was seated on his right. She was called Ellie by everyone and was Jane and Andrew's eldest daughter, born about a year after Annabeth and Joshua.

Before that, Jane and Andrew had been blessed with three sons. Andrew Reginald was born in March 1808, twins Richard William and George in February 1811. Ellie arrived in January of 1813. Until Ellie's birth, Jane had been convinced she would only have sons. After Ellie, almost three years later, Madeline joined the family. Four years after Maddie, Catherine and Paul were born.

The other blonde seated next to Edward was not one of Jane's daughters, but the eldest daughter of Mary and Richard Fitzwilliam.

~~~~~~~/~~~~~~~

Mary had come out just after her eighteenth birthday in April 1810. By the end of that season, she and Richard were courting one another, and they married in April 1811, a few days after her nineteenth birthday.

Mary had been overwhelmed by the gift from her sister, the expanded Longbourn which in size and earnings was only slightly less than their estate of Rosings Park. It would be turned over to Robby when he gained his majority.

SHANA GRANDERSON A LADY

Anne de Bourgh had signed Rosings Park over to Richard six months after he had taken up residence at that estate. She had lived there happily without any responsibility for running the estate. Once Mary and Richard married, she and Mary had become the best of friends, and until Anne's passing—more than ten years after her mother left the mortal world—in 1822, she had been aunt to the Fitzwilliam and other children in the expanded family.

Lady Catherine had not survived long at the asylum to which she had been relegated. In the winter of 1809, she caught a trifling cold, and regardless of her protestations, that one of her rank did not get ill, she had been very sick. It eventually became pneumonia and that malady had been what ended her delusional life.

Mary and Richard's first child, Lydia Anne, was born in June 1813. In April 1815, James was born. He was followed in August 1818, by Robert, Robby to his friends and family, by Bethany in March 1821, Priscilla in November 1823, and the babe of the family, George in September 1827.

Both Ellie and Lydia Anne, having large dowries and impeccable connections, had been relentlessly pursued since they had come out after they turned eighteen. Being close in age and best of friends, they had their coming out together. In the two seasons since then, they had refused every offer for a courtship. They had made a pact they would only accept one when they found a man they would be able to esteem, respect, and love, and who would return the same in full measure. Besides their own parents, there were too many examples of felicitous and loving unions among their aunts, uncles, and grandparents to ever settle for anything less. Even at twenty, neither worried. They had more than enough of a fortune if they never found a man to marry.

~~~~~~~/~~~~~~~

After Mary, next to marry was Kate in February 1813.

Kate had met Viscount Westmore, Lord Wes De Melville, at her coming out ball. He was already eight and twenty, ten years her senior, but that had not stopped their romance from blossoming. By November 1812, he had proposed and she, very much in love, had accepted him.

Given her husband would one day be the Earl of Jersey and have more than enough estates, Kate, like Jane, had refused Elizabeth's gifting her an estate.

As it was Wes's father who had sent *him* to hell, Elizabeth felt it was kismet that one of her sisters should marry him. So far the Earl and Countess of Jersey—Lord Cyril had passed away in 1824—had two sons and three daughters and Kate suspected she was with child again.

~~~~~~~/~~~~~~~

As only a few months separated them in age, Anna and Lydia had come out together during the little season in 1813. During the season of 1814, Lydia met Lord Mark Crieghton, Marquess Kingsford and son of the Duke of Devonshire.

Due to her love of the castle, Lydia accepted Castlemere from Lizzy, but left her sister and brother and their family living there until Papa Robert passed away and they moved to Pemberley.

The estate would go to her third son who did not have an estate of his own.

At around the same time, Anna met the young Earl of Granville, Lord Harry Smythe. The two couples met and were granted courtships within days of each other. They proposed to their respective ladies in January 1815. Both were accepted. Anna and Lydia were married in a double wedding in March 1815, a few days after Anna turned twenty.

Lydia and her Mark were blessed with a daughter born in late 1816, and a son born the same year—three months before—his grandfather went to his eternal reward. The late Duke of Devonshire passed away in 1819, making Lydia a

Duchess. Since then, Lydia had birthed two more sons and two more daughters.

Thankfully for Robert Darcy, Granville, Anna's husband's estate, was just across the Derbyshire-Yorkshire border in the latter county. As such, it was barely more than four hours in a coach for him and his Anne to visit Anna and her family.

To date Anna had four children, three girls and the youngest, a boy and heir. She suspected she was with child again.

~~~~~~~/~~~~~~~

Elizabeth looked across the aisle to where Charlotte, Lawrence, and the rest of their extended family were seated. Besides their daughter marrying Will, Charlotte and Lawrence had four more children, two girls and two boys. They were the owners of the Portnoy estate as Ernest Portnoy passed away in 1821.

Sir William had gone to his eternal reward three years previously. Elizabeth could not but smile when she thought how pleased he would have been to see his granddaughter become a duchess. Lady Lucas was seated next to Charlotte.

Of her uncles and aunts, only the Gardiners were still with them. Uncle Frank had passed away seven years ago and Aunt Hattie had followed him six months later.

Eddy Gardiner, married for six years now, ran his father's business with his younger brother Peter, also married. Lilly had married the owner of a large estate in Oxfordshire in 1819 and May, the youngest of the four Gardiner children, had waited until she was three and twenty to marry in 1827. From their four children, Madeline and Edward Gardiner had thirteen grandchildren—so far.

They had retired to a medium sized estate less than two miles from Madeline's beloved Lambton.

~~~~~~~/~~~~~~~

What of George Wickham you ask? He settled in New York and finally decided to get himself educated. After university, he read the law. He was one of the most sought after lawyers in New York and amassed quite a fortune.

He married and ended up having four children, a son and three daughters.

Wickham maintained a correspondence with his father, and when the latter informed him of his retirement in 1817, George sent an invitation to live with his family in New York. Contained within was not only the fare for a first class ticket, but a bank draft to Mr. Darcy repaying him in full for all debt markers that man held in his name. Having missed his son for so many years and once again being proud of the man he had become, Lucas Wickham accepted his son's invitation.

The ex-steward had lived with his son until his passing about a year past.

Other than a letter of thanks she posted him, Wickham never had any contact with Her Grace. He did follow the news about her and had been pleased, not envious, when he had read about William Darcy marrying her.

~~~~~~~/~~~~~~~

Charles Bingley and his wife Rebecca were attending the wedding.

After his sister ruined herself, Bingley had sent her to live with a spinster aunt in Scarborough. The day Caroline turned one and twenty, he released her dowry to her and washed his hands of her.

The still Miss Bingley lived with her sister at Louisa's husband's estate in Surrey. She never showed her face in London again.

Once Bingley had proved he had grown a backbone, the friendship with William Darcy had been rekindled, although not at the same level it had been before. The Bingleys had four daughters and one son.

Bingley had remained in trade and was doing very well for himself having decided entry into the landed gentry was not for him.

~~~~~~~/~~~~~~~

Clem William Collins had attended a seminary and after a few years, taken orders. He had begun as the curate at the church in Wiltshire, in the town where he and his mother lived.

Until he was awarded the living five years later, he had lived in the house he and Ophelia Collins had purchased. Not long after being preferred to the living, he had married a very sensible local lady. They had two sons and a daughter.

Between his mother and his wife, Collins became a lot less silly. Over the years, they would be invited to one of their high-ranking cousin's estates for a visit now and again.

~~~~~~~/~~~~~~~

At the rear of the church were the ever vigilant John Biggs and Brian Johns—among other guards present. They were into their fifth decade, but had not lost a step.

Thanks to Her Grace's generosity, as if allowing them and their families to live in spacious cottages at Castlemere was not enough, all of their children had enjoyed very good educations. This gave them entrée to employment that was not based on service or the males having to join the army.

Although they had never had to do so, after all of these years they would still do anything, including risking their own lives, if Her Grace, or any of her family was threatened.

For many years now they had been in command of the guards, some fifty men, who were employed to watch over the family. The Duchess paid them three or four times what they expected to be paid, but they had long ago learnt not to try and gainsay Her Grace as she could be rather stubborn when she wanted to be.

~~~~~~~/~~~~~~~

The wedding breakfast was being held in the Portnoy estate's ball room. The brides and groom's parents were seated at a table with Jane, Andrew, and Lady Anne.

"This is the first of the next generation to marry," Lady Anne remarked. "I can only pray He will allow me to meet some great-grandchildren before I see Robert again."

"Mama, I am sure you will see great-grandchildren born," Jane asserted.

Elizabeth watched her son and new daughter as they made their way around the room to greet each of the guests. "Thankfully Will looks much like his father. If one did not know the truth, they would never suspect my William was not his father by blood."

"By the Grace of God, he does not bear any similarity in looks or character to his birthfather," Charlotte stated. "Eliza, you told him the truth when he reached his majority, did you not?"

"I, no, we told him." Elizabeth looked at her beloved husband warmly. "He thanked us for sharing all with him. Then he said he had only one true father, and whatever happened before did not interest him."

"It was good that the former Prinny, the late King George IV, never mentioned the late duke at Will's official investiture when he reached his majority," Andrew noted.

"Speaking of the late King, how many times did he offer you a title, even a dukedom?" Lady Anne enquired of her son.

"It was four times, and like Father before me, I respectfully refused," William stated.

"Thankfully the late King had more discretion than that," Elizabeth recalled. She looked at her eldest son and his new wife again. "As much as I was wishing for a daughter so I would have been able to cast off the titles which had been forced on me, I will never regret for one second we were blessed with Will. He has already proved to be a man worthy of the titles he carries. A man who cares deeply for all those who depend upon him."

"You gifted him the three remaining satellite estates after you gave one each to Mary, Lydia, and the three Darcy sons born after Ben," Jane verified.

"Yes, that and more of the wealth I inherited were all part of his wedding gifts," Elizabeth confirmed.

"How many schools have you opened, and kept funded with the money you continue to set aside for charity?" Charlotte asked.

"I think it is over forty now," Elizabeth guessed. "It is the least I could have done to do some good with what I gained."

"As I have said before, in your case *Her Grace* is so much more than something referring to your rank," William stated lovingly.

"I, my one and only, forever true love, am not the only one at this table to display grace to others." Elizabeth looked at her husband of six and twenty years lovingly.

The others at the table could do nothing but nod in agreement.

~~~*The End*~~~

BOOKS BY THIS AUTHOR

A Change of Heart

Colonel Fitzwilliam Takes Charge

The First Mrs. Darcy

A Change of Fortunes (Republished & Re-edited)

Much Pride, Prejudice, and Sensibility
- Without Enough Sense

Lady Catherine's Forbidden Love & Love
Unrestricted Combined Edition

A Curate's Daughter

Mary Bennet Takes Charge

Admiral Thomas Bennet

Separated at Birth

Jane Bennet Takes Charge - 6th book
in the 'Take Charge' series

Lives Begun in Obscurity

Mrs. Caroline Darcy

Lady Beth Fitzwilliam – Omnibus Edition

Anne de Bourgh Takes Charge – 5th book
of the Take Charge Series

Mr. Bingley Takes Charge – 4th book of the Take Charge Series

The Repercussions of Extreme Pride & Prejudice

Miss Darcy Takes Charge- 3rd book of the Take Charge Series

Banished

Lady Catherine Takes Charge – 2nd book
of the Take Charge Series

A Bennet of Royal Blood

Charlotte Lucas Takes Charge – 1st book
of the Take Charge Series

Cinder-Liza

Unknown Family Connections

Surviving Thomas Bennet

The Discarded Daughter - Combined Edition

The Duke's Daughter: Combined Edition

The Hypocrite

Coming Soon

Anne de Bourgh's Best Friend –
January/February 2024

Made in the USA
Monee, IL
02 January 2024

50932980R00223